P9-BYN-989

She stood alone in the farthest corner of the gallery, beside the stone balustrade and beneath the shading branch of a nearby tree. The white of her gown was like a wisp of moonlight captured in the shadows, and he went to her at once, unable to resist. He'd no idea what he'd say or do, no idea at all except that he wanted to be with her, which should, he decided, be inspiration enough when the time came for doing and saying.

As he drew closer, she heard his footsteps and swiftly turned to face him. He thought she might have been crying; now he could see her hands had been knotted on the balustrade in frustration, not unhappiness. In an instant her expression changed from startled wariness to bewilderment to out-and-out wonder.

"It's you," she whispered, her eyes wide as he stood before her. "It's *you*."

"It is," he said. "And you're you, too."

"What absolute foolishness," she said. She smiled crookedly, displaying a single charming dimple, and then, to his eternal surprise, slipped her arms around his shoulders and kissed him.

By Isabella Bradford

When You Wish Upon a Duke
When the Duchess Said Yes
When the Duke Found Love

Books published by The Random House Publishing Group are available at quantity discounts on bulk purchases for premium, educational, fund-raising, and special sales use. For details, please call 1-800-733-3000.

When the Duke Found Love

Isabella Bradford

BALLANTINE BOOKS • NEW YORK

Sale of this book without a front cover may be unauthorized. If this book is coverless, it may have been reported to the publisher as "unsold or destroyed" and neither the author nor the publisher may have received payment for it.

When the Duke Found Love is a work of fiction. Names, characters, places, and incidents are the products of the author's imagination or are used fictitiously. Any resemblance to actual events, locales, or persons, living or dead, is entirely coincidental.

A Ballantine Books Mass Market Original

Copyright © 2012 by Susan Holloway Scott

All rights reserved.

Published in the United States by Ballantine Books, an imprint of The Random House Publishing Group, a division of Random House, Inc., New York.

BALLANTINE and colophon are trademarks of Random House, Inc.

ISBN 978-0-345-52733-2
eBook ISBN 978-0-345-52734-9

Cover design: Lynn Andreozzi
Cover illustration: Alan Ayers

Printed in the United States of America

www.ballantinebooks.com

9 8 7 6 5 4 3 2 1

Ballantine mass market edition: December 2012

For my two favorite
eighteenth-century duchesses,
Sarah Woodyard and
Abby Cox,
with thanks, regards, and affection

Acknowledgments

Many thanks are in order to:
Junessa Viloria,
blessed with the most awesome
of editorial superpowers.
Meg Ruley and Annelise Robey, agents extraordinare.
Janea Whitacre, Mark Hutter, Sarah Woodyard,
and Doris Warren of the Margaret Hunter Shop,
Colonial Williamsburg, wise in all matters
of eighteenth-century dress and decorum.
And last but certainly not least,
my fellow nerdy-history-girl, Loretta Chase,
supreme possessor of sanity, good humor,
and bargain-hunting prowess.

When the
Duke Found
Love

CHAPTER

 1

London
April 1764

Diana Wylder, the third and final daughter of the late Earl of Hervey, had never particularly believed in fate.

That is, she hadn't until the afternoon Mama explained to her about Lord Crump.

The afternoon began well enough, with a drive planned, to be followed by a stroll through St. James's Park with her mother and her older sister Charlotte. They were already waiting in the front hall as Diana hurried down the stairs, for as usual Diana was not precisely on time. To be sure, it was her hat's fault, not hers: a splendid new hat with a wide, curling brim and a crown covered with white ostrich plumes, coral satin bows, and small sprays of pink silk flowers. This hat required a great deal of strategic pinning so that the brim would tip at the exact fashionable angle over her face, yet still permit Diana (barely) to see. Her maid had taken a quarter hour to get it right, and though Diana considered this time well spent, she couldn't help but feel guilty as she saw Mama and Charlotte waiting for her.

"Forgive me," she said breathlessly, pulling on her

gloves as she joined them. "I didn't intend to take so long."

"So long as you're ready now," Mama said. "But don't you think you should push your hat back a bit?"

Ever helpful, Mama reached out to adjust the hat herself, but Diana scuttled backward.

"No, Mama, please," she said, holding the curving brim defensively. "Mrs. Hartley assured me that this is the way all hats are being worn this spring in Paris."

"You should care more for how hats are being worn in London, Diana, considering that is where you live," Mama said, but sighed wistfully to show she'd already resigned herself to defeat. "I only wish you wouldn't hide your pretty face away behind feathers and ribbons."

"She looks lovely the way she is, Mama," Charlotte said firmly, looping her arm fondly through Diana's. "Now come. It's far too fine a day to waste standing inside discussing hats."

That should have been a warning of sorts, for Mama generally wished Diana to show less of her person, not more, just as Charlotte, her older, married sister and the famously beautiful Duchess of Marchbourne, could seldom resist suggesting improvements to be made in Diana's dress. But Diana was in too good a humor to be wary, and instead she simply grinned and followed her sister and mother from the house and down the steps.

The sun was shining as it rarely did for April in London, and the air was so warm with the first true breath of spring that the side windows were down in the carriage. Charlotte's footmen, gorgeous in their pale blue Marchbourne livery, hopped to attention as soon as the ladies appeared. One of the footmen held the carriage door open and the folding steps steady as they climbed inside. As the youngest, Diana faced backward and slid across the feather-stuffed seat to the farthest side, claiming the window, where she could see and—more important—be seen. She'd no wish to have that splendid new hat be wasted where no one could admire it.

"I do like riding in your carriage, Charlotte," she said happily as they began. "Much better than Aunt Sophronia's."

"It's very kind of your sister to invite us to share it," Mama said, settling her skirts around her legs. Mama was young to be the mother of two duchesses—she wasn't even forty—and, with her golden blond hair and wide blue eyes, still sufficiently beautiful that people often mistook her for one more of the Wylder sisters instead of their mother. "It's also generous of March to have given Charlotte such a comfortable carriage for driving about."

"I like how everyone sees March's crest on the door and makes such a fuss over us because of it," Diana said, watching how even now people on the pavement were bowing and curtseying as they passed by. "It's as good as being a duchess, but without any of the responsibilities."

"You could do with a few responsibilities, Diana," Charlotte suggested gently. "You're eighteen now, no longer a child. It wouldn't hurt you to concern yourself with more important things than new hats."

Diana looked dolefully at her sister. Ever since Charlotte had married four years ago, she'd become more serious, more proper, more . . . well, dull, and it was all because of *responsibility*. To Diana, Charlotte's entire life now seemed so dutiful and ordered, without even a morsel of excitement. Charlotte and March's marriage had been arranged long ago by their fathers, and it was already well sealed with the birth of an heir, plus three other babies besides. As March's wife and duchess, Charlotte oversaw his four households, his servants, his female tenants and their children, his journeys, his charities and subscriptions, his dinners for his friends, and likely many other things that Diana didn't know about. From what Diana observed, Charlotte worked harder at being a duchess than her maidservants did in the scullery, and Diana didn't envy any of it—except perhaps this carriage.

"Don't make a face like that, Diana," Mama said. "Charlotte is only speaking the truth. Unless you wish to return to Ransom Manor—"

"I'm not going back to Ransom," Diana said quickly. Ransom Manor was the only true home that Diana had known, a rambling, ancient house on the southern coast where Mama had retreated from London to raise her three fatherless daughters—or, more accurately, where they'd raised themselves. It had been a splendid childhood, filled with pony riding and boat rowing and tree climbing and numerous pets, and very little of the education expected for the daughters of peers. But there were no suitable young gentlemen near Ransom, especially when compared to the absolute bounty of them to be found in London. "You can't expect me to go back there unless you wish me to marry a—a *fisherman*."

"Really, Di," Charlotte said mildly, opening her fan. "As if anyone would expect that of you! Though an honest fisherman might be considered an improvement over some of the rogues you've let attend you."

"They weren't rogues," Diana said, folding her arms over the front of her bodice with bristling defense. It was true that she'd been guilty of a few minor, *minor* indiscretions, but nothing worse than most young ladies indulged in to amuse themselves. "They were all gentlemen, every one of them."

"It's of no consequence now," Mama said quickly. "Those, ah, gentlemen are all better forgotten."

"Exactly," Diana said, pleased that for once Mama had taken her side. "*Much* better to think of all the other ones who will be riding through the park today, ready to admire my hat."

She smiled, tipping her head to one side as if already displaying the hat's magnificence. On the seat across from her, Mama and Charlotte exchanged glances, which only made Diana smile more. They knew there would be young gentlemen striving to capture her attention in the park, just as she would be smiling winningly at them in return from beneath the curving brim of her hat. Such attention followed her everywhere she went in London—in parks, in shops, in theaters and playhouses, at the palace, and even in church—and it had been like that since she'd first come to London to stay two years before. No wonder Diana found her life so amusing, and no wonder, too, that she smiled now at the prospect of the afternoon before her.

But Mama wasn't smiling in return, and neither was Charlotte.

"Diana, my darling girl," Mama said, a disconcerting tremor in her voice, "I know it's been my fault for letting you be so free, but now I hope to make it up to you in the best possible way."

"Nothing's been your fault, Mama," Diana said. "You don't need to make anything up to me, not now or ever."

"But I do," Mama said, pulling a lace-edged handkerchief from her pocket. "If your poor father had lived, he would have seen to this long ago, as he did for Charlotte and Lizzie. You're my baby, you see, my youngest and my last, and I haven't wished to let you go, even though I should."

"But you've always let me go wherever I pleased," Diana said, not understanding. "You are not making sense, Mama, not at all."

"Yes, she is," Charlotte said. "Mama has accepted an

offer for your hand from the Marquis of Crump. He is going to join us in the park so that you may meet him."

"But I do not *wish* to marry!" cried Diana, stunned. "Not now, not yet, and certainly not to a man I have never met!"

"You're more than old enough, Diana," Charlotte said, shifting across the carriage to sit beside Diana, taking her hand. "You're eighteen, the same age as Lizzie and I were when we wed. And we hadn't known March or Hawke, either, and look how splendidly everything turned out for us."

"But I thought I would choose my own husband," Diana protested. "I want to marry for love, not because I've been *offered* for!"

"Choosing is not always for the best," Charlotte said. "You do recall how narrowly you escaped the disaster of Lieutenant Patrick."

Diana blushed furiously. She had in fact been embroiled in a near disaster with the very handsome (and, as it was discovered, very rapacious and ungentlemanly) Lieutenant Patrick, but usually, by tacit agreement, his name was never mentioned in the family. "That was last year, Charlotte, when I was only seventeen. I'd never make the same misjudgment now."

"Oh, my dear," Mama said, also squeezing onto the seat beside Diana. "I know this must seem something of a shock, but Lord Crump is known to be a most kind and generous gentleman. He has the patience and gentleness to be able to guide you as a wife and lady, something none of those younger rascals could ever do for you, nor does he care about any of your past indiscretions."

"You mean Lieutenant Patrick again," Diana said, unable to keep the wounded reproach from her voice. "First Charlotte, and now you, too, Mama. Last year you said it wouldn't matter, that everyone would forget.

But now you're reminding me of him because you want me to marry someone else!"

Mama sighed. "We can put the misfortunes of your past behind us, Diana, because we love you. But others have not been as, ah, charitable, and you know how skittish gentlemen can be when it comes to choosing a wife. It's most admirable that Lord Crump has chosen to ignore the tattle and offer for you in spite of it. A sure sign that he will try his best to make you happy."

Frantically Diana shook her head. It was true that there'd been considerable talk about her last summer, talk that hadn't been very nice. Because of Charlotte being a duchess, Diana hadn't been completely cast out from polite society, but there was a decided chill to her reception in the most noble houses, a chill that would be cured only by an excruciatingly respectable marriage, preferably to an equally respectable peer.

And it was also true that both her sisters had had their marriages arranged for them, and equally true that their bridegrooms had been virtual strangers. But just because Charlotte and Lizzie had fallen in love with their husbands didn't mean that Diana would be so fortunate—especially not wed to a man named Crump, who was marrying her because no one else would.

"I'm sure that Lord Crump will come to love you, Di, and you him," Charlotte assured her, as if able to read her thoughts. "True, lasting love, too, and not silly flirtation."

"But why would he ask for me if he's never so much as seen me?" Diana asked plaintively. "He must be attracted only to my fortune, or my connection to you and March, or—or some other mercenary reason. He cannot care for *me*."

"But he will, Diana, just as we do," Charlotte said with a firmness that startled Diana. "Don't pretend you didn't know this would happen one day. You saw it with me, and with Lizzie, too. This is how ladies like us marry. We're not dairy maids or seamstresses, you know."

Diana bowed her head, hiding herself and her misery under the brim of her hat. Deep down she knew that everything Charlotte was saying was right, because she'd seen it in her own family. If being a lady and the daughter of an earl meant that she rode in a carriage and wore fine gowns and lived in a grand house on St. James's Square, then it also meant that she wasn't permitted to marry whomever her heart might lead her to.

Her marriage *would* be a mercenary transaction, a legal exchange of property and titles for the sake of securing families and futures. She would simply be another one of the properties to be shifted about by the solicitors in their papers. It didn't really matter that she was surpassing pretty, or that she possessed a kind heart and a generous spirit, or that she could ride faster than any other lady she knew, or that she always defended small animals and children, and it certainly didn't matter that she'd always dreamed of a handsome beau who would declare his love and passion for her alone.

No. She was no different from her sisters or her mother or any other lady of her rank. She must forget all the dashing young gentlemen who'd danced and flirted with her and sent her flowers with sweet little poems tucked inside. There would be no romance for her, no grand passion, no glorious love like the kind to be found in ballads and novels and plays.

For her there would only be Lord Crump.

And that was the exact moment Diana realized the grim, unforgiving nature of fate.

"There's nothing to weep over, Di, truly," Charlotte said, slipping her arm around Diana's shoulders. "You'll see. March knows Lord Crump from the House of

Lords, and says he's a steady, reliable gentleman, which is exactly what a lady wishes in a husband."

Steadiness was what Diana wished for in a horse. It was not what she dreamed of in a husband, though she knew better than to say that aloud.

"Pray do not misjudge Lord Crump, Diana," Mama said earnestly. "Let him address you and show you himself how fine a gentleman he is."

Still staring down at her hands, Diana sighed forlornly. "Is he handsome? If he were to ride by this window, would I take notice of him?"

Mama hesitated a moment, exactly long enough for Diana to know that Lord Crump was decidedly not handsome.

"Lord Crump is a good man," Mama said, carefully avoiding Diana's question as the carriage turned into the park's gates. "A most honorable gentleman."

"There he is, Diana," Charlotte said, leaning forward, toward the window. "Come to greet you, just as he promised. There, on the chestnut gelding. That is Lord Crump."

At once Diana looked up, her heart thumping painfully behind her stays. There was only one gentleman mounted on a chestnut gelding within sight, and he was riding purposefully to join them.

And—oh, preserve her—he wasn't handsome. The closer he came, the more apparent that became. He was stern and severe, his face beneath his white wig and black cocked hat without the faintest humor. His eyes were a chilly blue, his thin-lipped mouth pressed tightly shut, and there was a peppering of old smallpox scars over his cheeks. Diana could not guess his age, except that he was older than she: much older, perhaps even thirty or beyond.

"Oh, Charlotte, he—he frightens me," Diana whispered. "He's dressed all in black."

"He's in mourning, silly," Charlotte said, signaling for the driver to stop the carriage. "His older brother died last winter, which was how he came into the title. That's why he has such an urgent desire for a wife and marchioness."

"Smile, Diana, please," Mama whispered even as she turned toward the open window. Mama's own smile was as warm and irresistible as the sunshine as she nodded to the marquis.

But there was no smile in return from Lord Crump.

"Good day, Your Grace," he said solemnly to Charlotte, greeting each of them in turn by rank. "Good day, my lady. Good day, Lady Diana. I am your servant."

Unable to make herself speak—even if she could find words to say—Diana ducked her chin in a nervous small nod and smiled as best she could. It wasn't much of a smile, not at all, nor was it enough to thaw Lord Crump's grave expression.

"I trust you are well, Lady Diana?" he asked, his face looming in the window as he continued astride his horse.

"Oh, th-thank you, yes, my lord, I am," Diana stammered, her cheeks hot. "Very well. I trust you are also well?"

"I am well, Lady Diana," he said. "Indeed, I am grateful for your solicitude."

She had never felt more devoid of wit or conversation, more awkward or tongue-tied in her life—nor, she suspected, had Lord Crump as he stared at her, his pale eyes unblinking.

Not that Mama appeared to notice their discomfiture. "There now, Lord Crump," Mama said, beaming with overbright cheerfulness. "A fair beginning if ever there was one! But wouldn't it be better if you were to continue to converse beyond our ears? Diana, why don't you climb down and walk a bit along the path with his lordship whilst your sister and I take our turn about the drive. Does such a plan please you, Lord Crump?"

"It does, Lady Hervey." His face disappeared from the window as he dismounted from his horse, and Charlotte called for the footman to open the door.

Not daring to speak aloud from fear the marquis would overhear, Diana shot a look of desperate pleading to her mother. She did not want to walk a bit with Lord Crump; in fact, she did not wish to spend so much as a second alone in his company.

But her mother would not relent.

"Pray do not keep his lordship waiting, Diana," she said, her words full of unspoken warning. "Charlotte and I will come collect you on our way back, no more than a quarter hour's time. Though the paths are full of people this afternoon, I shall trust you to his lordship's care."

The footman opened the door and flipped down the steps. Another of their footmen was holding his lordship's horse for him, while his lordship himself stood waiting, his arms hanging against his sides, either with patience or with resignation.

Oh, preserve her, he had long arms. Dressed in black, he looked for all the world like a crow with folded wings, the black beak of his cocked hat overshadowing his face.

"Diana," Mama said in a warning tone. "Do not dawdle."

With a gulp, she took the footman's offered hand and climbed from the carriage. As she passed Charlotte, she felt her sister's hand press lightly on her back in silent sympathy. Yet instead of comforting her, the small gesture nearly made Diana burst into tears.

She fussed with her skirts, shaking out and smoothing the ruffled silk to postpone the moment when she must

take Lord Crump's arm. At last she couldn't put it off
any longer, and she looked up at him.

Still he stood without moving, his expression unchanging. He wasn't offering her his arm, either. With
any other gentleman, Diana would have been insulted,
but now she felt only relief.

"Shall we walk, my lord?" she said, striving to sound
cheerful.

He nodded and began to walk, clearly expecting her
to follow. She hurried to join him, her skirts billowing
around her ankles. She heard the door to Charlotte's
carriage close behind her and the driver call to the horses
to move on, and there she was, alone with the crow she
was supposed to wed.

No, she wasn't exactly *with* him. She was beside him,
which, fortunately, didn't appear to be the same thing
at all.

The very concept of a walk along the mall with a lady
seemed to elude Lord Crump. Instead of strolling at a
leisurely pace, enjoying the sun filtering through the
trees overhead and making genteel conversation, he
walked purposefully, with his head bent and his arms
swinging at his sides. While he was the same height as
Diana (although the nodding plumes on her hat gave her
a distinct advantage), his stride was almost a soldier's
clipped march, forcing Diana in her heeled shoes to trot
beside him to keep up as they dodged among the park's
other visitors.

But Diana was determined to keep pace, and determined, too, to begin some manner of conversation, if for
no other reason than to be able to tell her mother she
had tried.

"Do you like my hat, Lord Crump?" she asked breathlessly, the exact opening that worked with most tongue-
tied gentlemen. "It's new. You're the first to see it."

He stopped abruptly to consider the hat. "Do *you* like the hat, Lady Diana?"

"I do," she said. "Else I wouldn't have worn it, would I?"

"Ah," he said. "Then I resolve to like it as well."

He turned and began walking again, clearly considering his duty to both the hat and Diana complete.

But Diana would not give up, not yet.

"I am sorry for your loss, Lord Crump," she said. "Of your brother, I mean."

Again he stopped, and she stopped, too.

"My brother and I were not close," he said. "He was much older than I, and we were born to different mothers. He fell to smallpox, you know."

"I'm sorry, my lord," she said again. "It must have been a grievous shock."

"It was," he said. "I hadn't expected to marry at all, but now that I have inherited the title and all with it, I have no choice."

Diana made a small, wordless exclamation of surprise at such an ungallant confession. She felt more than a little pain, too. How could Mama have praised this gentleman when he'd speak so callously to her?

"No choice but to marry me, my lord?" she asked, her voice squeaking upward. "No *choice*?"

"No," he said bluntly. "You see I am not easy in the company of ladies, Lady Diana. I require a son, an heir, and for that I must have a wife. Your sisters have proven themselves to be fecund, and I trust you shall be, too."

Diana gasped, so shocked she could not bear to meet his gaze any longer, but instead stared down at the path beneath her feet. Of course it was hoped that every marriage would be blessed with children, and for noble marriages it was imperative. But for Lord Crump to speak so coldly and with so little feeling of her *fecundity*, as if she were a broodmare, appalled her. It wasn't that she was overly nice about how those noble babies were to be produced—lady or not, she'd been raised in the country, where there were no mysteries about such matters—but the thought of lying with this man as his wife and bearing his children horrified her.

She knotted her hands into fists at her sides, struggling to control her emotions. She couldn't make a scandalous scene here on the mall. Likely there were already people slowing to observe them, whispering behind their fans, preparing the tattle to share with friends. With a shuddering breath, she forced herself to look up, intending to meet his gaze as evenly as she could.

But Lord Crump wasn't even looking at her. Instead he was staring off down the path, his expression suddenly more animated and eager than it had been since he'd met her.

"By Jove, that *is* Merton," he murmured, marveling. "In the park, of all places."

"Who is Merton?" Diana asked innocently.

He frowned, clearly irritated to have her ask a question that was so obvious to him.

"The Earl of Merton, of course," he said, still looking down the path. "A most important gentleman in the House of Lords. I have been trying to meet with him for days regarding an important trade bill before it comes to a vote, and now—here, you will not object if I go speak with him, Lady Diana. I shall be only a moment, and will return directly when I am done."

He did not wait for Diana to reply, but immediately charged off in the direction of the elusive Lord Merton.

Speechless again, Diana watched him go. Although she'd hardly been enjoying his company, it was still preferable to being abandoned here in the middle of the mall. Already the fashionable crowd on the walk was beginning to gape at her, taking note of the astonishing sight of a young lady standing alone and unattended.

Anxiously she smoothed the sleeves of her gown and then her lace scarf over her shoulders. It was too soon for her sister and mother to return in the carriage, and she'd absolutely no desire to chase after Lord Crump and his precious Lord Merton.

Yet she could not remain where she was, as adrift as if she'd been cast off in a boat in the middle of the ocean. She looked down one way, then the other, and without hesitating any longer she turned from the main path entirely and ran off among the shady trees, not stopping until she was deep in the shade. Breathing hard, she leaned against the nearest tree and closed her eyes.

A moment alone to think, to calm herself, to swallow back her humiliation and despair. Only a moment, and then she'd go back and wait for the carriage.

But a moment was more than she'd have. She heard the rustling in the dry leaves first, the odd snuffling breathing that was suddenly around the hem of her skirt. She yelped with surprise and her eyes flew open. The white dog at her feet looked up at her, unperturbed and happy to have her attention. He was smallish, some manner of bulldog, with oversized pink ears like a bat's and a crumpled face that was so ugly it became endearing. His barrel-like sides quaked as he panted, and he seemed to be grinning up at her with his tongue lolling from the corner of his mouth.

"Whom do you belong to?" she said softly, crouching down before the dog to ruffle his ears. "Where is your master, to let you run through the woods like this?"

The dog closed his eyes and made such a grumbling groan of complete contentment that she laughed.

"What a delightful fellow you are," she said. He was obviously someone's much-loved pet: not only was he round and well fed (perhaps a bit too well fed), but he wore an elegant red leather collar with silver studs around his neck. There was a silver tag, too, and she tried to turn it around to learn his name. "Come, let me properly make your acquaintance, sir."

"His name's Fantôme," said a gentleman's voice behind her. "It seems he has made a more glorious conquest than his usual squirrels."

With a little gasp of surprise, Diana looked swiftly over her shoulder to the gentleman, and gasped again. He was young, not much older than herself, and he was every bit as handsome as his dog was not. He'd broad shoulders and the strong, even features that would make any woman walking along the mall take notice of him, but it was his smile that captivated Diana. The devil-may-care grin that reached his eyes made her smile at once in return.

"*Fantôme* is French for 'ghost,' isn't it?" she asked.

"It is," he said, crouching down to her level with the dog between them. He wore a blue coat and a red waistcoat, both cheerfully bright even here in the shadows, and his light-colored buckskin breeches were tucked into top boots. There were spurs on the boots, which showed he'd been riding and had somewhere shed both his mount and his hat to chase after his dog.

"Though I fear Fantôme's far too corporeal to be a real specter," he continued. "You've only to look at him to see the truth. Isn't that so, *Monsieur le Gros?*"

"Master Fat!" Diana exclaimed, translating for herself. "You'd call this fine gentleman by so dreadful a name?"

"I would," declared the gentleman soundly, patting the dog's broad back with fondness. "He is a French dog, and he is fat. And I do call him Monsieur le Gros, because it's true. All the best endearments are, you know."

"If you call your dog Master Fat," she said, "then I should not wish to hear what you would call your lady."

"Ah, but I haven't a lady, you see." He sighed deeply

and drew his brows together, trying to look sorrowful, but only succeeded in making Diana laugh again. "I've no need for endearments beyond those for Fantôme."

"I don't believe you, sir," Diana scoffed. "Gentlemen like you always have ladies."

"That's true, too," he agreed. "More truth: I do not have a lady at present, but I expect to have one again very soon."

Her cheeks warmed. It wasn't the same kind of miserable flush that she'd felt with Lord Crump, but the exciting glow that came from mutual interest and amusement. He was flirting outrageously with her, and if she were honest, she was doing the same with him. She shouldn't be permitting any of this, of course. She should rise and immediately return to the path and to Lord Crump or her sister's carriage, whichever returned first.

But she didn't. "Then we are quite even," she said. "I didn't have a gentleman when I rose this morning, but I do now."

"I congratulate you on your swift acquisition, ma'am," he said, clearly assuming she meant him. "Might I guess the fortunate gentleman's name?"

She shook her head, the flirtation as suddenly done as it had begun. Yesterday, and any other yesterday before it, she would have been gratified to see the interest on this gentleman's handsome face. Any other day, and she would have been pleased to see that he was as charmed by her as she was by him.

But today, now, she was promised to Lord Crump. She could vow she wouldn't marry him, that she'd rebel, but her conscience told her that she wouldn't. She'd be as dutiful in obeying her mother's choice as her sisters had been, and pray that her own marriage would be as happy as theirs. She would because, truly, a lady had no choice.

And she would never again sit beneath a tree to laugh and flirt with a handsome gentleman like this one.

She scrambled back to her feet. "I must go. I can't stay any longer."

He stood, too, making her realize how tall and broad and brilliantly male he was in his blue coat.

"You could stay if you wished it," he said as Fantôme, agitated, began to race around them. "Another moment or two. Please. You can."

She shook her head, looking back through the trees to the path. She saw Lord Crump, his black mourning standing out among the others as he waited for her.

"Please don't ask me," she said, beginning to back away. "Because I can't. I *can't*."

He caught her hand lightly to keep her from leaving.

"Only a moment, sweetheart," he said. He considered her hat, then plucked one of the tiny silk flowers from the crown, as if plucking a real flower from a garden. He tucked the wire stem into the top buttonhole of his coat and gave it an extra pat.

"There," he said softly, smiling. "For remembrance, yes?"

"No," she said, striving to harden her voice and her heart, and failing at both. "Good day, sir."

Then she turned and ran, back to the path, to Lord Crump, and to her fate as his wife.

CHAPTER

 2

There were very few people in this world (or the next, for that matter) who could influence the actions of George Charles Bramley Atherton, the fourth Duke of Sheffield. The groom charged with the breeding of His Grace's favorite horses was one, and his personal *chef de cuisine* in Paris was perhaps another. But the only mortal who, by way of a letter alone, could make Sheffield return to London on the night boat from Calais was his favorite cousin, the Duke of Breconridge.

Now, as the carriage slowed before Brecon's town house, Sheffield glanced down at the white bulldog dozing on the seat beside him and sighed. He'd slept late, and he'd taken his time dressing, and he'd even gone for a brief ride in the park to help compose his thoughts, and his defense, too. The shadows in the street were long and the day was very nearly done, and he couldn't keep Brecon waiting any longer.

"I fear it's finally time, Fantôme," he said, resigned. "Though the fair lady you found for me in the park certainly was a worthwhile diversion."

He touched the silk flower, still in his buttonhole. She *had* been fair, and with her golden hair and wide blue eyes, she'd been as delicious a creature as ever could be found in London. Yet there had been more to her beyond her beauty. It was hard for him to define exactly. He'd liked how she'd laughed, a rippling merriment deep in her throat, and he'd liked how she'd answered him with ease and with cleverness, too. She'd made him smile, and she'd made him laugh, which in his experience was both rare and pleasurable. Of course, when she'd crouched down to pet Fantôme, she'd also unwittingly displayed her well-rounded breasts as her lace kerchief had come untucked, and remembering that—or them—was powerfully pleasurable, too.

Not that anything would come of it. He sighed again. There was the man she'd mentioned, and Sheffield was sure she'd run off to join whoever it was. Besides, Sheffield must now vow to Brecon to be as chaste as a monk, at least until Brecon's ire had faded. He smiled ruefully down at the little silk flower and pulled it from his coat. Brecon would spot such a token at once, and Sheffield already had sufficient explanations to make without adding a mysterious girl in the park. But instead of casting the little flower into the street, he tucked it inside his waistcoat pocket for safekeeping.

"Don't tell Brecon, Fantôme," he said, still thinking of the girl as he glanced from the window. "Misbehavior of any sort will not be tolerated while we are in His Grace's domain."

Two years had passed since Sheffield had last climbed those white marble steps, two years that he'd spent traveling abroad, yet nothing had changed about Brecon's house. Nothing had changed, really, for as long as Sheffield could remember. The silver knocker, shaped like a curving dolphin, still gleamed mirror bright, and the carefully clipped yew trees in their marble pots beside the door never grew any larger. And Sheffield would have wagered a sovereign that at the precise instant his carriage's footman let his hand approach that black-painted door, the door would open, and behind it would be Brecon's butler, the improbably named Houseman, equally unchanged and unchanging.

Which was exactly what happened, though to Sheffield's regret, no one else had stood by to witness and take his sovereign wager.

"Good day, Your Grace," Houseman murmured as he held the door wide for Sheffield and Fantôme to pass. It was one of the miracles of Houseman that the butler could unerringly sense when a person of rank was calling, so that he could step in the place of the more usual footman to open the door himself. "Might we offer you a welcome upon your return to London, sir?"

"I'll be most happy if you do," Sheffield said, smiling. "I trust you are in good health yourself?"

"Tolerably well, sir." The butler wouldn't smile in return—he never did—but Sheffield never doubted the sincerity of the welcome. Everyone in his cousin's employ was cordial and well-mannered, a reflection of Brecon himself. Even Brecon's dogs were perfectly behaved and incapable of a misplaced yelp or a mess on the carpet, unlike a certain other canine of Sheffield's acquaintance.

"I'm happy you are well," Sheffield said, handing his hat to the footman. Uneasily he glanced about for Fantôme, who was sniffing at the base of a tall Chinese vase with malicious intent. He grabbed the dog by the shoulders and hoisted him up into the crook of his arm, away from mischief. "Is my cousin in the library as usual?"

"No, sir," Houseman said, giving his jowls a sorrowful shake at having to offer Sheffield a negative reply. "His Grace begs your forgiveness for being unable to be at home to greet you, but he was called away of a sudden on a private matter."

Sheffield's dark brows rose with interest. "For once it cannot have been me," he said. "At least not this night."

"True, sir," Houseman said. "I believe he was summoned by her ladyship the Countess of Hervey."

Now Sheffield was truly interested. Brecon must be in his mid-forties by now. He had long been a widower, and though he'd kept a succession of mistresses, each of those women had been as esteemed for her discretion as for her beauty. Brecon would never have become distressingly entangled with any true lady, especially not one so noble as a countess.

"Who is this Lady Hervey, Houseman?" he asked, his curiosity growing. "Is she handsome?"

Houseman blinked, his way of signifying that any dolt, including Sheffield, should have recognized the lady's name.

"Her ladyship is the mother of Her Grace the Duchess of Marchbourne," he explained, "and of Her Grace the Duchess of Hawkesworth."

"Ah, yes," Sheffield said, faintly disappointed. Lady Hervey was almost family since her daughters were married to his other two cousins. If the countess was old enough to have borne those daughters, she was also likely to be too old to amuse Brecon, at least in an interesting fashion. Instead he must have answered her summons in only the most courtly (and Brecon-ish) manner, ready to offer assistance to an aged, widowed gentlewoman. "The older ladies do need tending, don't they?"

"I will leave any further questions to His Grace to answer, sir," Houseman said, prim even for him. "If you please, sir, His Grace asked that you wait for him in his library."

Obediently Sheffield asked no further questions, and followed the butler into his cousin's library. This, too, had not changed: a dark-paneled retreat with enough books for a small college, the dark red armchairs, the framed portraits of ancient philosophers, and blind Homer's marble bust on the mantel. He set Fantôme before the fire, where the dog turned three times and instantly fell asleep. Sheffield himself had scarcely sat when a maidservant appeared with a light supper and a footman came to pour him his choice of Brecon's wines.

Thus fortified, Sheffield stretched his legs contentedly before the fire and beside his dog, and pleasantly thought again about the girl in the park. For this he was obliged to the Countess of Hervey, since if she hadn't conveniently fallen into distress this evening, then Sheffield himself would by now be the one receiving the full force of Brecon's patient concern.

Of course Sheffield believed he no longer required such supervision, having recently (and extravagantly) celebrated his twenty-fourth birthday. He was a peer of the realm, a gentleman of rank, educated and experienced in the great world. He looked after his own property and affairs and took his seat in the House of Lords. He even paid his bills on time. In return for all that ducal responsibility, Sheffield believed he was entitled to spend the hours that were left in his days however he pleased, and in the company—or bed—of whosoever pleased him.

But things were different where Brecon was concerned. Brecon had played the roles of a father and older, wiser brother to Sheffield for so long that he'd a difficult time giving it up. Brecon had been the one who'd come to the ten-year-old Sheffield to tell him his parents had been killed in a carriage accident. It had been Brecon who'd brought him home to this house on school holidays, and who'd bought him his first hunter, his first pistols, his first suit of full evening dress. Brecon had presented him at court and introduced him to society, helped him learn to manage his estates and other property, and generally explained and guided him through all the challenges and temptations facing a too-young duke.

Nor was he an ordinary duke, either, if there were such a creature. Sheffield and Brecon and their other two cousins, the Duke of Marchbourne and the Duke of Hawkesworth, were all descended from the same king, with his royal blood in their veins. To be sure, they'd also the blood of the four mistresses who'd shared that king's bed, but it was the royal contribution that separated them from the rest of the peerage. At court the four were considered nearer to being princes than other dukes, a difference that had only served to bind them more closely together. Was it any wonder, then, that Brecon had not only looked after Sheffield but understood him, too?

Sheffield smiled now, remembering how many times he'd been called into this very room to answer for some sort of schoolboy misdemeanor or another. He'd always be grateful for what Brecon had done for him—he'd be the world's most miserable ingrate if he weren't—and for that alone he'd returned to London and Brecon's library. Brecon's letter could not be ignored. But this time what Sheffield would have to explain wasn't firing guns beneath the proctor's window after curfew. No, this time his misdeeds involved a beautiful young French marquise and, unfortunately, the lady's jealous older husband as well.

Sheffield sipped his brandy and sighed, more with remorse for his own behavior than with any residual desire for the Marquise du Vaulchier. He didn't usually make mistakes like this one. He'd been impulsive where she was concerned, yes, but he'd thought he was still being discreet. He'd no idea the lady herself would trumpet their assignation across Versailles and directly into her husband's ear, and as soon as Sheffield had realized what she'd done, he'd broken with her.

He hoped that would be enough to placate Brecon, though Sheffield didn't really know what other penance he could be expected to do. Besides, the entire brief affair had taken place in France, not England, and what happened to young English gentlemen—particularly young gentlemen who were dukes—in France was generally overlooked at home. It was one of the reasons he was so fond of Paris.

"Sheffield!" Brecon came striding into the room to greet him, not pausing to first remove either his hat or coat. Whatever assistance Lady Hervey had required must not have been terribly arduous, for he was still dressed with his usual impeccable elegance, in a plum-colored silk suit with cut-steel buttons. Brecon was a gentleman very much in his prime, and Sheffield himself had observed how his cousin could make every woman, young or old, turn to look at him, and every man wish to be his friend. Brecon had *presence*.

"How glad I am to see you again, cousin," he said now, seizing Sheffield's hand, "and how sorry I am that I have left you to wait alone."

"It's fine to see you as well, Brecon," Sheffield said, grasping his cousin's shoulder with genuine affection. "You'd a good excuse, riding in like Galahad to Lady Hervey's aid."

He'd meant it as a small jest, picturing his cousin in full Galahad armor as he rushed to rescue the doddering Lady Hervey from whatever domestic trial faced her.

But Brecon didn't take it as a jest, his face growing grimly serious.

"What Lady Hervey required more than Galahad was a friend to listen to her woes, and I was happy to oblige," he said, shrugging free of his coat, which a footman behind him deftly caught. "Her youngest daughter is something of a trial to her, running after every manner of rogue. I fear that Lady Diana has been indulged all her short life, and now refuses to make a graceful transition from a headstrong girl to an honorable and obedient wife."

Sheffield raised his brows with surprise. It rather seemed to him that Brecon, with his long parade of mistresses, would hardly be the proper gentleman to offer such advice. "I cannot imagine that you would have much to say on the matter."

"I don't," Brecon agreed. He dropped into the armchair beside Sheffield's and sighed with pleasurable relief as another footman brought him a glass of sherry. "Having sired only sons, not daughters, I have little experience of my own in young female willfulness. Lady Hervey rather sought a friend's commiseration, not advice, and that I was happy to provide."

"Tell me more of this willful young lady," Sheffield requested. Both March and Hawke, the last of his cousins, had married daughters of the late Earl of Hervey through arranged matches. These ladies were beauties, but they were also now duchesses, and thoroughly respectable as such, even though Hawke had insisted on carrying his wife off to live in Naples. The notion of another, younger sister, one who was likely just as beautiful, but willful and impulsive, was intriguing to Sheffield. He'd always liked beauty unburdened by responsibility. "Is she as fair as her sisters?"

"Some believe her to be the loveliest of the lot," Brecon said, more with dismay than with admiration. "Golden hair, blue eyes with a winsome charm, and a lissome figure, too, much like her mother's. Oh, yes, she's fair, which only magnifies the misery she's capable of inflicting upon her family. She's had all manner of disreputable men sniffing after her, and there was one bounder in particular—an Irish officer, if you can believe it—who nearly coaxed her toward Gretna Green. All enough to scare off respectable suitors, and who can blame them? The chit's a handful. I've never seen poor Lady Hervey so distraught with worry."

Sheffield nodded, considering as he sipped his wine. From Brecon's description, this Lady Diana could be a twin to the girl that Fantôme had found for him in the park—as if any earl's daughter, however willful, would ever be found alone beneath the trees. But at least he'd the explanation for Brecon's involvement: a poor noble widow, distraught over her youngest child's fate. How could Brecon resist?

"It's a pity her father didn't have the chance to arrange a marriage for Lady Diana as he did for his other two daughters," Brecon was saying. "If he had only lived a bit longer, then everything would have long been settled, and there'd be none of this nonsense from the girl now about falling in love."

"Love is hardly nonsense, cousin," Sheffield suggested, sympathizing with the lady who possessed that golden hair and lissome waist. Perhaps she needed a champion, just like her mother. "What could be more important to a young lady than love?"

But Brecon knew Sheffield well—too well, really. He set his glass down on the table beside his chair and leaned forward, his expression serious.

"Sheffield," he said slowly, so there'd be no misunderstanding, "you are to have nothing to do with Lady Diana Wylder. Not. One. Thing."

Sheffield smiled, bemused. "She's as much as another cousin, Brecon. I do not see why I must keep from my own family."

But Brecon wasn't smiling. "You will heed me in this, Sheffield, family or not. I know how you are with women."

Sheffield shrugged to show that none of it was his fault. "It's rather how women are with me."

"I'm serious," Brecon said. "The girl's head is already

too full of sentimental ballads and tawdry novels. She doesn't need you addling her further."

Sheffield sighed, leaning back against the cushions. He rested his elbows on the arms of the chair and made a small tent of his fingers, bouncing them lightly against one another as he pretended to study the effect.

"Then tell me, Brecon," he said, musing, "for I am most curious. If not my own excellent company, then what would you prescribe for the lovesick lady? What do you believe she requires that I cannot offer her?"

Brecon made a grumbling, growling sound deep in his throat. "I know exactly what you'd offer Lady Diana, sir, and she is already sufficiently tottering on the precipice of ill fame without you pushing her over the edge. I can only imagine the two of you together. You are both too much alike to make anything but a disaster."

"You can't lock her away in a convent, you know," Sheffield said, thinking of the loquacious French marquise and rather wishing she'd retreated to a quiet place among the good sisters of someplace or another. "We don't do things like that to ladies in England."

"No." Brecon finished his wine and irritably motioned the footman to refill his glass. "But I have helped Lady Hervey in finding Lady Diana a suitable husband, a measured, responsible gentleman who can rein in her spirits."

"Pity," Sheffield said. "Her spirits sound as if they are part of her charm."

"They'll be the ruin of her, too, if she's not careful," Brecon said. "Fortunately, I was able to advise Lady Hervey in the financial arrangements of the settlement in a way that was beneficial to both parties. After all, the girl is the daughter of an earl, with ten thousand pounds, and through marriage she is now connected to us, as well as to March and Hawke."

Sheffield chuckled. "Some would question the value of such connections."

"No one would who wishes to prosper at court," Brecon said. "You must never forget the value of your heritage, Sheffield, or the influence that comes with it. Which at last brings me to your own situation."

Sheffield sat more upright in his chair, prepared to play the penitent. "By the time I'd received your letter, I had already ended the affair with the Marquise du Vaulchier, as you wished."

Brecon grunted. "What I wished should have been the least of your considerations in this matter, Sheffield. Where was your sense? With this latest conquest, you have managed to ruffle some very highly placed feathers in Paris as well as here in London. The Marquis du Vaulchier did not enjoy being cuckolded, and complained of you to his king, who has in turn complained to ours."

This was bad, far worse that Sheffield had ever imagined.

"Louis complained of me?" he asked. "A ruler who has let himself be ruled by his mistresses is shocked by my passing dalliance? Are you certain, Brecon?"

"How in blazes could I ever invent that?" Brecon said. "To be sure, the message was not spoken directly, but conveyed through their ministers, yet the gist of it was perfectly clear. You have brought embarrassment to His Majesty, and he is not pleased."

Sheffield dropped back in his chair and scowled, unwilling to accept the notion that he had somehow managed to outrage not one but two kings.

"Most every gentleman in His Majesty's court either keeps a whore or is dallying with some other gentleman's wife," he said defensively. "I do not see why I should be singled out as particularly offensive."

"You're singled out because of who you are," Brecon

said, his voice growing sterner with every word. "You've royal blood in your veins, Sheffield, the same as I do, the same as March and Hawke. We're not like every other gentleman at court. More is expected of us. More is expected of *you*."

"I've already told you I am done with the marquise," Sheffield protested. "I've come back to London. What more do you wish? Sackcloth and ashes and wailing my sins in the street?"

"It wouldn't be untoward," Brecon said, and to Sheffield's dismay his cousin wasn't jesting. "The king is weary of your bachelor antics, especially among the French. How many of those women have you bedded, anyway?"

Sheffield shrugged, which seemed safer than trying to come up with an actual number. His great-great-grandmother had been French, which likely explained his weakness for French women. The fact that his great-great-grandfather had loved her as his mistress rather than his wife might also contribute to his habits. The tendencies were in his blood and could not be helped.

Not that Brecon would accept that as an excuse. "You know His Majesty wishes to make the royal court less scandalous," he said. "He wishes to set an example for the rest of the country. You are not helping."

"It's all because His Majesty was forced to marry that German princess," Sheffield said. He had heard all about the king's new queen, who was whispered to be disappointingly plain. "He wants us all to become as tediously wholesome and German as he is himself."

Brecon sighed. "You can hardly fault His Majesty for wishing others to have the same contentment he has found in his own marriage."

"Thus I must give up my mistress for the sake of His Majesty's morality," Sheffield said. "Which I have done. What more can a lowly penitent do?"

"Marry," Brecon said succinctly. "The king wishes you to take a suitable wife who will both keep you from the beds of French noblewomen and provide you with an heir to secure your dukedom."

"Marry?" Sheffield repeated, feeling his comfortable bachelor existence being snapped out from beneath his feet. "Me? Marry?"

"It is, for most people, an agreeable condition," Brecon said. "It was for me, at any rate."

"But I am not you, Brecon," Sheffield protested. "Not at all."

"No, you most certainly are not," Brecon agreed, so quickly that in any other circumstances Sheffield would have been offended. "His Majesty suggests the oldest daughter of Lord Lattimore as being suitable, and I agree."

Abruptly Sheffield rose and went to stand at the mantel, staring into the fire. He'd always known he must marry. Producing the next generation of little Dukes of Sheffield was really the only obligation he had to fulfill. Noblemen were paired with noblewomen, like two-legged thoroughbreds. Future duchesses could never be the daughters of coal merchants or tavern keepers. Nor, God forbid, could they be mere actresses or milliners, no matter how charming those ladies might be in their person. Pedigree always trumped charm and beauty, and most especially it trumped love.

Love was never taken into account with noble match-making, yet Sheffield had always hoped it would be, at least for him. Was it such an appalling sin to actually love the woman one was to wed? For butchers and bakers and candlestick makers, it wasn't. Dukes didn't have that luxury, nor were they expected even to have romantic ideals. Sheffield's own parents had been the exception. They had fallen in love and scandalously eloped, and because it was a suitable enough match, their astonished families had not protested the marriage. Sheffield remembered their love, and how much more demonstrative they'd been with each other than any of his friends' parents. He also remembered how happy and secure their love had made his childhood, and equally how devastated he'd been when they were killed.

He'd always wanted—even coveted—the same sort of love and marriage for himself, expecting that when the proper time came, he'd fall in love and marry himself. Now it seemed he wouldn't. This match that Brecon proposed was inevitable, his fate, his doom, his curse, and he felt completely entitled to be melancholy about it. He was only twenty-four. He wasn't ready to marry, and he certainly wasn't in love with a young woman he'd never met. But if the king himself wished it, then he'd no choice. None.

And what the devil must be wrong with Lord Lattimore's daughter if she required a royal command to acquire a husband?

"You planned this, Brecon, didn't you?" Sheffield asked glumly, still staring into the fire. "I can see it now. That trumpery about the countess's daughter needing to wed, and all the time you'd begun crying the banns for me instead."

"The purest of coincidence," Brecon said, with such confidence that Sheffield didn't believe it for an instant. "At least there is not quite the same urgency as there is with a lady. No one is going to ruin you."

"No," Sheffield said, glumness turning to out-and-out gloom. "I'm already thoroughly ruined, thank you. What do you know of Lord Lattimore's daughter?"

"Lady Enid?" Brecon smiled warmly. "She's a fine, handsome lady with a pleasant manner. You will meet her and determine for yourself on Friday night at Lady Fortescue's rout. You've been invited, you know."

"Blast you, Brecon," Sheffield said with more resignation than genuine anger. "'A handsome lady with a pleasant manner'? How woeful must she be if that is the best you, the most charitable man I know, can say in her favor? A pleasant manner?"

But Brecon only smiled. "I do not wish to predispose you. All I ask is that when you meet Lady Enid, you bear in mind that duchesses are not to be judged by the same standards as, say, a French marquise."

Sheffield didn't answer. Though Brecon wouldn't believe it, the fact that Lady Enid was evidently no beauty—how could any woman named Enid be one?—did not distress Sheffield nearly as much as the cold-blooded nature of the arrangement. She was as much as being delivered to him on a silver charger, a respectable lady-wife, while he was doubtless being presented to her as the duke and fortune she should be honored to marry. It would be a match made by solicitors and other men of business, with the king hovering over all like a royal Cupid.

There'd be no chase, no hunt, no seduction, not an iota of the things that Sheffield enjoyed most to do with women. He liked the excitement of pursuit infinitely more than the predictable satisfaction of possession, and this sort of match would be unspeakably dreary.

He tried to think only dutiful thoughts, of how this was what he must do, but instead his thoughts insisted on running willfully off on their own, imagining all manner of inappropriate women whom he'd much rather be pursuing.

No, one inappropriate woman, one with a chuckling laugh and gold-colored hair and high, plump breasts that truly did belong on a woodland nymph—likely the most desirably inappropriate woman his imagination could muster before the undoubtedly plain face of Lady Enid.

"You're quiet," Brecon said at last, making Sheffield

start and wonder how long he'd been lost in his own reflections. "Are you stricken speechless by the prospect of behaving like a gentleman?"

Sheffield tried to smile. "How can I not be, when I feel the noose tightening around my throat already?"

But Brecon was no longer looking at him, or listening, either. Instead he was staring downward, to the vicinity of Sheffield's feet.

"What, pray, is *that*?" he demanded, simultaneously both mystified and appalled. "A *pig*? Have you brought a pig into my library, Sheffield?"

Sheffield looked down as well, to where Fantôme lay blissfully curled close to the fire's grate. Sheffield had to admit that, from where his cousin was sitting, the dog likely did resemble a small white pig, his well-rounded sides basking in the warmth. As if on cue, Fantôme rolled inelegantly onto his back and began snoring, his long pinkish ears fluttering gently. Sheffield smiled and slipped the toe of his boot beneath the dog's back, gently rubbing against his spine until Fantôme's snores became mixed with heady canine groans of pleasure.

"He's a dog, not a pig," Sheffield said fondly. "He's my dog, and his name is Fantôme."

"Fantôme," repeated Brecon, staring down at the groaning dog. "French?"

"*Mais oui*," Sheffield said, unable to resist.

"*Mais non*," Brecon said dryly. "You have no more taste in your dogs than you do in your mistresses."

"Now, now, Brecon, pray do not be unkind." Sheffield bent down to scoop the dog up into his arms, cradling him there like a fat baby. "If I vow to keep an open mind when I meet Lady Enid, then you must do the same with Fantôme."

"Sheffield, please." Brecon's expression was pained. "To speak Lady Enid's name in the same breath with that creature, even in jest, is ridiculous. Yet if it will make you consider the lady fairly, then I will gladly do the same for that—that handsome and noble dog."

The handsome and noble dog yawned, snuffled, and gave a leisurely swipe of his tongue across his crumpled nose.

Sheffield ruffled Fantôme's ears and sighed. He could turn his back on all that Brecon had said and the king had suggested. This was the eighteenth century, not the fifteenth, and he didn't have to marry His Majesty's choice of a bride or risk being tossed into the Tower until he obeyed. He wouldn't lose his titles or his lands. He could leave England anytime he pleased, and forget entirely about these marital expectations.

But if he didn't care what the king said, he did care about Brecon's opinion. Indeed, he cared more than he'd likely ever admit. Brecon was the closest thing he had to family, to both a father and a brother, and Sheffield would never sever that attachment, not for all the willing ladies in France. Brecon was also the most honorable gentleman he'd ever met, and ever since Sheffield was a boy, he had always wished to be like Brecon. He hadn't come close to succeeding, but he'd tried, and he was willing to try again in regard to Lady Enid.

Gently he set Fantôme back down on the carpet. He squared his shoulders, resolved to smile, and held his hand out to Brecon.

"As you wish, cousin," he said softly. "Regarding the marquise, and Lady Enid, and this ball, and marriage, and all the rest. Whatever you wish."

CHAPTER

 3

"There now, Diana, you look quite perfect." Charlotte gave a final critical tweak to one of the ruffles on Diana's gown. "Lord Crump will be dazzled."

"Lord Crump will take no notice at all," Diana said. They were standing in the small room that Lady Fortescue had set aside for ladies to leave their cloaks and make general repairs before they joined the rest of the company. The air was thick with the scent of perfume and the drifting dust of hair powder. They were far from the first guests to arrive for the rout, and the room was crowded with ladies all striving to stand before the same looking glasses at the same time.

All, that is, except Diana. Her gown was lovely, a cream-colored silk damask embroidered with pale pink carnations, her hair had been perfectly arranged high on her head in a cascade of curls, and her coral and pearl necklace and earrings made her pale skin glow. Charlotte had overseen two lady's maids and a hairdresser to make sure her youngest sister looked her best this evening, but Diana hadn't cared at all. Why should she, when Lord Crump wouldn't, either?

"I could be wearing a ragged scrap of homespun and he'd say nothing, Charlotte," she said. "If he had no opinion on my hat the other day, he won't even see my gown."

"He might not see the gown, no," Charlotte said, tucking a stray wisp of her own hair beneath a spray of diamonds and feathers pinned into it. "But he will see you in it, and that's far more important. March never really notices my gowns or hats or shoes, but he is very aware of the overall effect. I'm sure it's the same with Lord Crump."

"Lord Crump is not March, Charlotte," Diana said firmly. "Not at all."

Two days earlier, when she'd rejoined him in the park, he had told her of his conversation with his friend Lord Merton. He hadn't apologized to her for abandoning her, nor had he asked how she'd spent the time when he'd been off with Lord Merton.

Which, if Diana were honest with herself, was probably for the best. She was not good at dissembling, and if Lord Crump had inquired too closely about her time alone, she doubtless would have told him about the fat white dog and his handsome master. She'd certainly thought enough about the dog's owner, about his broad shoulders in the bright blue coat and the wicked, sly glint he'd had to his eyes, and how he'd made her laugh and blush. She'd thought, too, how vastly sad it was that this handsome, nameless gentleman might be the very last she could think such things about. According to Charlotte, once she was wed, she'd have to banish all charming gentlemen like him not only from her life but also from her very thoughts—though Charlotte also said that once she loved her husband, that would take care of itself.

"Lord Crump is more like March than you know, Diana," Charlotte said, straightening the heavy pear-shaped pearls, crowned with diamonds, that hung from her ears. "When we first wed, he was so stuffy and proper that I despaired. But I persevered, and you see how love has changed him."

"But March is handsome," Diana protested. "Even if he was stuffy and proper, he was pleasing to gaze upon. There's nothing pleasing about Lord Crump."

"Nothing that you've yet discovered," Charlotte said. "I'm sure he has his qualities. I've told you before, Diana. A flirtation can happen in an instant, but love takes time to build. Which would you rather have: a bright flower blossom that withers and loses its petals and scent after a day or two, or a diamond that must be wrested from deep in the earth but which, once possessed, keeps its beauty forever?"

"The diamond," Diana admitted grudgingly, then looked at Charlotte's earrings. "But I'd much prefer a flesh-and-blood husband to either."

"Oh, Diana, please." Charlotte rolled her eyes with dismay. "I pity Lord Crump having to cope with you! Now come, let's join the others, and pray try to be agreeable to that poor gentleman."

With a sigh, Diana followed her sister from the tiring room. As far as she was concerned, she'd much rather have the instant pleasure of flirtation that she'd discovered with the stranger beneath the trees than endure the stupefying process of finding something lovable in Lord Crump.

Lady Fortescue was known for her fashionable entertainments, and her grand old house—one of the last along the Strand to remain from the former century—was arranged almost entirely for the accommodations of large numbers of guests. Each of the spacious rooms opened into the next, creating a long, lavish space for dancing, dining, drinking, and conversing. Most important, Fortescue House was unrivaled for displaying one's self to the very best advantage, with large looking glasses to reflect both the candlelight from the chandeliers and London's most fashionable society as its members strolled from one room to the next.

Even though Lady Fortescue had characterized this evening's gathering as only a rout, not a full-fledged ball, there were still plenty of jewels. Most of the ladies were dressed formally, with wide, swaying hoops beneath their skirts. The gentlemen were every bit the male peacocks, their jackets and waistcoats glittering with silk embroidery and jeweled buttons.

Charlotte moved confidently through the crush, the crowd always making way for the Duchess of Marchbourne. Diana followed in her wake, as was both proper for their ranks and necessary, since with their wide hoops it was almost impossible for them to maneuver through a crowded room side by side. Since she'd turned seventeen, Diana had been accompanying Charlotte more and more in public, and she no longer gave thought to deferring to her older sister as a duchess.

Yet tonight Diana sensed that things had somehow changed. Was she imagining it, or were the other guests looking at her differently, with a new interest and respect, because of Lord Crump? Were they whispering behind their fans about her, not Charlotte? She should have known that word of their match would have raced through the small circle of well-bred London. Only a few days had passed since she herself had learned of his proposal. Had she already made the subtle shift in society's eyes, moving from being one more unmarried younger sister to a lady with a peer as her intended?

"Ah, there they are," Charlotte said, smiling. "March, and Mama, and Aunt Sophronia. And of course your Lord Crump."

"He's not *my* Lord Crump," Diana said automatically. "Not at all."

"But he shall be," Charlotte said with supreme confidence. "I'm certain we'll be discussing a wedding date before long."

Silently Diana prayed that "before long" would mean a long, long time in the distance. He stood there with his hands clasped behind his back, the one grim face in a room filled with gaiety. It didn't help that he stood beside March, so effortlessly handsome and ducal that Diana didn't wonder that Charlotte loved him so much. To be sure, Diana respected Lord Crump's black mourning for his brother, but if he'd made the decision to attend Lady Fortescue's rout and to join her family's party here, then she wished he'd at least try to arrange his features more pleasantly. *If* he could; perhaps it was beyond him.

Oh, please, *please*, let him not ever be her Lord Crump!

"Here's my little golden butterfly now," Aunt Sophronia said, smiling as she presented her lined but rouged cheek for Diana to kiss. Aunt Sophronia was their father's oldest sister as well as the dowager Countess of Carbery, and a fearsome force in London society. She was a prickly lady, not only in her manner but also in the number of sharp-edged jewels she always wore like a kind of glittering, gaudy armor. Yet she had always shown great fondness for Diana, her clear favorite among the sisters, and in turn Diana had never been intimidated by her the way Charlotte and Lizzie still were.

Now she took Diana's hand, drawing her close. "I am so glad to see you here at last, my dear," she said. "I have been having the most delightful conversation with your Lord Crump."

"If you please, Aunt Sophronia," Diana protested. "He's not my Lord Crump."

"Bah," said her aunt with a wave of her strongly scented handkerchief. "Do not be modest about conquests, my dear. It's not flattering to the gentlemen, especially one as fine and knowledgeable as Lord Crump.

Do you know that he could tell the exact mine in India where my sapphires were found?"

She touched the large blue stones in her necklace as she beamed at Lord Crump. He did not smile in return, but merely bowed in grave acknowledgment.

"Lord Crump has interests in the East India Company, Diana," March said, "which explains his expertise where sapphires are concerned."

"You honor me, sir," Lord Crump said. "Jewels are an excellent investment. I am familiar with many of the precious stones to be mined at present in India— sapphires, emeralds, diamonds, and rubies—though perhaps I do not possess the expertise that you would credit to me."

"Oh, yes, Lord Crump, you do," Aunt Sophronia said eagerly. "Pay heed to that, Diana. A husband with a knowledge of fine jewels is a jewel himself."

Everyone laughed, except for Lord Crump and Diana. How could she if he didn't? Why didn't anyone else understand that she'd much prefer a husband who smiled with her than one who could cover her with jewels?

"The musicians have returned," Mama said, looking over her shoulder to the next room which had been cleared for dancing. "I can hear them beginning to tune again. My daughter is a graceful and accomplished dancer, Lord Crump. Perhaps you would care to lead her through the next set?"

"Mama, please," Diana said, mortified. She'd never had to beg for a partner before, and she'd no wish to begin now. "If Lord Crump wishes to dance, then I'm certain he'll ask me himself."

"I'm sure he wishes it," March said heartily, resting his hand on the other man's shoulder as if ready to propel him toward the dance floor. "What man wouldn't wish to dance with a girl as pretty as Diana?"

"Forgive me, sir, but I do not dance," Lord Crump

said. "Dancing is a frivolous, idle pastime, requiring much practice for little purpose."

"The purpose, Crump, is to please the ladies," March declared. "There can be no more honorable pastime than that. The sooner you learn that, the happier your wedded life shall be."

"Very well, sir," Lord Crump said, visibly steeling himself. "If it pleases Lady Diana, then I shall. Would you care to dance?"

Diana took a deep breath, then took his offered hand. "Thank you, my lord, I am honored."

He nodded, holding her fingers as lightly as was possible, and together they passed into the room where the dancers were gathering.

"I do thank you, my lord," Diana said shyly when they were beyond the hearing of her family. It did please her that he'd agreed to dance; she hadn't expected it. Even if he was not a skilled dancer, she'd do her best to help him along and make it easy for him. "For doing this for me, I mean."

"His Grace asked me," he said without looking at her. "I could not refuse."

That stung, and it took considerable effort for Diana not to pull her hand free.

"Forgive me," she said, unable to keep the disappointment from her voice. "I thought you wished to please me, not March."

His eyes widened a fraction with surprise. "But there should be no confusion, Lady Diana. Because of His Grace's superior rank, I am bound to obey his wishes."

She looked down, struggling to compose herself for the dance. "I do not understand, Lord Crump, how you can be so charming with everyone else, but so—so disagreeable to me."

He sighed. "You are very young, Lady Diana."

"I am eighteen, my lord!"

"Very young," he repeated. "Not that I believe age is any hindrance in a wife."

"No, no," she said unhappily. "So long as I am *fecund*."

Before he could answer, the music began, and the dance with it. Though the complicated minuets were done for the evening, this country dance was a cotillion, with steps and turns and changes that would make any further conversation impossible. It was doubly impossible for Lord Crump, who was insisting on dancing the steps as he chose, whether they were the proper ones or not, and stiffly blundering this way and that.

Diana watched him with ever-growing despair. At least the dance would soon be done, but a marriage—ah, that would be forever.

Sheffield could not recall the last time he'd been nervous before a woman—any woman. It simply did not happen.

Yet here he was standing in one of Lady Fortescue's infernally overcrowded reception rooms, sweat prickling along his back beneath his shirt and his heart racing as if he were sixteen again. Brecon was making the introductions, and also standing ready to keep Sheffield from bolting. He was vaguely aware of other witnesses, the hazy faces of parents who were bowing and scraping and generally delighted to give their daughter to a duke.

But now at last, yet also too soon, the moment he could no longer avoid: here was the woman he'd been ordered to make his wife.

"Sheffield," Brecon was saying, "Lady Enid Lattimore."

She was curtseying low before him because of his rank, something he never enjoyed despite being a duke. Automatically he held out his hand to her to help raise her, and as she stood she finally lifted her face and looked him squarely in the eye.

He smiled and let out a great, gusty sigh of relief. Dressed in blue, she wasn't exactly a beauty, but she was pleasing enough, with round, rosy cheeks, a snub nose with a dusting of freckles, and a determined chin. Perhaps a little too determined, now that he considered her more closely. She was not smiling—not even a hint of it—and he'd guess from the set of her chin that she was determined not to.

"Your Grace," she said, and that was all. She wasn't being shy or reserved; she was resentful, even angry.

It was not the most fortuitous beginning.

"I am most honored, Lady Enid," he said with his most irresistible charm. He raised her hand and kissed the air over it, smiling up at her over her fingers. He'd never met a woman who didn't melt at that.

Until now, with the woman he was supposed to marry. Instead Lady Enid remained stone-faced, her fingers tense in his hand, as if she were barely able to refrain from jerking them free.

"Why don't you walk about with Lady Enid, Sheffield?" Brecon said, choosing to ignore the lady's unhappiness. "Surely there are things you'd wish to say to each other without us listening. That is, if Lord and Lady Lattimore can be persuaded to part with their lovely daughter."

"Of course, sir, of course!" Lord Lattimore exclaimed, patting his waistcoat-covered belly. "Whatever His Grace desires!"

With an endorsement like that, Sheffield had no choice but to lead Lady Enid away, holding her hand as gingerly as he could. In silence they made their way through the crowded room toward the tall windows that lined one wall. The spring evening and the crush combined to make the room so warm that the windows had been thrown open to the balcony, and guests strolled freely back and forth. Moonlight spilled over Lady Fortescue's gardens, down to her private river gate and the star-dappled Thames beyond. Sheffield considered taking Lady Enid outside with the hope of the moonlight thawing her humor.

"It's a lovely evening on the river, isn't it, Lady Enid?" he said. "Would you care to step outside to view it?"

She glared at him. *"Docti viri es?"* she demanded. *"Graece et Latine dicis?"*

"Eh?" Sheffield frowned. He recognized that she was addressing him in Latin, but beyond that he was lost, his days of classical study at university a shaky memory at best. *"Docti* what?"

"I asked Your Grace if you were a learned gentleman," she said, unable to keep the triumph from her voice. "I asked if you read Latin and Greek."

His frown deepened. "Why? And why ask me in that ancient mumbo-jumbo?"

"Quia nunquam a dominus qui non nubunt," she answered in the same mumbo-jumbo, then helpfully translated. "I could never marry a gentleman who couldn't. Read Greek and Latin, I mean. Clearly you cannot, sir, and therefore I cannot marry you. I will *not* marry you."

"I can speak, read, eat, and sleep in both French and Italian, Lady Enid," he said, unable to keep irritation from creeping into his voice. He could do a good many other things in those languages, too, not that this grim bluestocking would ever wish to experience them. "Do those account for nothing by your reckoning?"

"No, sir," she said firmly. "French and Italian are frivolous modern tongues, without rigor or tradition."

Sheffield's smile had become a grimace. Blast Brecon for getting him into this, and blast His Majesty, too. He cleared his throat, blatantly buying more time to think.

"Lady Enid," he said finally. "Lady Enid, there seems, ah, to be a certain misunderstanding here."

"No misunderstanding, sir. None." Her face had become so red that Sheffield feared she'd burst into tears. "I understand everything, sir. Despite what Father says, I am a lady of virtue and honor, and I could never resign my happiness to a gentleman who—who is a wastrel and a rake, and who cannot read one word of Latin!"

"Where the dev—that is, who told you that?" he demanded, taken aback. "Your father?"

"Not Father, no," she admitted. "But everyone else speaks of it. From the servants clear to His Majesty. Everyone knows you live for scandal and intrigue and—and low, faithless women."

"For a lady who considers herself so virtuous, you're remarkably well informed." Swiftly he steered her through the nearest door out onto the gallery, not for the romantic moonlight but for the privacy that this peculiar discussion required.

"Where are we going, sir?" she asked, flustered and trying to wriggle away from him. "What do you intend?"

"Not one blasted thing, Lady Enid," he said, "except to learn exactly what is behind this sermon of yours."

"It's not a sermon, sir, but the truth," she said, her voice becoming less strident and more squeaky. "Father says I must marry you because you are a duke and very wealthy, sir, but I say you are no gentleman, and I will not do it."

Sheffield sighed. He should be insulted and angry, even furious, at being rejected with such vehemence. He was a duke with royal blood, and dukes were supposed to be proud and ever mindful of their rank and position.

But while his knowledge of Latin might be lacking, his experience with women wasn't. As soon as he saw how her determined chin had begun to tremble, he understood.

"Come, Lady Enid, tell me the truth," he coaxed. "You love another, don't you?"

"Yes!" she wailed, covering her face with her hands. "Oh, he's such a fine, learned gentleman, not at all like you!"

"I'm sure he is," Sheffield said dryly. He pulled a handkerchief from his pocket and handed it to her. "But despite the fellow's many qualities, your father does not approve."

"How—how did you guess, sir?" she sobbed, and blew her nose into his handkerchief, directly onto his embroidered ducal crest and coronet. "Joshua—that is, Dr. Pullings—is the most perfect gentleman imaginable, yet because he is only an ordained minister and scholar without any fortune instead of a fine lord, Father would never consider him fit for me."

"What earl would?" Sheffield said, hoping he sounded sympathetic. He was, too. Weren't they both trapped on the same high-bred marriage-go-round? "How did you come to fall in love with Dr. Pullings?"

"He was my brother's tutor," she said, "and I was permitted to join them for lessons. Even though I was a female, Josh—Dr. Pullings, that is—took an interest in my education . . . and in me. And though we did not wish it, we soon fell in love."

Could there be a more predictable tale? "But your father refused to listen to your poor vicar's suit."

Fresh torrents of tears spilled down her cheeks, and as she shook her head, they scattered over the front of her gown. "Father grew angry, cast out Dr. Pullings without notice, refused to give him the parish living he'd promised, and ordered me to marry you instead, and I—I will not. I will *not*!"

"You needn't be quite so forceful about it," he said, and with resignation offered his second handkerchief, always carried in the event he encountered weeping ladies such as this one. "Not that I wish to sound ungallant, but I have no more interest in marrying you than you do me."

Her teary eyes widened. "Do you love another, too?"

"At present, no," he said, feeling sheepish to admit such a thing. "But because I subscribe to the unfashionable notion of loving one's bride for herself rather than her bloodlines, I would rather wait to marry until I do."

She nodded eagerly. "Then come with me, sir, so that we might tell my parents, and end this foolish match now!"

"No, Lady Enid, I will not," he said, holding her back. "Nor shall you. I may be a wastrel and a rake, but I also have a conscience, and I don't wish anyone to whisper nonsense of you, or claim you were jilted."

"Oh, sir," she said softly, and he had the uneasy impression she was seeing him for the first time, there in the moonlight. "That's most kind of you. I did not even think of it."

"That's because you're a lady of virtue and honor," he said wryly, unable to keep from repeating her earlier words to her, "and I live for scandal and intrigue. If you can bear it, let us continue as if we mean to obey our elders and wed. What better way to avoid matchmaking schemes than to have been matched already?"

"Can we do that, sir?" she asked uneasily. "Pretend that way?"

"I can if you can," he said. "The ruse will benefit us both, at least until I can think of a respectable way for us to part."

How exactly he'd manage that would be a puzzle. Thanks to Brecon's influence, he really was a rake with a conscience, an uneasy combination if ever there was one. He was perfectly happy to pretend that he and Lady Enid were betrothed if it gave him a respite from other matchmaking schemes, and in fact he'd like to see her wed to her educated tutor, parsing Latin together forever and ever. If he didn't want to marry without love, then he saw no reason she must do so, either, no matter what her father dictated. Besides, Sheffield rather enjoyed the notion of playing Cupid for such an unlikely couple, especially if it meant he would be free.

Clearly Lady Enid was thinking, too. "I'll send word to Joshua to let him know the truth," she said, "so he may stop worrying about me."

"You remain in contact with him, despite your father's wishes?" Sheffield asked, surprised. "You know where he resides?"

"I do, sir," she said, the determined chin returning. "I will remain ever faithful in my love. He is here in London, serving as tutor to a thick-headed merchant's son in Cornhill, the only position he could obtain because of Father."

"Why, Lady Enid," Sheffield said, liking her better after this declaration. "That sounds as if you're conducting a bit of intrigue yourself."

"I would do anything for Dr. Pullings, sir," she said vehemently. "*Anything*. And thus I will pretend to be betrothed to you, sir."

"Even that?" Sheffield asked, amused but also touched by her devotion. It wasn't that he longed for her particular devotion—he didn't—but when he considered all the ladies in his own past, he wasn't sure any of them had been quite so loyal as this.

"Even that, sir," she said firmly, and slipped her hand into his arm. "Shall we share our happiness with my parents?"

They walked back into the house, squeezing their way past the guests who'd gathered to watch the dancers. Sheffield glanced at them, too, his gaze irresistibly drawn to the sight of graceful women dancing. But one in particular caught his eye, a girl with golden hair and a gown of cream-colored damask with pink flowers, and this time he didn't need Fantôme to find her.

"What is it, sir?" Lady Enid said. "You look as if you've seen a ghost."

"Not quite," he said, chagrined that she'd noticed. "But do you know that lady dancing in the white gown, the one with the fair hair?"

Lady Enid looked at the lady, then stared at him, incredulous. "You truly don't recognize her?"

"I wouldn't ask if I did," he said. "Remember, I've been abroad, and a good many fair new faces have appeared in London since I left. Including your own, Lady Enid."

She laughed. "An excellent recovery, sir," she said. "But you should know the lady in white, for she's practically part of your own family. She's Lady Diana Wylder, and her older sisters are Lady Marchbourne and Lady Hawkesworth."

"*That's* Lady Diana Wylder?" he asked, stunned that London could be such a small place. How could it be that Fantôme's lady in the wood was the same lady Brecon had mentioned as being a trial to her mother?

"It is, sir," Lady Enid answered, laughing again at his astonishment. "But I wonder that you do not know her for her history alone, for truly you must both be cut from the same scandalous cloth. Her name has been linked with several of the most unfortunate men, from a ne'er-do-well Irish officer to a Covent Garden actor. She's said to be quite . . . *impulsive.*"

"I'd no notion," he murmured, watching the girl with renewed interest. No, not merely renewed: doubled, or even tripled. He'd already been intrigued by her beauty and her laughter (and her breasts—he'd an undeniable male interest in those), as well as the mysterious circumstances of finding her unattended in the park. But to learn that she was also the same girl whom Brecon had forbidden him to see—ah, perhaps that interest had grown tenfold.

"Actors and Irish officers," he said. "What better way to a dubious reputation?"

"Indeed, sir," Lady Enid said, with perhaps more relish than he'd expected. "It's said that Lady Diana would be considered quite ruined by now if Lady Marchbourne weren't her sister."

"Who's that sorry-looking fellow in black dancing with her now?" Sheffield asked. The man was grim and awkward as he dragged her about the floor, not even bothering to attempt the proper steps. Lady Diana in turn was trying hard to make the best of the dance, and of him, but her misery was clear enough. Even from across the room he could see that her smile was too fixed, her eyes too bright, for real happiness. "He can't possibly be an Irish officer."

"Oh, no, sir," Lady Enid said promptly. "That's Lord Crump, her betrothed, or at least he will be her betrothed any day now. It's said that he's the only unwed lord who's stern enough to offer for her hand."

So this was the man she'd meant when she'd said she wasn't free, there beneath the trees. In Sheffield's estimation, Lord Crump had no business at all offering for Lady Diana's hand, despite how stern he might be. Or rather, because of how stern he was. Sheffield couldn't believe that Brecon had encouraged this foolishness. A spirited girl such as Lady Diana deserved to be amused and charmed, not broken like a recalcitrant nag.

"It's considered a most favorable match for them both, sir," Lady Enid was saying. "She's very beautiful and well-bred, and he's likewise titled and wealthy and willing to overlook her indiscretions for the sake of heirs."

More overheard gossip and scandal: yet this time Sheffield heard the unmistakable wistfulness in Lady

Enid's voice, a wistfulness that drew him sharply back from his thoughts of Lady Diana.

"Not so very different from our own situation, is it?" He patted her fingers on his arm, determined not to be a boor. "But ours will have the happier outcome, Lady Enid, I'm sure of that."

She only sighed, her gaze following Lady Diana.

That would not do; there were few things more depressing than one woman mooning after the lot of another.

"*Gallia est omnis divisa in partes tres,*" he said solemnly.

She looked at him in confusion. "What are you saying?"

"*Gallia est omnis divisa in partes tres,*" he repeated. "That's Virgil, you know."

"'All Gaul is divided into three parts,'" she translated. "It's Julius Caesar, not Virgil."

"It's also the complete sum of the Latin I can recall from school," he said. "All the proof you require regarding me as a possible husband. You deserve a gentleman like Dr. Pullings, Lady Enid, one who will appreciate you for who you are. I swear to do my best to arrange it, too. You have my word."

"*Audentis fortuna luvat,*" she said softly. "That *is* Virgil."

He tipped his head quizzically to one side. "Meaning exactly what?"

"'Fortune favors the brave,'" she said. "Meaning that I thank you for everything, and that I hope you find your lady to love, too."

She smiled up at him, full of trust and gratitude, and she was smiling still when they rejoined her parents.

"How joyful you two look!" Lady Lattimore exclaimed with a great measure of joy herself. "Your Grace, I have never seen my daughter more delighted."

"We were parsing Latin, Lady Lattimore," Sheffield

said, purposely bland. "I have never before met a lady-scholar like Lady Enid."

Beside him Lady Enid barely smothered her laughter, turning it into a mangled, choking cough.

"I do not like the sound of that, Enid," Lady Lattimore said, frowning with concern. "You are quite flushed. She never flushes, Your Grace. Never. Enid, here, let me feel your forehead. Are you unwell? Are you feverish?"

"She's fine as a fiddle, my dear," Lord Lattimore said, winking broadly at Sheffield. "Ladies, hah."

But Lady Lattimore would not be deterred. "She is feverish, sir; the excitement of love has made her so. Summon our coach, if you please. Your Grace, we must beg our leave, for Enid's sake."

There was a bustle of farewells and apologies, a promise that he'd call soon, a final, hurried smile from Lady Enid, and then they were gone, leaving Sheffield much freer than he'd expected from this night—free, really, in every way that mattered.

He raced back to the room with the dancing, to where he'd last seen Lady Diana. He wasn't exactly sure what he'd do when he saw her again. His options were decidedly limited. He wasn't in Paris any longer. Whether she was family or not, he and Lady Diana had yet to be introduced to each other, and even if they had been, they were both supposed to be bound to others. He couldn't address her, separate her from Lord Crump, or ask her to dance, not without causing great scandal. He couldn't even bow to her from across the room. About all he could do was watch her dance from a respectful distance and pray she'd look his way and notice him.

But as soon as he'd managed to work his way through the crowd, the dance ended, and the musicians put aside their instruments to show that the set had ended. Like waves coming into shore, the crowd of guests turned away from where the dancing had been and pushed back against him, looking for more diversions, other friends, and the supper room. Over their heads, he saw Lord Crump's stiff bow before Lady Diana, and her curtsey. Then abruptly she turned away and left him, disappearing through another of the tall open doors to the gallery.

At once Sheffield followed, ducking through the nearest door and onto the same gallery. The evening had grown cooler, and a mist had begun to rise from the river and veil the moon, the same moon that had shone without magic on him and Lady Enid. The chill had driven the other guests back inside the house, leaving the gallery empty except for Lady Diana.

She stood alone in the farthest corner of the gallery, beside the stone balustrade and beneath the shading branch of a nearby tree. The white of her gown was like a wisp of moonlight captured in the shadows, and he went to her at once, unable to resist. He'd no idea what he'd say or do, no idea at all except that he wanted to be with her, which should, he decided, be inspiration enough when the time came for doing and saying.

As he drew closer, she heard his footsteps and swiftly turned to face him. He thought she might have been crying; now he could see that her hands had been knotted on the balustrade in frustration, not unhappiness. In an instant her expression changed from startled wariness to bewilderment to out-and-out wonder.

"It's you," she whispered, her eyes wide as he stood before her. "It's *you*."

"It is," he said. "And you're you, too."

"What absolute foolishness," she said. She smiled crookedly, displaying a single charming dimple, and then, to his eternal surprise, slipped her arms around his shoulders and kissed him.

CHAPTER

 4

Without thought or hesitation, Diana closed her eyes and kissed the stranger.

It was bold of her, and brazen, and not like her usual self at all. Despite what the gossips whispered, she wasn't in the habit of kissing men willy-nilly, and certainly not men whose names and history she did not know. In fact, if pressed, she could likely only count a half-dozen boys and men whom she'd kissed in all her eighteen years. Perhaps the number was greater than for other, more saintly ladies, but surely it was not enough to qualify her as slatternly or overly free.

At least not until now. Now she was standing in the moonlight on the gallery of Lady Fortescue's house with the breezes from the river tossing her skirts and her hair and her arms curled wantonly around the shoulders of a man who was a complete and total stranger to her.

No, she must be honest: he was not a complete stranger. She might not know his name, but from his speech, dress, and manner, she knew he was an English gentleman. She knew he had a white French bulldog named Fantôme. She knew he was gallant, and amusing, too, and she knew he was wonderfully handsome and that his shoulders beneath her arms were broad and manly and very nice to rest upon. She knew he'd a charming smile, and that she'd wanted to kiss him the first time he'd smiled at her, and ever since, which was part of the reason she was kissing him now.

Most of all, she was kissing him because he wasn't Lord Crump.

But then, to her surprise, the gentleman began to kiss her in return, a beguiling, seductive kiss that coaxed her to follow his lead. He settled one hand around her waist and another at the small of her back as familiarly as if they'd been there scores of times before, and leaned into her, gently pushing her back against the trunk of the overhanging tree. As he drew her body closer to his, he deepened the kiss, slanting his mouth over her lips until with a little catch in her breath she parted them for him. Instantly the kiss changed into something deeper, hotter, more demanding, and far, far different from the kisses she'd shared with those other half dozen boys and men. It almost made her dizzy, this kiss. It was exhilarating and it was passionate, and it was complete and utter madness.

As swiftly as if she'd been burned, she jerked her mouth away from his and twisted herself free from his embrace, adding an extra, emphatic little shove to his chest that was more from her own mortification than from anything he'd done.

He stared at her, his mouth open with bewilderment and confusion—a confusion that she certainly understood. Then he visibly collected himself, squaring his shoulders and bowing before her.

"I beg your forgiveness, ma'am," he said. "To take advantage of you as I did is—"

"But you *didn't*!" she cried, shamed beyond measure. "I was the one who took unfair advantage of *you*, forcing my attentions on you like a—a *harlot*!"

His brows rose with surprise. "I do not believe it is

possible, ma'am, for a lady to take unfair advantage of a gentleman. Nor did I ever consider you as a harlot."

"But I *kissed* you, sir," she said. She pressed her palms to her cheeks, striving to calm herself. "If that wasn't unfair of me—"

"It wasn't unfair, ma'am," he protested. He was standing so the moonlight washed across his face, making him so handsome that she could have wept. "You did not see me pushing you away, did you?"

"No." She closed her eyes for a moment, trying to shut out the memory of the entire appalling scene. "But it is the nature of a man to take whatever is offered, while it's the lady's part to refuse, or at least not to kiss him like that. That is, to kiss you. Oh, sir, what I've *done*, and for what? For what?"

"Because you liked it," he said, and grinned. "I did."

He held his hand out to her, but she shook her head in furious refusal.

"No, sir, no, *no!*" she said. "I only kissed you because I was angry and frustrated with—with someone else, and with my passions unsettled, I kissed you because I—oh, I do not know why."

"I understand entirely, ma'am," he said, as if her explanation were perfectly logical. "Combine a surfeit of passion, a fury, and the moonlight, and there you are. Or rather, there we were."

"But never again," she said, desperation making her nearly breathless. If Lord Crump learned of what she'd done here, he'd reject her—she was certain of that. Every other of her little indiscretions would pale beside this. She'd be completely disgraced, and worse, she'd break her mother's heart. "Never."

"I don't believe I care for the finality of that," he said wryly. "It's not terribly flattering."

"I beg you, sir, this is no jest," she pleaded. "You must forget that this has ever happened between us, else

I shall be quite ruined, and disappoint all those who care most for me."

"Very well, then. You have my word of honor that no one will ever hear of this." With his hand still outstretched, his grin settled into a more understanding smile. "Not so much as a whisper, Lady Diana."

She gasped with fresh dismay. "You know who I am?"

He let drop the offered hand she'd ignored, and bowed again.

"I always learn the name of the most beautiful lady in the room," he said, and the way he said it made her sure he'd done exactly that. "Besides, we should know each other, considering that—"

"Please don't tell me," she begged. "I don't wish to know. It will make it easier to pretend I do not know you if ever we meet again."

"Very well, Lady Diana," he said, lowering his voice to a confidential whisper. "It shall be our private secret."

He smiled again, so charming in the moonlight that she couldn't begin to tell if he was teasing or not. Ladies were not supposed to share secrets with gentlemen, any more than they were supposed to kiss them, and she could only pray he'd keep his word. What choice did she have now except to trust him?

"Thank you, sir," she said. "I thank you."

She turned and fled, leaving him behind on the gallery as she slipped through one of the doors and back inside. She did not look back, not wishing to encourage him if he'd dared to follow, but she did glance at one of the gold-framed looking glasses as she passed it, and he wasn't behind her. Relieved, she swiftly found her family where she'd left them, with Charlotte, Mama, and Aunt Sophronia all sitting in armchairs with plates of sweetmeats and pastries in their laps. March wasn't there, doubtless off discussing some male business with a friend, but watching over the ladies in his place was his older cousin, the Duke of Breconridge, leaning over the back of Mama's chair as he told some witty story that had sent all three ladies into peals of laughter behind their fans.

Diana smiled as she rejoined her family, relieved that none of them seemed to have been worrying about her, or even missed her. Perhaps she could simply slip into listening to whatever story Brecon was telling and pretend that she'd been there all evening. Perhaps, if she laughed at his drolleries along with her aunt and sister and mother, no one would ask where she'd been or what she'd been doing.

And perhaps, too, pigs would sprout feathered wings and fly from their sties up to the moon.

"Here you are at last, Diana," Aunt Sophronia said, twisting around to face her. "I trust you're feeling better now?"

"Thank you, Aunt, yes," Diana said, barely remembering that she'd escaped Lord Crump and yet another dance by claiming she needed fresh air. "I'm quite recovered now."

Charlotte leaned forward, looking over her fan. "But where is Lord Crump, Diana? He told us you'd been suddenly taken ill, and he was going to make inquiries at the ladies' cloakroom, to see if you'd gone there. He was quite concerned for you."

Belatedly (and guiltily) Diana realized that Lord Crump was nowhere to be seen. She hadn't meant to abandon him as long as she had; she was fortunate— *very* fortunate—that he hadn't come out onto the gallery to look for her there.

"I didn't intend to worry him," she said, hoping her face wouldn't betray her. "All I needed was a moment or two alone after the dancing."

"Never leave a gentleman to his own devices, my dear," Aunt Sophronia warned sagely, her rings glittering as she shook an admonishing finger at Diana. "Even a fine and honorable gentleman such as Lord Crump can find mischief."

Diana flushed. She doubted that Lord Crump would so much as recognize mischief, let alone seek it out, while she herself seemed to tumble into it as naturally as breathing.

"I'm sure he'll return to us here, Aunt Sophronia," Diana said. "The rooms are so crowded that it's difficult to move through them."

"I certainly hope he will return to you, my dear," said her aunt. "It would not do for you to lose your betrothed the way you would mislay an old glove."

Charlotte took Diana's hand in a show of sisterly support.

"Lord Crump would never wander far from Diana, Aunt Sophronia," she said. "What gentleman would?"

Smiling, she gently pulled Diana's hand, drawing her closer so she could whisper to her.

"I do not know where you've been, Di, or what you've been doing," she said so softly that none of the others could overhear, "but there are leaves in your hair."

Immediately Diana's hands flew to her head. Charlotte was right. There *were* bits of leaves in her hair, doubtless left from kissing the stranger beneath the tree, and as quickly as she could she pulled them out, twisting the curls back into place with her fingers.

Charlotte suddenly smiled, looking past Diana and releasing her hand.

"Here's March," she said. "Goodness, look who he has with him!"

Expecting March to have returned with Lord Crump, Diana didn't turn at once, taking an extra second to compose herself. She had to smile and look welcoming; at least she could be grateful she wouldn't have to dance with him again that night.

"I knew he'd returned to London," March said, "but I didn't expect to find him here tonight. You recall my wicked cousin Sheffield, fresh from conquering Paris?"

Another cousin of March's; sometimes it seemed to Diana there was always another, the way they kept popping up in company. But at least it wasn't Lord Crump, and she exhaled with relief.

"Be more honest, March," Aunt Sophronia said with an arch little huff. "Your cousin's fresh from a single lamentable conquest. Though I'll admit that scandal agrees with you, Sheffield. You're even more handsome than I remember. No wonder that dreadful French lady was so besotted."

"Ancient history, Lady Sanborn," the newcomer replied confidently, "ancient history, and all in my past. Handsome or not, I'm thoroughly reformed, and as safe and tame as your own little dogs."

Everyone laughed, except for Diana. She recognized that voice, that easy charm, and her heart squeezed tight in her breast. It couldn't possibly be true, could it? Could her luck have run so incredibly badly as this?

"You know His Grace the Duke of Sheffield, don't you, Diana?" Charlotte asked, a gentle prodding intended to make Diana turn about and be civil. "He has lived abroad for a great while and you have been tucked away in Dorset, but surely you must have been in London to have met at least once, yes?"

Oh, yes, we've met, thought Diana grimly. But, family or not, it was never polite to keep one's back toward a duke, and with a deep breath she turned swiftly around to face him.

"Your Grace," she murmured, bowing her head and making the curtsey that was proper when greeting a duke. "Forgive me, for I do not believe I've yet had the honor."

"Ah, well, that's easily remedied," March said. "Sheffield, this is Charlotte's little sister, Lady Diana Wylder. Diana, my cousin, the Duke of Sheffield."

So Sheffield was his name, and he was a duke. She shouldn't be surprised, not really. He'd that kind of easy, inborn confidence that usually came with titles and good fortune. Here in the candlelight, she could see how costly his clothing was, perfectly tailored to his height and broad shoulders, and richly embroidered to add to the overall impression of luxurious wealth. She should have recognized the resemblance between him and March and Brecon. They'd the same strong jaw and dark coloring, and the same preference for wearing their own nearly black hair instead of a more fashionable wig. The long-ago king who'd been their shared ancestor surely had sired a splendid crop of handsome gentlemen, so handsome that it almost seemed unfair to the rest of the peerage.

And, of course, their indisputable charm gave them an unfair advantage over all the ladies as well—as Sheffield was proving even now.

"Lady Diana," he said, taking her hand to raise her. "If I'd known you were here in London, I would not have lingered so long in Paris."

He kissed the air over the back of her hand, exactly what was respectfully correct for the circumstances. But there was little that was respectful about how he looked up at Diana over the back of her hand, his gray eyes filled with conspiratorial amusement.

Had he known all along who she was? And had she really played so neatly into the hands of such an infamous scoundrel that even Aunt Sophronia knew of his reputation?

Blast him—and blast herself, too, for kissing him like one more in his parade of conquests!

"Do not be frightened by Sheffield's boldness, Diana," Brecon said, clearly misinterpreting her simmering silence for wariness. "He cannot help himself, you know, and speaks such palaver to all ladies from habit, not genuine intent."

"True, Lady Diana, all true," Sheffield said, solemnly agreeing, though again the engaging merriment in his eyes betrayed him. "My cousin Brecon tells only the truth, especially about me."

"I am thankful for it, sir," she said, finally remembering to pull her hand free of his. Heavens preserve her, one look from those gray eyes with their dark lashes was more seductive than an outright caress from any other man! "There can never be too much truth in this deceitful world of ours."

"Wisely spoken, my dear," Brecon said, though he seemed to be concentrating more on Sheffield than her. "But for once Sheffield was also speaking in perfect honesty when he said he'd become tamed. He is to be married."

All around Diana the rest of her family was exclaiming with amazement and congratulation, but all she cared for was what Sheffield told her.

"More truth, sir?" she asked, her voice trembling with emotion that could be anger, indignation, or even simple misery. He loved someone else, and he loved that someone so deeply that he'd asked her to marry him. She felt double the fool now for having kissed him, a man promised to another lady. "This is no idle tale, and you are to wed?"

"I am, Lady Diana," he said evenly. "I have come to an understanding this very evening with Lady Enid Lattimore."

Did a cloud of regret flicker across his eyes and dim his smile, or was she only wishing it there? Worse yet, could he see the same disappointment mirrored in her own?

"May I offer my congratulations to you, sir," she said,

somehow saying what was expected, "and my best wishes for your happiness with Lady Enid."

He began to bow in acknowledgment, but as he did, Lord Crump finally reappeared, showing a much better sense of timing than he'd displayed earlier while dancing. He seemed to be overly warm, likely from the crush of the crowded rooms and from looking from her, and beads of sweat glistened on his temples around the edge of his wig. Standing among the tall, handsome cousins in their silk coats, he looked even more like an ungainly crow.

"Here you are, Lady Diana," he said, managing to sound both solicitous yet faintly scolding. He blotted his forehead with his folded handkerchief. "I trust you are recovered?"

"Thank you, Lord Crump, I am." She smiled warmly and slipped her hand into the crook of his arm, ignoring his obvious surprise. "You've joined us just in time."

"I have, Lady Diana?" He smiled uneasily in return.

"Yes, indeed," she said, raising her voice so that all around her would be sure to hear. For the second time this evening, she was acting impulsively and letting her emotions race roughshod over her common sense. Two wrongs would never make a right, especially not in this case. But just as she'd kissed Sheffield without a thought for the lasting consequences, she'd make her declaration now exactly the same way, bravely and boldly and because she wished to do so. Who cared if Sheffield had found his future wife? Didn't she have a husband-to-be waiting for her, too?

"I'll grant that our family has much to celebrate with His Grace's betrothal," she said, pausing until she was certain she'd everyone's attention. "But His Grace is not the only one with joyful news. Tonight I—I have accepted Lord Crump's offer of marriage."

"Dear Lady Diana!" exclaimed Lord Crump, his

eyes round with astonishment. "How happy you have made me!"

Diana tried to smile. He'd every right to be surprised: not only had she not accepted his proposal of marriage, he hadn't made one. She was trusting he wouldn't share that little fact, and he didn't. In fact, he seemed perfectly willing to pretend that he had. Perhaps he was even relieved that he wouldn't actually have to do so now.

He took her hand in his, giving her fingers a clumsy pat.

"Dear Lady Diana," he said again. "How grateful I am for your regard, and how agreeable to have matters settled between us so soon."

"Oh, Diana, I am delighted!" Mama exclaimed, rushing forward to wrap her arms around Diana. She was weeping with joy, which made tears sting in Diana's eyes, too. Soon Charlotte and Aunt Sophronia had joined them, all hugging and weeping in a wonderful, womanly display of rejoicing and love.

At least it would have been wonderful if Diana had truly loved Lord Crump. With every blessing and kiss of good wishes that she received on her cheek, the reality of what she'd just done struck her more keenly.

Over her mother's shoulder, she saw Sheffield again. He was standing to one side, watching her. When his eyes met hers, he didn't smile as she'd expected. Instead he held her gaze for a moment longer, his expression thoughtful. Then he looked away and joined the other gentlemen.

That, and no more.

The next morning, Sheffield sat alone at a small table near the coffeehouse's window, idly glancing over a week-old paper from Paris as he sipped his coffee. The coffee was better than he expected, the beans well roasted and the brew murky-dark and thick, the way he liked it, and the news was not so old that it failed to entertain.

The coffeehouse keeper had not recognized him beyond being a gentleman, and so while he'd been shown to a favorable seat, he hadn't been badgered with the obsequious attention that often followed dukes. He was thankful for that. His meeting here this morning would be far more agreeable without any ducal fanfare, which was why he'd dressed plainly and hired a hansom instead of rolling out in his coach with the gold-picked crest on the door. With Fantôme curled asleep against his feet beneath the table and the spring sunshine warm on his shoulders, he felt comfortably at ease. Simplicity definitely had its pleasures.

Besides, he'd earned a small respite in this day. The morning still wasn't done, yet he'd already accomplished much. He'd risen early to meet with Marlowe, his primary man of business here in London. Although Sheffield was conscientious about his properties and affairs even while abroad, there were still many things to review with Marlowe: changes in the household staff of his London house; the latest progress on the new stables at Oakworth, his country house in Hampshire; recommendations regarding the apple trees in his orchard; and the arrangement of new statues in the garden. There was also a stack of letters from petitioners and acquaintances, and appeals from worthy charities to consider.

Once he'd finished with the most urgent of Marlowe's business, Sheffield had an inquiry of his own. He'd a vague memory of a church living tied to the parish that served his tenants at Oakworth, plus other families in the nearby village. Dispensing livings to worthy clergymen wasn't generally one of Sheffield's interests, and while Marlowe had expressed modest surprise when Sheffield asked, he still gave the answer that Sheffield had hoped for.

But that hadn't been all. Sheffield had also arranged this meeting here, and on his way he'd stopped at his favorite bookseller's. There he'd found exactly what he wanted, or rather, what he thought Lady Enid would want: an exquisite old edition of Homer's *Odyssey*, bound in red leather. He'd written a brief inscription inside to Lady Enid and had it sent to her. Then, because it didn't seem right sending only a book to a lady, he'd also had a large bouquet of red roses, fresh from the country, delivered to her as well. He'd no more intention of marrying Lady Enid than she did him, but the rest of London didn't know that, and Sheffield wished to maintain his reputation as a thoughtful lover.

Which, reputation or not, he was. He liked women too much to be anything else, whether from Brecon's influence or his own French blood. His life would undoubtedly be much less complicated if he'd a harder heart where women were concerned. He knew plenty of gentlemen who put their own pleasure first and gave not a thought for the poor woman who'd done the pleasing, but he wasn't one of them. He enjoyed discovering the little differences and nuances that made every woman special, and which, to his mind and his cock, made seduction such an endlessly fascinating experiment.

But that joy of discovery could also turn into a trial. How else to explain last night, and now this morning? Even as he'd been assiduously considering and choosing the perfect small gift to send to Lady Enid, his shameless thoughts kept racing back to kissing Lady Diana.

No, it went back further than that, to the afternoon when Fantôme had found her in the park. He had been fascinated with her then, and last night had only served to increase that fascination. She was an undeniable beauty with her golden hair and wide blue eyes, and of course her delectable breasts, but it was her impulsiveness that truly intrigued him. Most ladies were wary with strange men, but she wasn't, not at all. What was the word that Brecon had used? *Willful*. To him, she wasn't so much willful as direct. Clearly she did what she wanted, when she chose, and with whom. Little wonder that Brecon and her mother were so concerned. Lady Diana was completely, charmingly unpredictable. He'd never come across another woman who behaved like that, and as a man, he was irresistibly drawn to the challenge.

He smiled, thinking of how she'd kissed him. He'd been surprised, yes, but what had surprised him far more was tasting her inexperience. She'd kissed him freely, but she wasn't in the habit of doing it. He'd realized it from the instant he'd begun to kiss her in return, and how startled she'd been by the intimacy of it. He'd wager a hundred guineas that she was a virgin, despite the tattle. She hadn't backed away, though, and she'd learned quickly and eagerly. How much more he'd like to teach her!

So why, then, was she so determined to wed a dry old stick such as Crump?

"Begging pardon, sir," a waiter said, bowing slightly beside the table. "That gentleman, there at the door, he says he's to meet a gentleman with a white dog. Do that be you, sir? He said his name be Dr. Pullings, sir. Do you know him, sir? Should I show him here, sir, or send him away?"

Sheffield leaned to one side so he could see the door and the newcomer beside it: a young man with an open, round face, plain dark clothes rusty with wear, a flat, uncocked hat, and the kind of shapeless, dun-colored wig with a limp black ribbon that was favored by impoverished clerics.

"Yes, I'm the man with the white dog," Sheffield said, bemused to be described in such a way, "and yes, I am expecting Dr. Pullings. Show him here directly."

The waiter went to fetch Dr. Pullings, and Sheffield refolded the paper and put it to one side. He hadn't been reading it much, anyway. His own life at present seemed far more dramatic than anything a mere Parisian journalist could contrive.

"Good day, Dr. Pullings," he said, offering the other chair. "I thank you for joining me on such short notice."

"Good day, Your Grace, good day," Pullings said, bobbing a nervous bow. "It is I who must be grateful, Your Grace, and forever in your debt."

The waiter's head twitched at that doubled "Your Grace." So much for anonymity, thought Sheffield wryly; the entire coffeehouse would soon be attempting to eavesdrop on their conversation.

"You're hardly in my debt yet, Dr. Pullings," he said. "Here. Sit. What shall you have? Coffee, tea, chocolate?"

"Tea, Your Grace, thank you very much," Pullings said, sitting on the edge of the other chair with his hat on his knee. He was younger than Sheffield had expected, younger even than he himself. His nose and cheeks were lightly freckled, adding to his boyishness, and he had an insistent Adam's apple that betrayed his nervousness. His clothes were even shabbier than Sheffield had first thought, the seams of his coat faded and the fraying cuffs of his shirt turned at least once. He was the perfect model of an impoverished scholar-cleric, and exactly the sort of young man certain to horrify Lord Lattimore as a suitor for Lady Enid.

"I realize I said little in my letter," Sheffield began. "I'm sure the entire arrangement must seem peculiar to you."

"No, Your Grace, no, no," Pullings said. The tea appeared before him, and with an anxious clattering of the spoon in the cup he stirred in his sugar. "That is, I'd a letter last night from—from the lady involved, who explained everything."

Sheffield wished there were some polite way to explain that he needed to be addressed as "Your Grace" once, and thereafter an everyday "sir" would suffice. But despite his nervousness, the poor fellow had taken care not to use Lady Enid's name in public, and Sheffield approved.

"I'm glad the lady explained it all, Dr. Pullings," he said wryly, "because in all honesty, I'm not sure I could do the same."

Pullings's face fell. "You've changed your mind, then, Your Grace," he said with obvious despair. "I cannot blame you. It was too generous of you to be true."

"I haven't changed my mind," Sheffield said quickly. "That is, so long as our conversation goes as I hope, then I haven't."

This *was* a deuced odd circumstance, interviewing the sweetheart of the woman he himself was committed to marry. No matter how desperately Lady Enid had sworn she was in love, Sheffield wanted to make sure that Pullings was worthy of her attentions before he tried to bring them together. On principle he'd no wish to side with Lord Lattimore, but he didn't want to see Lady Enid be swept away by a Greek-and-Latin-spewing fortune-hunter, either.

"I swear to whatever you wish, Your Grace," Pullings declared. "I will not surrender the lady, not to you or anyone else."

"Even if she came to you without a farthing to her name?" Sheffield asked, feeling like the devil's advocate. "I understand her father will give her nothing if she marries against his wishes."

"I would take her in her shift alone, Your Grace," he said, his eyes flashing with an unministerly fire. "She is that dear to me. Our souls, our hearts, are as one, and will be so forever, no matter what the Fates may conspire to keep us asunder."

"No need for things to be quite so, ah, dramatic," Sheffield said, thinking how closely Pullings's words echoed Lady Enid's. Clearly these two spent a great deal of time declaiming their devotion to each other, and quite poetically, too. Yet in a way he envied them. He'd been in and out of love for years, but he'd never once felt this strongly for any woman, and he doubted that any of those women in his past would have said the same about him, either.

"No need for drama, nor poetry," he continued. "Consider this simply a way for all of us to oblige one another."

"Love is never an obligation, Your Grace," Pullings said earnestly. "It is a joy, a blessing, a—"

"Well, yes, all that," Sheffield said, thinking how he'd never want to sit before Pullings as he was preaching a sermon. "Here is my offer. There is a small parish connected to my property in Hampshire. The present vicar is an elderly fellow who plans to withdraw at Midsummer's Day to spend the rest of his days with his son's family. The living's yours, and the lady, too, if you will permit her to act as my intended until that time."

Pullings's jaw fell open. "A parish in Hampshire," he whispered. "A living of my own . . . Oh, Your Grace, I do not have words to thank you for your generosity, your munificence, your—"

"The lady," Sheffield said. "You must agree to that part, too."

Pullings frowned. "Forgive me, Your Grace, but I must beg your assurance that if the lady acts this part, then you will show her the utmost respect."

"Not so much as a kiss on the cheek," Sheffield said soundly. "You've my word of honor on that. I respect the lady too much to disrespect her in that way. In September you two can elope and set up housekeeping in

Hampshire, easy as can be. No one shall know the truth but us."

It wouldn't really be easy as can be, not exactly. Sheffield knew that, even if the young man across from him didn't. It would be a huge, raging scandal—an earl's daughter running off with her brother's old tutor, a duke abandoned at the altar (almost), a disappointed king— but nothing that Sheffield couldn't weather. Besides, he'd never been the wounded party in a love affair. He was actually rather looking forward to the experience as a diversion.

"It will be a grievously large deceit, Your Grace, with many untruths necessary for success," Pullings said slowly, his palms pressed flat on the table on either side of his teacup, as if bracing himself. "And yet it may be the only way."

Sheffield sighed impatiently. "If you wish to marry the lady, then yes, it likely is the only way."

"Then I shall accept, Your Grace," he said finally. "On behalf of both of us, I accept. We shall evermore be in your debt."

"Excellent!" Sheffield smiled and held his hand out to the other man, who took it gingerly. "I shall be honored to play your Cupid, Dr. Pullings."

"I—we—are the ones who are honored, Your Grace," Pullings said solemnly. "It is bold of me to say so, but our Heavenly Lord in His wisdom cannot smile on the holy sacrament of matrimony debased into a union of titles and fortunes."

"Exactly so," Sheffield said, surprising himself by being in complete agreement.

"I am glad you agree, Your Grace," Pullings said. "I can only pray that this ruse of ours will be of benefit to you and the fair lady you truly love as well."

Even as Sheffield began to deny the existence of such a lady, the image of Lady Diana Wylder abruptly appeared in his thoughts, a vivid memory of her determined smile as she'd reached up to kiss him. It was the damnedest thing. He didn't love her. How could he, when he scarcely knew her? He didn't love anyone, not at present.

"*Omnia vincit amor,*" Pullings said solemnly. "Love conquers all. Virgil knew the truth, didn't he? Surely this marvelous day is proof of that, Your Grace."

"Perhaps," Sheffield said thoughtfully. "Perhaps."

He couldn't shake the memory of Lady Diana, nor, really, did he want to. He had promised to call upon March's wife, Charlotte, and her sister was bound to be there as well. All he wished today was to see her again, to watch her smile and hear her laughter. As for tomorrow, who knew what might happen?

Omnia vincit amor. . . .

CHAPTER

5

Diana woke to the scrape of the bed-curtain rings across the metal rod as her lady's maid, Sarah, pulled them aside for the day. She'd already opened the curtains at the window, and the bright morning sun streamed in across the bed and into Diana's eyes.

Squinting, Diana rolled over again, burrowing her face back into the pillows and pulling the coverlet over her shoulders. Her cat, Fig, also awakened against her will, stretched and resettled close against Diana's hip, ready to return to sleep as well.

"Good day, my lady," Sarah said briskly. She moved Diana's breakfast tray onto the little table beside the bed, purposely (or so it seemed to Diana) rattling and clattering the porcelain cup and saucers and the silver chocolate pot to make the greatest possible noise. "It's half past ten, my lady. Pray recall that you are to join Her Grace, Lord Pennington, Lord Fitzcharles, and Lady Amelia in the garden at eleven."

Diana groaned. She had in fact forgotten she'd promised to meet Charlotte and her children: Lord Pennington, known in the family as Jamie, and his twin sister Lady Amelia, were both three, and their younger brother Georgie, Lord Fitzcharles, was two. (The third boy, Edward, Lord Powys, was only five months, and still banished to the nursery.) The plan for the morning was to sail toy boats on the wide garden pond behind Marchbourne House, where Diana was idolized as the most accomplished commodore of the family. Being with her nieces and nephews was one of the best parts of staying with Charlotte and March while she and Mama were in town, and on most days Diana would have already been at the side of the pond, eagerly planning the regatta.

But this morning was different. They had all stayed at Lady Fortescue's house long after midnight, and Diana had not been undressed and in bed until nearly three. Yet as exhausted as she'd been, her thoughts—and her conscience—were far too tangled to let her sleep, and the sun was just beginning to rise when at last she'd drifted off. All she wished now was to return to blissful sleep and forget about the Duke of Sheffield, Lord Crump, and everything she'd said and done with them both.

"You've only twenty-five minutes now to eat and dress, my lady," Sarah warned, the chocolate pot in her hand poised to pour. "Unless you wish me to send Her Grace your regrets."

"No, no, Sarah, I'll rise." Diana pushed herself upright, sending a disgruntled Fig sprawling to one side. "I cannot disappoint the children, and Charlotte will remind me of it all the day if I am late."

She took the cup and saucer that Sarah offered, sipping from it before setting the cup alone back down on the tray. While Sarah watched in silent disapproval, Diana filled the deep-sided saucer with the extra cream intended for the chocolate, then set it on the bed for Fig. With a chirrup of pleasure, the little cat settled down, her tail straight behind, and began to lap the cream while Diana gently ran her hand along the silky fur of her back. Fig had come with her from Ransom, one of her few remaining connections with their old life in

Dorset. As cats went, Fig was no beauty—no matter how much cream she ate, she remained small and bony and her fur an irregular patchwork of tawny brown and black and cream—but she was afraid of nothing, and as devoted to Diana as Diana was to her.

"Best leave that cat be, my lady," Sarah said, "and come to your dressing table so I may begin your hair."

Obediently Diana climbed from the bed, slipped her arms into the silk dressing gown that Sarah held up for her, and plucked an iced raisin bun from the plate. As soon as she'd sat on the cushioned bench before the looking glass, Sarah had begun pulling apart Diana's long nighttime braid and began brushing furiously at her honey-gold hair.

"You needn't do anything fancy, Sarah," Diana said, wincing from the brushing as she ate the bun. "I'll just be in the garden."

"There's undress for Dorset, my lady, and then there's undress for London," Sarah said, deftly smoothing and twisting Diana's hair. "Her Grace expects you to present yourself as is proper for Marchbourne House."

Diana sighed wistfully, pulling the raisins one by one from the bun. In the old days at Ransom, she and Charlotte would have chosen ragged boy's breeches, oversized sailor's jerseys, and bare feet, and they'd have been as happy and free on the beach as the gulls wheeling over their heads. But now Charlotte was the Duchess of Marchbourne and the mistress of this house and two more besides, and she was required to dress in silk and furs and jewels. Although a marquis was not so grand as a duke, Diana supposed the same would be expected of her once she married Lord Crump.

Lady Diana, Marchioness of Crump. Oh, she did not want to be reminded of what she'd done! Desperately she tried to put it from her mind and think of something, anything, other than how last night she'd announced to her world that she was going to marry Lord Crump.

But what—or who—came to mind at once was far worse: the Duke of Sheffield, his dark hair tousled and his gray eyes shining with merriment as he smiled at her, sharing the secret of how she'd boldly, wantonly kissed him.

She closed her eyes for a moment and gave her head a fierce shake, then with a deep breath looked around for any distraction.

"What are those, Sarah?" she asked. One of the large silver salvers from the front hall was sitting on a nearby chair. The salver was piled high with cards and folded letters, and even without reading any of them, Diana could tell from the well-bred penmanship and the crowns and coronets pressed into the sealing wax that they'd come from some of the most noble addresses in London.

"Lady Hervey said they're for you, my lady," Sarah said, her mouth bristling with hairpins as she dressed Diana's hair. "Her ladyship says they're congratulations upon the announcement of your coming marriage, all delivered this morning."

Unhappily Diana looked at the piled salver. Each of those letters and cards represented one more person she could not disappoint, and every good wish they contained sealed her betrothal to Lord Crump a bit more firmly, bound her a bit more inexorably to him.

"Her ladyship ordered them brought up to you," Sarah continued, "for you to read and acknowledge, my lady."

Mama would expect her to answer them all this afternoon. Only a sentence or two would be required, and likely the same sentence or two. But written over and over, it would be like a schoolroom punishment—especially since it would be a sentiment of joy that Diana did not feel.

With her hair done, Sarah dressed her quickly. Her days of boy's breeches might have passed, but at least she wasn't expected to wear silk for paddling in the pond. Instead she wore a plain dark red linen jacket over a blue-and-white-striped linen petticoat, and a kerchief printed with roses over her shoulders and breast. To keep the sun from her face, she pinned on a wide-brimmed straw hat with red ribbons tied at the nape of her neck.

She was taking another bun from the breakfast tray just as the clock on the mantel struck eleven. Quickly she stuffed the rest of the bun into her mouth, scooped Fig from the bed and tucked her into her arms, and hurried from her bedchamber and toward the stairs.

Marchbourne House was very large and very grand, and even at a swift pace, it took her several minutes to race along the corridor from her bedchamber, past bowing footmen and maidservants, and down the marble staircase. The garden door was within sight when a footman hurried toward her.

"Lady Diana," he said. "Lady Hervey wishes you to join her now in the green room."

"Now?" Diana stopped abruptly. "But I am on my way to join Her Grace in the garden."

"Forgive me, my lady," he said, bowing again as if to apologize. "Lady Hervey said now."

"Now," she repeated with resignation. At least Charlotte would understand, considering it was Mama delaying her. "Very well. Please tell Her Grace in the garden that I shall be with her as soon as Lady Hervey releases me."

She left him and headed back to the green room, a small chamber to the front of the house that her mother used as her office and sitting room whenever they stayed with Charlotte. With walls papered in a pattern of over-sized white and yellow tulips, the little room seemed always washed with sunshine, its cheerfulness very much like Mama herself.

Today Mama shared the green room with another. She sat in one of the curving armchairs that flanked the fireplace, and in the other was Brecon. Diana wasn't surprised; the duke was often with her mother. They'd both lost their spouses early in life, and Mama seemed as willing to turn to him for advice about business and legal affairs as Brecon was eager to offer it. Diana understood perfectly well why her mother would like a gentleman-friend such as Brecon. She was fond of Brecon, too, enjoying his company as if he were a favorite uncle who told silly stories over dinner. He was amusing and gallant and relatively handsome, for all that he must be at least forty, though Diana could never be sure with older people.

But Brecon and Mama certainly seemed happy enough now—so happy, in fact, that Diana had the uncomfortable feeling of interrupting as she stood in the doorway.

"Come in, lamb, come in," Mama said. She was dressed to make calls or visit shops, in a painted silk morning gown, a frilled linen cap, a lace scarf over her shoulders, and matching worked mitts on her hands, while her pelisse and hat lay ready on her desk. Smiling, she patted the seat of the chair beside hers to encourage Diana to join her. "There's no need to look so uncertain. We've only the pleasantest matters to discuss."

"How is Mistress Fig this day?" Brecon asked. He, too, was dressed to go out, in a dark blue coat, dark beaver hat, and tan buckskin breeches, or perhaps that was simply what he'd chosen to wear to call here. "Her whiskers are looking particularly glossy."

Diana grinned, taking the chair beside her mother. When Brecon smiled at her like that, she saw at once the cousinly resemblance between him and Sheffield: a most inconvenient observation to make this morning, and one she tried hard to forget.

"If Fig's whiskers are glossy, it's because she has had an especially large saucer of cream this morning," she said as the little cat circled around and around on her lap before finally settling. "Likely there's still some on her whiskers."

Brecon laughed, but Mama's expression was a bit wryer.

"It would seem Fig's not the only one wearing her breakfast," she said, not so much scolding as observing. "Truly, Diana, sometimes I do despair. I know poor Sarah does her best with you, but here you are, scarce out of bed, yet already covered with crumbs and cat hairs."

Already knowing what she'd find, Diana glanced down at her jacket. The dark red linen was sprinkled with white crumbs and a smear of sugar icing, added to a scattered dusting of Fig's fur.

"Forgive me, Mama," she said, brushing her bodice as best she could. "I didn't intend to be untidy. But all I've to do this morning is sail boats with Charlotte and the children, and I doubt they'll care."

"But you should, Diana." Mama sighed. "One day you've plumes in your hat as tall as Westminster's towers, so fashionably dressed that you'd give a Parisian lady pause, and the next you look ready to muck the stables. There should be some balance. A true lady draws admiration for herself, not for what she wears."

Now Diana sighed, too, for this was not a new conversation. "You mean you wish me to be more like Charlotte."

"No, I do not," Mama said. "I wish you to be yourself, Diana. Only a less extreme version, if you please."

Diana sighed again, thinking how there was enough

sighing between her and Mama this morning to blow a ship across the Channel. Mama wasn't being particularly honest, either. Diana was certain she'd much prefer her to be a precise copy of Charlotte. What mother wouldn't? Charlotte always did the proper thing, whether choosing a suitable gown, arranging guests for a formal supper, or producing sons to secure March's dukedom, and she did it so pleasantly that few realized how impossibly perfect she was. Of course Diana did, having to follow after such an exemplary older sister. Even if she wished to be like Charlotte, she could never be as *dutiful*. It simply wasn't in her blood.

"You must think of Lord Crump now as well as yourself," Mama was saying. "I'm sure he would much prefer to have his wife as an ornament at his side, rather than drawing stares of amazement from strangers."

"I could put plumes in my nose, and I doubt Lord Crump would take notice. Tall curled ostrich plumes, dyed crimson."

Brecon laughed, until Mama shot him a look of warning that made him smother it into a restrained cough.

"Certainly Lord Crump would notice," Mama said. "Gentlemen always take notice of what ladies wear. They simply don't feel the need to comment on every scrap. Still, if you were to wear your cherry-colored silk tomorrow night when Lord Crump attends the theater with us, I doubt even he will be able to resist smiling at you with pleasure."

"You have asked him to come with us, Mama?" Diana asked faintly, her heart sinking. "Tomorrow?"

Mama nodded, smiling warmly. "I thought he would enjoy it, and heaven knows there's plenty of room in March's box. We never begin to fill the chairs."

"It's not that his lordship wouldn't enjoy the play," Diana said, looking down at Fig in her lap. "It's only that, ah, I do not wish us to appear too forward. Last night I thought he seemed somewhat, ah, *startled* that I'd accepted his proposal as quickly as I did. Perhaps he needs a bit more time apart for considering. To be completely certain in his choice, you know."

That was her only hope now: that Lord Crump would have second thoughts and break off the match. A gentleman could do that, and though he'd be faulted for a while, he could still marry someone else. But a lady would forever be known as a jilt if she changed her mind and went back on her word, a reputation that would keep away all other suitors.

To be sure, it was a slender hope, and Brecon soon squashed it flat.

"Nonsense," Brecon said briskly, leaving no further room for doubt. "What has the man to consider? A most delightful young lady has accepted his proposal of marriage. I'm sure he's as proud as the day, and with every good reason, too."

Mama leaned forward eagerly. "Most likely he was simply stunned by his good fortune, that was all. I saw not a hint of reluctance from him. But I thought that was why we should include him in our party tomorrow night. The sooner we welcome him into our family, the sooner he will feel at ease among us."

Diana ran her fingers along Fig's spine, ruffling her fur back and forth. "I'm not sure Lord Crump feels at ease anywhere."

"Clearly he does in your company," Mama said, resting her hand gently on Diana's knee. "And no wonder, when you are being so very thoughtful and considerate for his sake. Oh, Diana, I am so happy for you!"

"We all are," Brecon said. "I'm sure your head was spinning too fast to hear it, but there was nothing but praise for the match last night at Fortescue's. It's most satisfying to see such a creditable arrangement made between two young persons of rank."

"That's it exactly, Brecon," Mama agreed, then turned back to Diana. "But it's not only about having you become a marchioness, lamb. It's that you have appreciated Lord Crump's virtues in a mature and sober manner. You and I both know that you've often preferred a handsome face above all things, and I cannot begin to tell you how proud I am to see you put aside impulse and frivolity and make such a wise decision about your life."

There was a little trembling in Mama's voice that betrayed the depth of her emotions. Diana knew that if she looked up from Fig's patterned fur even for a second, she'd soon be crying, too, not from emotion but from the truth.

She hadn't made a wise choice, not at all. Instead she'd made the most important decision of her life based on exactly the kind of impulse and frivolity that Mama thought she'd outgrown. Worse still, she'd done it because of the handsome face of the Duke of Sheffield, and she'd acted entirely in reaction to his own announcement.

"The carriage is here," Brecon said, glancing through the window as he rose to leave.

"The carriage can wait," Mama said lightly, her hand still on Diana's knee. "I'll be there soon enough."

Over and over Diana ran her hand over Fig's fur, feeling the vibrations of the little cat's purr beneath her fingers. She could still confess everything to Mama, from how she'd first met Sheffield and Fantôme in the park to how she'd kissed him last night, and most of all, how she despaired of ever being happy with Lord Crump for her husband. Last night, as she'd tossed sleeplessly in her bed, she'd imagined doing exactly that.

And if she did? There would be tears and unhappiness and abject misery, but in the end, likely nothing would change. Mama wouldn't understand, at least not enough to make a difference. Instead Diana must be like every other lady of her class. She must be obedient, and she must marry Lord Crump, just as everyone expected, and make the best of it. All a confession now would accomplish would be to upset and disappoint Mama, and that Diana did not wish to do.

Perhaps, after all, she was more like Charlotte than she'd ever realized.

With a shuddering gulp, she forced herself to look up from Fig and meet her mother's gaze.

"Thank you, Mama," she said, determined to be strong. "I am grateful for your faith in me, however undeserved."

"You deserve everything, lamb," Mama said, slipping her arms around Diana to kiss her forehead. "You'll see. You're not as happy as you should be now, but in time, you'll have the love and the life that you deserve."

But as Diana buried her face against her mother's shoulder, she didn't believe she deserved anything at all.

Sheffield followed the servant through Marchbourne House with Fantôme at his side, his footsteps and the click of Fantôme's claws echoing as they crossed the patterned marble floors. This was the largest of the town houses—it was really nearer to a palace—belonging to the cousins, and the grandest as well. The last time Sheffield had been here, soon after March and Charlotte had been married, the place still had felt like a bachelor's residence. March, too, had absorbed the lessons of diligence and responsibility from Brecon, and this house had shared the same dull and dutiful air: beautiful, lavish, filled with exquisite paintings and furniture, but with all the cheer of a tomb.

Somehow Charlotte had managed to change that. Sheffield couldn't begin to guess how, but just as she'd thawed March, she'd also done the same with Marchbourne House. The marble floors were the same, as was the army of servants, and the same somber ancestors stared down from the walls. But now there were fresh flowers in porcelain vases everywhere, and in the rooms they passed Sheffield saw how the chairs were invitingly cushioned and drawn close around fireplaces, and that there were smaller, more cheerful paintings of family pets and laughing children among the portraits of long-dead ancestors. Less tangible was the new sense of a family at home here, with four lively young children plus Charlotte's mother and, most noteworthy, Lady Diana.

Would a wife make the same transformation in Sheffield House? His own London house was smaller, elegant rather than grand. Though it was all Sheffield's, and had been for many years, in a way he still thought of it as his parents' house, with everything virtually unchanged since his mother had arranged it. It was just as well that Lady Enid would not become the next duchess; she'd probably want to put busts of Homer and Virgil in every room and turn the ballroom into the library. He smiled, thinking of what his mother would have made of such additions.

"Through these doors, sir," the footman said, opening them and standing aside for Sheffield to pass. "Her Grace will receive you by the pond."

Sheffield stepped outside, blinking at the sunlight. He pulled a leash from his coat pocket and clipped it to Fantôme's collar. He trusted the dog to behave with the children—Fantôme was by nature too lazy to do otherwise, and would patiently submit to every indignity from sticky small hands, including throttling hugs, pets and tugs on ears, and even being ridden like a short, stout pony—but the leash would reassure Charlotte and any overprotective nursemaids who might be lurking.

With his usual snuffling nosiness, Fantôme had found

a dusty yellow ball, overlooked by both children and servants, beneath a lacquered Chinese chest-on-chest, and he trotted proudly with his prize bulging from one side of his mouth. At least they'd make an entrance, Sheffield thought as they followed the footman. He expected the ladies to be in some sort of shaded summerhouse or garden folly, genteelly taking tea out of the sun the way ladies did.

What he found, however, completely and utterly surprised him.

In the middle of the garden was a large garden pond, really more of a canal, framed by neat marbled edging and close-clipped grass. The water was covered with small wooden boats, the kind that could be bought for a penny at the Bartholomew Fair. The boats were painted red, green, and blue, and their square paper sails were carrying them every which way like excited ducklings. Three small children—two lordlings and a little lady— in white gowns ran shrieking up and down along the grass, with three nervous nursemaids hovering to keep them from toppling into the water. Like a queen on her throne, Charlotte sat in an armchair at one end of the pond beneath a makeshift canopy, holding an infant in a cap and trailing gown in her arms as she called an endless, anxious stream of cautions to the other children by the water.

But the real queen of this penny armada ruled not from land but from the waves. In the middle of the pond stood Lady Diana, the skirts of her petticoat looped up through the pocket openings of her skirts. A wide-brimmed straw hat was pulled low to shade her face, and from exertion, the knot of her hair was frizzled and loose along the nape of her neck. The water wasn't deep, perhaps a foot at most, and her slender, pale legs were bare to the knee— confound him, to the *knee*—as she waded through it.

Water splashed up onto her legs, droplets sparkling in the sunshine as they trickled down her bare calves. The hems of her petticoat weren't tucked up quite far enough to escape the pond water, and the wet linen clung closely to the little hollow at the back of her knee. More water had splashed onto the kerchief around her neck, making a dappled pattern of near-transparency over the swelling tops of her breasts.

He stared, and stared some more. He'd never seen a lady like this. She held a long bamboo pole in her hands to help guide errant boats, leaning forward to prod them away from the shore, to the noisy encouragement of the children.

"Avast, you foul sea dogs!" she shouted with piratical relish. "Avast, me hearties, and pull to the lee!"

The children jumped up and down and shouted with her, and when she tipped the end of the pole into the water to flick droplets in their direction, they squealed and ran about with delight.

With so much activity, no one had noticed Sheffield's arrival, forcing the discomfited footman to raise his voice over the din.

"His Grace the Duke of Sheffield!" he bellowed, loud enough to be heard clearly in St. James's Park.

"Sheffield!" Charlotte rose at once, thrusting the baby to one of the nursemaids and hurrying around the edge of the pond to greet him. "Good day to you! Pray forgive us for this shambles. My only excuse is that I never thought you'd appear before the afternoon."

"Forgive me for disturbing you," Sheffield said, smiling as warmly as he could. "If this is an inconvenient hour, then I can return another time."

He liked Charlotte, a beautiful, witty lady with lovely eyes and an excellent humor despite being married to March. Under any other circumstances, he would have enjoyed conversing with her. But now all he could think

of was how her wide hat and hooped silk skirts and fluttering lace shawl were blocking his view of her sister,
still standing in the pond. At least he guessed she must
be; he hadn't heard any untoward splashing to indicate
that she'd left it, and there was no honorable way he
could crane his neck to peek around Charlotte to be
sure.

No, Lady Diana must still be in the pond, with her
skirts clinging wetly to her thighs and the water trickling
slowly down her shins and her dampened kerchief half
untucked from her bodice and—

"It's not inconvenient at all, Sheffield," Charlotte was
saying, reaching up to pat his shoulder. "You are
March's cousin and a member of our family, and always
welcome here, whatever the hour. Is this your dog?"

Abruptly Sheffield dragged his thoughts back, blinking in a way that must have been so obvious as to be
reprehensible. Blast, let Charlotte not have read his
thoughts, or rather, let his thoughts not have showed so
readably on his face.

To be certain, he knelt down beside Fantôme, grateful
for the diversion—and also grateful for the wide sweep
of Charlotte's gown, hiding even a hint of the distract-
ing Lady Diana.

"This is Fantôme," he said, rubbing the dog's broad
chest until he closed his eyes and made a low grumble of
contentment. "Do not mistake his ugliness for fierce-
ness. He's as mild as a lamb."

As if to prove it, Fantôme gave one final rumble and
collapsed over onto his side, the yellow ball still crushed
to one side of his jaws, his eyes closed, clearly begging to
be further petted. Charlotte laughed, but still Sheffield
lightly coiled the leash around his wrist as her children
came forward. As much as he trusted Fantôme—which
was to say completely—it was always better to be safe
around small, erratic, noisy creatures.

"Jamie, Amelia, Georgie, here." Charlotte and the nursemaids steered the children into a shuffling line before him. "This is His Grace the Duke of Sheffield, and he is your Uncle Sheffield. Now come, present your honors to him."

"That's not necessary," Sheffield said quickly, but Charlotte insisted. The older boy and the girl managed to bow and curtsey reasonably well, but the younger boy needed prodding and whispers before he managed a stiff little bow. Sheffield stood and nodded in acknowledgment, feeling at least a hundred years old before the wide-eyed children.

"Well done," Charlotte said proudly. "My sister Diana is here somewhere. I know you two met last night. Diana?"

She turned, and at last gave him a clear view of Diana. Surrounded by the little boats, she was still standing in the pond with the bamboo pole in one hand and her other cocked on her hip, making no move to join them. She didn't smile, either, but as soon as she saw him watching her, she bent low into the water in a beautifully executed curtsey—beautiful, that is, until she rose, water streaming from her skirts.

The children laughed uproariously. "Look at Aunt Diana," one of them said. "She's all *wet*."

"Yes, she rather is, isn't she?" Sheffield agreed. She was, and he couldn't look away. At his distance, he couldn't judge her mood. At first he'd thought she was embarrassed to be caught in such dishabille, but that couldn't be it, not since she'd made no move to cover herself. Was she not smiling to be playfully serious, or was she truly unhappy with him? He hadn't given her any reason for displeasure. She couldn't possibly be angry at him for announcing his betrothal to Lady Enid, since she'd done exactly the same thing with hers to Lord Crump.

Lord Crump. How could a lady as delightful as this wish to wed a man like that?

"Is your dog sleeping?" asked the little girl.

"Ah, no," Sheffield said, reluctantly looking away from Diana as he tried to remember what her name was. Amelia, that was it. "He's simply lazy, Lady Amelia, that is all."

"He's *fat*," said the older boy, scowling, the same one who'd announced that Diana was wet. "*And* he's stupid-looking."

"He is a little stout," Sheffield admitted, thinking how Jamie, Lord Pennington, was clearly destined to be a stalwart in the House of Lords with his magnificent gift for stating the obvious. "You may pet him if you wish. That's what he's begging for."

Bravely Jamie reached down and began scrubbing hard at Fantôme's barrel-shaped side. His sister joined him, doing the same, while Fantôme groaned with pleasure.

But the younger boy, Georgie, Lord Fitzcharles, hung back beside the nursemaid and leisurely worked one finger inside his nose.

"Ball," he said finally. "My ball. Doggie has *my* ball!"

"Oh, Georgie," Charlotte said with dismay. "I believe that ball belongs to the doggie now."

"No!" wailed Georgie, turning shrill. "My ball! Want my ball!"

"Fantôme will give it back," Sheffield said, bending down again beside the dog. "Drop it, Fantôme."

Without opening his eyes, the dog's jaws opened with a click, letting the ball fall out into Sheffield's hand. The ball had been dusty and worn when Fantôme first found it. Now it was also crushed on one side and sodden with dog slobber. Still, in the name of peace, Sheffield offered it to Georgie.

Glowering at Sheffield, Georgie grabbed the ball and promptly hurled it into the pond.

Suddenly Fantôme awoke and scrambled to his stubby legs with a snort that made Jamie and Amelia rush back to the safety of the nursemaid's skirts. With more energy than Fantôme had shown in weeks, he jerked the leash from Sheffield's hand and bounded after the ball, leaping into the pond with all the grace of a white cannonball. The resultant splash was so large and widespread that it was a wonder any water remained in the pond. Charlotte gasped as the water hit her, Diana backed away, the children screamed, and the baby began to shriek.

"Oh, hell," Sheffield muttered, already pulling off his shoes and stockings and coat and watch to go in after the dog. "Fantôme, here! Here! Blast you, come *here*!"

It was no surprise that Fantôme chose to ignore him. Instead he bounded up and down in the water, bringing massive maritime destruction to many of the penny boats. Diana tried to grab him, sloshing through the water, but the dog considered it all a splendid game and deftly eluded her.

Only Georgie seemed unperturbed, holding his hand out impotently toward the mayhem in the pond.

"Ball," he said plaintively. "My *ball*."

While his nursemaid tended to his siblings, he swiftly toddled off to the edge of the pond, jumped, and instantly sank beneath the water.

Charlotte screamed, but Sheffield was already there, wading into the water to grab the little boy and hoist him, dripping and howling, into her arms.

"Thank you, Sheffield, thank you so much," she said apologetically over the din of the four wailing children. "I believe it best if we withdraw now, and wish you good day."

With Charlotte leading the way to the house, they

made a noisy procession of weeping children and shushing nursemaids. Sheffield's final glimpse of George was of him sobbing over Charlotte's shoulder, still grasping at the air toward the infernal ball.

"You see what your wretched dog has done, Your Grace," Diana said, speaking to him for the first time. "He has spoiled everything. Can't you catch him?"

"I'll try," Sheffield said gallantly, turning to face her. She was thoroughly soaked now, her expression murderous. "Fantôme, here."

He tried to grab the dog, then the trailing leash. The bottom of the pond was slick, and each time he lunged after Fantôme, his feet slipped beneath him. His own clothes were growing wetter with each attempt, and his irritation with Fantôme was growing, too.

"Chase him toward me, Lady Diana," he said, "and I'll try to intercept him."

She didn't move. "He is your dog, Duke, not mine."

"Thank you," Sheffield said, letting her share a bit of his general irritation as well. "You're most helpful."

The yellow ball that had started it all floated near his leg. Sheffield fished it from the water and held it up for the dog to see.

"Fantôme!" he shouted, making sure he had the dog's attention. "Fantôme, fetch!"

He threw the ball onto the grass, and at once Fantôme went after it, dragging himself from the pond and running to the ball. He seized it again in his mouth, shook the water from his fur, and promptly collapsed in happy exhaustion on the grass.

"Well, there's an end to that," Sheffield said. He held his hand out to Diana, offering to help her from the pond.

But she was in no humor to be helped, and seemed determined to let him know the reason.

"Why didn't you tell me you were betrothed?" she

demanded. "Why did you let me make such a fool of myself first?"

"You did that quite readily without any help from me," he said. "If you recall, you didn't wish me to tell you so much as my name. Why would I have told you about Lady Enid, too?"

"Because a gentleman would have, *Duke*," she said, her face flushed. "Because I never would have kissed you if I'd known you were promised to another lady. I never would have done that, ever!"

"Then what of your own betrothal?" he asked, incredulous. "What manner of lady who is engaged to wed goes about kissing strangers?"

"How dare you throw that back at me," she sputtered with incoherent rage. "How dare you, when you—you—oh, *you*!"

She reached out and with both hands shoved his chest as hard as she could. Caught off balance, he found his feet sliding out from beneath him, and down he went on his backside into the pond. His remaining clothes—his shirt and breeches and waistcoat—were instantly, thoroughly soaked, and he could already feel the muck from the bottom of the pond seeping into the sodden cloth.

It was not pleasant.

She stared down at him, her eyes wide and one hand clapped over her mouth with shock. But the shock didn't linger, and after a moment or two, he realized that behind her hand, she'd begun to laugh.

At *him*.

He leaned forward, resting his arms on his bent legs, and she only laughed harder.

"I'm glad to have offered so much amusement to you," he said. "In return you might at least offer to help me up."

He held his hand up to her, the water streaming from

his sleeve. She looked down at him pityingly, then finally took his hand.

"Thank you," he said, and pulled her down into the water beside him with almost as great a splash as Fantôme had caused.

She yelped, flailing her arms as she instantly scrambled back to her feet, leaving her hat floating behind her like a giant straw lily pad. She wasn't laughing any longer, but he was.

"Turnabout's fair play, ma'am," he said, amazed that she'd fallen for so old a schoolboy trick. "Sauce for the goose, sauce for the gander."

She snatched her hat from the water. "You are perfectly welcome to consider yourself as a gander, Duke," she said, "but for my part, I will never be a goose."

With her head high and her hair hanging in a half-pinned clump down her back, she stepped from the pond and marched resolutely down the path toward the house, leaving a trail of pond water behind her.

Still laughing, Sheffield watched her, thoroughly enjoying how her wet skirts clung to her wiggling, indignant bottom. No goose, not at all. Not at all.

His smile faded as she finally disappeared from sight, his mood turning more thoughtful even as he still sat in the water. He should not pursue her, he must not, and he'd as much as promised Brecon he'd keep clear of her. She belonged to someone else, and in theory, so did he.

Yet there she was, Lady Diana of the clinging skirts, as great a temptation as he'd ever met, and after this afternoon, he could not wait to see her again.

CHAPTER

 6

"You sit here beside me, Diana," Charlotte said, pointing with her furled fan to the nearest chair in the row before the rail, "and we'll leave that one for Lord Crump, when he arrives."

Diana nodded and took the seat beside her sister, the frothy ruffles of their gowns mingling. As Mama had suggested, Diana had worn her new cherry-colored silk *robe à la française* tonight, and because they were attending the theater, she'd been permitted to wear the gown without a lace neckerchief tucked into the low, squared neckline for modesty. She was very aware now of how her breasts were pushed up by her stays and how much of them showed for a fashionable display, and she felt both stylish and adult, enjoying the undeniable attention that the gown brought her. As Mama had said, she wasn't a girl any longer, but soon to be a married woman, and entitled to dress like other noble-born ladies, including Charlotte beside her.

What Mama hadn't said (but Diana had guessed) was that she was hoping that the sight of Diana's largely uncovered bosom would inspire a bit more lover-like ardor in Lord Crump. Except for when they'd danced, he'd scarcely so much as held her gloved fingertips. Now that they were considered betrothed, he'd be expected to show more devotion, and clearly Mama hoped this gown would be the necessary little nudge of encouragement that Lord Crump required.

But cherry-colored silk could only do so much, and Diana had resolved to try to begin anew with Lord Crump. Charlotte had told her again how she and March had had a difficult beginning, yet had persevered to become the happiest married couple that Diana knew. Perhaps if she was more agreeable and less defensive with Lord Crump, then they would be, too. He was held in the highest regard by everyone else in their world; surely there must be some side of him that she could thaw and mold into a loving husband.

That much Diana had told to Charlotte, and Charlotte had applauded her resolve. But what Diana hadn't confessed was how her new resolution had more than a little penance woven into it. She'd been furious when Sheffield had asked her yesterday what kind of betrothed lady went about kissing strangers, but he'd been right. She still didn't know what had possessed her to kiss him that night at Lady Fortescue's, but she was determined never to do such a thing again. She was also determined never to trust him in a garden pond again, either, but then that was another resolution entirely.

Now she sighed, wistfully looking about as the theater began to fill. Her family was seated in March's box on the first tier, not far from the royal box, giving Diana an excellent view of the other theater-goers—which, really, was often as interesting a performance as the one on the stage. But tonight it seemed that everywhere she looked were happy couples: men bowing over women, or whispering secrets behind fans, or sinking back into the forgiving and private shadows of boxes for an even more private interlude. Even March and Charlotte beside her were laughing softly over some shared jest, their hands twined familiarly, and across the aisle, Brecon, too, was entertaining Mama with some story or another.

But all she had beside her was a pointedly empty chair. How was she to be more agreeable to Lord Crump if he wouldn't appear? She looked down at her fan, fussing with the ivory blades and desperately wishing he'd conclude whatever business had delayed him and join her here.

"Look, Diana, to our left, at the Earl and Countess of Wentworth," Charlotte said, leaning toward her. "Do you think those sapphires around her throat are real or paste?"

Grateful for something to consider besides Lord Crump's absence, Diana eagerly leaned forward for a better view. "They're vastly large for real stones. Is Lord Wentworth known for his generosity?"

Charlotte raised her brows over the curving edge of her fan.

"If they're real, he must be very generous indeed, or else very guilty," she said, laughing as she glanced around at other boxes. "Oh, my, Diana, look. There's Sheffield, sitting with Lord and Lady Lattimore. That must be his Lady Enid with him, too."

Diana looked. She might even have stared. How, really, could she not? When she'd last seen Sheffield, he'd been sitting sprawled in the middle of the garden pond with penny boats bobbing around him. His clothes had been soaked, his linen shirt clinging to his chest and shoulders, his silk waistcoat ruined, and his dark hair wet and trailing in unruly, shining waves. Few men would have appeared at their best in such circumstances, yet Sheffield had looked effortlessly, unbearably handsome, smiling up at her as if sitting barefoot in a pond were simply one more customary engagement in his daily calendar.

But now he sat in Lord Lattimore's box between Lady

Lattimore and Lady Enid, looking much more civilized. He wore a dark jacket with the exact amount of silver embroidery to sparkle subtly by the candlelight, his white linen flawlessly arranged and his hair sleeked back.

Compared to such manly perfection, Lady Enid seemed small and plain, her face round and unremarkable and her ochre-colored gown having no style at all. Yet Sheffield was being endlessly attentive to her, his arm resting casually but possessively over the back of her chair and his smile for her alone. No wonder she was smiling with such pleasure up at him. Why shouldn't she, with a lover like Sheffield hanging on every word she spoke? Lady Enid hadn't needed cherry-colored silk ruffles or a well-displayed bosom to capture his interest and secure it, and Diana felt herself sinking into her chair with discouragement.

"Brecon says that Lady Enid is a brilliant bluestocking who reads voraciously and can discourse in ancient languages," Charlotte said. "Clearly Sheffield finds her enchanting. Brecon says that even His Majesty is in favor of the match, especially in light of Sheffield's recent indiscretions."

"Indiscretions?" Diana asked, unable to resist. "Is that what Aunt Sophronia meant by his 'lamentable conquests'?"

"Yes." Charlotte hesitated, clearly considering whether it was proper or not to repeat this particular bit of gossip. "Sheffield has had his share of romantic liaisons. Perhaps more than his share, if even half of the number that has been credited to him is to be believed. Recently, however, he became entangled most unfortunately with a married French noblewoman. Brecon says it was an enormous scandal in Paris, and that Sheffield was fortunate to escape without having to fight the husband in a duel."

"A duel!" Diana said, impressed. Though she'd heard of hot-tempered gentlemen who challenged one another, duels weren't as common among the English aristocracy as they were among the French. His Majesty did not approve of his noblemen killing one another, and discouraged it as best he could. Long ago, March had been forced to fight one to defend Charlotte's honor, but the circumstances had been considered justified, and besides, no one had been killed. But imagining Sheffield having to avoid an irate French husband with a sword in his hand added an extra bit of excitement to his character.

It also, unfortunately, explained why Diana had found him so appealing. She'd always had a weakness for charming, handsome rogues, and worse, she was the sort of lady that charming, handsome rogues tended to pursue. The more she learned of Sheffield, the more she realized how precisely those three words defined him.

"March says the king himself insisted on Sheffield breaking off with the woman and returning to London," Charlotte continued. "That's why he's marrying Lady Enid, you see, as a way of proving he's changed. If anyone can reform a rascal like Sheffield, it will be a clever, sober lady such as Lady Enid. From the look of them together, he does seem to find her intriguing. Oh, here's Lord Crump at last, and just in time for the play, too."

Quickly Diana turned, her smile ready as he entered the box. He bowed and greeted everyone else first—proper since everyone else was of higher rank, but not exactly displaying the eagerness that Diana had hoped for. Still, she greeted him warmly when he finally sat beside her.

"Good evening, my lord," she said, fluttering her fan with nervous intensity. "I'm so vastly glad to see you! I'd begun to fear you would not be able to join us."

"Good evening to you, Lady Diana," he said with his

usual dry, dutiful manner. "I am fortunate to be here at all. The streets around Drury Lane are so congested that it makes passage an absolute trial. I cannot tell you how long it took my carriage to travel here from Westminster."

"Westminster, my lord?" Mama had always advised that the surest way to make a gentleman believe you were witty and wise at conversation was to ask him about his own interests. "What manner of business kept you in your office so late? Is there a ship new arrived from the Indies that takes your attention, or—"

"Oh, nothing that need concern you," he said lightly. "Suffice that it kept me there so long that the streets between there and Drury Lane were nearly impassable. One more reason for a sane man never to bother with the playhouse."

This was hardly an auspicious beginning, but Diana remembered her new resolution, and persevered.

"But tonight's play will feature the celebrated Mr. Garrick," she said. "I vow he is so accomplished that he can bring me to tears."

"Then you must be of a most tender nature, Lady Diana," he said severely, making it clear that he found tenderness a grievous fault, not a virtue. "To be moved to tears by the false emotions of an actor! You would do well to direct those inclinations toward charitable work rather than the idle amusements of the playhouse."

Diana's smile faded. Everyone she knew enjoyed the playhouse. How could he not?

"But surely one cannot be somber all the time, my lord," she insisted. "Laughter and pleasure are not bad things. After a day's labor on behalf of the country, don't you wish the amusing respite of a play?"

He glanced at her sideways with patent disbelief. "I find such satisfaction in my work that I require no respite," he said. "Certainly not the kind that comes from the playhouse. It's not that I disapprove, as a Puritan would. Rather, it would seem to be a sorry waste of the precious hours in every day."

Diana's fan stilled as she fought the urge to strike him with it. "Laughter is not a waste, my lord."

He paused, and finally smiled indulgently. "Indeed, Lady Diana," he said. "But then, you are still young."

She bit back the obvious conclusion: that if she was young, then he was a dry old stick. She intended to be laughing still when she was as old as Aunt Sophronia, or even older, and how she longed to tell him so! Instead she lowered her fan to her lap, turning so that the candlelight from around the stage would shine on her bosom to best effect. If she could not beguile him by discussing Mr. Garrick's magnificence or the play they were to see, then the cherry-colored silk and her breasts would surely succeed. She'd never met a gentleman who could withstand such an onslaught.

But though Lord Crump kept the same indulgent, thin-lipped smile on his face, his glance didn't waver or dip below her face. Not so much as a single stolen glance, not even when Diana heaved a purposeful, monumental sigh that threatened to raise her breasts free of her stays.

Nothing.

Almost as if in sympathy, the orchestra began to play, signaling the beginning of the performance.

"Here's the play at last, Lady Diana," he said. "I trust it will bring you the diversion and amusement you seek."

She forced herself to smile and tried to forget her frustration as she turned to watch the play, called *The Enchanter: Love and Magic*. She couldn't help but think how she'd need a sizable portion of magic before she'd ever coax Lord Crump to love. She certainly was no enchanter, at least not where he was concerned, and her frustration simmered, making it impossible to concentrate.

Late in the first act, she heard a shuffling beside her. Lord Crump had taken several letters—business letters filled with numbers and accounts, from what she could see—from inside his coat and was actually *reading* them during the play, tipping them toward the stage so he would have sufficient light.

"Cannot that wait until later, my lord?" she whispered. "Is it so very urgent that you won't put them aside to enjoy the play?"

He stared at her, clearly startled that she'd dare question him. He blinked, then smiled and tucked the letters back into his pocket. He clasped his hands in his lap and dutifully turned toward the stage.

Daring greatly, Diana reached out and rested her hand on his forearm. She'd hoped he'd take her hand in his, or at least cover hers. Instead he glanced down at her hand as if it were some exotic winged insect that had inexplicably landed there. He unclasped his fingers and clumsily patted her hand—one, two, three times—with more obligation than affection or real regard. Then he clasped his hands together again and stared once again at the stage.

It wasn't exactly that he'd rebuffed her, or that he was by design being cruel or mean-spirited. Rather, it was that Lord Crump simply did not know what to do with her, or likely any woman, for that matter. In a way, that ambivalence was the most hurtful reason of all.

Slowly Diana withdrew her hand from his sleeve and bowed her head with frustration. How could she be more attentive, more agreeable, more wifely, to a man who seemed to take no notice of her?

Charlotte sensed there was something amiss, even if Lord Crump did not. As soon as the applause had died down for the conclusion of the act, she leaned across Diana to address him directly.

"Dear Lord Crump," she said, "March and I are going to walk about during intermission. There may perhaps even be ices. Would you and Lady Diana care to join us?"

No one refused Charlotte, not even Lord Crump.

"Very well, Your Grace," he said, unfolding from his chair. He stepped into the aisle and offered his hand to Diana. "If you please, Lady Diana."

"Thank you, my lord," Diana said, flashing a quick smile of gratitude to Charlotte as she took his hand. At least now he couldn't drop her hand; he'd have to keep it until they returned to their seats. "You are most kind."

Many others from the boxes had likewise chosen to stroll between the acts, and the corridor was already filled with people—or, rather, filled with gentlemen, ladies, and the ladies' wide hooped skirts, which made each lady occupy the space of three. The doors to the boxes had been thrown open and hooked, not just permitting the occupants to leave with ease but also letting friends visit, making the boxes serve as temporary reception rooms.

"Faith, what a crush," Charlotte said over her shoulder. She was holding tight to March, not only because he was a tall man but because the crowd bowed and parted for him as soon as he was recognized. Diana also held tight to Lord Crump, though she kept close to Charlotte and March as well. A marquis might be a peer, but there was nothing like a duke to clear a useful path.

"How much farther must we go, Lady Diana?" Lord Crump asked, raising his voice. "Could we not have sent a lackey for these ices you desire?"

"I suppose we could have, my lord, yes," Diana said.

From his pained expression, she knew she could add strolling the corridors during intermission to the ever-growing list of things he did not enjoy doing. "But if we'd stayed in our seats, then no one would see us, or we them."

There was little doubt they were being seen now—or rather, she was. Lord Crump might have said nothing about her bright silk gown, but the gaze of every other gentleman in the theater seemed to find her, and stay there, too. She supposed the attention was flattering, but in truth she would have traded all that random admiration for a single compliment from the man she was to marry.

"We're almost to the counters with the ices and wines, my lord," she said. "Then we can—oh!"

Without warning, Charlotte and March had stopped in front of them, and Diana, having turned to speak with Lord Crump, barely avoided crashing into her sister from behind.

"Sheffield, here you are," Charlotte exclaimed. "And Lady Enid! How much I've heard of you, my dear. Diana, here, it's Lady Enid, ready for us to welcome her to the family."

Diana squeezed forward, still holding Lord Crump's hand. Because of the crowd around them, they all stood unavoidably close together in a small circle, or at least as close as the ladies' gowns would permit. As Diana soon realized while Charlotte made the introductions, it had been one thing to watch Sheffield with Lady Enid at a distance, but quite another to have them standing only a few feet away. Lady Enid wasn't nearly as plain as she'd seemed from a distance, or perhaps it was simply her glowing happiness that made her round face more appealing. Of course she'd be happy. She'd Sheffield beside her.

There was no denying he was the most devastatingly

handsome man in the theater, or at least he was in Diana's eyes. Devastating: yes, that was the inexplicable yet undeniable effect he now had upon her. It didn't matter that he was standing with his betrothed and she with hers, or that the last time she'd seen him she'd wanted to throttle him for pulling her into the pond.

When he laughed at something that Charlotte said, tipping his head back so his dark hair slipped over his forehead, all she could think of was how silky that hair had felt beneath her fingers when she'd kissed him. She looked at his elegant dark silk coat, embroidered with swirling silver vines along the edges and spangled here and there with blue-gray stones that exactly matched his eyes, and thought not of the coat but of how well it fit him, how broad his shoulders were and how narrow his waist and hips, how strong and leanly muscled he was beneath that silk coat, and how wonderful he'd been to lean against in the moonlight.

All these shameful notions raced through Diana's head in the handful of moments that presentations and greetings took. She prayed that no one—least of all Lord Crump—would observe her fluster, and to control it she ordered herself to think only stern, somber, non-devastating thoughts, such as the sermon she'd heard at church last Sunday.

But then Sheffield smiled directly at her, and his gaze at once dipped to her breasts. Manfully, he forced himself to look again at her face, but only for a moment, and (perhaps this was the truly manful part) then back his gaze dropped. She felt her cheeks grow hot, her heart beat faster, and a part of her deep inside turn soft and melt like wax in the sun. He couldn't help it, and neither could she.

But Sheffield, blast him, didn't seem to care about hiding it.

"I trust you are recovered from your maritime exercises, Lady Diana?" he asked, his voice studiously bland but his eyes full of spark. "When last I saw you, you'd taken on water and were listing badly."

"And you, Your Grace, had sunk straight to the bottom, an unsalvageable wreck," she answered succinctly, refusing to let such a comment go unanswered. "You were a woeful sight indeed."

"Sadly true, Lady Diana, sadly true." He sighed dramatically and shook his head, then let his gaze once again wander to her breasts. "Ah, if only I'd been able to continue to battle, and not been forced to strike my flag before your broadsides!"

"Whatever are you saying, Sheffield?" asked Lady Enid, clearly confused as she looked from Sheffield to Diana and back again. "You're speaking complete nonsense."

"Oh, Lady Enid," Charlotte said quickly. "You must pay them no attention. My children were playing with toy boats in our pond yesterday, and Sheffield and my sister joined them. This is doubtless no more than a reference to the children's games."

Charlotte smiled, eager to dismiss the conversation as child's play, though the glance she shot at Diana should have been warning enough. Diana understood entirely; she'd lived her whole life as the target of warning glances from her older sister.

But understanding was not the same as obeying, especially not when Sheffield wasn't about to stop, either.

"Scuppered, Lady Diana," he said with relish. "That's what I saw in that pond. Bows up, and scuppered."

Diana grinned wickedly, unable to let him have the last word. She'd forgotten so entirely about everyone else that they might as well have been alone in the corridor.

"Aye, aye, if you must, admiral," she said. "But I'd rather that than being run aground and dismasted."

Sheffield laughed, but no one else did, and too late Diana realized how badly she'd just erred. Making bawdy sailor jests in company was not acceptable, and it didn't take long for Lord Crump to speak.

"You astound me, Lady Diana," he said. "I'd no notion you were so familiar with the language of common seamen."

"Forgive me, my lord," Diana said swiftly, bowing her head. She could only imagine what Lady Enid must be thinking, and she didn't dare look her way. "I misspoke."

"You spoke like yourself, Diana, with no harm done," March said, striving to redeem the conversation just as Charlotte had. "This is a hidden gift of the Wylder sisters, Crump. Having been raised near the sea, they naturally developed an affinity for the language of seafaring folk. My Charlotte will banter with me in such a fashion as well whenever she wishes to amuse me."

But the teasing jests between a husband and wife at home that March described were far different from what she and Sheffield had just done. That hadn't been banter. That had been flirtation, and even Lord Crump must have heard the difference.

"Indeed," he said now, his voice withering with disapproval. "I would never have believed the daughters of a peer would have anything in common with base sailors."

"I should not be so quick to fault sailors, my lord," Lady Enid said evenly, her hands clasped before her waist. "You might recall that Odysseus, that most noble of ancient heroes, was a mariner. If the voyages of Odysseus were a sufficient inspiration for Homer's poetry, then I would scarcely think there's merit in scoffing at sailors as 'base.'"

Startled, Diana looked at Lady Enid with fresh appreciation. Charlotte had called her a bluestocking, and from her manner of speech, there was no doubt that she was educated and intelligent, too. But there was also a challenge in her voice that Diana liked at once, a spirit that Diana could entirely embrace. In spite of still holding Lord Crump's hand, Diana smiled at Lady Enid.

Lord Crump drew back so far that his chin pressed against his tightly wrapped neck cloth. "As impressed as I am by your familiarity with the classics, Lady Enid, I intended no such slander as you imply against the great poet Homer."

"Forgive me, Lord Crump, but I never said you slandered Homer," Lady Enid said, her eyes bright with tenacity. "It was sailors you scorned as unfit company, not Homer."

"But assuredly they are unfit company for ladies," Lord Crump protested, using the authoritative voice that he likely employed when addressing the full House of Lords. "You cannot deny that sailors are drawn from the lowest ranks of society and can hardly be considered fit company for persons of rank and equality."

"The fishing folk I knew at Ransom were as decent as any I've met in London, my lord," Diana said, staunchly joining Lady Enid's defense. "More so, really. I may not have read Homer, as Lady Enid has, but I do know that the holy disciples in the Bible were fishermen and sailors, and that when Christ would sail in their company on the Sea of Galilee, He never scorned them as base or unfit."

Now it was Charlotte and March who were staring at her, clearly uncertain of what might next spill from her mouth. To be honest, Diana wasn't entirely sure herself.

Beside her Lord Crump grumbled and muttered. "Agreed, Lady Diana, agreed," he said grudgingly at last. "I cannot contest such an argument."

Diana only nodded and said nothing more, not wishing to test the good fortune that had let her wriggle free. Nor did she dare look at Sheffield. If she truly didn't wish to test her luck, she'd never look at Sheffield again.

"Pray tell me, Lady Diana," Lady Enid said, making it clear that she considered the discussion with Lord Crump finished, "are you accomplished in other marine matters, too? If necessary, could you put to sail in a boat yourself?"

Diana nodded. "A small one, that is," she said, thinking of how insignificant an accomplishment that must seem beside being able to read Homer. "Charlotte and Lizzie—that's our other sister—and I all know how to sail and row boats, from living near the sea."

"I can quite vouch for her skill, Enid," Sheffield said, which was not exactly true. That poking about with toy boats yesterday had had nothing to do with real ones, and Diana permitted herself one sour glance at him to show what she thought of his empty opinion. His expression was blandly noncommittal, and he, too, was purposely not looking toward her. She supposed she was relieved.

But what Diana did notice was how he and Lady Enid were standing slightly apart, she with her hands held before her and he with his clasped behind his back. It was curious, more the posture of an amiable brother and sister than of a future husband and wife; even Lord Crump was holding her hand, however perfunctorily. Sheffield wasn't generally so reserved where it came to women. Far from it. At least he wasn't when it came to her.

"His Grace has only seen me with toy boats, Lady Enid," she said, "but I'm perfectly capable with the real ones, too."

"Then you must explain it all to me, Lady Diana,"

Lady Enid said eagerly. "I know nothing of such things, and wish to learn."

"Enid and I will be walking in St. James's Park tomorrow," Sheffield said mildly. "Perhaps Lord Crump and Lady Diana would wish to join us?"

"Oh, yes, please do," Enid said. "What a fine way to learn more of one another, since we are all to be of the same family."

Diana gulped. She would in fact like to spend more time with Lady Enid, but to do so with both Lord Crump and Sheffield together might be more than she could bear.

"How cordial of you, Lady Enid, and you, too, Sheffield," Charlotte said, beaming. There were few things that Charlotte liked better than to have the ever-growing family be happy together. "If this warm weather holds, you shall have a splendid day for walking."

Diana glanced anxiously at Lord Crump. "Thank you, Lady Enid, and such a diversion would be most enjoyable, except that his lordship is not much given to—"

"It matters not, it matters not," Lord Crump interrupted with an impatient wave of his hand. "I would never be able to free myself from my business for walking idly about in the middle of the day."

Diana tried to look regretful instead of relieved. "You see how it must be, Lady Enid," she began. "I must regret that we—"

"You may go, Lady Diana," Lord Crump said. "I encourage you to do so."

"Truly, my lord?" Diana asked, surprised and dismayed. Was there any less comfortable number in a carriage than three? "You wish me to go without you?"

"Yes, yes," he said with another wave of his hand. "I give you leave to go with His Grace and Lady Enid.

Why shouldn't I? Sharing the discourse of a learned lady such as Lady Enid will occupy you profitably."

"Then it is settled, Lady Diana," Sheffield said heartily. "I shall gather Enid first in my carriage, and then you from Marchbourne House. We'll make a party of it, won't we, Lady Diana?"

Diana smiled with little enthusiasm, and thought only of how once again good luck and fortune had deserted her.

CHAPTER

❧ 7 ❧

"You're the third bridegroom I've attended at this chore," Brecon said the next morning, claiming the second chair at the jeweler's counter. "First March with those rose-cut diamonds for Charlotte, then Hawke and his rubies. Or rather, Lizzie's rubies. I'm eager to see what you select for Lady Enid."

"So shall I," Sheffield said, striving to tamp down the uneasiness that had been plaguing him all morning. It was Brecon's insistence that Lady Enid needed a betrothal ring to display before the world that had brought him here this morning to Mr. Boyce's shop. Boyce, his sons, and their ancestors had been serving all the ducal cousins and their ancestors, including the king that had sired them all, for at least the last two hundred years, and there'd been no question that Sheffield would come here now to arrange for what should be one of the most important jewels he'd ever give. The shop was small, quietly well appointed, and discreet, as befitted its titled customers.

Sheffield had already had Marlowe bring the most promising pieces of family jewelry here for Boyce's refurbishing, and Boyce himself would add several of the choicest new precious stones from his stock for consideration. Given Sheffield's rank and the value of the stones that would be displayed, Boyce had obligingly closed the shop to all other customers for as long as was necessary. An assistant hovered behind the counter if needed, and Boyce had even had coffee brought in. Two chairs had been waiting for the two dukes, and a black velvet cloth was already spread across the counter. Everything, in short, was arranged to make the selection as easy and agreeable as possible, but as Boyce began to bring out the small, rounded ring boxes, Sheffield could scarcely control his restlessness, nor the powerful urge to jump up and flee.

It was not that Sheffield was exactly a neophyte at buying jewels for women. Far from it. He'd been buying costly trinkets for females since he'd been a mooncalf schoolboy with his first mistress. Nor, unlike most men, was he concerned over the price he'd likely pay. Cost truly was no object, not with his income. To be sure, a betrothal ring for a duchess was not a choice to be taken lightly, as Brecon had been relentlessly explaining to him for the last hour, but not even that was the real cause of his uneasiness.

No, it was more than that, worse than that, and Sheffield prayed he'd get through this morning without Brecon guessing the real reason.

"Let's see the Atherton family rings first," Brecon suggested. "A ring with a history is an elegant way to welcome a lady to the family."

Sheffield nodded, and at once Boyce set a small tray on the counter, presenting a dozen or so rings each in its own fitted plush box: garnets, diamonds, sapphires, and rubies, all of which had graced the fingers of former Duchesses of Sheffield.

But the only ring that Sheffield saw sat in the center of the tray. It wasn't the largest or the most dramatic, but it meant the most to him. It was a brilliant blue-green emerald, surrounded by smaller white diamonds. Swirls of gold held the stones, then slipped like waves down the shank and around the back. Carefully he took it from the box seeing how the gold was worn on the sides and smoothed by the last owner's fingers.

"A beautiful stone, sir," the jeweler said, quick to approve his choice. "A Brazilian emerald from the Portuguese mines. Considerable clarity and the color make it a rarity, sir. We seldom see emeralds of this quality here in London. Most never leave Lisbon."

"That was your mother's ring, wasn't it?" Brecon asked softly.

"It was," Sheffield said. "It was."

He remembered how he'd always been fascinated by the ring as a child, and how he'd turn his mother's hand to watch the emerald sparkle. His father had invented a thrilling tale of how the stone had been destined for a Portuguese princess but had instead been captured and claimed by a fierce pirate for the most beautiful duchess in England. Sheffield had believed every word, even when his mother had laughed and scolded his father for telling preposterous lies to their son.

He turned the ring in his fingers now, seeing the familiar shifting colors in the stone. His father had given it to his mother when they'd eloped, and Sheffield could not recall ever seeing her without it on her finger. He'd always assumed the ring had been buried with her, fourteen years ago. To see it now was like having his mother here again as well, a sensation so powerful that he didn't trust his voice to describe it.

No, he could sense the presence of both his mother and his father, for the ring had so strongly symbolized their love and marriage that even now he couldn't think of one without the other. Their initials were engraved within, blurred with time and wear, but there still.

"The emerald can be reset for the lady, sir," Boyce

suggested. "Something more in keeping with present tastes that will better show the stone."

"No," Sheffield said, more sharply than he'd intended. He couldn't imagine ever changing this ring, wiping away the wear from his mother's fingers or the engraving his father had had put inside. "The setting should never be altered."

"I agree that it's beautiful as it is, replete with sentiment," Brecon said. "Is this the ring you wish to give to Lady Enid?"

He couldn't think of anything he'd like less to do. The sheer wrongness of it struck him like a blow, compounding the churning of his uneasy conscience.

That was it, really. All his uneasiness was the fault of his conscience, an article that most dukes with royal blood quite happily did without. Society generally expected gentlemen of his rank and wealth to do whatever they pleased without consequences, and Sheffield had been no exception. Brecon had tried to instill certain honorable limitations, but for the most part, Sheffield had led a life cheerfully untrammeled by rules, laws, expense, or worrying overmuch about the feelings or concerns of others.

When he'd first contrived it, his plan to avoid marrying Lady Enid Lattimore by arranging for her to marry her lowly vicar instead had seemed like a lark, a droll way to outfox the king's interfering desire to see him wed. He'd also liked the idea that his escape would bring two other thwarted lovers together, like a hero tidying up the secondary characters in some cleverly overplotted play.

But before long he'd realized that what blithely seemed like a lark to him was thoroughly serious to Lady Enid and Dr. Pullings because they loved each other. Because of that love, they were willing to risk anything for its sake—even to trust him.

He'd always claimed he believed in love, true love, yet he'd never done anything but make a sport of it. Love affairs were not love. He saw that now. He certainly hadn't experienced anything like what his parents had shared or the devotion that Brecon had felt for his wife, or what existed between Lady Enid and Dr. Pullings. Even March and Charlotte seemed to have it. And every one of those couples had been willing to face whatever challenges came their way and do whatever they must for the sake of love.

He'd never had to do anything, because women had always flocked to him. He'd had more than his share of dalliances, infatuations, desires, flirtations, affections, attractions, seductions, and conquests.

But not love. Not once.

It was most sobering.

Yet the longer he looked down at his mother's ring, the clearer—and more enjoyable—his thoughts became, because they were filled with Lady Diana Wylder. Until now, he'd tried not to think of her at all, pleasurably or otherwise. She wasn't some actress or milliner's apprentice, and she wasn't another man's bored, promiscuous wife, either. She was a lady, the daughter of a peeress, and most important, she was by marriage a member of his own extended family. She was betrothed to the Marquis of Crump. According to Brecon, she was also headstrong and difficult, teetering precipitously on the edge of dishonorable disaster, and a trial to all who cared for her.

But Sheffield liked a headstrong lady, especially one who was impulsive enough to kiss him the way Lady Diana had. In fact, he liked most everything about Lady Diana, from how she laughed and how she'd teased him in nautical fashion to how wickedly attractive she'd been with her clothes sopping wet and clinging to her in all the proper places. He liked those proper places, too, for the thoroughly improper activities that they suggested. In short, he liked *her*, liked her very much. Even Fantôme liked her.

But did he like her enough to upset their entire interwoven family by pursuing her? He'd told himself that his sole reason for this ruse with Lady Enid was to free himself from marriage, at least for the time being. He knew he was too young, too unsettled. He simply wasn't ready. Yet no matter how attracted he was to Lady Diana, any dalliance with her could end only one way, and that must be with marriage—and a marriage with an exorbitant amount of ill will and scandal attached to it, too. Hardly the most auspicious way to find true love, or to begin a shared life, either, and as he stared into the glinting stone of his mother's ring, he wished the emerald were like some Gypsy's crystal ball, able to predict his future.

"Sheffield, please," Brecon said, jovial but insistent. "We cannot keep Boyce waiting all the day whilst you reflect on the charms of your betrothed. Do you wish to give your mother's ring to Lady Enid?"

"I think not." Purposefully Sheffield closed the lid on the velvet-covered box, holding it in his palm just a moment longer. He would give his mother's ring to his future wife, whomever she turned out to be, but not to Lady Enid. "I do not believe it's to Lady Enid's taste."

"As you wish, sir," Boyce said, crestfallen. "Can you enlighten me as to her ladyship's taste?"

"Come, Sheffield," Brecon said, clearly exasperated. "Let's hear what you've determined."

"An amethyst," Sheffield said, suddenly certain of what Lady Enid would wish. "A stone that's a Roman purple. Regal. With diamonds, of course. She likes antiquity, things with a classical bent. Have you anything of that nature, Boyce?"

"Indeed I do, sir," Boyce murmured, relieved and now

encouraged that he might have a sale rather than a refurbishing. Quickly he put aside the Atherton family
rings and disappeared for a moment into the back room,
returning with yet another small plush box.

"Perhaps this might better please her ladyship, sir," he
said. He opened the lid with a graceful flourish and held
it out to Sheffield. "The stone is an amethyst, sir, as you
requested, a deep, regal purple of the highest cardinal
grade. If you look closely, you will see that the back has
been delineated with an intaglio of an ancient goddess."

"Not Venus, I trust?" Brecon asked, dubious. "That
would not be appropriate for a lady."

"Oh, no, sir," the jeweler said quickly. "I cannot answer as to precisely which goddess she is, but I assure
you she is fully covered, quite chaste, and appropriate
for a lady's hand."

Sheffield slipped the ring from the box and held it to
the window's light. The sizable stone was exactly as
Boyce had said, a rich purple, faceted lightly on the
front, but not so much as to obscure the classical lady
carved on the reverse. Diamonds surrounded the amethyst, and the gold band had even been engraved with a
Greek key pattern. The ring *was* appropriate for a lady,
exactly as Boyce had said, and Sheffield could not imagine a more perfect ring for Lady Enid. It was even sufficiently untraditional for a betrothal ring that she might
wish to wear it after she'd married Dr. Pullings.

"This one," he said. "I'll take it with me to give to the
lady today."

"Very good, sir," Boyce said, bowing deeply. "And
might I offer my very best wishes to both Your Grace
and her ladyship?"

"Thank you, Boyce," Sheffield said, rising to leave
with a sense of accomplishment. With any luck, he'd be
back here soon to reclaim his mother's ring for his true
bride.

"Well done, cousin, well done," Brecon said heartily, clapping Sheffield on the shoulder as they left the shop. "At last I believe you are acting with purpose and honor."

With a grin, Sheffield nodded. For once, he couldn't agree more.

"I do not wish to go, Charlotte, that's all," Diana said. It was past noon, but she was still in her dressing gown, sitting cross-legged on her bed with Fig clutched tightly against her shoulder. "How can you believe I would?"

Summoned by Sarah, Charlotte stood in the doorway, her expression perplexed. "But you seemed to like Lady Enid well enough last night."

"Lady Enid's one thing," Diana said. "But having Sheffield there, too, will make things *difficult*."

"I do not see why," Charlotte said, coming to sit on the end of the bed. "He's betrothed to Lady Enid, and you to Lord Crump. There's no reason for difficulty, at least not the usual difficulties you have with gentlemen."

With a groan, Diana flopped backward against the pillows, letting Fig scramble away. The last thing she wished was to have to listen to an enumeration of her past peccadilloes with gentlemen, even from Charlotte.

"But you saw how Sheffield was last night," she said. "He baits me, torments me, and willfully makes me look foolish before others."

"You're exaggerating," Charlotte said mildly. "Especially since you did much the same thing to him."

"I did not," Diana said. "I merely replied."

Charlotte's brows rose with skepticism. "To tell a gentleman he is 'dismasted' is not an ordinary reply," she said. "You're fortunate Mama didn't hear you say that."

Diana grimaced. So she truly had said "dismasted." She'd been rather afraid that she had, and hoped against hope that she'd only *thought* of saying it, instead of actually letting the words leave her mouth.

"It was Sheffield's fault, not mine," she said defensively. "That is what I mean about how he provokes me."

"He can hardly be blamed for what you said, Diana," Charlotte said. "But I will agree that you two are flint and steel to each other, and far too similar to be at ease in each other's company."

"Similar to Sheffield?" Diana repeated, incredulous. "How could I possibly be like him?"

"The two of you are charming, impulsive, and irresponsible," Charlotte said with more frankness than Diana had expected, or wished to hear. "You're both overly fond of flirtations, too. It's perfectly understandable that you would not be at ease in each other's company, considering how you're both betrothed to other people. Still, I trust that for the peace of the rest of us, you will find a way to put aside your differences and be civil."

Diana stared glumly up at the gathered center of her canopy. None of this was her fault. She was more than willing to put aside differences, and these supposed similarities, too, and forget the past entirely. It was Sheffield who insisted on being so provoking.

"You should be preaching to Sheffield, Charlotte," she said, wounded. "Not to me."

"I'm not 'preaching' to either of you," Charlotte said, the first trace of irritation showing in her voice. "I'm only remarking that, because of our family ties, you and he will often be brought together in the future, and it will be happier for us all if you can manage to be agreeable to each other."

Instantly Diana thought once more of how they'd kissed on Lady Fortescue's gallery. In some ways she and Sheffield were definitely agreeable to each other—*too* agreeable—which was much of the problem. And then other times, such as when he'd pulled her into the pond, he was nothing but a vexing trial. She wished she could confide everything to Charlotte so she'd understand, but how could she explain how she felt about Sheffield to her sister when she couldn't untangle it for herself?

"But to be in his carriage today with him and Lady Enid will be impossible," she said. "Please don't make me go. Please, Charlotte. Please tell them I'm ill or some such."

"You'll go, Diana, and you'll be gracious about it," Charlotte said, using the same voice she employed with her children. "I know you're jealous of Lady Enid, but that's no—"

"Jealous of Lady Enid?" Diana cried, appalled that Charlotte could even suggest such a thing. "Over *Sheffield*?"

"Jealous because she'll have Sheffield there beside her, and you won't have Lord Crump," Charlotte said, as if there could be no other explanation. "Now come, make yourself ready. No matter what you think of Sheffield, he is still a duke, and it would be barbarously ill-mannered of you to keep him and Lady Enid waiting."

"But I'm your sister, Charlotte," Diana said wistfully, "and if you cared for me, you wouldn't make me go. Please, Charlotte."

But as the oldest sister, Charlotte always had been able to make Diana do what she wanted, and today was no different. At precisely three o'clock, Diana was walking down the white steps of Marchbourne House to where Sheffield's carriage waited.

Despite dressing quickly, she'd chosen her clothes with care, hoping to dazzle everyone in the park so thoroughly that they wouldn't notice that Lord Crump wasn't with her. She wore a *robe à l'anglaise* of pale blue silk brocade, flowered with a pattern of roses, and over it a short cape of yellow silk ottoman, clasped at the throat and embroidered with more flowers and twisting vines. Deep drawn-work flounces were attached to the hems of her sleeves, and at least a dozen pins anchored her wide-brimmed hat at an exact slanting angle over her forehead. Though it was a warm afternoon, she carried a swansdown muff, too, not for warmth, but as the last frivolous touch to her dress. As she came down the steps, she could feel everything—her silk skirts, flounces, and cape, the ribbons on her hat and the feathers of her muff and the two long golden curls that fell over her shoulders—fluttering gracefully in the breeze as if she herself might drift away up into the blue sky over London.

Which, considering the afternoon before her, she rather wished she could.

As she'd expected, Sheffield's carriage was expensively elegant, its curving lines showing it had been built in Paris, not London. The carriage lamps were polished silver, as was the hardware around the door and windows. The carriage's dark green lacquer gleamed in contrast to the red wheels, the spokes and trim picked out in gold and his arms painted on the door. One of Sheffield's footmen, dressed in green and gold-laced livery that matched the carriage, had come to the door to escort her down the steps, and two more stood at attention on either side of the door, ready to unlatch the door and help her climb the three steps of the stone block and into the carriage.

To her surprise, Sheffield himself reached out the window and opened the door, then climbed out to the pavement to hand her into the carriage himself. He was dressed informally, much as he had been the first day they'd met in the park, in a well-tailored blue coat, dark red waistcoat, and white deerskin breeches. She remembered those breeches, how closely they fit to his thighs and certain other unmentionable regions besides, and she couldn't help but notice them again as he descended from the carriage.

"Good day, Lady Diana," he said cheerfully, his gaze sweeping from the plumes in her hat to the tips of her shoes, and returning to linger on the triangle of skin framed by the flaring edges of her cloak—a triangle that happened to include the curving swell of her breasts over the squared neckline of her gown.

"Good day to you, Your Grace," she said, striving to follow Charlotte's advice for a genteel truce, even as she fought the urge to snatch her cloak closed. "How kind of you to include me today."

"The kindness is yours in joining Lady Enid and me," he said, matching her bland politeness with his own. His expression, of course, was neither bland nor polite, his eyes full of teasing merriment and his smile very nearly a leer. "Truly we are honored, Lady Diana."

As he stood on the pavement and she climbed to the top step of the carriage block, his face was unavoidably level with her breasts. Lady Enid was not two feet away, yet he shamelessly smiled with such approval that Diana blushed. *So much for truces,* she thought, and as quickly as she could she squeezed her skirts through the door and into the carriage to join Lady Enid.

"Good day, Lady Diana, good day!" Lady Enid said, her face pink with happiness. Her clothes were costly but plain—a dark blue riding habit with pewter buttons and an unadorned matching hat—but Diana guessed that any lady who was as scholarly as Lady Enid likely didn't have time to spend with a mantua maker or milliner.

"Good day, Lady Enid," Diana said, automatically beginning to take the seat across from her, the one that faced back. She assumed that Lady Enid and Sheffield would wish to sit side by side, and by rank the forward-

facing seat was theirs. At least that was the arrangement
with Charlotte and March.

But not, it seemed, for Lady Enid. "Here, Lady Diana,
sit by me," she said eagerly, shifting to one side and patting the cushions. "We'll let His Grace sit with Fantôme."

At the sound of his name, Sheffield's bulldog wandered out from behind Lady Enid's skirts and jumped
onto the opposite seat, where Sheffield soon joined him.
Charlotte settled beside Lady Enid, the footman latched
the door, and the carriage drew away from the house
and into the road.

"How does Monsieur Fantôme?" Diana asked. Of all
the occupants in the carriage, she was most at ease with
the dog, and she leaned forward to ruffle his ears.
"Handsome boy!"

"Oh, hardly," Sheffield said. "Even I wouldn't dare
call him handsome. But he makes up for his face with a
worthy soul. Isn't that so, Fantôme?"

The dog lay down beside Sheffield's thigh and rolled
on his back, his paws in the air and his pink tongue lolling from his mouth.

"Shameless, shameless," Sheffield said, obligingly
scratching the dog's belly. "You see how the company
of ladies debases him. Enid, my dear, show Diana your
ring."

Diana noticed how he'd left off their titles, instantly
making the conversation more intimate and familiar,
but also more awkward. She was still deciding how to
react when Lady Enid thrust her hand out before her,
holding it so that Diana was sure to see the ring.

"Sheffield gave it to me this morning to mark our betrothal," she said proudly. "That's the goddess Athena
carved in the stone. Could there be a more perfect ring?"

"It's lovely," Diana murmured as she dutifully leaned
over the other woman's hand. The amethyst and diamond ring wasn't to her own taste—she didn't care for

purple, even in a precious stone—but Lady Enid clearly adored it, which was all that mattered. Or almost all: the choice of the ring had been so thoughtfully made with consideration for her interests that Diana was impressed. Clearly Sheffield's aim had been to please Lady Enid, and he'd succeeded.

In comparison her own finger remained woefully bare, and she thought how Lord Crump would never be able to make a similarly appropriate choice. He knew next to nothing about her, nor did he seem interested in learning more, either. But then March had scarcely known Charlotte when he'd chosen her ring, so there was still hope.

"Yes, it is lovely," Lady Enid said softly, then with a sigh covered the ring with her other hand. It was a curious gesture, peculiar for any lady who'd just been given such a ring from the man she was to wed.

But equally curious was Sheffield's behavior. To begin with, he'd chosen to sit with his dog rather than with the woman he'd promised to wed. He was courteous to her, but nothing more. He didn't even attempt conversation, which Diana knew was most unusual for him. Instead each of them stared from different windows, each lost in their respective thoughts. Diana wondered if they'd quarreled or had some other misunderstanding; yet there was none of the tension that usually accompanied such unhappiness, none of the ill will, and certainly no recriminations or name-calling. The three of them might have been strangers traveling in a post-road coach.

Fortunately, Marchbourne House faced Green Park, with St. James's Park adjacent, and their drive to St. James's gates was a brief one. Once inside, they joined the afternoon parade of carriages, and finally there was plenty to say. With the carriage windows dropped, the three of them nodded and smiled at the noble-born passengers of other carriages. Because Sheffield had been away for so long on the Continent and Lady Enid was indifferent to society, Diana was the one who identified the most faces. It became something of a game, with her not only spotting the owner of each passing carriage but supplying a scrap of identifying history, too, which Sheffield instantly embroidered. Before long the three of them were laughing uproariously together, and in every other carriage in St. James's that afternoon the conversation inevitably included the charming high spirits in the Duke of Sheffield's carriage, how handsome His Grace had grown whilst away, how remarkable Lady Enid Lattimore and Lady Diana Wylder were for their beauty, and how dreadfully ugly the dog was that stood on the seat with his paws out the window.

When they reached the farthest end of the drive for the third time, Sheffield drew an elaborate gold watch from his waistcoat.

"Is it time, then?" Lady Enid asked, her voice abruptly taut.

"It is." Sheffield smiled and tucked the watch back in its pocket. "Nearly four o'clock."

"Time for what, Duke?" Diana asked. "Must we leave so soon?"

"Not at all," Sheffield said, signaling to the driver to stop. "I thought we should like to walk beneath the trees for a bit. One never knows whom one might meet in the shadows."

Diana narrowed her eyes at him, for of course he must be referring to how they'd first met—not that she would say so before Lady Enid.

"True enough," she said instead. "All manner of rascals can be found lurking in the shadows."

"Not so long as the sun is with us," Sheffield said, letting Fantôme jump down from the carriage first. "But I'll grant you that no one of fashion walks at this hour.

Other than the nursemaids walking with their charges, we'll have the trees to ourselves."

They climbed down and soon left the carriage behind, the two women walking together and Sheffield slightly ahead, letting Fantôme wander. He'd been right about the hour, and there were few others walking beneath the elms and the oaks, their shadows stretching long in the dappled sun. It seemed to Diana the perfect time to walk, but beside her Lady Enid seemed strangely agitated, looking anxiously about in every direction as if fearing some giant lion or other beast would leap from behind the next tree.

"You needn't worry, Lady Enid," Diana said, wishing to calm her. "His Grace is right. I've walked here scores of times before at this hour, and we're perfectly safe."

Lady Enid only shook her head, not daring for an instant to be less vigilant and look at Diana. "I have no fear of outside attack, Lady Diana, but rather I fear my own weaknesses and lack of fortitude, which might keep me from the happiness that—oh, forgive me, I must go to him!"

Abruptly she abandoned Diana and began to run away, heedless of how her skirts flew about her legs or her hat bumped on her hair.

"Lady Enid!" called Diana, beginning to follow her. "Come back, I beg you!"

But she'd only taken a few steps when, to her astonishment, she saw a soberly dressed reverend gentleman step from a tree and hurry toward Lady Enid. He swept his black hat from his head, holding his arms out to her, and she flung herself into his embrace, holding him as tightly as was possible. The next instant they were kissing with as much passion and devotion as a man and woman could, while all Diana could do was watch with complete bewilderment.

"Who is he?" she demanded when Sheffield joined her. "I don't understand at all, Duke. Who *is* he?"

Sheffield watched them, too, his smile broad. "That's the Reverend Dr. Joshua Pullings, the gentleman Enid intends to marry."

"Marry?" Now Diana stared at Sheffield. "But I thought *you* had promised to marry her."

"Oh, I have," he said easily. "She's duly promised to marry me as well, but Dr. Pullings will be the one who will actually become her husband."

Diana shook her head, unable to find any logic in this nonsense. "That's impossible," she said. "Lord Lattimore would never condone it."

"No, he wouldn't," he agreed. "In fact, he has expressly forbidden that match, and much prefers the one between Enid and me. Lattimore will be furious when he learns the wrong man has won his daughter, but then, he didn't count on love, did he?"

Lady Enid and Dr. Pullings had stopped kissing now and were talking. Though they stood too far away for their words to be overheard, it was clear from how they smiled and gazed upon each other, how she rested her palm so trustingly upon his chest and how his arms circled her waist with such tenderness, that their conversation must be nothing but the sweetest endearments and promises. The difference in their fortunes and stations didn't in the least concern either of them. All that mattered was love. It was one of the most romantic sights that Diana had ever seen, and as confused as she was by exactly how it had come about, she still couldn't help but wish she'd a measure of the same tenderness and devotion from Lord Crump.

"People like us don't marry for love," she said wistfully. "It's not permitted."

"It will be this time, because I'm doing the permitting," Sheffield said. "Or at least the arranging. Come, let's grant them their time alone, and I'll explain."

He offered her his arm, and when she didn't take it immediately, he gently took her hand and tucked it into the crook of his arm to lead her away. She sighed and followed, matching her steps to his.

"You've a great deal of explaining to do, Duke," she said. "You say that they are lovers who will wed, but how did they come to know each other? How did they fall in love without Lord Lattimore hearing of it? Tell me all, sir, tell me now!"

He chuckled, clearly enjoying the role of storyteller as they walked away from the paths and across the lawns, with Fantôme racing in big looping circles around them. "You're quite demanding," he teased, "and you ask a great many questions."

"I am, Duke," she said, unashamed to admit it, "and I do. I know ladies are supposed to be demure and accepting, but how else is one to learn anything if one does not ask questions?"

"A fair point," he said. "Very well, I'll answer your questions, on the condition that you'll cease giving me the respect due to a doddering uncle. I give you leave to forget that I'm a duke, and recall instead that we're practically family. Call me Sheffield instead, and I shall call you Diana."

She did not agree at once. To leave off his honorifics as he requested was wickedly familiar, just as strolling about the park unattended except for Fantôme as their chaperone was far too familiar as well. True, they were practically family, but while Charlotte could call him simply Sheffield because she was a duchess and equal to him in rank, Diana had no such privilege.

"Call me Sheffield," he said again. "It's wonderfully easy, a single word. Please, Diana."

"Very well, *Sheffield*," she said with dramatic emphasis. She adjusted the brim of her hat and peeked out from beneath it, liking how she had to look up to meet his gaze. It was hardly Lord Crump's fault that he was much the same height as she was, but she did enjoy walking with a man who was taller. "Now tell me everything, as you promised."

"It's not that long a tale," he said. "Dr. Pullings was tutor to Enid's brother. Because she showed a prodigious interest in learning, she was permitted to share the lessons. Soon the shared interest turned into love, and she and Dr. Pullings asked for Lord Lattimore's blessing."

"Which Lord Lattimore most certainly refused," Diana said. None of her own little romances had ever progressed so far, but she could sympathize entirely. "Oh, poor Lady Enid!"

"Poor Enid indeed," Sheffield said wryly. "She was ordered to marry me, while equally poor—or perhaps literally poor, considering he's a parson without an income—Pullings was dismissed without references. Fortunately, I'd no more wish to marry her than she did me, and thus we came to our agreement."

"To pretend to be betrothed?"

"Yes," he said, smiling proudly. "I agreed to help her meet Pullings with the aim of them finally marrying, while I am free of the meddlesome matchmaking of others who wish me married. It's quite ingenious, isn't it?"

But Diana shook her head and stopped walking to meet his gaze.

"No, it is not," she said firmly, removing her hand from his arm and slipping it instead into the muff. "You've encouraged her to defy her father and follow after an unsuitable man who will ruin her and their children, no matter how much he loves her. You've offered the two of them empty hope, and that you've made them *lie* so that you can continue to amuse yourself isn't brilliant at all. It's low and deceitful, and—and *appalling*."

"Appalling?" he repeated, surprised. He bent down, took the stick that Fantôme offered, and hurled it off across the grass. "That's putting a rather harsh face on it, isn't it?"

"It isn't just Lady Enid and Dr. Pullings," she said. "You've made me part of your duplicity, too. If Lord Crump had come with us, then you wouldn't have dared do this. He wouldn't have tolerated this, not for a moment."

"I know Crump," he said, pointedly looking out at the dog and not at her, "and knew he wouldn't squander his time coming to the park, even if he were asked a thousand times."

That stung, especially from Sheffield, for she was sure she'd heard an unspoken implication that Lord Crump simply didn't care to come to the park with Diana. She scowled, her chin dipping lower over the front of her cloak.

"But you knew that *I* would," she said, anger and bitterness mixed in her voice. "You believed that if I rode in your carriage like a—a *chaperone*, everyone would take note that the three of us had been in the park."

"It was never that calculated," he began, but Diana had heard enough.

"You thought I'd oblige you and be complicit with your plans," she said, fuming. "You were certain I'd become one more liar and help you keep your precious bachelor freedom intact. But I won't, sir, and I mean to put an end to this directly."

She turned away and headed off in the general direction of Lady Enid and Dr. Pullings. She didn't exactly run, because the curved heels of her shoes kept sinking into the grass, but determination made her move at a brisk pace, her arms swinging at her sides. She would tell them she wanted no part of this whole ruse, and she'd demand that—

"Diana!" he shouted. "Halt, blast you!"

She heard him come after her, but she didn't turn, and she certainly wouldn't stop after being addressed in that way.

"Diana!" He grabbed her arm to make her stop. His hand tightened on the swansdown muff on her wrist, and when she instinctively pulled her arm away from his grasp, she slipped free of the muff and of him, too.

She looked over her shoulder just in time to see him staring down in disbelief at the fluffy white muff in his hand. Any other time, she would have laughed—would have, at any rate, until he threw the muff away in frustration. At once Fantôme came racing on his short, stocky legs, every stick, branch, and squirrel in the park forgotten in favor of the delectable white muff.

The thought of that lovely muff crushed in Fantôme's jaws and covered with dog slobber stopped Diana more sharply than Sheffield could. She wheeled around, barely seizing the muff from the grass before it became Fantôme's prize, and leaving him whining and disappointed at her feet.

"Come with me," Sheffield said, taking her firmly by the upper arm. "I mean to give those two excellent people their time together, and I'm not going to let you interfere."

"Why should I do anything you say?" she demanded as he forcibly led her away.

"You'll do it not because I say so but because it's the proper thing to do," he said, stopping before a bench shaded by a large oak with smaller trees around it. "Now sit, so I may talk to you in a civilized manner, and not as if you're some raving bedlamite."

He released her arm. She didn't sit, but she didn't run away again, either.

"I'm not Fantôme," she said, folding her arms across her chest. "You cannot order me to sit as if I were."

He made a rumbling noise of exasperation. "Very well, then, stand. But sitting or standing, you *will* listen to me."

He swept his hat from his head, tapping it lightly against his thigh for emphasis. He couldn't possibly have become out of breath from chasing her a dozen paces, not a man as large and strong as he was, but she could think of no other explanation for the three deep breaths he took before he spoke.

"I believe no one should be forced to marry another," he began, "simply because their properties need joining or their fortunes combining, or because they have the same bloodlines, like horses. I do believe men and women should marry for love alone, which is why I won't marry Enid, and why I'll do my best to see her and Pullings wed instead."

She stared up at him from beneath her hat's brim, not sure whether to believe this tirade from him or not. Why couldn't he accept that people of their rank didn't marry for love? It was the same for them all, and she couldn't understand whether he was truly being rebellious or only saying such a thing to capture her attention. He had managed that much; she couldn't recall ever having heard a gentleman make such a speech to her. But then, it was difficult to remain objective when he looked like this, his hair tousled and tossed by the breeze, his profile sharp against the late afternoon sky.

"You believe in love?" she asked warily. "You? With your married French mistresses galore?"

He winced. "You know of that?"

"Who in London does not?" She felt vastly worldly, speaking of such things to a man like him. It was also dangerous, exactly the sort of conversation that the future Lady Crump had no business conducting. "Everyone speaks of it."

"Everyone," he repeated more softly. "But you're not everyone, Diana."

There was something in his voice that made her shiver, an implied intimacy that should not be there between them. She knew she should leave him now and go find the others. She knew she must not be alone with him any longer.

And yet she did not move.

"What I did with her wasn't love." His voice was rough with urgency, as if it was important that she understand every word he spoke. "She might have been any doxie on the street instead of a marquise for what existed between us. It was a simple divertissement, a careless passion, a carnal desire—"

"No more," she said, swiftly turning away. "I—I can't listen to any more."

"Diana, please," he said, catching her once again, and she let herself be caught. "Diana."

And then, as she'd known from the beginning he would, he drew her close and kissed her.

CHAPTER

 8

Sheffield hadn't intended to kiss Diana. In fact, he'd vowed to himself that morning that he wouldn't, that he'd treat her more honorably than he generally treated women. If true love wasn't won without challenge or sacrifice, then it likely required noble restraint, too.

Those thoughts, however, had taken place while he and Brecon were sitting in the jeweler's shop, and it had been easy to make resolutions about noble restraint with his mother's ring in his hand. Being alone with Diana, however, was an entirely different matter. It wasn't as if she was trying to be enticing, not today. She'd been solemn and stern because she hadn't agreed with what he'd done on behalf of Lady Enid and Pullings, and she'd even been judgmental about it, too.

But to his bewilderment, Diana being solemn and stern was a hundred times more enticing than any other lady being purposely seductive. She simply *was* enticing, even with Fantôme jumping around at her feet, trying desperately to steal her muff. She was perfectly confident, perfectly assured, her skirts ruffling around her legs, that foolish flowered cape fluttering lightly around her shoulders, and the ribbons on her hat rippling like pennants. She'd tipped her head with equally perfect skepticism and disdain, her single dimple adding punctuation as she looked up at him from beneath the curving brim of her hat with her lips pursed and her bright blue eyes slightly narrowed.

It was the pond at Marchbourne House all over again. Nothing was going as it was supposed to be between them. The more she acted as if she'd no gainful use for him, the more captivated he became.

All he'd intended to do was explain how cleverly he'd arranged matters between Enid and Pullings. He'd expected her to be impressed. She wasn't, and when she wasn't, he went babbling on about love. Damnation, about *love*, the single most perilous word a man could ever utter. He hadn't intended that at all. He didn't love her, not to go bandying the word about like that. He was only considering loving her, a very different thing, at least in his head.

Then she'd folded her arms to demonstrate her determination and inadvertently offered him an engrossing display of her breasts, raised beneath her forearms and framed by the sides of her cloak. That was enough—more than enough—to make him stop thinking with his head and let his cock take over instead. He'd been left so confused that before he'd realized it, he was explaining carnal desire and the Marquise du Vaulchier. Clearly words could no longer be trusted, not where Diana was concerned, and in desperation he'd automatically done what he knew never failed: he'd pulled her into his arms and kissed her.

She made an odd mumbled sound of protest that might have been his name, or might have been something much less flattering. He didn't care, and after a moment, she didn't, either. Her hands—and that infernal muff—fluttered briefly against his chest, not from anger, but more from amazement, and then they stilled, trusting him more than she should. He kissed her purposefully, brazenly, ignoring that they were standing in the middle of St. James's Park. This was one thing he knew how to do supremely well, and there couldn't be any misguided mentioning of love this way, either.

But the longer he kissed her, the more he felt that confident control fraying and unraveling. This time, she required no gentle coaxing for her lips to part, but instead her mouth opened freely, welcoming him. She was somehow both innocent and eager, inexperienced but not shy, and the combination of curiosity and passion was like a torch to his own desire. This time, too, she didn't rest her hands on his shoulders, but boldly reached inside his coat, allowing her palms to roam across his back, pressing her body closer to his.

He slanted his mouth to deepen the kiss further, and she made a small, maddening purr of excitement. At least it made *him* mad, mad with unabashed lust, mad enough for his hand to slide away from her waist, lower, past the hard edge of her stays to the wonderful softness of silk skirts over the full, rounded curves of her buttocks. His fingers spread, caressing her and pulling her hips closer to his. Despite the layers of clothes between them, she couldn't ignore the hard length of his desire now, nor did he wish her to. He'd hoped to make her forget that unseasonable mention of love, and he'd certainly done that. There wasn't any flowery, romantic love in what they were doing: only lust, white hot and ready and—

"*Oooh!*" she gasped abruptly, pitching against him so hard that she nearly toppled them both.

"What in blazes?" he exclaimed, grabbing her by the waist to steady her.

"It was Fantôme," she said breathlessly. The heady spell of desire had been broken, and she swiftly stepped apart from him. "He jumped and struck me. I suppose he still wanted the muff."

"Hell." There stood Fantôme, shifting from one front

foot to the other as he grinned up with endless devotion, completely unaware of the almost unbearable frustration he'd just created. "Thunder and hell."

"I'm sorry." Her face was flushed, her lips were red and swollen from kissing, and her hair was coming unpinned—the very picture of a desirable woman half tumbled. "I'm sorry."

"I'm sorry, too," he said, though he'd the distinct impression they weren't sorry for the same things. His voice was gruff as he struggled to tame the beast raging in his breeches. Her general dishevelment wasn't helping, either. "Damnably sorry."

"Yes, I'm sorry," she said, taking a deep breath to compose herself. "Yes. No. Oh, whatever am I trying to say?"

"No more apologizing," he said. He picked up a stick and threw it as hard as he could, more for himself than for Fantôme. "That would be a start."

"Yes," she said again. "I suppose we are even now. I have kissed you, and you have kissed me."

He stared at her, stunned by such confused logic and still incapable of thinking with his head. "We're *even*?"

"Yes," she said, reaching up to try to shove her hair back to rights. "We've both erred, haven't we? Two wrongs do not make a right, but they do balance things out. Goodness. My hat's all askew, isn't it?"

"The devil take your hat," he said. "The devil take your argument, too."

"Perhaps I should consign you to the devil as well, and be done with it." She sighed and sank onto the bench, staring down at her hands instead of him. "You realize that this must never, ever happen again. Not if you wish to see this preposterous scheme for Lady Enid to a respectable ending."

"It's not in the least preposterous," he said, grateful for a topic other than why they should never kiss again.

"There is a small parish attached to my property in Hampshire. The living is mine to grant, and the present vicar is withdrawing at the next quarter day. I've told Pullings it's his, to put him beyond Lattimore's vengeance. All Pullings must do is marry Lady Enid, who seems eager enough to become the Greek-reading wife of a country parson."

She looked up at him from beneath her still-crooked hat's brim. "You would do that for them?"

"I told you I would." He joined her on the bench, taking care to keep a safe distance between them. "No one should have to marry against their wish. I told you that, too."

Again she looked away. "I didn't believe you."

"You should." He wanted her to believe him. He didn't know why it suddenly seemed so desperately crucial that she did, but it was. He wanted her to believe him in this, and in everything else as well.

But all she did was shrug and shake her head. "It's not just a question of Lady Enid's happiness. Pray recall that I am promised to Lord Crump."

"I do recall it," he said, more adamantly than he'd intended. "Every minute of the day."

"As do I," she said softly, sadly. "It's good that I do, too, before I make another ruinous misstep like that last one."

He frowned, for this was not what he wished to hear. "You consider kissing me a ruinous misstep?"

"Oh, yes," she said. "*Most* ruinous, if it were to become known."

He had no answer for that, because she was most likely right. Kissing him would be ruinous to any betrothed lady. Even a month ago, such distinction would have made him proud, or at least laugh, but not now.

Damnation, how could she have turned him so completely wrong side out?

"It's not just Lord Crump himself," she continued, interpreting his silence as a request for more explanation. "It's my mother and sisters and aunt, too. They wish only the best in life for me, and have persuaded me to see the reason in marrying an admirable gentleman like Lord Crump. Their own marriages were arranged with success, you know, excellent examples for me to follow. And then there's also March and Brecon."

"March and Brecon?" he repeated. "What do they have to do with this?"

"Because I cannot disappoint them, either," she said, sounding determined yet defensive. "Because they are acquaintances of Lord Crump and applaud our match as a most admirable one for us both. Brecon in particular was most helpful to Mama with the legal arrangements."

Belatedly Sheffield recalled his first night back in London, and how Brecon had been with Lady Hervey, discussing the betrothal of her difficult daughter. Sheffield had been amused and intrigued at the time. Now, knowing both the daughter and the future groom, he was instead horrified that Brecon's habitual helpfulness had led to this match.

"But this is exactly what I mean," he insisted. "We are all too bound by conventions of our class, and too accepting of marriages that are arranged not from love but from power and economics. Why should you accept Lord Crump if you do not love him?"

"Because I must," she said. "Because ladies like me cannot afford to rebel like that, or we will never marry. Because I've already done too many things I shouldn't have, and now only a gentleman as impeccable as Lord Crump can redeem me."

He hated hearing the resignation in her words, her acceptance of a fate that seemed unspeakably dire to him. Crump might purify her reputation, but he'd also crush her spirit and rob her of any happiness in life. All that fire and passion he'd tasted in her kiss, along with her wry humor and impulsiveness and beauty, would be completely wasted on a husband like that.

"Consider Lady Enid," he urged. "She's not afraid to break free of her match."

"Our situations are entirely different," she said firmly, but now there was a bitterness in her voice, too. "I love my family and therefore respect their choice. I do not have a gentleman like Dr. Pullings waiting for me, nor would his lordship be nearly so obliging and generous as you are to Lady Enid. No, I will marry him, because I must. I must."

He wanted to save her. How could he not? He wanted to be her hero, to tell her he'd find some way to help her free herself of her betrothal, to miraculously do the same for her that he'd done for Lady Enid. But she was right. Her situation was different. Her personality and their intertwined families made matters infinitely more complicated, and he thought again of how the only possible way to rescue her would be to marry her himself.

Even if he were to pursue such an irrevocable step, she seemed so thoroughly resigned to her fate and so determined to obey her family's wishes that he wasn't sure she'd accept. She believed she needed redemption by way of a saintly husband, and he couldn't offer that, not by half. And there he would be, the dashing Duke of Sheffield rejected in favor of the sour-faced Marquis of Crump.

He'd be worse than merely ruined. He'd be an out-and-out laughingstock.

But when Sheffield watched her now, leaning over to welcome Fantôme back to the bench, he knew he wouldn't abandon her. She might not want him, but he wanted her, and for now that was what mattered.

"Good dog," she murmured, smiling at his dog if not at him. In return Fantôme snuffed and snorted with a stick in his mouth that wasn't the one Sheffield had thrown. Proudly he dropped it at Diana's feet instead of Sheffield's, and added a pretty bow as well.

"Fine fellow," she continued, reaching out to ruffle his ears as she praised him. "Fine, handsome fellow. If it weren't for Fig, I'd wish for a dog exactly like you."

Sheffield sighed and tried not to think how ridiculous it was to be jealous of his own dog. "Who or what is Fig?"

"My cat," she said, running her fingers beneath Fantôme's collar to make him lean against her knees and groan with pleasure. "She is much like Fantôme, in that she is beautiful only to me."

Sheffield sighed again, thinking how woefully low their conversation had sunk that it now dwelled upon pets. On the other hand, he'd gladly grovel like Fantôme if it meant that he, too, could press his head against her knees like that.

"Fantôme likes cats," he said. "But then, Fantôme likes everyone."

She looked up at him with frank skepticism, her wide blue eyes entirely capable of squeezing his heart.

"Fantôme can't possibly like cats," she said firmly. "Fantôme is a bulldog, and bulldogs kill cats, given half a chance."

"Not Fantôme," Sheffield said. "He can't even kill a spider. He is the mildest, meekest-tempered bulldog in creation. That is how I acquired him. His last owner— the keeper of a tavern in Boulogne—had hoped to prosper by fighting him in the pits. Fantôme had demonstrated neither interest nor aptitude for fighting, and the tavern-keep was attempting to improve his fighting spirit by whipping him bloody. I was a witness, and bought the dog to stop his suffering, unaware of what a lazy beast I was acquiring."

"He was flogging this sweet dog?" she asked, horrified by the story. "Poor, poor Fantôme! Oh, Sheffield, how fortunate that you saved him."

That was likely more praise than he deserved, but he'd take it. "If you rub the fur on his back the right way, you can still see the scars. Proof that there are tender-hearted bulldogs."

"I accept your proof, though I'd never have thought it possible," she said, her sudden smile unexpectedly shy. "You are *kind*, Sheffield. I accept that, too."

As if Fantôme understood—and Sheffield was willing to believe he did—the dog pulled himself up on the bench beside him, squeezing in on the far end and forcing Sheffield to move closer to Diana. It was neatly done, and *almost*, almost sufficient for him to forgive Fantôme for jumping against Diana earlier. With a contented sigh, the dog rested his jaw on Sheffield's thigh and rolled his eyes upward so obviously that Sheffield chuckled.

"You see how he is," he said. "Entirely docile and tame. Pray remember that reputations are often given, not earned."

She glanced at him uncertainly from beneath her still-crooked hat. Blast, did she think he was speaking of *her* reputation?

"I meant Fantôme's reputation," he said quickly, and he was rewarded to see how she relaxed.

"Indeed," she said, fussing with her skirts, but somehow in the process managing to slide a fraction closer to him on the bench. There was that single, sudden dimple, a winsome little beacon in her cheek as she watched him from beneath her lashes. "Does that mean that the scandalous Duke of Sheffield is at heart docile and tame as well?"

He chuckled, as much from the sight of the dimple as from what she said.

"Docile and tame?" he said, resting his hand along the

back of the bench, and incidentally behind her back as well. "No, I fear not. It's not in my blood."

She didn't move away. She smiled and brushed aside a random wisp of hair that was dancing against her cheek.

"Perhaps not," she said. "But you are . . . *kind*."

Hell. She thought he was *kind*. Being kind was for elderly tea-drinking aunts. Being kind did not earn invitations into ladies' bedchambers.

He kissed her anyway, curling his arm around her shoulders to draw her closer. Almost at once the desire returned to ignite between them, instant, undeniable lust that made him want to devour her. This time he impatiently pushed the hat clear from her head and thrust his fingers into the golden tangle of her hair to cradle her head. Freed of the hat, she tipped her head to one side to make their mouths match more perfectly. She curled one hand around the back of his neck, slipping her fingers beneath his queue to lightly stroke his nape. He'd never thought of the scruff of his neck as being particularly sensitive, but when she touched him there, he felt a startling shudder of excitement race down his spine.

He groaned as his mouth ground against hers, and at that point it seemed like the most natural thing in the world to slip his hand into that tantalizing opening in her capelet and beneath her linen kerchief. At once he found her breasts rising from her stays, the flesh warm and rounded and even more wondrous than he'd imagined it to be. She didn't squirm away like some women would, but instead arched into his caress and made a low purr of pleasure that was at once charming and seductive.

Forcibly he reminded himself that they were on a bench in St. James's Park in the afternoon, which was not exactly the best place for undressing an earl's daughter. But when she kissed him like this, he was tempted, sorely, painfully tempted, to forget they were in an open, public place and toss up her skirts and do exactly what he wanted with her—and what she wanted, too, from the way she was pressing her breast into his palm.

At least he was considering it when Fantôme abruptly leaped from the bench and began to bark.

He pulled away from Diana, intending only to be interrupted long enough to scold his dog.

"Quiet, Fantôme, quiet!" he shouted, but the dog was already racing away across the grass toward Lady Enid and Dr. Pullings.

"No, no, no," Diana said breathlessly, tucking her kerchief back into her bodice. "Why did they need to return *now*?"

"Because it's the time we agreed, that's why," Sheffield said, his mood black. Twice he'd been interrupted while kissing her, twice in less than an hour, which was two times more than any man should be expected to bear. He retrieved her hat from where it had fallen behind the bench and handed it to her. "I expect you'll want this."

"Goodness, yes," she said. She was twisting her hair back into some semblance of decency, clumsily shoving hairpins in willy-nilly and making it clear even to him that she never dressed her hair by herself. Finally she gave up, stuffing her hair back into her cap and pushing her hat on top. "If Mama or Charlotte ask questions, I'll have to blame the wind."

He loved how she looked, disheveled and flushed, but no mother would ever accept her appearance as having been caused by the wind. "They'd believe that?"

She sighed. "Do I look that mussed?"

"Yes," he said, reaching out to tuck a few last wisps of hair back under her cap. *Mussed* was far too genteel a word for how she looked. *Tumbled* would be more apt, even *ravished*, if they'd had another ten minutes alone. "But you were with Lady Enid the entire time, and that makes for a sufficient explanation."

"I trust so." She glanced back at the two others approaching, making sure they were still out of earshot. "We *are* even now. I kissed you, then you kissed me, and that last—I believe we kissed each other. But that must absolutely be the last time."

He sighed. "You said that before."

"Yes, but I mean it now." Pointedly not looking at him, she drew herself up, sitting very straight and folding her hands in proper ladylike fashion. "It must be that way, Sheffield, for all the same reasons I said before. It must. I hope Lady Enid will not guess that I've been kissing you."

"She won't," he said, not about to agree to never kissing again. "Look at Enid. She's just as, ah, mussed as you are."

In fact, both Lady Enid and Pullings looked much more the worse for wear than Diana and he did, and Sheffield would wager ten guineas that they hadn't been interrupted by a watchful dog. It wasn't that their clothing had a certain haphazard air; both of their faces were still flushed, with that drowsy look of satisfaction that Sheffield recognized from his own experience. Clearly the preacher hadn't stayed up in his pulpit, but had ventured into his congregation, not that the congregation seemed to have objected.

"I suppose she is," Diana agreed slowly, less adept than Sheffield at reading the obvious.

Sheffield smiled. "Ah, loving in the park beneath the wide blue sky," he said to no one in particular. He stood, ready to greet them. "Good day to you two. I trust you have amused yourselves?"

"Good day, Sheffield," Enid said, and she blushed an even deeper shade of crimson. "I, ah, I came across Dr.

Pullings whilst walking. He was my brother's tutor, you see, and I haven't —"

"It's not necessary, Enid," Sheffield said as gently as he could. "Diana knows all."

Enid's eyes widened with dismay. "All?" she said faintly, her gaze darting toward Diana. "Everything?"

"As much as I know," Sheffield said, more honestly than the rest of them realized. Who exactly knew what would make for an interesting discussion? Obviously Enid and Pullings knew about each other, as he did himself. Now Diana also knew about Enid and Pullings, but the latter two didn't know about Sheffield and Diana— if in fact there was anything *to* know, which Sheffield had to admit he didn't know, either. It made his head ache.

Fortunately Diana had no such reservations.

"I'm so vastly happy for you, Lady Enid," she said, rising to embrace Enid and do the instinctive cheek kissing that women used to seal agreements instead of shaking hands. "Now you must introduce me to Dr. Pullings."

The introduction was made, with Pullings managing to be courteous, if a bit confused. Sheffield wasn't surprised. Although Diana was on her best and most generous behavior, a lady as beautiful as she was could leave even a parson in a state of confusion.

"I cannot tell you how grateful Lady Enid and I are, my lady, and we shall forever be in your debt," he said, his bow stiff and formal. "You and His Grace together have brought us not only happiness but hope for our love."

"His Grace and I have not exactly acted together, Dr. Pullings," she said, smiling to keep the rebuke a gentle one, "but rather in concert. Pray recall that I am betrothed to the Marquis of Crump, and *together* is a word that should only link my name to his."

Poor Pullings squeezed his eyes shut in mortification. "Please, please forgive me, my lady," he said. "I never intended to slander either you or his lordship."

"I don't believe you did," Diana said, glancing back at Sheffield. "I only wished everything to be perfectly clear."

She was smiling still when she looked at him, but there was a touch of defiance, too, or was it a challenge? It did seem like a damned curious time to think of Crump. Still, Sheffield smiled in return, wondering what the devil she was plotting next. She could hardly blame him for what had happened here at this bench, for she'd been every bit as eager as he. Hadn't she said herself that they were even?

"Perhaps next time Lord Crump can join us, too," Lady Enid said, eager to smooth the waters as she clung to Dr. Pullings's arm. "In Sheffield's carriage, I mean. In the park."

"Another time, yes," Sheffield said blandly. The last thing any of them should wish for was Crump's gloomy presence, but he'd no wish to go into that now. Instead he glanced at the lengthening shadows across the grass and drew his watch from his waistcoat; the hour was, as he'd suspected, much later than it should be.

"Nearly five, Enid," he said. "I fear I must dutifully return you to your home before your father himself comes hunting after us."

"I fear so," Enid murmured, her round face puckered with regret as she clung all the more tightly to Dr. Pullings. "I wouldn't wish Father to react violently, and yet I fear he'd do exactly that."

"Come, Your Grace, let them say their farewells in peace," Diana said, lightly tucking her hand into the crook of Sheffield's arm to turn him away. "Lady Enid can join us when she's ready."

Sheffield nodded. "Don't dally with the good-byes,

Pullings," he said over his shoulder. "I've no wish to face Lattimore's temper. Here, here, Fantôme, you're included, too."

He looked down at the dog, who had seemingly fallen asleep leaning against his leg after his long and busy afternoon of interrupting. Sheffield gave Fantôme a gentle prod to roll him into action, and let Diana lead the way. Generally he didn't like women who tried to take command, but with Diana he had already learned that she'd be leading him somewhere interesting.

Besides, her hand on his arm was likely going to be the last opportunity he had to touch her today, and he covered her hand with his, just to make sure she didn't escape as they slowly headed toward where they'd left the carriage. He liked walking with her. She was exactly tall enough at his side, and likely because of that unconventional upbringing in the country, she had a long, brisk stride, and she'd no trouble keeping pace with him.

"You know Lord Clump will never join us," she said, clearly striving to sound stern and practical again, in contrast to her tousled state. "You've said that yourself. Besides, if he did, you couldn't send Lady Enid off alone with Dr. Pullings. His lordship would never condone such an arrangement."

"Never, never, never," Sheffield said mildly. "I warrant he'd never condone you kissing me, too."

Her cheeks pinked again. It was so easy to make her blush, and so charming when it happened, too.

"I told you, Sheffield," she said. "That can never happen again. If it were possible and you weren't part of my family, I would remove you entirely from my life and never see you again."

"By Jove," Sheffield said. "Another never! Your obsession with finalities astonishes me."

"Stop it, Sheffield," she said crossly. "You know exactly what I'm saying."

"Perhaps," he said, giving her hand a fond little squeeze. "But that is not to say that I agree with it."

"You must," she insisted. "You have no choice in the matter."

"But I do." He smiled down at her. "And where you are concerned, I will never, ever say never."

"Here I am," Lady Enid said, hurrying to join them. "Forgive me, but—but it was so difficult to part."

"Only for a short while, Enid," Sheffield said. Mindful that they would soon be near the carriage, he eased his arm free of Diana's hand and replaced it with Lady Enid's. "We were just planning our next jaunt when you joined us."

Diana shot him a murderous glance. He merely smiled.

"Oh, how vastly fine of you both!" Lady Enid exclaimed, grateful teariness in her voice. "You've made me so happy. I shall never be able to repay you, you know."

His smile widened, and he made sure it reached Diana as well as Enid.

"Never say never, my dear," he said. "Never, ever say never."

CHAPTER

 9

"What is your judgment, Di?" Charlotte turned her head to one side, the better to display her hat, an elegant black one meant to accompany a riding habit. "You know March's tastes as well as I do. Will he like it or think it too severe?"

Diana studied her sister critically. They were sitting on the square stools at the counter at Hartley's, the finest millinery shop in Bond Street, with Mrs. Hartley herself—dressed in her customary deep plum silk—assisting them. The Wylder sisters (and their mother) all were very fond of hats, and while Mrs. Hartley was a talented milliner who created styles instead of following them, she was also a shrewd tradeswoman and understood the advantages of counting the Duchess of Marchbourne, the Duchess of Hawkesworth, and their sister and mother among her choicest customers. All of which was why, even with the shop crowded with other ladies, Diana and Charlotte sat in splendor on the two best stools, at the center counter, with what seemed like half the shop's stock of hats, caps, plumes, and ribbons brought out for their consideration.

"I like it, Charlotte," Diana said at last. She enjoyed going to shops with Charlotte, having her older sister's company to herself the way it had been when they'd been girls. It was so much like the old times that in the carriage earlier she'd almost—almost—been tempted to tell Charlotte about what had happened with Sheffield three days ago in the park. "But I think you might wish to try it cocked a bit further to one side, to show your profile against the black."

"Like this?" Charlotte asked, sliding the hat to one side.

"If you'll forgive me, ma'am," Mrs. Hartley said. "The current fashion is to wear the brim low, and calculated to beguile."

Deftly she adjusted the hat to sit more forward on Charlotte's hair, tweaking the brim to an elegant curve that flattered Charlotte's profile. An assistant at once held up a framed looking glass for Charlotte to consider her reflection.

"That does look better, Charlotte," Diana said. Being tall and beautiful, Charlotte *looked* like a duchess, and because she had a duchess's fortune, too, and never inquired after prices, shopkeepers and tradespeople always produced their very best pieces for her. "Without a doubt."

But Charlotte hesitated. "I do not know, I do not know! I fear it looks heavier somehow, more suited to a gentleman than a lady."

"It's not supposed to resemble a gentleman's hat, but a jockey's cap," said Diana, being a religious reader of all the newest ladies' magazines. "That's the fashion for this season."

Charlotte wrinkled her nose with dismay. "A jockey! Oh, Diana, I don't believe March would approve of that."

"Not truly a jockey, ma'am, not at all," Mrs. Hartley said swiftly. "The aim is to give a sporting air to the hat, in perfect sympathy with the lady's habit. If I might suggest it, ma'am, a sure way to a more feminine insouciance is to add a curled plume or two here, over the crown."

She beckoned to another assistant, who took down a covered box from one of the shelves and brought it at once, holding it reverentially in her hands as if it contained the greatest treasures imaginable—which, to milliners and ladies, it did.

"These have arrived this very week from Africa," Mrs. Hartley said, carefully taking a plume from the box. "The finest of ostrich feathers, curled and dyed to my own specification."

Diana let out a small sigh of wonder. The plume was gorgeous, a cluster of large black ostrich feathers, nodding gracefully and bound together at the base of their quills like a rarified bouquet.

"Now if we add this to the crown, ma'am, like so," the milliner continued, holding the plume in place for Charlotte to see, "we have an altogether more noble effect."

Charlotte smiled happily at her reflection. "Exactly," she said. "Please add the plume, Mrs. Hartley. Is it possible to have it finished so that I might take the hat with me?"

"As you wish, ma'am," Mrs. Hartley said, adding a small bow. "It shall be done at once." Taking both the hat and the plume with her, she hurried off to the shop's workroom upstairs. Several assistants stepped forward, eager to help Charlotte with other selections, but Charlotte smiled and waved them away, preferring instead to pass the time with Diana.

"So, that is done," she said briskly, as if buying feathered silk hats were a base chore to be conquered. She leaned closer to the mirror, smoothing her hair back in place beneath her lace-edged cap. "Is there anything you require, Di?"

Diana shook her head. As soon as she'd been consid-

ered old enough to go into company in London, Mama
and Aunt Sophronia had bought her an entire new and
fashionable wardrobe, so extravagant that there were
still things she'd yet to wear. Even her hat today had
been worn only once before, the day she'd first met Lord
Crump. He hadn't liked it, and she gave the largest silk
bow a pat, as if to reassure it that *she* still loved it.

"Then nothing for you today," Charlotte said with
obvious regret. "But think of all we must purchase for
you before your wedding! Mama—and March, too—
will insist on sending you off to Lord Crump in the very
best style."

"But not yet," Diana said quickly. As hard as she was
trying to accustom herself to the idea of marrying Lord
Crump, she would still rather think of their wedding as
a distant event. "Not for months and months."

"Months and months?" repeated Charlotte with surprise. "I'd thought Lord Crump wished to be wed sooner
rather than later. There's little to be said for a long betrothal, you know."

"His lordship's still a stranger to me, Charlotte,"
Diana protested. "I'd rather come to know him first,
and for him to know me."

"I've told you before how little I knew of March on
our wedding day, yet it couldn't have turned out any
more happily." Charlotte smiled, lightly stroking the
narrow fur stole draped over her shoulders. "The only
true way to begin to know a gentleman is to spend time
alone with him, Di, and that will not happen until you
are wed."

But instead of thinking of Lord Crump, Diana's
thoughts at once returned to Sheffield. Guilty thoughts
they were, too, the same guilty thoughts that had been
plaguing her ever since she'd returned to the house after
their afternoon in the park. To her relief, both Charlotte
and Mama had been occupied and hadn't seen the state

of her hair or cap as she'd raced up the stairs to her own rooms. She'd no idea how she would have explained her appearance, not without spilling Lady Enid's secret as well as her own.

Because whether she wished it or not, she now did have secrets where Sheffield was concerned. As Charlotte had just said, the one sure way to know a man was to spend time alone in his company, and again and again she seemed thrust into exactly that with the duke. If she were honest, the real problem wasn't how often they were alone; it was what happened when they were. She should know by now, since it was always the same. Within minutes in his company, she ceased to be able to think of him as wretched, infuriating, or provoking. Instead her resolve melted away like morning dew before the rising sun, and before she realized it was happening, she was kissing him. Again. *Kissing* him, in the most harlot-like fashion imaginable, and worse, he was kissing her with a wicked, seductive, delicious purpose.

She knew the difference, too, even if she wasn't supposed to. Gentlemen kissed ladies as a sweet sort of salute on the lips. Men like Sheffield kissed only as a prelude to—to *ravishment*. Kissing him was like being devoured. Her head spun and her heart beat faster and her knees grew so weak she had no choice but to hold him more tightly.

Worst of all, kissing Sheffield made her long to be ravished, especially since he'd be the one doing the ravishing. That was the guiltiest thought of all, the thought that would not leave her alone each night, but made her feverish with longing for something she'd never had. When Sheffield kissed her, she didn't want to stop him, the way a lady should, because she suspected—no, she *knew*—that if kissing was any indication, he would be extraordinarily skilled at ravishing.

Perhaps Charlotte was right. Perhaps she should marry

Lord Crump as soon as was possible, so she'd stop this improper nonsense with Sheffield. Surely becoming the Marchioness of Crump would do that.

But why was she equally sure that there'd be not a hint of delirious ravishing to be found in Lord Crump's bed?

"There now, Di, you were thinking about being married, weren't you?" Charlotte said gleefully, giving Diana a fond little poke in the arm. "I could tell by the expression on your face *exactly* what you were thinking, you naughty young miss!"

She laughed, and Diana blushed furiously, grateful that Charlotte's thought reading wasn't quite as accurate as she believed. *Blast* Sheffield for doing this to her!

"Good day, Duchess," said Lady Farrish, one of Charlotte's friends. "How splendid to find you here, my dear!"

She curtseyed, then bent to kiss Charlotte's cheek before taking the stool beside her. Before long they were busily lost in discussing their husbands and their children, much to Diana's relief. She supposed she'd soon have those same topics to discuss, too, and she let her thoughts wander, idly sliding the rows of coral beads in her bracelet up and down her wrist. But once again, instead of Lord Crump, her traitorous brain offered up Sheffield's handsome face, laughing as he teased her about some foolishness or another with Fantôme snuffling around his feet.

"Your Grace, good day," Mrs. Hartley said, returning with the now plumed hat in her hands. But she wasn't addressing Charlotte as she curtseyed, her assistants curtseying with her. She was looking past her, and past Diana as well. She was smiling warmly, more warmly than was perhaps required, her expression clearly dazzled.

Diana turned, and there was Sheffield, standing behind her and towering over all the women. He wore a fawn-colored coat with a pale blue waistcoat and his customary white buckskin breeches, all of which had been exactly tailored to flaunt his broad shoulders and lean, muscular form. His neckcloth was tied with haphazard nonchalance, and his hat sat at a devil-may-care angle. Somehow he managed to look perfectly well dressed without seeming to care that he was. He was such a glorious specimen of English manhood in its prime that he inspired a soft, collective sigh of approval from all the women—a sigh that included Diana's own breathy contribution.

While most men would be overwhelmed by a place where they were so decisively outnumbered, Sheffield only smiled his most charming smile, as confident as any pasha with his harem. In return every woman smiled back. Even the sun, bright through the shop windows, seemed to smile upon him.

Belatedly Diana rose and curtseyed, too, joining all the other women (except for Charlotte) to spread her skirts and bow her head.

"Good day, ladies, good day," he said, his greeting warmly encompassing even the lowest young apprentice. He turned to Charlotte, taking her offered hand to kiss the air above.

"Duchess, good day," he said. "You are more lovely than all the goddesses of ancient times combined."

"And you, Sheffield, are more full of puffery," Charlotte said, laughing. She offered her cheek for him to kiss, and then presented her friend Lady Farrish. Finally it was Diana's turn.

"Good day, Lady Diana," he said, greeting her in exactly the same manner as he had Lady Farrish. He did not take her hand to kiss, nor was there any special smile or wink meant only for her.

"Good day, Your Grace," she murmured, looking down. She knew she should be thankful he hadn't singled her out, yet irrationally she felt a bit wounded that he hadn't. Perhaps all those kisses yesterday by the bench had meant nothing to him. Perhaps he truly was the hopeless rake that everyone said, and she'd been no more than another woman to dally with.

"How might we serve you today, sir?" Mrs. Hartley asked. "What might we offer you to please a lady?"

"Why, mistress, I'd wager every article in your shop would accomplish that," he said, sweeping his hands wide to encompass the entire stock. "But I do have a special article in mind, and I hope you will oblige me in my request."

"Anything, sir," Mrs. Hartley said, a fraction too eagerly. "Whatever you require."

He nodded. "You have heard that I am to be married. Lady Enid is a jewel beyond price, a model of virtue, honor, and accomplishment."

"May I offer my congratulations, sir?" Mrs. Hartley said, clearly hoping to secure the custom of one more duchess. "We shall be honored to supply her ladyship in every way possible. If you could but tell us what pleases her, then—"

"A hat," he announced. "That is what I wish for Lady Enid. A hat that is exactly the same as Lady Diana's."

Diana looked at him sharply, expecting mischief. Why had she regretted being ignored?

"You can't do that, Sheffield," Charlotte said, faintly scolding. "No lady wishes to have the same hat as another. Better you should bring Lady Enid here so that she may make her own decisions."

"But I like this hat of Lady Diana's," he said, walking slowly around her stool and gazing at her hat like a connoisseur with a fine work of art. "The color, the ribbons, all those—those flowery things on the top. This hat *amuses* me."

Diana watched him warily from beneath her hat's brim.

"Charlotte's right, Sheffield. Lady Enid won't want to copy me. It's insulting to her to think she would. We're very different ladies."

"Indeed you are," he said. "But I haven't forgotten that hat, not since I saw it first in the park."

Diana gulped. No one else knew they'd met that first time in the park. Charlotte was already raising her brows with interest.

"You're mistaken, Sheffield," Diana said quickly. "I've worn this hat but once before, and then only in the company of Lord Crump."

"Did you," he said with mild surprise. "Did Crump like it as much as I?"

"No, he didn't," she admitted. "I do not believe he liked it at all."

"Well, then, there you are," he said expansively, claiming the empty stool beside hers. "Everything is explained."

Nothing was explained as far as Diana was concerned. She was sure there was some deeper purpose to Sheffield's insistence regarding her hat. He didn't do or say anything without purpose, and she wondered when this particular purpose was going to appear.

"Might we fashion another hat for you for Lady Enid, sir?" Mrs. Hartley said, refusing to abandon the chase. "If not identical to Lady Diana's hat, then in the same spirit and whimsy?"

"I suppose that is the best path to take, Mrs. Hartley," Sheffield said with a certain resignation. "Not the same hat, but similar. Lady Diana shall advise me."

"I shall?" Diana said, startled. Now that Charlotte's hat was completed with its new plume, Diana had thought they'd leave and she'd be done with Sheffield. She certainly hadn't planned on lingering to advise him on anything.

"Yes," he said, smiling, and confident that she'd agree.

"You'll understand the proper names for all these fripperies."

Diana began to tell him no, that she'd no desire to help him choose a hat for Lady Enid, who wouldn't really care one way or the other, but Charlotte leaned forward before she could.

"What a splendid idea, Sheffield," she said, beaming at him past Diana. "I'm weary of you two being prickly with each other, and so is the rest of the family. If you can manage to be agreeable together here, then we'll all be grateful."

"Oh, we will, Charlotte," Sheffield said. "Lady Diana and I can promise you that. You have my word of honor."

He winked at Charlotte slyly, which made her laugh. Shaking her head, she turned away, back to her friend and Mrs. Hartley, while Diana was left with Sheffield. He'd rested his elbow on the counter and leaned his jaw against his hand, the better to focus entirely on her.

She wished he wouldn't do that. She really wished he wouldn't.

"Do you truly want to give Lady Enid a hat?" she asked, lowering her voice so no one else would overhear. "It seems a rather curious gift from a gentleman. Or are you here only to provoke me?"

He sighed. "I've given her a book written by an ancient Greek, which pleased her, and I've given her a ring, which was also well received. I do not see why a hat cannot be next."

He hadn't answered the question about provoking, but then he didn't need to. He *was* being provoking, without even trying—if sitting here close beside her, looking vastly more beautiful than any man had a right to, could possibly define provoking.

She tried concentrating on his ear—an ordinary male ear, really—in an attempt to calm herself.

"Lady Enid and I may have only the briefest acquaintance, Sheffield," she said, "but she strikes me as an eminently practical lady, and I am quite certain she'd never step from her house in a hat as frivolous as mine."

He smiled, drawing her attention helplessly away from his ear to his face. "You see, that is why I require your advice. As a lady, you are naturally more astute about other ladies than I shall ever be."

If even half of what she'd heard of him was correct, he knew far more about far more ladies than she ever could—not that she'd remind him of it here.

"Very well, then," she said instead. "I'll attempt to please Lady Enid's taste, though mind you, I'll offer no assurances."

She turned to Mrs. Hartley's assistant, who had been waiting patiently behind the counter through all of this. "I would like to see a hat with a moderate brim, of the finest Milano straw."

The assistant nodded and brought out several choices. Diana chose the most conservative of the three, then asked to see purple silk ribbons.

"To match the amethyst in her betrothal ring," she explained to Sheffield. "To show that you remembered it. Isn't purple also the color of fidelity? Lady Lattimore will take notice of that, even if Lady Enid doesn't."

"You are a genius, Lady Diana," he murmured, paying absolutely no attention to the ribbons. "What would I do without you?"

"You'd probably be charged a good deal more for your ignorance," Diana said wryly. She swiftly selected a dark purple silk moiré that was neither too wide nor too narrow, and requested that it be used for the ties as well as for the edging that bordered and bound the brim. Next she chose several small clusters of silk violets as trimmings, to be sprinkled with hand-sewn glass beads like dewdrops.

"I want this hat dressed with elegant taste," she explained to the assistant. "Nothing gaudy or coarse, to be sure. The lady for whom it is intended wishes to present a handsome appearance without being a slave to fashion."

"Yes, my lady, we can make it so," the assistant said. "Will you return for it tomorrow, my lady, or shall I have it sent?"

"We'll wait," Sheffield said. "I wish Lady Diana to approve the finished hat before it is sent."

"Forgive me, Your Grace, but that could take several hours," the assistant said anxiously. "A hat is not like a gown. Only one milliner may work on it at a time, and to maintain the quality—"

"Why don't you pin things in place and then show it to me?" Diana suggested. "I'll be able to judge well enough from that to assure His Grace."

The assistant made a quick curtsey before she left and took the hat to the workroom upstairs to be dressed.

"I cannot wait until it's finished," Diana said, coiling one of the ribbons left on the counter around her fingers to give herself something to do that wasn't staring at Sheffield. "When Charlotte leaves, I must go with her in her carriage."

"You could come with me in mine," he said. "I wouldn't object."

She frowned at him. "I could not," she said firmly. "That would not be proper, as you know perfectly, perfectly well."

He sighed, and shook his head. "True enough. You might be tempted to throw yourself upon me and kiss me again."

"Hush!" she whispered fiercely, glancing around to make sure no one else had heard him. "What has possessed you to speak so?"

"No one is paying any attention to us at all," he said.

"Look around you. They're all far too engrossed in the breathless pursuit of beribboned folly to listen to our tedious conversation."

He was right, blast him. Once the sensation of the arrival of the Duke of Sheffield had faded, the women had returned intently to their own business and conversations, and while the shop remained crowded, she and Sheffield might have been alone in an empty field for all that anyone else was eavesdropping. Absently she released the end of the ribbon wrapped around her finger and watched it spiral wildly free before it dropped to the counter.

A warning, a caution: She must stay tightly wrapped and not slip, not even for a moment, or she, too, would unravel and fall.

"No one will listen so long as you do nothing foolish to draw attention to yourself," she warned, shifting back on her stool as far from him as she dared. Because they were in a crowded shop, he was sitting much closer to her than he ever would in a drawing room, his knees touching her skirts. No one else thought anything of it, but she was almost painfully aware of his proximity, the peril of all that potent maleness simmering beside her. "You must not draw attention to me, either."

"Oh, I won't," he assured her. "I've given my word to your sister that I would be on my best behavior, and I couldn't possibly break my word to March's wife."

The way he was smiling did not put her at ease. She'd forgotten (or tried to forget) his eyes, their gray-blue color made the more striking by his dark lashes. Whenever he smiled, the warmth showed in his eyes, too, and made it almost impossible not to smile in return.

"If you vex Charlotte," she warned, "then they'll all know. March, and Mama, and Aunt Sophronia, and Brecon, too. She'd probably even let Hawke and my other sister Lizzie know, clear in Naples, so they could be unhappy, too. You know how such things happen in families."

"I don't, actually," he said. "I have no brothers or sisters, and both my parents are dead. Except for Brecon, I've been my own family for so long that I have no grounds for knowledge."

She could tell he was trying to keep his voice light, to match the rest of their bantering conversation, but he couldn't quite do it. His smile had faded and his eyes had become less teasing, and she sensed that, despite making a jest of it, he would much prefer to have a family than not.

"I'm sorry, Sheffield," she said softly, unable to imagine her own life without her sisters or mother, and she longed to place her hand on his arm, or make some other little gesture of comfort. "I'm sorry."

"For what?" he asked, instantly retreating from the confidence. "It's not your fault. It's simply how things are."

"It is," she said, "but you needn't be so—so fateful about it. My father died before I was born, yet I will always regret not having him in my life, to love and guide me as a father should."

He was watching her closely, carefully, as if waiting for her to say something that would wound. "You have your sisters and mother still."

"I do, and now you have us Wylders for family as well." Why should he be so defensive? She knew better than to pity men, but she hadn't thought there'd be harm or shame in saying she was sorry. She'd simply shown sympathy for his lack of family, that was all. "Whether you wish it or not, you're bound to us now, too, through Charlotte and Lizzie."

"So I have noticed." He relaxed, his charming smile once again firmly in place. "I dally in France for a few years, and when I return, there are Wylders sprouting everywhere, like mushrooms after a rainy night."

"Mushrooms?" she repeated, laughing in spite of herself. While it was not very flattering to be compared to a mushroom, his observation was so outlandish that she couldn't help but be amused, imagining her mother and her sisters with pale, spreading mushroom hats on their heads. "Is that how you think of us?"

"In a way," he said, clearly teasing now. "It's rather apt, considering how quickly your sisters have sprouted on our family tree, and adding children willy-nilly, too. Worst of all, once you marry, we'll have Crump there, too, bobbing away like a sour apple from one of the farthest branches. Faith, to think I'd ever be related to that man, however distantly!"

Now Diana was the one who grew guarded, wishing for all the world that Sheffield had not introduced Lord Crump into what had been a wonderfully silly conversation.

"You will be linked to his lordship only by marriage," she said, "and most distantly at that. And where is the shame in being connected to such a good and honorable gentleman?"

"Because he hated your hat," Sheffield said. "That's reason enough."

Her hands flew up to her hat, as if to protect every silk flower and bow from disparaging men, especially in a milliner's shop.

"His lordship did not exactly say he hated my hat," she said. "Rather he asked if I liked it, and I said I did, and then he said he liked it, too."

"Which is to say he hated it," Sheffield said with relish. "Despised it outright, and wished it straight to the devil, never to be seen on your head again."

Diana gasped, her eyes wide.

"Do not put words into his lordship's mouth!" she

exclaimed, doubting that Lord Crump ever wished so much as a flea straight to the devil. "I don't recall you praising my hat, either."

His gaze rose at once from her face to the hat. "But I do like it. I like it very much. Why else would I have wanted its twin made for Lady Enid?"

"Why indeed?" Perplexed, she lowered her voice and leaned closer to him, so close that likely the most exuberant bows on the hat in question were somewhere over his own head. "Pray recall who I am, Sheffield, and, more important, what I know. Why *would* you insist on giving Lady Enid such a hat—or any hat, for that matter—when in truth she won't give a fig about any of your gifts unless they come from—from another?"

He frowned and did not answer beyond heaving a monumental sigh. Then he shook his head and stared down at the counter, lightly drumming his fingers on the polished wood.

It all seemed overly dramatic to Diana. "So is it another secret, Sheffield? A secret so heinous you cannot share it?"

He raised only his glance to look at her, leaving his face turned down in a doleful manner.

"It's not a secret," he said. "It's more of a confession."

"A confession?" she said uneasily. She could scarcely imagine the kinds of confessions Sheffield might make. "Are you certain Mrs. Hartley's shop is the best place for confessing?"

"You asked earlier if I meant to provoke you," he said, "and I did. I called at Marchbourne House, and when the footman told me you and Charlotte were here, I followed."

"You asked for me?" she repeated, startled. The footman naturally would have told Mama, and Mama would have not been pleased to hear of it.

"I asked for Charlotte," he said. "I guessed you'd be

together, and you were. The hat is no more than an excuse, a reason for me to enter this shop. There seemed no other way to see you, considering how you've been avoiding me these last days."

"I haven't been avoiding you," she said. "That is, I have been going about my own life, without thought of you one way or the other."

That wasn't true, not when she'd spent the last nights awake and thinking of him. But that was what she *should* have done, however, so there could be no real harm in saying so. Besides, he was the one determined to confess, not her.

"I wanted to see you," he said, more moody than confessional. "After the park, I'd have thought you wanted to see me as well."

Now she frowned, too, wishing he didn't sound so much like a spoiled boy—albeit a handsome and virile one—who wasn't getting his way. Of course, dukes *were* spoiled boys who generally did get their way; she'd seen that often enough with March and Charlotte. But in this case, Sheffield wasn't going to.

"What I want, and what you want, doesn't matter," she said, as patiently as if she were addressing one of her nephews. "Your betrothal may be a sham, but mine is not. I belong to Lord Crump. You have no right to see me, and it will be much better for us both if you don't."

"It's your fault," he said mournfully. "If you hadn't kissed me that first time, none of this would have happened. Now you have bewitched me, and it's your obligation to help me recover."

"Sheffield, please. You are not serious, are you?" she asked, incredulous and overwhelmed, too. At first she'd thought this was more of his flirtatious teasing, but now she wasn't as sure. Yet she couldn't believe he was saying such things with such conviction, especially not in this shop with a score of other women around them. "Or are you simply mad?"

"If I am mad," he said sadly, "then that is your fault, too."

She had to pause for a moment to control herself, to be sure she did not raise her voice with frustration. The more he talked like this, the more confused and uncertain and unhappy she became herself.

And, heaven save her, a mournful, melancholy Sheffield was ten times as devastating as a jolly one.

"It can't be my fault, Sheffield," she said at last. "At least not how you paint it."

He nodded gravely, letting her believe he agreed.

"Another confession, then," he said. "And I will agree that it wasn't your kiss that bewitched me."

"I am thankful for that," she said, rubbing her fingers nervously over her beaded bracelet. "I'd not wish myself to be such a—a demon as that."

"No demon kiss," he agreed. He sat upright on the stool and reached into the inner pocket of his waistcoat, the one where gentlemen kept their valuables. "You recall that first afternoon, when Fantôme found you amongst the trees?"

"You're supposed to have forgotten that day, as should I," she said softly. She couldn't guess what he'd drawn from his pocket. Hidden by his fingers, it looked like a small scrap of linen, wrapped around something else.

"But you haven't, have you?" he said. "Nor have I. Look. Here's the proof. I've carried it with me ever since."

He put the little linen bundle in his palm and opened it. There in his hand lay the silk flower he'd plucked from her hat that first day, a perfect match to the ones that were still blooming on her crown now. She could not believe that he'd kept it. Most gentlemen who claimed tokens like that didn't, especially from women whose names they did not know.

But Sheffield had. And he'd done it because the flower had belonged to her.

Stunned, she looked from the flower to his face. His expression was an odd mixture of sheepishness and pride, with a measure of defiance, too.

"You're going to laugh," he predicted grimly. "You think me a great sentimental oaf, don't you?"

"Here is the hat, my lady, as you requested," the assistant said, returning with the newly trimmed hat for Lady Enid. "To be sure, it is not finished, my lady, not as we like our hats to be here at Hartley's, but her ladyship can consider the placement of the flowers."

At once Sheffield covered the flower in his hand and stuffed it into his pocket. He turned away from Diana to greet the assistant, visibly composing his face into a charming smile for her sake.

"Truly you have wrought a miracle," he declared, his smile warming as he saw her smile. "Lady Diana, do you approve?"

"Yes—yes," stammered Diana, not yet adept at making such a swift transition. She stared down at the hat, striving to make a coherent comment. "The color of the ribbon is as handsome against the straw as I'd hoped, and the flowers are most cunningly arranged. But perhaps another bow behind them, as a frame?"

"An excellent suggestion, my lady," the assistant said, nodding. "Does her ladyship wish to review the hat again?"

"I'm sure it will be acceptable," Sheffield said. "As soon as it is completed, have it sent to Lady Enid Lattimore."

"I am finished, Diana," Charlotte announced cheerfully, standing to go. She glanced down at the small gold watch at her waist. "My, look at the hour! Come, we must be off."

"Yes, Charlotte," Diana murmured, sliding from her stool. She wished Sheffield would look at her again, just her, the way he had before. Now she almost wondered if she'd imagined the little flower in his hand.

"Sheffield, good day," Charlotte was saying, giving him her hand to kiss. "I trust we shall be seeing you again soon. Pray bring Lady Enid to me, too. Diana has sung her praises so highly that I cannot wait to meet her."

"I should be honored," he said, bowing over her hand, "and so shall Lady Enid, I'm sure."

"And her ring!" Charlotte said. "I do so wish to see her betrothal ring. Diana told me it was quite magnificent. I pray that Lord Crump will soon give her one to equal it."

Diana winced. Doubtless Sheffield had noticed she'd yet no ring on her finger, but still she wished Charlotte hadn't called his attention to it so obviously.

"I'm sure his lordship will soon, Charlotte," she said. "You know how his affairs occupy his time."

"Indeed," Charlotte agreed, and with obvious approval, too. "It's the price a gentleman must pay if he wishes to accomplish grand things in this world."

"I'm certain Lady Diana understands," Sheffield said, taking her hand in farewell. "The wife of such a gentleman pays a similar price. Good day, Lady Diana, and thank you again for your opinions."

She smiled at him, but his smile in return was the same one he'd granted to Mrs. Hartley and her assistants, the smile of perfunctory charm that came to him without thinking. As delightful as it was, there was nothing in that smile that spoke of shared secrets or confidences, or of kisses stolen and given. There was certainly none of the vulnerability that he'd dared to let her glimpse when he'd shown her the silk flower from her hat.

Was Sheffield protecting her by treating her like all the others, without any special respect or regard? Or were his earlier confidences—"confessions," he'd called them—only the guile of a worldly gentleman too practiced in pleasing ladies?

She did not begin to know, and as she joined Charlotte in their carriage, her thoughts were in almost as great a confusion as her emotions.

"Sheffield looks well," Charlotte said as the carriage drew away from the shop. "There's a new purpose and direction to his manner that is most pleasing. Clearly he has finally found the one woman to make him forget all the others, exactly as Brecon and March had hoped for him. Though who can truly know the heart of a gentleman like Sheffield?"

She chuckled, but Diana did not join her. Who indeed truly knew the heart of the handsome, charming Duke of Sheffield?

Not I, she thought miserably, *not I*.

CHAPTER

10

A blithering, babbling idiot.

Nearly two weeks had passed since Sheffield had watched Diana leave the milliner's shop, yet he still could not recall that afternoon without coming to the same judgment regarding himself. She'd told him she did not want to be alone with him, she'd defended her betrothed, she'd told him to forget they had ever kissed. He'd responded by behaving like a mooncalf, telling her how he was bewitched and befuddled by her, how he could not put her from his mind, how he was desperate to see her alone again. He'd confessed it all, even used that very word, *confession*, as if he needed to grovel for her approval and absolution.

Then, as if that had not been enough, he'd showed her the silk flower that he'd plucked from her hat the first day he'd seen her, before he'd even known who she was, the flower he'd kept like a talisman ever since. No wonder she'd been left speechless by that. What could any lady say?

Nothing. Except that the Duke of Sheffield, famous for his charm and the ease with which he could seduce the most worldly of women, had been undone by a country-bred virgin who'd promised to wed the dullest man in all Britain.

Oh, yes, he was a blithering, babbling idiot, and no one was going to persuade him otherwise.

Which was why he was now in a place specially designed for other idiots like him, or at any rate, for gentlemen with more money than sense. It was a house so exclusive that it had no real name, but everyone for whom the door would open knew of it, and where exactly in Covent Garden it was. The main sport was gaming, with tables arranged in several rooms, but also available was an assortment of overpriced wines and unsavory food pretending to be French. Equally overpriced and unsavory women paraded among the gentlemen, paying the most attention to those who won or who flashed the largest wagers. Because Sheffield did neither, they generally ignored him. But then he drank little of the wine, ate less of the food, and took part in none of the games, either; his entire reason for being there was so that he would not have to go home just yet to a vast house that was empty except for servants.

He'd spent the earlier part of the evening dining with Lady Enid and her parents, a strained and dutiful meal if ever there was one. He'd created this false betrothal, and now he had to abide by it, at least for the time being. He had kept his distance from Diana and the rest of the family, and to his regret, she'd likewise made no effort to contact him. When she'd asked him to keep away, he somehow hadn't realized that she'd intended to do the same.

Surely Diana must have felt the same joy that he had when they'd been together, the same spark between them. Surely it hadn't been all pretending, and she hadn't been able to put that attraction entirely aside for the sake of duty and Crump. Surely she hadn't forgotten him, for he had not been able to forget her, nor did he wish to.

The longer he'd sat at the Lattimore dining table beside Enid, the more he'd thought of Diana, just as Enid likely was thinking of her Joshua. Perhaps the characters in a Shakespearean comedy enjoyed this sort of complicated dissembling, but Sheffield was rapidly discovering that he didn't, not to this degree.

Now he stood to one side of the gaming house's garishly painted wall with a glass in his hand and pretended to watch the roiling scene before him. A few old friends greeted him, but they quickly moved on when they saw he was in no humor for merriment. He was alone with his thoughts in a crowd, exactly as he wished it.

Until the one man he most wished not to see in such a place suddenly appeared before him.

"Sheffield," Brecon said. "I rather expected to find you here, though I'd hoped I wouldn't."

"Brecon," Sheffield replied, sipping from his glass. "If I have so grievously disappointed your hopes, then perhaps you would do better to leave and pretend you'd not seen me at all."

"Too late," Brecon said. "I have seen you, and spoken with you, and withstood the impact of your sourness. That is too much to ignore or pretend away."

Sheffield motioned for a servant to bring Brecon a glass of wine. "Then if you are determined to stay, you must drink with me and offer some reasonable company. Where is Mrs. Greene? I recall she'd a wicked taste for piquet."

Mrs. Greene was the most recent of Brecon's companionable mistresses, a plump, discreet woman with chestnut hair and intelligent eyes. Better to speak of her, Sheffield reasoned, than be forced to speak of himself.

"You're right," Brecon said, taking the offered glass. "That dear lady did enjoy her piquet, and what was better, she seldom lost at it—though I pray never in a house such as this. But it matters no longer, for she and I have parted ways."

"Then her doubtless worthy successor is with you instead?" Sheffield asked idly, looking about the room for any woman who might be remotely to Brecon's taste.

"No," Brecon said. "At present there is no successor. I am here alone, having dined at March's house. Charlotte does keep a most excellent table, and wine that's a good deal sweeter than this vinegar."

He puckered his mouth with comical disgust at the wine, but Sheffield was instantly on guard. This was Brecon, and Brecon wouldn't mention March and Charlotte without a reason. Had Diana said something to him?

"I fear the same cannot be said of Lady Lattimore and her cook," he said, determined to reinforce his supposed ties to Enid. "Though the company this evening was quite fine, the table was abysmal."

Brecon smiled pleasantly, abandoning the barely tasted wine on a nearby table. "You dined with the Lattimores?"

"I did," Sheffield said. "This night, and last night, and several others in these past two weeks besides."

Brecon's smile continued its pleasantness, which made Sheffield all the more wary. "You continue to be pleased by the match? The lady is agreeable to you?"

"Completely," Sheffield said, hoping he wasn't being too emphatic. In truth, spending time with Enid had only convinced him that they were not suited. Oh, she *was* agreeable, exactly as he'd told Brecon, and pleasing, but they had little in common. Her nature was too solemn for him, or perhaps his was too lighthearted for her. Worst of all was that he felt absolutely no hint of desire for her or her person, a serious challenge if they actually did wed. Fortunately that would never be an issue, for Enid and Pullings were planning to elope in September—that is, if Sheffield didn't expire from boredom first.

And then he thought of Diana again. He couldn't help it. His traitorous brain was determined to focus on her, no matter how sternly he ordered it not to. He liked how she looked at him sideways from beneath her lashes, appraising and challenging at the same time, and altogether as enticing as hell. He liked how she laughed, and how she found amusing the same things that he did. He liked how she wasn't afraid to jump into a pond, or kiss him until her hair fell down, or do most anything merely because she wished to. He liked how she was bold without being brazen. He'd even like her loyalty, loyalty being a great rarity in the women he'd known; he only wished she were being loyal to him instead of Crump.

And it went without categorizing that he liked her neatly rounded figure, too, or what he'd seen of it so far, her narrow waist and well-curved hips and breasts. Those breasts could make any man smile, imagining how they'd fill his hands, the exact perfect size and weight and warmth for his—

"So the lady does please you," Brecon said, marveling. "It's writ plain as day across your face. I've never seen you like this, Sheffield, and I am glad of it. Lady Enid will make you an excellent duchess."

Jarred back from his thoughts of Diana, Sheffield could only smile and pray that guilt was not writ plain across his face as well. He could not lie to Brecon; he'd never been able to do it before, and he couldn't now, nor, really, did he wish to.

"You'll agree, then, that I'm in need of an excellent duchess," he said, taking great care to adhere to the truth.

"You are indeed," Brecon agreed heartily. "Once you have a wife waiting for you at home, you won't bother with unseemly dens like this one. Have you set a date to wed?"

"Lady Lattimore wishes September."

"September!" exclaimed Brecon. "That's a powerfully long time to wait for your bride. Why would Lady Lattimore wish to keep you on tenterhooks for months more? At least Lady Hervey has a good reason for postponing her daughter's wedding, not wishing the girl to wed in mourning for her groom's brother. But I cannot see why Lady Lattimore would do the same."

"How does Lady Hervey's daughter?" Sheffield asked, unable to resist asking about Diana.

"Lady Diana?" Brecon said. "Oh, she has become the very picture of a docile, willing bride. It's exactly as her mother had hoped. Crump has already been an excellent influence on her, persuading her to follow the path to become a modest and honorable lady-wife. She scarce spoke a word at table unless bidden by him to speak. The change has been remarkable."

Sheffield did not believe it. He thought of the fiery Diana he knew, and could not fathom how Crump could persuade her to do anything she didn't wish to do.

"She is that much changed?" he asked. "How could a man like Crump achieve such a transformation?"

"She is indeed changed," Brecon said, obviously approving. "I understand that Crump has put aside his other affairs this past fortnight to devote himself to her, and that this was sufficient for her to want to please him in turn."

Sheffield didn't answer. He couldn't believe this, nor did he wish to. How could the Diana he remembered so vividly—laughing, teasing, bold, and witty, whether falling in the Marchbourne pond or kissing him on the park bench—ever willingly become this meek, obedient creature that Brecon was describing? No, he refused outright to believe it, not unless he saw the proof himself.

"Love works in miraculous ways, Sheffield," Brecon was saying. "You of all men must know that."

Brecon meant his supposed love for Enid, but it was

only Diana who filled Sheffield's thoughts now. How she'd asked him to keep away, how he'd miserably obeyed, what Brecon was saying now: none of that mattered. He had to see her again and judge for himself, and as soon as was possible, too. He would take Lady Enid to call at Marchbourne House tomorrow. He couldn't afford to wait. If he did, he could truly lose her to Crump, and that he refused to do.

"*Omnia vincit amor,*" he murmured, more to himself than to Brecon.

But Brecon heard, and looked at him curiously. "Latin from you, Sheffield? Truly love does conquer all, if Lady Enid can make you spout Virgil where a score of schoolmasters failed."

Sheffield smiled. "*Omnia vincit amor,* Brecon," he said, caring only for the truth in the words, not the language. "That says everything, doesn't it?"

The next day, Diana sat in the morning room, taking breakfast with March, Charlotte, and Mama. There was some sort of complicated conversation taking place involving a new fence and the drainage of the apple orchard at Greenwood, the Marchbourne country house, and the details of the conversation seemed to be of a great worry and concern to everyone except Diana. She was concentrating instead on carefully holding spoonfuls of cream for Fig, seated in her lap like a furry princess and eager to lick them up with great delicacy. Diana was happy to do this for Fig, considering not only that Fig loved cream but also that she was the sole individual at the table who was paying any attention to Diana whatsoever.

It wasn't the first time, either. Since she'd dedicated herself this last two weeks to making the best of her betrothal to Lord Crump, she'd discovered that the more dutiful she tried to be, the more invisible she'd become within her own family. It wasn't exactly that they took her for granted, nor did she doubt that they still loved her. But they did seem almost relieved that she'd soon be Lord Crump's entire responsibility, not theirs. Mama in particular spoke often about how happy marriage would make Diana, and how pleased Mama herself was to see Diana so agreeably settling into her new role.

Diana had smiled, but with every word like that her heart had sunk a bit lower. The sad, sorry truth was that by striving so hard to please everyone else, she'd also managed to make herself miserable, nor did she see any way free. Lord Crump's notion of a dutiful wife meant that she must be as obedient to him as if she were the lowest servant in the house. All her opinions and wishes must now mirror his, as if he were determined to subdue every last scrap of the Diana that she'd always been in order to create the perfectly proper Lady Crump.

There was never any unseemly laughter or loud talk in Lord Crump's company, let alone any teasing or flirtation. He still addressed her as Lady Diana, and he'd yet to give her leave to call him anything but "my lord." All remained precisely, formally correct between them, and if he'd come to feel any genuine affection toward her, he'd yet to show it. He'd not so much as held her gloved hand. The one time March had jested with Lord Crump about stealing a kiss (a kiss she would have freely given, too, for the sake of experimentation), he'd demurred, and said such demonstrations must be reserved for marriage.

She should have been grateful for such genteel regard, such respect, as Mama told her. She should have been honored.

Instead all she thought of was the one thing that was neither genteel nor respectful, and that was Sheffield. Sheffield, who teased and flirted and kissed and manhandled her at will; Sheffield, who beguiled and amused and infuriated her; Sheffield, who could make her pulse race and her body tremble and her lips sigh for more.

Sheffield, who would never, ever be hers.

She bowed her head a little further over Fig so that no one would see the tears she felt sting her eyes. She had done the right thing, and so had he. When he'd tried to explain his desire for her, she'd sent him away, and he'd obeyed. That was how it should be, must be, yet even as she admonished herself for the thousandth time, a single wet tear of misery slid from her eye and down her nose, and fell, glistening, onto Fig's back.

"Did you even hear me speak, Diana?" Mama asked, and quickly Diana wiped her fingers across her cheek and looked up. Mama was watching her with patient indulgence, as were March and Charlotte. "Perhaps it's time you stopped bringing Fig to the breakfast table, if you can pay no more attention to conversation than this."

"I was paying attention," Diana protested, holding Fig more closely in her arms. "You can't fault poor Fig. I was listening."

Mama raised a single skeptical brow. "If that were so, lamb, then you would likely be a good deal more excited than you are at present."

She motioned to the footman standing at her side, a footman bearing the polished salver that always delivered letters and messages at Marchbourne House. He came around the table and, to Diana's surprise, stopped before her. A single folded letter lay on the silver salver, addressed to her in a hand she did not recognize.

"I believe the seal belongs to the Lattimores," Mama said. "Aren't you curious?"

At once Diana seized the letter and cracked the seal, swiftly scanning the few lines written within.

"It's from Lady Enid," she said, her heart racing. "She

is inviting me to join her this afternoon to drive through the park."

"Alone?" Mama asked. "Won't Sheffield be joining you?"

"Ah—yes," Diana said, guiltily looking back down at the letter as if only now noting Sheffield's name, instead of it being the first she'd seen. "The duke will be joining us."

"Poor devil." March grunted in sympathy as he sipped his coffee. "Riding in the carriage with the pair of you gossiping away."

"Hush, March," Charlotte said mildly. "You know you'd like nothing better than to spend the afternoon in the company of two such lovely young ladies. It's a pity that poor Lord Crump is occupied today and cannot join Diana and Lady Enid."

"It is a pity," Diana echoed faintly, holding the letter up out of range of Fig's too-interested paw. "Without his lordship's company, there is no question of me accepting."

"Whyever not?" Mama asked with surprise. "I'm sure he wouldn't object to you joining them."

"I don't believe he would like me to," Diana said, desperate for an excuse. She'd done her best to banish Sheffield from her life and she'd succeeded. But she knew all too well that if she saw him again—especially in the park, alone, like last time—then every careful resolution she had made to be an honorable lady would be gone as quickly as ashes in the wind. "I don't believe he'd approve."

"Oh, of course he would," Mama said, absently twisting one of her still-golden curls back under her lace-edged cap as she waited for the footman to fill her teacup again. "I have heard him say myself that Lady Enid is an excellent person for you to have among your acquaintances."

It wasn't Lady Enid who worried Diana. "That is true, yes," she admitted. "But to be the third party with her and Sheffield—"

"Oh, I shouldn't let that concern you, Diana," Mama said. "Sheffield may only have eyes for his intended, but they'll both be mannerly enough toward you. Brecon tells me it's quite the miracle to see how Lady Enid has tamed Sheffield. You cannot begin to know how gratifying it is for us older folk to see you children grow wiser in your choices."

"Oh, Mama, please," Charlotte said, laughing. "Diana and I are hardly children any longer, while you are scarcely in your dotage! Faith, you make yourself sound as if you're as old as Aunt Sophronia."

Mama sighed, so deeply that Diana couldn't help but feel the weight of it, too.

"There have been recent times when my youngest daughter has taxed me so much that I felt every bit as old as your aunt," she said, then smiled fondly at Diana. "But I worry no longer, now that I know she'll be safe with Lord Crump."

That was more than Diana could bear, and she pushed her chair back from the table.

"Pray excuse me, but I have matters to tend before I go riding with Lady Enid," she said, settling Fig neatly against her shoulder. "Duty must come before amusement, as his lordship would say."

"And frequently does, too," March said dryly, earning a swat on the arm by way of reprimand from Charlotte.

"You are excused, Diana," Mama said with approval. "Fig, too."

Diana curtseyed quickly and hurried up the stairs to her room, carrying not only the little cat but a heavy conscience as well.

"Oh, Fig, Fig," she whispered unhappily into the cat's fur. "Whatever shall I do?"

She desperately wished Fig had an answer, because she hadn't one for herself. Even as she'd quoted Lord Crump, her thoughts had been completely occupied by imagining Sheffield, and were still. Lady Enid's invitation might indeed be no more than what it appeared, a pleasant ride through the park. Diana could only pray that it was; for the sake of her respectable future as Lady Crump, she must pay no special attention to Sheffield, nor permit him to do so to her. She must be as dignified and reserved as Lord Crump himself, no matter how tempted she might be to feel otherwise. That was her future, and she could not dare risk it for the sake of a single afternoon's merry flirtation.

At least that was what she told herself, over and over, for the rest of the morning: *Dignified and reserved, dignified and reserved . . .* She kept repeating it as if it were some magical incantation, as if the words themselves could make it so and protect her from the handsome, amusing temptation that was Sheffield.

She was still silently repeating it to herself as Sarah dressed her for the afternoon. Even though they'd be in a carriage and not on horseback, she chose to wear a staid (at least for her) riding habit of dark gray wool trimmed with black velvet. Ordinarily she wore the habit with a wide red silk sash fringed in silver, and red leather gloves with silver embroidered cuffs, but today she'd waved those away as too frivolous. The snug-fitting jacket was cut like a man's military coat, with a double row of tiny gray thread buttons that would surely defy even Sheffield, no matter how adept he was at removing a lady's clothing.

"Would you like your black riding hat, my lady?" Sarah asked as she tucked the last pin into Diana's hair. "Or since you'll be in a carriage, would you prefer something less severe?"

Diana studied her reflection in the looking glass. With

her hair drawn tightly back and the dull habit, she *did* look severe. Dressed like this, she could be some drab, mean-spirited governess instead of a future marchioness. She sighed forlornly. How could being respectable be so challenging?

"Perhaps I should try a more engaging hat, Sarah," she said. "Perhaps something with a few flowers?"

"Yes, my lady," Sarah said, retreating briefly into Diana's dressing closet before returning with another selection. "Will this do, my lady?"

Diana turned. The hat in Sarah's hands was the same one she'd worn the first time she'd met Sheffield beneath the trees, the one from which he'd plucked the single silk flower as his souvenir. At once she remembered how he'd shown the flower to her in the hat shop, how he'd smiled at her, how for that instant he'd made her believe he actually cared for her.

"Not that one, Sarah," she said hastily, hoping to banish those inappropriate memories along with the hat. "I believe I'll wear the black hat after all."

"As you wish, my lady," Sarah murmured, yet still managing to make it clear that the black hat would definitely not be her own choice. It wouldn't have been Diana's choice, either, under ordinary circumstances, and she couldn't help but grimace at her reflection as Sarah pinned the black hat with its single cockade in place. The black above the gray habit made her appear sallow and grim, but then sallow and grim would be far safer. Before she could have any second thoughts, she turned from the glass and pulled on her plain black gloves.

"There's His Grace's carriage now, my lady," Sarah said, glancing from the window. "Exactly on time."

Diana nodded, and deliberately took her time walking along the passage and down the stairs to the front hall. Lord Crump had admonished her for being too hurried and rushed, and she was striving to correct herself. But though she held her head high and paused for a second on each of the marble steps, her heart was racing almost painfully with anticipation, and it took all her will not to bolt down the stairs pell-mell as she used to do.

"Why, here you are, Diana," Charlotte said, standing in the hall with a footman beside her. "I was just sending for you. Sheffield and Lady Enid are here for you."

"I saw them from the window." Diana kissed her sister's cheek in farewell. "I'll be back in time to dress before we dine."

"I should hope so." Charlotte's curious glance took in Diana's gray habit. "I wouldn't wish you to play the gloomy gray lady at my table. Why so somber, Di? If ever there's a gentleman who'll appreciate a fancy hat, it's Sheffield."

"It's what *I* wished to wear," Diana said defensively. "I must go, Charlotte."

She turned and hurried through the door, accompanied down the house's front steps to the carriage by one of Charlotte's footmen on one side and one of Sheffield's on the other. Lady Enid's round face smiled at her from the window above the gold-tipped crest on the carriage door, and Charlotte was saying something else to her from inside the house.

Whatever it was, however, Diana didn't hear, because there, suddenly, was Sheffield himself.

CHAPTER

 11

Sheffield clambered eagerly from the carriage and came striding forward to take Diana's hand and welcome her. To her dismay, there were few sights more glorious, nor more hazardous to her resolve. He was dressed as he always was for day, in cream-colored buckskins that fit close around his thighs, boots, a dark tailored jacket, his neckcloth tied with careless elegance, and his dark hair held back with a plain black ribbon—the same clothes that scores of other gentlemen in London and the country wore each day as well. Yet not one of those other men would look as he did now, like a veritable god coming to rescue her. He was so blindingly, sinfully handsome that she nearly gasped aloud, as if a bright light had flashed into her eyes in a darkened room.

Only two weeks had passed since she'd seen him last. How could she have forgotten his effect upon her?

And why, why, did she never feel the same when she saw the man she was to marry?

"Good day, Lady Diana," he said, taking her hand.

She'd been imagining this moment since she'd opened the letter at breakfast, yet not like this. In the few seconds that it had taken him to leave the carriage and join her, everything had changed. That first anticipation she'd seen in his face, that eagerness, had vanished. Now his smile was exactly as it should be and no more, his expression pleasantly bland, and he didn't even squeeze her fingers as he handed her into the carriage.

Perhaps the dull gray habit had done its task, she thought as she smoothed her skirts, or perhaps two weeks apart had been sufficient to cure him of whatever interest he'd once had in her. She told herself it was all for the best, that this was how things should and must be between them, and tried to congratulate herself on such a tidy conclusion.

Tried, and did not quite succeed.

But they'd barely driven half a mile before Diana sensed that much more had changed than simply Sheffield becoming disinterested in her. The joyful love that she'd remembered glowing from Lady Enid was gone, and though she again had made room for Diana to sit beside her, this time she seemed drawn, with unmistakable shadows of sleeplessness beneath her eyes.

"Forgive me for speaking plainly, Lady Enid," Diana said gently, "but I cannot help but notice an, ah, uneasiness about you today. If you are unwell, then please tell me, so that we might turn about and—"

"Oh, no," Lady Enid said swiftly. "No. I'm perfectly well, and I would not miss this drive for all the world."

"Of course she is well," Sheffield said. "It's not as if I'd force her to be here against her will. This is meant to be a pleasurable diversion, not torture in the Tower."

Yet Lady Enid still wasn't smiling, which made Diana wonder all the more. "Will we be driving through the park again?"

"Indeed we will," Sheffield said as he leaned back against the squabs. "There is no better place than Hyde Park for us to be observed and remarked by the world, or at least the gossiping part of it."

Diana nodded, for that was certainly true. "Will Dr. Pullings be joining us there as he did last time?"

"No," Lady Enid said softly, looking down at her embroidered mitts, one folded back to display the meaningless amethyst betrothal ring. "Not in the park."

Diana had sisters and friends enough to understand how much more must be hiding beneath those few words, and at once she placed her hand gently over Lady Enid's to offer sympathy. "I am sorry."

"Why should you be sorry for anything?" Sheffield asked, mildly incredulous. "There is nothing wrong, and certainly no reason for sorrow. We'll drive once through the park, and then we'll return to Sheffield House, where Dr. Pullings will be waiting for us. You needn't be inventing grief where there isn't any."

"I wasn't," Diana said defensively. "Judging by Lady Enid's demeanor, I guessed that she was not happy, and I offered my solace. Where is the invented grief in that?"

"There isn't any," he said with too-studied patience, "save for the threat of it hovering about this carriage like some marsh-born miasma."

Diana pressed her lips tightly together, struggling to control her temper. She should not let him irritate her like this.

"Then there is no grief, no sorrow, no illness," she said, each word crisp. "Except, that is, the vexation that you have this moment created."

He sighed deeply, crossing his arms over his chest. "There is no vexation. Lady Enid expressed a desire to converse with Dr. Pullings in more privacy than an open park. I offered her the use of my home. She agreed."

"Oh, yes," Lady Enid said. "Sheffield has been most generous."

But Diana had already forgotten grief and sorrow. How had she become so distracted that she hadn't heard they were to meet Dr. Pullings not in the park but at Sheffield House?

"We will go to your house, Sheffield?" she asked warily.

"We will," he said. "It is, I believe, an agreeable place. Even you shall find it so."

"I'm sure it is," Diana said. Whatever her feelings might be toward him, he was a duke, and in her limited experience the London houses of dukes were more accurately palaces, rather than mere places, and she doubted Sheffield's was any different. "But agreeability is not the issue. For me to enter your house as an unaccompanied lady—"

"You won't be unaccompanied," Lady Enid said quickly. "You'll be with me."

"But not for long," Diana said, determined to be firm. "Once you leave me to converse with Dr. Pullings, then I shall be quite unaccompanied, save for Sheffield. It would be quite improper, and intolerable."

She began to rise from the seat, intending to signal the carriage driver to return her to Marchbourne House.

"Please, Lady Diana, do not desert me now," begged Lady Enid plaintively. She seized Diana's hand, curling their fingers together to draw her back. "I beg you, for the sake of my love and happiness!"

Diana hesitated, swaying with the carriage's motion and torn with indecision. "Forgive me, but I do not believe Lord Crump would approve if I were to—"

"Your Lord Crump will have absolutely no grounds for offense," Sheffield said, pointedly gazing from the window and not at her. "It's clear you have become completely devoted to that gentleman, with modesty and reserve now your guiding lights. I saw the change as soon as you stepped from March's house. You have my word that I will respect you, and your virtue as well."

Diana stood another moment, looking at him even if he would not look at her. Was she really so altered that he had seen it at a glance? Did she carry some sort of invisible brand that marked her as belonging exclusively to Lord Crump, something that all other gentlemen could see with such ease?

She really wished Sheffield would look back at her. As it was, she couldn't tell if he meant this as a compliment, or a jest. Sheffield being Sheffield, she could not tell.

Blast him, why wouldn't he *look* at her?

"Please come with us, Lady Diana," Lady Enid pleaded softly. "Please."

Diana sighed, and at last sank back down onto the seat, her gray woolen skirts spreading around her.

"Very well, Lady Enid," she said. "For your sake, I'll come."

"But not for mine," Sheffield said, his voice carrying a world-weary resignation. "I take note of the exclusion, Lady Diana."

He'd finally turned from the window, but his expression was so shuttered that he might as well have continued to look away. His blue-gray eyes were half closed, as if he could scarce be bothered to open them further: the perfect, handsome mask of a London gentleman determined to betray nothing.

And, without doubt, to infuriate her further.

But she could play that game as well. After so much time in Lord Crump's company, she could match anyone at being excruciatingly polite.

"I am so grateful that you understand, Sheffield," she said, smiling serenely. "I'm certain his lordship would be pleased by your assurances as well."

He made a low grunt of agreement, or surprise, or disgust, or perhaps all three combined, and then turned back to whatever was so endlessly fascinating in the street outside their carriage. Lady Enid said nothing more, and Diana didn't, either. What could she say in such an uncomfortable silence?

Clouds began to gather overhead as if to mirror their

mood, and the spring afternoon that had begun with bright sun was now gray and blustery with a promise of rain. As they drove through the park, crowded with other carriages and riders on horseback despite the worsening weather, Diana was sure they must have appeared the most grimly unhappy party imaginable. If the point of the drive was to be observed, then they most certainly were, and she could well imagine the kind of gossip that would be spread through fashionable London later that evening.

Did you see the Duke of Sheffield this day with his intended, Lady Enid Lattimore? They neither of them spoke, not a word, and with Lady Diana Wylder sitting there, too, dressed all in drab and as solemn as a tomb!

One turn about the park was more than enough to accomplish their purpose, and Diana was almost relieved by the time the driver turned and headed toward Sheffield's house. Diana knew his property lay to the north of the city, and from the window she watched as they passed Golden Square and crossed St. Giles to Great Russell Street, near Montagu House. At last they came to the tall, weathered brick walls that enclosed Sheffield's land, and passed through the ironwork gate to the drive and the yard.

Unlike the lavish newness of Marchbourne House, Sheffield House was clearly much older, having been built on a slight rise when the land it stood upon was still open countryside, not part of London. But in the century since then, the city had grown and expanded around the thick brick walls, leaving the house and its gardens like an island in a sea of much newer buildings. To be sure, the neighborhood remained a prosperous one, with elegant town houses inhabited by titled families and the wealthiest merchants, but there was no question that the home of the Dukes of Sheffield rose proudly above them all, like an omnipotent older king surrounded by younger courtiers.

She'd quick glimpses of the house as they circled the yard before the steps: brick, white stonework, rows of tall windows. The carriage stopped precisely before the front door; the footman opened the door for Sheffield, who descended and then handed Lady Enid out first. Next it was Diana's turn, and as she stood in the carriage's doorway, she'd her first real view of the house, over Sheffield's head.

She caught her breath with admiration, for truly this was the most perfect house she'd yet to see in London. It wasn't the largest, the grandest, or the one with the most elaborate carvings. But to her eyes it was certainly the most beautiful: rosy brick walls framed by pale white stone pilasters, the exact number of windows to be most pleasing, and the handsomest doorway beneath a scrolled pediment. The hipped slate roof sat neatly across the eaves like a well-made hat, and stone urns with stylized flames like oversized finials crowned the corners. Even the gusting wind and gray sky only made the house more appealing as a sanctuary surrounded by old oaks.

It was, in short, an altogether charming, elegant house, and she couldn't help but wistfully envy the unknown lady who'd someday be its mistress.

"You gasp and founder, Lady Diana," Sheffield said dryly, still standing with his hand raised to help her. "Must I summon a surgeon, or else stand here the day long?"

"Oh, hush, Sheffield." Belatedly she took his hand to step down, but held it only until the instant her foot touched the ground. "I cannot believe I'm the first guest to be awed by your house. It's surely one of the loveliest houses in London."

He smiled, the first genuine smile she'd had from him that afternoon. "I did say it was an agreeable place."

"It's far beyond agreeable," she said, "and you know it, too, else you wouldn't be so modest."

He looked back over his shoulder at the house, his expression as fond as a father's for a favorite child.

"I can take no credit for any of this," he said with a shrug, shaking away her praise. "I'm blessed to have come from a family with taste to equal their fortune."

Yet the house itself said otherwise. The window glass was spotless and gleaming, the white marble steps immaculate, the stones in the drive raked and weeded: all surprising niceties for a bachelor household, even a ducal household, and especially one where the bachelor was so often abroad. Men usually didn't notice things like that. Diana certainly hadn't expected such care from Sheffield, given his general devil-may-care character.

The earlier breeze had sharpened, twisting and fluttering her skirts around her legs and tugging at the brim of her hat. She grabbed the crown to keep the hat pins from tearing free from her hair, and with the other hand caught her skirts, turning into the breeze to keep stray strands of hair from blowing into her eyes.

"We should go inside before we're carried off by the wind," she said, beginning to hurry toward the door as the first drops of rain fell. "Besides, we've kept Lady Enid from Dr. Pullings long enough."

Indeed, Lady Enid hadn't waited while Diana and Sheffield had been admiring the house, but was already ahead of them at the bottom of the steps, the agitation on her face unmistakable. Meaning to calm her, Sheffield took her arm and guided her inside, while Diana followed.

"He will be here, Enid, I am sure of it," Sheffield said gently, turning to the footman who held the door. "Barker, has Dr. Pullings arrived?"

"Yes, Your Grace," the footman said, bowing. "He is waiting in the library."

"I must go to him at once," Lady Enid said, tugging on Sheffield's arm. "Take me to him, please, please!"

"It's not far," Sheffield said, waving aside the footman and leading the way to the library himself. The library door stood open, with Pullings waiting before the fire. With a cry of purest happiness, Lady Enid ran into the room and into his arms. Although Diana had feared the worst for their love, this reunion proved that whatever was distressing Lady Enid, it wasn't Joshua Pullings.

"There," Sheffield said, gently closing the library door shut. "Best to leave them alone together. I'm sure they'll amuse themselves well enough without us."

"Oh, yes," Diana said, acutely aware now of how she and Sheffield were likewise alone together, without even a hovering footman or maidservant. In the carriage he'd pledged to be the model of honor and regard, but she did not trust him, or herself, either. "Yes, yes."

"Yes," he repeated, and smiled at the unintentional echo. "Yes."

Diana nodded, smoothing her gloves over her hands. This was exactly, *exactly* why she'd wanted to excuse herself from this day. Sheffield was doing nothing but standing before her, as respectful as Lord Crump himself. But then Sheffield doing nothing was still a thousand times more seductive than Lord Crump trying his hardest to please—which, to be honest, she'd yet to experience. Sheffield simply stood there in the empty hall, his dark hair unruly from the wind, raindrops glistening across the broad shoulders of his dark coat, and the creases in his close-fitting breeches radiating from a place she'd no business looking. He stood before her, and smiled. That was all, and that was everything.

"I'd intended to show you my gardens," he said. "Early as the season is, I understand that there are actually a few flowers to be admired, but alas, the weather is not cooperating."

"It's not," she said, briefly glancing past him to where rain was drumming against the window at the end of the hall. If she'd any sense, or at least decency, she would demand to return to the carriage and sit there by herself, rain or not, until whenever Lady Enid was ready to go home as well. She should, but she didn't.

Suddenly she heard a scrabbling of claws along the tiled floor behind her, and an overwrought canine panting. She turned just in time to see Fantôme propel himself up into Sheffield's arms.

"Here you are at last, Fantôme, by all that's wicked and unholy," he said, catching the dog with a grunt. "I vow you're getting fatter every day, old gentleman. Have you been begging in the kitchen again, eh? Everywhere you go you're spoiled, aren't you? Fantôme, Fantôme, Monsieur Le Gros, yes, yes!"

The dog wriggled joyfully in his arms, trusting Sheffield to keep holding him. Sheffield did, happily letting himself be covered with hair and slobber as he cradled his dog in his arms like an adored, oversized, and unattractive baby, and unabashedly lavishing baby talk on him, too.

"Do you like pictures?" he asked over Fantôme's ecstatic snuffling. "I have a great many of those. I've as much French and Italian blood in my veins as English, which explains the collecting, you know. My ancestors must have been utterly helpless when confronted by paintings, because it seems they never passed by any that they didn't buy. I could show them to you, as many as you'd like."

She took a deep breath. Paintings were safe. March had paintings, too, and Hawke likely had more than the king himself. As long as she and Sheffield looked at pictures, she would be fine.

"Then please show me your pictures, Sheffield," she said. "I wish to see them all."

* * *

She wishes to see them all. Sheffield crouched down to set Fantôme on the floor, and to buy himself a few moments to think as well. He was determined to behave honorably, and he couldn't forget it. Yet when he'd anticipated this afternoon, he'd intended to spend this time alone with her strolling through the garden. The flowers (for he'd been assured by his gardener that there would indeed be flowers in bloom) would have provided a genteel backdrop for what he would say to her.

But then the rain had come to confound him, and remind him of the ultimate futility of making plans. He should have known better; in his experience, planning never was very successful where women were concerned, given their nearly universal unpredictability, a fine match for the English weather. He'd always done better improvising, anyway, and letting the lady herself guide his words and actions. No lady could object to a gentleman's behavior if she believed that behavior had been her own idea, and with Sheffield, they never objected.

But looking at pictures would be much more of a challenge to his honorable intentions remaining honorable than the flower gardens would have been. The house's picture gallery was upstairs. Also upstairs, on that same floor, were the family's bedchambers. Reaching the gallery would require passing several of those bedchambers, including his own, with its enormous ducal bed.

Fantôme whined, demonstrating his unwillingness to be put down by making his legs go limp beneath him. Sheffield swore beneath his breath, struggling as hard to make the dog keep his feet as the dog was determined not to.

"What is wrong with him?" Diana asked with concern. "Why can't he stand?"

"Because he doesn't wish to, that's why," Sheffield said,

still wrestling with the dog, and with his own thoughts, too.

It wasn't really the proximity of his bed that was the greatest challenge to behaving honorably. It was Diana herself. She'd rigged herself out as severely as a nun— he'd wager it was because of him, too, and not Crump— yet still he found her irresistible. The entire time they'd been in the carriage, he'd been trying not to think of how much he'd enjoy slowly unfastening every one of those little buttons on her bodice, like unwrapping some splendid gift. Even now, kneeling on the floor with his infernal dog, he couldn't help but glance at her feet before him, her red leather shoes with curving heels and silver buckles and her neat ankles in white stockings. He wondered what kind of garters she wore, and if she tied them over the knee or below, which led him to imagine her thighs, and how soft the skin must be—

"Are you sure he's well, Sheffield?" she asked, bending down beside him and gently stroking the dog's head. "Poor Fantôme! What ails you, puppy?"

"Determined sloth," Sheffield said with resignation. Giving up, he finally let the dog loll over onto his back, and stood upright himself. "I've told you before he is the laziest creature in Christendom. Come, leave him. If he wishes our company, he'll find his legs fast enough and join us."

She gave the dog one final pat, then stood, too.

"Shall we look at pictures, then?" she asked, clearly determined to keep to a definite agenda. That was wise of her, considering how Sheffield had been studying the way her skirts had tucked in beneath her as she'd sat beside his dog, how even that grim gray wool could look beguiling when it was pulled taut over the rounded swell of her bottom.

"We shall," he said. "The picture gallery is upstairs,

but we should have plenty of time. I was counting on granting the lovebirds at least an hour alone."

He offered her his arm, the way he would any lady.

She pretended she didn't notice it, instead walking slightly ahead of him, back the way they'd come.

It was not an auspicious beginning.

"An hour will likely seem as nothing to Lady Enid," she said, looking about the house rather than at him. "Earlier I'd feared there was something amiss between her and Dr. Pullings, she seemed so distressed, but obviously there was some other cause."

"Obviously," he said, determinedly walking beside her. "I'd venture it was due to Lord and Lady Lattimore insisting that she spend so much time in my company this past fortnight. Poor Enid learned what manner of gentleman I am, and that must have been what nearly did her in."

She laughed. "Most mothers would not wish their daughters in your company, while most ladies would be charmed by it."

He sighed dramatically, hoping to keep her smiling. "Most ladies are not Lady Enid. I fear she finds me an empty-headed dullard, a tedious fellow who has read nothing and knows even less."

"Then it's fortunate for you both that she'll marry Dr. Pullings and not you," she said, the smile disappearing. "Your house is very handsome, Sheffield, inside as well as out. You impress me."

She'd stopped in the front hall to gaze about her, taking the time now that they hadn't had when they'd first entered with Lady Enid. The space was open and soaring, designed to impress guests even as they were welcomed into the house. The floor was black and white marble, inlaid in the pattern of a spreading compass rose, and directly overhead was a splendid oculus through which the sun shone, or would have if the rain hadn't been drumming against the leaded glass. Even without the sunlight, the gilded carving on the balustrade of the great stair gleamed like burnished old gold, and the huge old hunting tapestry that hung on the landing gave everything a certain palatial air.

It was all warmly familiar to him, for it had been his home for as long as he could remember. But Diana would be accustomed to the more modern grandeur of March's house, and uneasily Sheffield wondered both what she honestly thought of his house and why he should care so desperately.

"Do you mean that I impress you by my own splendor," he said, striving to keep his voice light, "or that I impress you because my house impresses you?"

She smiled again, making him realize he'd do most anything necessary to keep that smile beaming in his direction.

"I suppose I'm impressed on both counts, Sheffield," she said. "I find your house most elegant and original, but I'm also impressed by how well it is kept, considering how seldom you're in residence."

"Of course I keep it up," he said. "Why should I not?"

"Because men generally don't pay heed to housekeeping matters," she said with a small shrug that hinted at many other reasons that she'd rather not share. "And you, Sheffield, are a man."

"I'm also my parents' only child," he said. "They were proud of this house, making endless improvements and refinements, and that's reason enough for me to keep it as they'd have wished."

She smiled and nodded: evidently that was the right answer, though he'd be damned if he knew why. At least it made for a genteelly safe conversation, and he plunged on.

"Do you see that oculus?" he asked, pointing up

toward the ceiling. "My mother was especially proud of that. My father called it the apple of her eye. Being too young to understand, I would stand about beneath it, waiting for apples to drop. Ah, I told you Fantôme would join us soon enough."

The dog ambled across the black and white floor toward them. He stopped beneath the oculus and snuffled at the floor, finally beginning to lap at the small puddle that had gathered in the center of the compass pattern.

"Oh, hell," muttered Sheffield, staring up at the leaking oval glass. Here Diana had just praised him for looking after his property, and then this had to happen. A footman hurried forward, accompanied by a scullery maid with a wooden bucket and a bundle of rags. The footman bowed—an apologetic bow if ever there was one—and the maid curtseyed before she dropped to her knees, pushed Fantôme aside, and began to wipe up the puddle. Looking upward, the footman strategically aligned the bucket beneath the drip, pushing it across the floor inch by inch with the toe of his shoe.

"The oculus has always leaked when it rains," Sheffield said by way of apologizing to Diana, just as the footman had silently apologized to him. "It always did in my parents' time, and I expect it always will."

"Have you any pictures of them?" Diana asked.

"Pictures of what?" he asked, still distracted. Why was it the windows had never leaked when he'd been with a mistress? "Of this mess?"

"No, of your parents," she said. "I should like to see your parents' portraits, if they are here."

"They're here," he said, relieved. "The best ones are in the Sultana Room."

"The Sultana Room," she repeated with relish. "I like the sound of that. Would you show me their portraits, Sheffield? I should like very much to see them. Please?"

"Very well," he said. "This way."

He began up the stairs, and this time she slipped her hand into the crook of his arm, letting him lead her. She'd also inadvertently solved his dilemma for him. The Sultana Room was at the opposite end of the house from the gallery and from the bedchambers. Neither were the matching portraits of his parents in the same suggestive category as the nymphs and satyrs.

"Here we are," he said, and as soon as she'd entered, he closed and latched the door after them.

She turned around at once, her blue eyes wide and troubled. "Why did you do that?"

"What, close the door?" he asked. "Because if I didn't, some servant or another would come bumbling in to disturb us. You live with servants. You should understand."

She swallowed, glancing back at the closed door. "But to be alone with you like this is—is not right."

"Is it right that I don't wish Fantôme to follow us in here?" he asked. "He will mistake the cover sheets for bushes, and misbehave. Besides, you would be alone with me anywhere in the house. No one will know unless you tell them. And didn't I give you my word earlier that I would respect both you and your Lord Crump?"

She frowned, thinking. "Yes," she admitted reluctantly. "Yes. All that is true. I suppose a single door doesn't matter."

"It doesn't," he said, looking around the room as his eyes adjusted to the murkiness. As in every great house, the furnishing in unused rooms were draped with linen cloths against dust and the heavy curtains closed tight against sunlight and fading, curtains that he now pulled open himself. Even on this gray afternoon, the view was magnificent, over the house's gardens, orchards, and outbuildings, and further across the fields north of the city. The worst of the rain had passed, leaving rolling low clouds of mists and the palest of sunshine over the spring-green plantings and trees.

"How vastly beautiful, Sheffield," Diana said, forgetting her wariness to join him at the window.

"This was my mother's favorite room," he said, "and because it was hers, it was my father's, too. We often took breakfast together here, the three of us. It does have the best vantage in the house."

She leaned her fingertips lightly on the window's frame as she gazed out, her face delicately lit by the pale daylight. "I don't wonder that your mother loved it."

"I wonder if she'd like the view as much now," he said. He hadn't been in this room for years, and he realized now how much he'd missed it. "Look there in the distance, beyond the last of our walls. You can just make out the New Road, the turnpike built not long ago for the farmers coming to the London markets. A convenience, they say, but it means the town itself soon will follow, and with it will come an end to our green country view."

"A convenience, and progress," Diana said softly, her voice echoing his own melancholy. "It cannot be helped, to be sure, but still I often wish things would stay as they were and never change."

She stood hugging her arms closely around her body, and he fought the almost irresistible urge to slip his own arms around her and pull her close. He'd never wanted to hold a woman more, nor desired one more, either, and restraining himself like this around her was a torment that, as a duke who'd always gotten what he desired, he'd never before experienced.

And as if she sensed it—or even felt the same—she abruptly turned away from the window and him to walk across the room to the pictures on the farthest wall.

"So these must be the portraits of your parents," she said, her voice as full of deference as if she were meeting them. "By these I'd venture you're the sum of them both."

"That's inevitable, isn't it?" he said, chuckling. "Parents beget children in their likeness."

He pulled the dust cover from the wide settee across from the portraits and sat, leaning back to look up at the portraits. Like his parents, the pictures had always been side by side and never separated. These weren't the grand ermine-draped duke and duchess portraits that hung in the ballroom downstairs, but smaller and informal, the way he remembered his parents. His mother was dressed as if for a masquerade, in the red and gold spangled sultana's costume that had given the room its name, and with a magnificent green emerald on her finger. She was turned to look over her shoulder, laughing as if she'd just heard a merry tale or jest, or was simply reveling in the wonderful, wanton silliness of her costume. His father wore his country clothes, the same kind of wool jacket and buckskin breeches that Sheffield himself favored, with his two most devoted hunting dogs beside him.

But the likenesses went beyond mere clothing. It was eerie, and unless Diana had mentioned it, he doubted he would have seen it for himself. His mother's smile and eyes, his father's dark hair and jaw, all jumbled together to make his own face.

"They loved each other very much, didn't they?" Diana continued. "You can tell by their faces. They're happy, and they're in love, and it shows."

He'd never thought of the pictures quite in that way, but she was right. He remembered his parents' endless affection for each other, almost as if they'd been lovers instead of husband and wife.

"It was a love match," he said thoughtfully, looking at the painted faces and remembering the real ones. The longer he looked, the more he remembered, and the clearer his own thoughts were becoming in other ways, too. "They eloped, which must have been quite the scandal. But yes, they were happy. Always."

She came to sit on the settee with him, albeit with a sizable distance between them. She leaned back, as he had done, and bumped her hat against the carved back. She unpinned the hat and pulled it off, and then, unencumbered, she leaned back once again with a sigh.

"My parents were the same," she said. "Not that I can recall, for my father died before I was born. But Charlotte remembers, and says it was so. Mama has never remarried, because she says there will never be another man she'll love as much as she loved Father."

He nodded. Her reminiscences were a perfect match for his, as was so much else about her.

"The same," he said. "The same."

"And that's why you wish to marry for love yourself," she said softly. "I did, too."

He turned, his arm outstretched along the settee's carved back toward her.

"You did?" he asked. "You no longer do?"

Blindly she looked down to avoid his gaze, while her hands curled together into tight little fists in her lap.

"I believe that love will come with marriage," she said carefully, without emotion, as if reciting by rote. "I believe that I will in time come to love Lord Crump, and that he will love me in return."

"Look at me, Diana," he said, his voice low and rough with urgency. His earlier resolutions were forgotten now, as was his promise to respect her as Crump's future wife. All that mattered was what she said now. "Look at me, and tell me you believe that."

Still she did not look up, her head bowed and her shoulders bent as she warred with herself.

"Lord Crump is a good man, an honorable gentleman, who respects and admires me," she said, her voice trembling. "He will in time love me. They all say so. He *will* love me."

"But do you love him, Diana?" he demanded. He'd no right but every reason to ask, and he was not going to give up until she answered him. "Do you love him as a wife, as a lover? Damnation, do you love him as a woman should love a man?"

At last she looked up to him, her eyes bright with tears, and shook her head.

"No," she whispered fiercely. "I do not love him, and heaven help me, I never will."

It was exactly what he'd been waiting to hear, and now, at last, he'd wait no longer.

CHAPTER

12

Diana had meant to carry the truth about not loving Lord Crump as a secret forever, buried deep beneath her conscience and somewhere below where her heart had once been. She'd vowed to herself and to her family that she'd try as hard as she could to be the wife and marchioness that Lord Crump deserved, the path that all assured her would be the way to her happiness. She had tried to be as dignified, reserved, and refined as a noble lady must, the wife, daughter, sister, and someday mother of peers and peeresses.

She had tried, and tried harder, and this was what had come of it. For while there was no doubt that Lord Crump was a good man, she was not very good in return. The abundant proof of her not-very-goodness was on display here, now, on a blue silk damask settee in the late Duchess of Sheffield's Sultana Room, where she was inelegantly and shamelessly entangled with the present Duke of Sheffield, who was kissing her as if his very life depended on it.

Perhaps it did. She knew her own life was hanging in a precarious balance, desperate for the love of a man whom she loved in return. No, not simply *a* man, but Sheffield, the man whom no one else wished her to have, and the only one she'd ever truly wanted.

All of which was why she was kissing him every bit as fervently in return. He held her with his arm around her, cradling her in the crook of his arm at the exact angle that made her reach out for him, her hands splayed against his chest, the soft wool of his waistcoat covering the hard muscles of his chest. She was always both startled and pleased by how strong his body felt, how different it was from her own—and how much she liked that very difference.

She made a happy, wordless purr of contentment, which he resourcefully employed to part her lips and slip his tongue inside her mouth. Ah, another of the things that fascinated her about him: how he tasted, warm and male and charged with desire. She slid her palms along his chest to rest on his shoulders, letting him draw her closer as he deepened the kiss. She opened her mouth eagerly, taking him deeper. It was almost as if he wished to devour her, and really, if she were honest, that was how she felt about him, too. Kissing him made her heart race and her breath quicken and her body twist against his in a way that only made her long for more of it, and him.

"Do you know how you've captured me, Diana?" he whispered hoarsely, breaking away from her mouth to kiss the side of her throat, a place she'd no idea could be so divinely sensitive. "From the first time I saw you, sweet, the first time. I could never put you from my mind."

"So it was with me as well," she whispered in return, nearly breathless from joy. "Oh, Sheffield, I cannot begin to tell what I feel for you!"

She cupped her hands around his face and brought his mouth back to kiss him again. She had slipped back farther on the settee, against a cushion as well as his arm, and Sheffield wasn't so much as sitting beside her any longer, but across her. She was twisted about, her hip and her hoops awkwardly pressing into him, and she shifted to try to become more comfortable. At once he moved forward to settle directly on top of her, drawing his arm from beneath her shoulders. Now he could brace his weight without crushing her, but it also meant that she was lying on her back as if lying in her bed—a bed that now included Sheffield lying with her.

A tiny fragment of her conscience howled at this, warning her of exactly how vulnerable her position could be, yet the rest of her ignored it. How could she not, when at this precise moment she was also made aware of how the row of tiny thread buttons on her bodice were not the impenetrable armor that she'd thought? He'd not only deftly unfastened them all, but had slipped his hand inside and was now doing the most bold yet wondrous things to her breast, teasing and tugging and caressing her nipple and the flesh around it until she arched up against his hand as if to beg for more.

"Do you know I love you, Diana?" he said fiercely. "Do you know that of me?"

Her eyes widened, filling with tears as she gazed up at his handsome face, so close over hers. She remembered all the times he'd spoken of how he'd only marry for love, as his parents had done, and of how much he valued a love like that. Is that what he meant now when he said he loved her? Is that what he was offering to her now, the kind of love that would last a lifetime, and not simply for a single achingly perfect afternoon?

"I love you, Diana," he said, more firmly, as if he'd heard her unspoken doubts. "I love you."

She gulped, overwhelmed by emotion. *He loved her*: three words that were more than enough to bring back the impulsive part of herself, the part that she'd tried so resolutely to subdue, but had never quite gone away. She would never again be tempted to abandon everything for the sake of love, of passion, not wed to Lord

Crump. She'd only have this one chance with Sheffield—if she dared. She knew what she'd be granting in the name of love, too—she might be an innocent, but thanks to her sisters' conversations regarding their husbands, she wasn't ignorant—and she knew the risks of consequences and scandal.

But Sheffield loved her. He loved her, and for that moment, with him, nothing else in all the world mattered more.

"Oh, Sheffield," she confessed, the words spilling out straight from her heart. "I love you, too. I've always loved you."

"Then let me love you as you deserve," he said, his voice so low and full of promise that she shivered with anticipation. "Be mine, Diana, here, now. Be only mine."

"Yes, oh, yes," she murmured, the only words she could speak before he was slanting his mouth hard over hers once again. He'd shoved aside her bodice entirely and pulled down her shift and stays, leaving her breasts entirely exposed. Easing lower down her body, he kissed each in turn, then licked and nibbled at her nipples until she gasped with the pleasure of it. She tangled her fingers into the dark silk of his hair, freeing it from his once-tidy queue as he suckled at her before claiming her mouth again.

Somehow—she wasn't sure when—he'd shed his coat, and now when she grasped his shoulders, there was only the fine Holland linen of his shirt beneath her fingers. She moved her hands along his back, relishing the feel of his muscles as he moved over her, all coiled masculine strength and power. She wished he'd shed his waistcoat, too, and as they kissed she reached between them, fumbling a bit as she blindly undid the buttons and shoved the waistcoat across his shoulders.

He grunted with approval, and shrugged the waistcoat free and to the floor. Now when he pressed down on her, her bared breasts grazed against the linen, the last thin barrier between them. Daringly she pulled his shirt free from his breeches and slipped her greedy hands inside the billowing linen. His skin was hot beneath her touch as she explored him, the long hollow of his spine, the bunching of his muscles. Even his scent intoxicated her, all heated male overlaid with the faint fragrance of bay leaves and lime from his shaving soap.

She felt her hairpins snag on the cushion as her hair came undone, and she did not care. She felt her skirts slide high over her knees and higher, and then his hand trailing along the inside of her bare thigh. Instinctively she tried to squeeze her legs closed, but he was between them, holding them apart.

"Let me please you," he said, his words warm against the shell of her ear. "Let me love you."

Love, love: that was the magic word for her, the word that only he could offer, and with a shuddering sigh she relaxed and gave herself over to the love he promised, and her body desired.

And she did desire it. His touch on her thigh was gentle but insistent, coaxing little circles that swiftly inched higher and higher. She gasped with surprise when his hand covered her most private place, and gasped again as he gently parted her to caress her more intimately. She clung to his shoulders as he kissed her again. No one had ever touched her here, pressed her here—oh, heavens, stroked her *there*.

"My own love." His voice was rough with a fresh urgency, his gaze intent upon her. "Love me, sweet, and let me love you."

He eased a finger into her, then a second, finding deliciously sensitive places within her that she'd never known were there. Charlotte had told her that March's lovemaking could make her lose her wits, and now, at last, Diana understood what her sister had meant. The more Sheffield touched her, the more the sensations seemed to coil through her whole body, making her writhe shamelessly against him. She didn't care that her skirts were around her waist, or that she'd looped one leg over the back of the settee, or that her garter had come untied and her stocking drooped around her ankle.

Nothing mattered but him. Her whole being now centered on his caresses like a maddening sweet torture, and she felt herself grow shamelessly wet, as if to ease the way for his fingers. She was pushing against him now, her breath coming in sharp little cries as she struggled for the great prize he was offering, just out of her grasp.

"Sheffield, oh, please," she cried, begging. "Please!"

She clung to him, reaching, reaching, then suddenly the sensations crashed within her, wave after glorious wave of pleasure. It was beyond imagining, beyond everything, and all because of him. Her eyes closed, she sank back against the settee's cushions, boneless and dazzled and gasping for breath, and let the last delicious shudders fade through her.

"Oh, Sheffield, how you love me," she murmured, too blissfully sated to manage more. "How you love me!"

She was only vaguely aware of the settee creaking beneath her as Sheffield repositioned himself, of him saying more endearments, more reassurances, more promises of love, all of it jumbled in her pleasure-sodden brain. She knew there would be more to lovemaking, and that he was right to say they'd only begun. But oh, if it were all as wondrous as this, then she'd eagerly follow wherever he led. He was touching her again, and with languid anticipation she raised her hips a fraction to meet him. He was pushing into her swollen, sensitized again, but this time it wasn't his fingers. This was larger, much larger, and much hotter and more demanding, and her eyes flew open just in time to see it all: Sheffield with his breeches undone and his shirt shoved aside, kneeling between her outstretched legs to thrust his very sizable member into the core of her innocence.

Or what had been her innocence. She gasped and tried to scuttle backward, but struck against the arm of the settee. By then it was too late, anyway. He was already in her, thrusting once, twice, and then he was buried deep within her. That lovely, spangled pleasure had disappeared, and in its place she felt stretched and filled and pinned to the settee with all the graceless futility of a flopping, broken butterfly.

"Damnation, I'm sorry if I hurt you, Diana," he whispered, his breath ragged as he lightly brushed kisses across her cheek. "I'll make it better now, I swear."

"How, Sheffield?" she asked, her voice squeaking with her rising panic and the surprising sting of discomfort scattering the haze of her first pleasure. "How can it ever be better?"

"Because I love you," he said hoarsely, "and you love me."

There was more he planned to tell her, much more, not that Sheffield saw the point of further conversation now. In their present situation—and with the need pounding through his body—demonstration would accomplish far more than any mere words. He was accomplished at pleasing women, and he would make sure that he pleased her, the one woman he loved beyond all others. He regretted the fear he saw in her eyes, the tears that were even now sliding sideways down her cheeks and into her hair. Only a few moments before, she'd been so blissfully beautiful, lost in the pleasure of her spending. Now he'd have to do his best to take her back to that, and join her, too. Yes, he'd make it better, infinitely better.

He kissed her again, moving slowly within her to let her accustom herself to the feel of him. Damnation, she was tight and sleek, and it took every fiber of his will-power to hold back. He had to make this good for her. He had to be gentle, no matter how much he longed to ram himself into her.

He moved slowly, wanting her to discover the plea-sure as his cock stroked her from within. Her scent was the headiest perfume he could imagine, the purest scent of sex and desire. He plunged deeply, then withdrew, letting her learn that sweet agony for herself. He knew the exact moment she did from the catch in her breath and the wondering look in her eyes. He kissed her again, nibbling at her lower lip as he drove her a fraction harder, and this time she curled her hands around him. Another stroke, and she rewarded him with a gasp of startled but unmistakable pleasure.

That was what he wanted, what he sought. He wanted this to be for her. He shifted his angle, seeking to inten-sify the sensation. She gasped, her fingers clutching rest-lessly at his waist, and he knew he'd succeeded. He dragged his tongue along her throat, there on her pulse, and felt her shiver and twist beneath him. She'd begun to move with him now, unable to resist the rhythm, and her first gasps had changed to a sound that was halfway between a moan and a sigh, the most wanton little sound any man could ever hope to hear. She wanted more. No, she wanted *him*, and as he gazed down at her, her cheeks flushed and her breasts bare and quivering with each of his thrusts, her nipples red and taut from his kisses and her long, lithe legs curled around his waist—ah, what more could he ever want in return?

His ballocks told him quickly enough. She was so tight, so slick, so hot, that no matter how he might wish to make this last forever, he couldn't. Bracing himself against the back of the settee, he slipped his hand be-tween their bodies and caressed her there, where they were joined, and where she was most swollen and sensitive. At once she cried out, arching against him, signaling that her crisis was nearing as well.

He needed no more than that. He forgot gentleness, forgot everything but carrying her with him to the end. He drove relentlessly, his own groans mixed with hers, as he pushed her harder, and harder still. Her body tightened beneath his, around his cock, and then with a wordless cry she tumbled over the top, pleasure spinning out from her. That was the last spark he needed, that inner caress of hers. With a roar, he surged forward one final time, burying himself as deeply as he could to come within her. She truly was his now; there could never be any further question of that.

Panting with exertion, he bowed his head over hers and wearily kissed her, a gentling sort of kiss that barely grazed her lips. His hair hung damply around his face, and his shirt clung to his sweat-soaked shoulders. Diana was breathing hard with him, her breasts rising and falling against his chest and her lips sweetly parted. But her eyes were still closed, her lashes feathered across her cheeks, making it impossible to tell her mood.

It should be fine, he reasoned with himself. More than fine. Even in his usual post-sex haze, he could understand that. She'd just given her maidenhead to a man who loved her, and by his reckoning she'd spent twice, and quite pleasurably at that. Many women could never make either of those claims, not once in their entire lives.

None of this, however, was what he'd planned. He'd intended merely to show her paintings, as she'd asked, and then, as they discussed the pictures, he'd find a way to tell her he loved her. In a measured and respectful manner, he would have explained why he believed he'd be a far better husband for her than Crump could ever be, and then he'd ask her to become both his wife and his duchess. He'd even planned to kneel before her to do it, the way the swains in poetry did it, here in the Sultana Room before the painted versions of his parents.

But things hadn't exactly gone that way. She had that effect on him. He really shouldn't be surprised, since nothing ever did seem to proceed as planned where Diana was concerned. It was only one of her many charms, and he could quite safely predict that she would never, ever bore him.

He smiled down at her now, imagining their life together, and thinking how much more agreeable it would be to make love to her on the generous acreage of his ducal bed, instead of on this infernally narrow settee.

"My own Diana," he said softly, and kissed her again, not on her lips, but on her forehead. "I love you, sweet."

He'd never meant the words more than he did now, and he never intended to say them to any other woman. Given the circumstances, he expected she'd say the same in return to him.

She didn't, leading him to try again. "I love you, Diana."

But instead of replying, she pressed her hand over her mouth and squeezed her eyes more tightly shut.

He frowned, fearing she felt ill. Damnation, he'd never done *that* to a woman. His sated cock slipped free of her body, and with a sigh he sat back from her, wiping himself with the tails of his shirt. With a shuddering sigh, she swiftly sat upright, too, shoving her petticoats down over her bare legs and nether regions, then pulling her bodice back over her breasts. He was sorry for that; he'd been enjoying looking at her, yes, but he'd also enjoyed the intimacy that had come with it.

"Diana, my love," he began again. "If I have hurt you, by all that's holy, I—"

"No, Sheffield," she said, looking everyplace except at him. "No."

She was buttoning her bodice with furiously swift fingers, putting herself back together with a haste that women rarely possessed. He buttoned the fall on his breeches and retrieved his waistcoat and coat from the floor. He pulled his handkerchief from his coat's pocket and handed it to her.

"If you would like to, ah, tidy yourself," he said. "There's no washstand in here, I know, but let me send for—"

"No servants," she said quickly. "We haven't time. The others will be waiting for us."

She found her hat from where it had fallen on the floor, and pinned it back onto her head, pushing stray locks of hair back under the brim. She stood, briskly shaking out her skirts and smoothing them down before she headed toward the door. It wasn't that she was angry with him. She'd been angry before, but this—this was different.

"Diana, look at me," he said. *"Look at me."*

She stopped but did not turn.

He took her arm, pulling her back, and at last she looked up at him, her face enough to break his heart.

"Listen to me, Diana, I beg you," he said gruffly. "You can't pretend this hasn't happened. I love you, and you love me, and that's enough—"

"Please don't, Sheffield," she said, and though her eyes were dry, he heard the tears in her voice. "I can't listen to you, not now, not after I—after we—oh, a pox on it all!"

"Everything will be fine and right, Diana," he said firmly, bending over to kiss her, and prove to her it was. "You'll see. I'll make it so."

But instead she twisted free, stepping backwards away from him, her arms crossed over her chest as if to comfort herself.

"You can't, Sheffield," she said, shaking her head. "No matter what you wish, you can't change what has happened. I do not blame you, for I was most willing, but—"

"And where is the sin in that?" he demanded, following her. "Diana, listen to me, and—"

"It's all my fault," she said, her voice breaking. "Everything, and—and—oh, if only I did not love you so!"

She threw open the door and hurried into the hall, her steps so fast she was nearly running.

Running from *him*. No one did that.

"Diana," he said, matching her strides. "If you love me, then there is no problem, because I love you, too. Diana, please. You must hear me."

"No," she said, staring straight ahead and quickening her pace even more as she ran down the stairs. "I must sort this out for myself. I have listened far too much to you, Sheffield, and no more, not now. No *more*."

They were at the library now, and a waiting footman instantly opened the door for them. At once Lady Enid and Dr. Pullings rose, turning to face them. Sheffield couldn't help but notice how Pullings had his arm protectively around Lady Enid's shoulder, and how she pressed against his side, trusting him completely.

The way Diana should be with him.

"Pray forgive us for keeping you so long," Diana said, forcing herself to smile for their sake, not his. "But Sheffield was showing me his family's paintings, and we lost all sense of the hour."

Automatically Sheffield glanced at the gold clock on the mantel. Hell, it was nearly six: they had lost sense of the hour, and everything else, too. Now he'd have to contend with an angry Lattimore, and likely March, too, for keeping the ladies out so long.

"I'll have the carriage brought," he said curtly, nodding to the footman who remained at the door.

"Thank you, Sheffield," she murmured, finally glancing his way, and pleading in silence to keep the truth their secret.

Secret, hah, he thought glumly. Anyone who looked

at her would know what she'd been doing, and it wasn't looking at pictures, either. Beneath her hat, her gold-streaked hair was a tangled mess that no decent lady's maid would claim. Her skirts were crushed into telltale creases, her mouth was ruddy from his kisses, and despite her inexplicable misery, she had the sated glow of a woman who'd recently been well pleasured. She'd never looked more achingly lovely to him, nor more desirable, plaguing both his heart and his cock.

She could deny it all she wanted, but she felt it, too. The devil take him if she didn't. If she'd really been so determined to cast him aside, she wouldn't still be looking at him now, her blue eyes wide and unwilling to break their gaze. Almost imperceptibly she shifted; whether she'd admit it or not, she was likely feeling the traces of their lovemaking on her thighs, as fine a memento as he could ever leave her with.

He could, grudgingly, understand why she wouldn't want to speak to him right now. Everything had happened so deucedly fast, she was bound to be somewhat confused. He had to remember that, as impudent as she could be, she wasn't another of his customary lovers, but an earl's daughter and a virgin. Rather, she was still an earl's daughter, but she certainly wasn't a virgin any longer. But because of Lady Enid and Pullings, he'd have until June to persuade Diana that they truly did belong together. He'd woo and win her properly, the way an earl's daughter deserved—or, actually, how he was pretending to woo Lady Enid.

Except with Diana, and with luck, he'd be able to intersperse that wooing with a few more afternoon interludes like the one they'd just had.

He smiled. He couldn't help it. And though she steadfastly didn't smile in return, she did blush, which was almost better.

"Forgive me, Your Grace," Pullings said. "But there are things that must be said."

"Then say them," Sheffield said, still intent on Diana. He'd never think of the Sultana Room in quite the same way again. She was his sultana now, and never was a sultan more blessed. "You're free to speak, Doctor. No one's stopping you."

Pullings cleared his throat, seldom a fortuitous sign with a preacher.

"First, Your Grace," he began, "Lady Enid and I wish to express our boundless gratitude for your most magnanimous generosity toward us in our plight, both in spirit and in action. We shall never be able to repay you for the kindness, the possibilities that you have seen fit to lavish upon us."

"It is nothing, Pullings," Sheffield said, only half listening, his thoughts still on Diana and the Sultana Room. He'd especially enjoyed how she'd hooked her knee over the back of the settee. He'd have to ask her to do that again. "Recall that you've obliged me as well."

He was obliged, too, more obliged than Pullings could ever guess for that gift of time. Diana was sure to come around by June, sure to realize that they belonged together.

Pullings bowed deeply. "You are too kind, Your Grace. Second, Lady Enid and I beg to thank you for your munificence regarding your offer of the living on your estate."

"You're most welcome," Sheffield said. Perhaps he'd bespeak a sultana's costume for her, with those filmy full breeches the heathen ladies in harems favored. He could just imagine Diana in those, parading about and being queenly like a proper sultana. He wished he could ask her now, but likely he should wait until they were wed.

"Truly you have extended a haven to us, Your Grace,"

Pullings was droning on. "A salvation, a refuge in our hour of need, and—"

"Yes, yes, Pullings," Sheffield said, striving to hurry him along. "The parish will never have been so well served."

Pullings bowed again. "You honor me, Your Grace. Third—"

"Joshua, please," Lady Enid interrupted gently. "If you cannot bring yourself to tell His Grace and Lady Diana, then I shall. I know it was agreed that Dr. Pullings and I would wed in June, but regrettably, that is no longer possible, and our little masquerade must come to its end."

"Oh, no, Enid, no," Diana said with sympathetic dismay. "Surely you have not had a change of heart?"

Blushing, Lady Enid smiled shyly and shook her head. "I'm with child," she said. "Joshua's child. We mean to wed as soon as can be arranged."

Sheffield was stunned. Enid was with child, she and Pullings meant to wed, the masquerade was done. The amusing house of cards he himself had contrived was about to collapse into an unsavory welter of scandal, and as soon as the world—*his* world, anyway—learned of it, he'd become the butt of every cuckold jest known to raucous mankind.

But worst of all was knowing he'd lost his excuse for seeing Diana alone.

Hell. Hell, hell, *hell*.

CHAPTER

13

"Where are my sister and mother?" Diana asked even as the Marchbourne House footman was closing the door after her. "Are they at home? Are they dressing?"

Not waiting for his answer, she hurried across the hall toward the stairs, leaving him to follow after her.

"Her Grace and her ladyship are in the nursery, my lady," the footman said, calling after her as she raced up the stairs. "Shall I send for your maid, my lady?"

"No—yes," she stammered, even though his question was the most natural in the world. "That is, yes, thank you."

She was lucky, ridiculously lucky, that Mama and Charlotte were in the nursery with the children and not in one of the downstairs rooms as they often were at this time of the afternoon. She never would have escaped them otherwise. She would have been called in to share her afternoon, to tell whom she'd seen and where she'd gone and what she'd done, the usual ritual in her family. But this afternoon she couldn't have begun to tell what she'd done. Most likely she wouldn't have had to: Mama's eyes, sharp for signs of misbehavior, would have seen it all at once, and then—oh, Diana did not want to consider what would have happened then.

Even now, as she ran down the long hall to her own

bedchamber, she was acutely aware of how wrinkled her clothes were and how her hat was barely pinned to her tangled hair. She'd been in such haste to dress that she hadn't realized she'd left behind a garter, and her left stocking had sagged and shimmied its way down her leg to end up as a grubby wad around her ankle. But the worst was feeling the stickiness of Sheffield's seed between her thighs with every step, making her remember every thrust, every caress.

Not waiting for the footman who had stepped forward to open the door to her chamber for her, she threw the door open herself and then latched it closed. She didn't bother to light candles, relying instead on the last dusky light of the fading day through the windows and the embers of the fire in the grate. She tore off her hat and rushed to the washstand in her dressing room, pouring water from the pitcher into the bowl. She'd only have a few moments of privacy before Sarah appeared to dress her for supper, and as quickly as she could she did her best to clean away the last traces of Sheffield's lovemaking. Yet no amount of water and lavender-scented soap could clean away the reality of what she'd done, and with a little whimper she sank down on her dressing table bench.

Like countless other girls before her, she'd let herself be led and seduced, swayed by pleasure and the promise of love. Worse yet, she'd been nearly as eager as Sheffield, shamelessly embracing the pleasure he'd offered like the lowest Covent Garden trollop. If she'd jumped feet-first from the center of Westminster Bridge, she couldn't have behaved more rashly. Sheffield could speak all he wished about love and marriage, but every warning she'd ever heard about men from her mother, her aunt, her sisters, told her he couldn't mean it. To gentlemen like Sheffield, love was only another sport, pursuit and chase and capture, and then on to the next quarry. He'd made lofty vows to marry only for love, and then the next moment he'd boasted of how cleverly he contrived his pretend betrothal to Lady Enid to free himself for more pursuits. Hadn't her family warned her of the danger of his charming ways, even before she'd known who he was? Yet she hadn't listened, she hadn't heeded, and now, because for a few false moments when she'd let herself believe he truly loved her, she was ruined.

Ruined. Of course she'd heard the single word, whispered by ladies in horror behind open fans, but she'd never thought it would mean her. The women in her family bred with remarkable ease; both of her sisters had conceived their first children within the first month of their marriages. The notable fertility of the Wylder sisters had in fact been her greatest attraction for Lord Crump. But he wished for an heir of his own blood, not of the Duke of Sheffield's, and she could not imagine being so reprehensible as to try to pass Sheffield's child off as Lord Crump's. Besides, they were not to wed until the autumn, and if she was with child, by then all the world would know of it.

No. Her betrothal to Lord Crump would be broken with some excuse that would fool no one, and she would be sent abroad, banished into discreet seclusion to bear her bastard. The child—*her* child—would vanish forever from her life, to be raised by well-paid caretakers. In time she might return to England, but she would never marry. No honorable man would have her. Instead she'd wither and fade into lonely, outcast spinsterhood, pitied and scorned and ultimately forgotten.

Even if she miraculously did not conceive, she could be equally ruined if Sheffield let slip so much as a whisper of what had happened. It wouldn't even have to be a whisper, really. If he simply *looked* at her again before others the way he'd looked at her when she was leaving his house—why, even a simpleton would guess what they'd done. The gossip in London about Sheffield and the married Frenchwoman had been gleeful enough; it would be a hundred times worse if the Earl of Hervey's youngest daughter were discovered to be the guilty lady. The result would be nearly as dire as if she'd borne Sheffield's bastard. She might be slightly less ruined, if there were degrees of ruination, but not by much. Surely Lord Crump would break their betrothal, and be applauded for it, too. No peer desired or deserved a bride who was not a virgin, while she—she would become a pariah, an outcast from her class, and a spinster.

Fig sleepily appeared from beneath the bed to rub against her leg. Diana gathered the little cat up and settled her in her lap, where she promptly closed her eyes, curled her tail around her feet, and began to purr. Nothing disturbed Fig, and as Diana held her close, she wished that she, too, could find peace with such ease.

She had told Sheffield she never wished to see him again, but it was already too late. She loved him. She loved how he smiled and laughed and how he could make her laugh, too. She loved his kindness and she loved how much he cared for fat, lazy, ugly Fantôme. She loved how generous he'd been to Lady Enid Lattimore, and how he'd offered a living and a church to Joshua Pullings. She loved how he'd kept the flower he'd plucked from her hat, and she loved that he'd noticed the hat in the first place. She loved how he respected his parents' memory. And she loved how he kissed her, and how he'd touched her, and how he'd made her body sing with joy in ways she'd never imagined, and how he'd held her and told her he loved her, and given her the shared intimacy that had been the most glorious moment of her life.

Oh, yes, she was ruined. For how could she ever love any other man after she'd loved Sheffield?

"Diana?"

That was Charlotte's voice, in her bedchamber, and quickly Diana set Fig down and began unfastening her bodice as if she'd been undressing all the time.

"Here you are," Charlotte said, coming to join her in her dressing room. She might have been in the nursery earlier, but she was already dressed for evening in a gown of deep blue silk brocade with serpentine trim, her favorite pearls around her throat and swinging from her ears. "Why are you undressing yourself here alone in the dark? Where is Sarah? She should be here with you, not dawdling belowstairs."

"She'll be here soon, I'm sure," Diana said swiftly, wishing to save Sarah from Charlotte's ire. "I've only just returned home."

"So I was told," Charlotte said. She poked at the fire to make it flame enough to light a taper, which she used in turn to light the nearest candlesticks: remarkable independence for a duchess. More duchess-like, she then sat gracefully in an armchair, spreading her skirts with a silken *shush*. "Why were you so late?"

Pulling the remaining pins from her hair, Diana turned on the bench to face the looking glass and the window. Outside, grooms were climbing ladders to fire the high lanterns that hung at the house's gates and on either side of the door, just as maidservants inside would be moving through the halls and rooms to draw the curtains and light the candles against the coming night. Lanterns lit and curtains drawn, Fig in her lap and Charlotte's pearls: strange how the routines and habits of life continued without pause, while for her, nothing would ever be the same.

"There were a great many carriages in the park today," she said, which was true. "And then it rained so suddenly, and you know how the streets become."

"Impassable," Charlotte said, agreeing. "At least you'd fine company to pass the time. How does Lady Enid?"

"Well," Diana said, again offering careful truth, "she seems very happy about her coming marriage."

"I'm certain she does," Charlotte said. Fig rubbed against her leg, and heedless of her blue silk, she lifted the little cat into her lap. "But what of Sheffield? Brecon swears he's changed completely, that he's become the perfect, tamed bridegroom, but I cannot conceive of it. Not Sheffield. I've always thought that of the four dukes, he is the only one who seems to have inherited the old king's roguish taste for variety in his ladies."

Diana prayed she didn't blush as she tried to guide her sister away from the topic of Sheffield. "You should be grateful March didn't inherit such a quality."

"I am," Charlotte said, lightly stroking Fig's ears. "Mightily glad. But do you believe that Lady Enid has reformed Sheffield, as Brecon says?"

"He appeared vastly content to me," Diana said, more wistfully than she'd intended. "He spoke often of—of love."

"Then Lady Enid is indeed a clever lady as well as a learned one," Charlotte said. "Who would have thought that Sheffield would finally be reined in by Homer and Sophocles? I must invite her and Sheffield to dine with us, so that we might all come to know her better. Perhaps next week, and I shall ask Lord Crump as well. They'll both be part of our family soon enough, though faith, I've no notion at all of what conversation will please such a lady-scholar."

"Quite ordinary things, truly," Diana said, thinking of how Lady Enid would likely wish nothing better than to discuss babies and breeding with an experienced expert like her sister. "It's not as if she carries musty old books about with her to the park."

"I'm glad for Sheffield's sake she doesn't," Charlotte said, but it was clear from her voice that she was no longer thinking of Lady Enid. "Look at me, Di, if you please."

Diana laughed nervously. Did it show in her face that she was no longer a virgin? Could Charlotte see some new wantonness or experience in her expression that hadn't been there before?

"I don't know why you wish it, Charlotte," she said, reluctantly turning toward her sister as she'd been bid. "You know my face as well as anyone."

"Perhaps instead I know it too well," Charlotte said, studying her thoughtfully. "When you left today, all I saw was that dreadful dull habit, plain enough to make a Quaker dowdy. But now I see how lovely you've grown, Diana."

Tears welled in Diana's eyes. "Oh, Charlotte," she said. "You needn't say such things."

Charlotte smiled fondly. "Why shouldn't I, when they are true? You've changed so much, and here I've scarcely noticed. You're not my little country sister any longer, but a true London beauty. Ah, Sarah, at last, and high time, too. You'll have to hurry to make Lady Diana presentable for supper."

The maid dropped a guilty curtsey. "Forgive me, Your Grace," she murmured, already beginning to lay out Diana's clothes for the evening. "Her ladyship will be ready, I promise."

"I trust so," Charlotte said. She set Fig down on the floor and rose, pausing to smile over Diana's shoulder at their reflection, side by side, in the looking glass. "My dear little Di! If Lord Crump's affection has already wrought such a change in you, then I can scarce wait for the magnificent transformation once you're wed."

She kissed Diana's cheek and turned to go, leaving Diana too choked with roiling emotion to do more than nod in return.

Oh, how she wished that Charlotte hadn't reminded

her of Lord Crump! If there was any true change to her, it would be Sheffield's doing, not Lord Crump's, more to her sorrow. But Charlotte wouldn't know that, or anything else. For one long, tantalizing moment, Diana considered confessing all and unburdening herself to her wise older sister, the way she'd done so many times before. Charlotte would know exactly how to make the best of this disastrous situation. With her usual calm efficiency and discretion, she'd take over from Diana and arrange everything that needed arranging.

But not yet: not yet. For now her best path was to hope that she wasn't with child, and hope, too, that Sheffield could keep their secret.

And heaven preserve her, it was a great deal to hope for, on both counts.

The next evening, Sheffield sat before the fire in his library, listening closely while Marlowe explained all he had accomplished on Sheffield's behalf during the day.

"The hackney's driver will collect Dr. Pullings at the gate on the north side of St. Anne's, sir," Marlowe said, standing before Sheffield with his book of notes in his hand. "Thence the driver will stop on the opposite side of Bedford Square from Lattimore House, where Dr. Pullings will step down and cross the square by foot. At the stroke of one, Lady Lattimore will leave her house by the garden door, sir, and meet Dr. Pullings, and they will leave together in the hackney."

Sheffield leaned forward in his chair, drumming his fingers on the mahogany arm. Marlowe was generally very good with details, but he'd never planned an elopement before, and Sheffield did not want this one to have any flaws.

"You are certain the driver is to be trusted?" he demanded. "He will keep his silence?"

"Given what he is being paid, sir, I believe he will,"

Marlowe said. "He will convey her ladyship and Dr. Pullings to the dock, where they will take their passage to Calais. Then the decoy couple will take possession of the hackney and will make their way broadly across the country toward Scotland. Their goal will be to make themselves remembered, so as to leave a trail if Lord Lattimore chooses to pursue."

"Oh, he will," Sheffield said. "Lady Enid is his only daughter, and he already has a strong dislike for poor Pullings. The captain of the vessel has agreed to wed them?"

"Yes, sir," Marlowe said, briefly glancing at his notes. "Captain Stewart. He was most obliging."

"Good, good," Sheffield said with satisfaction. The captain had been his suggestion, and he was proud of it. The laws against clandestine marriages had tightened considerably since his own parents had eloped, requiring banns to be published and church weddings for a marriage to be valid. But having the marriage performed by a ship's captain could still override those stipulations, even if a marriage on board a ship in the Thames stretched the definition of a wedding at sea. "By the time Lattimore discovers Lady Enid is gone, they should be safely wed and beyond his reach."

"Indeed, sir," Marlowe said, sharing Sheffield's satisfaction. "I have also taken great pains to keep from any mention of your name. Everything has been arranged as if by Dr. Pullings, and no other."

"Then all we can do has been done," Sheffield said, smiling. "It's up to them to be married and live their lives in conjugal bliss."

This all sounded tidy and neat, and with the ever-competent Marlowe to do the tidying, it doubtless was. Yet while conjugal bliss lay before Lady Enid and Pullings, a whirling firestorm of scandal would face Sheffield in the morning when word of their elopement spread through London. Sheffield wasn't dreading it. In fact, he was almost looking forward to weathering the scandal for the sheer novelty of the experience.

First he expected a chagrined and furious Lattimore to arrive soon after breakfast, bearing the letter for him from Enid explaining that she was terribly sorry, but she was breaking their betrothal to marry Dr. Pullings. He would then make the most grievous long face imaginable before Lattimore, and sigh and groan as if he truly were a disappointed bridegroom.

By noon, he expected the first inklings of the elopement would have begun to creep through society, no matter how hard Lattimore would try to suppress it. Scandals often had a perverse life of their own, and this one was bound to grow and spread like a noxious weed.

By nightfall, it would be discussed by everyone in his acquaintance as they dressed for the evening. By the time they left their houses, their servants would be speaking of it, too.

By midnight, he'd be the butt of endless jests and bawdy cleverness at his clubs, and by dawn, the whole tale would be trimmed and embellished and served up for breakfast reading in every lurid paper in the city. Asterisks would take the place of the letters in his name to stave off the charges of libel, but they'd fool no one. The handsome, womanizing duke, abandoned by his noble-born bride for a dull country parson: how could tattle be juicier than that?

Before this, Sheffield had always been depicted the villain in such pieces, the sly thief of virtue preying on unhappy wives. Now the proverbial shoe would be on the other foot, and for every person who might pity him, he imagined there would be a goodly number of husbands (even ones whose wives he'd never poached) who'd gloat and say he deserved this treatment. Not being wed to Lady Enid, he didn't believe he was actually entitled to cuckold's horns, but he was also certain there'd be at least one crudely drawn cartoon that would give him a rack of fresh antlers anyway.

None of it mattered. He'd bear ten times—no, a hundred!—the abuse and mockery for the sake of the same prize. Diana, his Diana, or so she could fairly be now. He'd give the scandal one day, perhaps two, and then he would call at Marchbourne House and ask for her hand.

He'd thought of little else since they'd parted. It wasn't just that she'd knocked him nearly senseless with her delicious eagerness when he'd made love to her, or how beautiful she'd been with her blue eyes heavy-lidded and her gold hair tousled and her clothes half torn away, or the breathy moan that she'd made of his name, or even how he'd thought he'd truly found paradise buried deep in a woman's body. It wasn't even that he'd been the one to claim her virginity.

Well, if he were honest, it *was* all those things. But mainly, absolutely, it was because she was the woman meant to be his companion through life. It was as simple, and as complicated, as that. He'd found her, and this would be the end of his searching. He had no concern for Crump, or the marquis's claim to Diana. Sheffield wanted her, and he was confident she wanted him in turn, and that was that. She was fated to be his lover, his wife, his duchess—even his sultana.

His Diana.

"You have the ring from Boyce's?" he asked Marlowe, his thoughts already racing onward to the moment he'd slip his mother's emerald on his own bride's finger.

Marlowe bowed slightly and drew the familiar shaped box from inside his coat. "I kept it close, sir."

"Very good." He took the box, opening it slowly, as if fearing the magic of the ring would somehow have disappeared. No: it sat nestled in the velvet, as bright with fire and memories as it always had been. He studied the ring, smiling to himself, and thought of how proud he would be to see it on Diana's hand.

It was so pleasing a thought that he must have thought it a good deal longer than was realized—long enough that Marlowe finally had no choice than to make the gentlest of throat-clearings to draw him back. He closed the box, setting it on his knee.

"Thank you, Marlowe," he said, smiling still because he could not help it. "You have executed everything with your customary thoroughness, and I'm grateful for it."

"Thank you, sir," Marlowe murmured, bowing his thanks in return. "It is my pleasure and my duty."

Sheffield was indeed satisfied to have so trustworthy a man to handle his affairs, no matter how complicated those affairs became. Yet to his surprise, Marlowe seemed to be hovering, with something unsaid left in the air between them. That was not like Marlowe, who was generally the very soul of discretion.

"That is all, Marlowe," Sheffield said, not chiding, but making it clear that their conversation was done.

Yet still Marlowe remained, with whatever he longed to say making him linger. Almost imperceptibly his gaze flicked down to the ring box.

Then Sheffield understood. All that Marlowe knew was that his master was going to great pains to extricate himself from an engagement, yet he had been asked to retrieve the late duchess's ring, a ring of considerable value and history with no lady to wear it. Marlowe knew nothing of Lady Diana Wylder that would explain either the ring or Sheffield's smile. No wonder he dared to be so inappropriately . . . curious. That same curiosity would only be shared and endlessly magnified tomorrow by the rest of London.

He looked down from Marlowe to the box on his

knee and, smiling still, covered it with his hand, cupping his palm protectively over the box and the ring inside. He was sorry that Marlowe felt so curious, but not so sorry that he'd explain. Until the ring was safely on Diana's finger, his secret—no, *their* secret—would remain exactly that. When the time was right, the whole world would know. He'd shout it to the highest church spires himself.

But not yet. Not yet.

The next day, Diana sat in the garden of Marchbourne House with Charlotte and her children and an assortment of nursery maids. Sheltered by the tall brick walls, the garden was warm and filled with sunshine, with the leaves in the trees still a bright spring green and no sign of the rainstorms from earlier in the week. Simply dressed in her old country clothes, which were well covered with Fig's fur, and with her feet bare, Diana sat on the grass and tossed a stuffed ball back and forth to Jamie, Lord Pennington. Jamie was more enthusiastic than skilled, and though he waved his arms and thrashed about and made a good deal of noise, he seldom actually caught the ball, forcing Diana to go crawling after it. Not that she minded. Chasing after a stuffed ball helped to take her thoughts from Sheffield and everything else—and there was considerable everything else—connected with him.

Chasing the ball or not, she thought of Sheffield constantly. She could not help it. She looked at the pond, and remembered how he'd pulled her into the water with him. She sat on the settee in her mother's sitting room and thought of how wickedly and thoroughly and divinely Sheffield had made love to her on his mother's settee. She thought she heard his laughter and his voice wherever she turned, and imagined his carriage drawing up before the house when none was there.

She had as good as banished him from her life, yet still she longed to see him again, and she'd been disappointed that he'd sent no little fond letter yesterday, no acknowledgment of what they'd shared on that settee. Perhaps that silence was customary with him and ladies once he'd made a conquest. She didn't know; she'd no experience with being conquered. But although she'd told him she'd no wish to hear him declare his love for her, that was exactly what she craved most.

To be sure, she realized the perversity of such desires. Just because she'd been a fool once with him didn't mean her foolishness carried over into all other corners of her self. But it did seem that the more she tried to be firm and stern with that self, the more she pined after what would be ruinous to have.

And so she tossed the ball to Jamie and praised him even when it fell through his chubby fingers, and tried her hardest not to think of all that she, too, had let slip away.

"You almost had it that time, Jamie," she said, striving to sound encouraging. "Toss it back to me now, and we'll try again."

"I have it now, Aunt Diana," he said, holding the ball tightly in both hands. He wrinkled his snub nose at her, making what she guessed was a fierce and menacing face. "I have it, and I'm going to *su'prise* you."

She made a face back at him, curling her fingers into claws. "You cannot surprise me, little man," she boomed in a deep, ogre-ish voice. "No one surprises *me*!"

He shrieked with delight and hopped backward, still clutching the ball. "I will! You'll see, Aunt Diana, I will, I will!"

"Oh, my dears, my dears!" exclaimed Mama, coming so fast into the garden from the house to join them that she was nearly running. "You cannot begin to imagine the terrible thing that has happened!"

There was an uncharacteristic urgency to Mama's voice, enough to make Diana turn at once toward her. Something wasn't right, that was clear. She knew Mama had been out to her mantua maker's and must have just returned, but she hadn't paused to put aside her parasol or remove her hat, and her breathlessness only added to Diana's foreboding.

"What has happened, Mama?" asked Charlotte anxiously, rising with the baby Georgie in her arms. "Is March—"

"No, Charlotte, no, it's not March," Mama said, "nor is there anything amiss with Lizzie or Hawke or their family. It's poor, poor Sheffield. He has been jilted."

"Sheffield?" Diana repeated, her own voice becoming traitorously breathless, too. "Sheffield's been jilted?"

Jamie's ball hit her squarely on the side of her face, knocking her sideways.

"Did so su'prise you, Aunt Diana!" he called, cackling gleefully. "Did so!"

"Hush, Jamie, hush," Charlotte said impatiently. "Grandmother is trying to talk. Where did you hear this, Mama? Sheffield jilted by Lady Enid! Oh, I can scarce believe it. Poor, poor Sheffield."

"Poor Sheffield indeed," Mama said, sitting in a chair that a servant had brought for her. "I heard it first from Lady Salford at Mrs. Cartwright's, but the entire shop was fair buzzing with the tale. It appears that Lady Enid ran off in the night with her brother's old tutor, a lowly parson, and left poor Sheffield with nothing but a letter and her betrothal ring. Poor, poor Sheffield!"

"At least she left her ring," Diana said, rubbing her face where Jamie's ball had struck it and praying the sore spot wouldn't blossom into a full-fledged bruise there on her temple. She'd known all along this would happen, but she was still taken aback by the haste, even with Lady Enid's revelation. "The ring was very pretty."

"A ring is nothing compared to a wife," Mama said with scandalized relish as she arranged her skirts. "They say Lord Lattimore is mortified by his daughter's behavior and has set out after her and her—her *paramour*—to Scotland, while poor Lady Lattimore has taken to her bed with the vapors from the shock. And poor, poor Sheffield! To be used so cruelly and abandoned like this!"

Poor Sheffield, hah, thought Diana. Likely he was laughing every bit as gleefully as her little nephew Jamie. He'd gotten exactly what he'd wanted, which was to be as free a bachelor as he had been before. But then hadn't he once told her that he always did get everything he wished?

"What is the matter, Diana?" Mama asked. "You're making dreadful sour faces. Do you have a headache?"

Diana sighed, seeing little point in blaming Jamie when most of what troubled her was Sheffield.

"No, Mama," she said. "No, I am fine."

"Then tell us, Di," Charlotte said eagerly. "You were last with Sheffield and Lady Enid. Did you see any hints of this break? Any unhappiness or dissatisfaction when they were together?"

"None," Diana said carefully. "I would never have guessed she loved another."

She didn't, that is, since there'd been no need for guessing, not with everything explained by Sheffield himself.

"It is *dreadful*," Mama said, her voice dropping lower with confidential horror. "I would never have thought such a thing of Lady Enid. For a lady to leave a gentleman whom she has promised to wed—why, it is every bit as disgraceful as if she left her husband!"

Diana shook her head, thinking wistfully of how happy Lady Enid and Dr. Pullings were together, and how well suited they were to each other.

"But what if Lady Enid loved the other gentleman

more, Mama?" she said. "Wouldn't it be equally disgraceful for her to marry Sheffield?"

"Really, Diana," Mama said, clucking her tongue with dismay. "How many times must we repeat this? The happiest marriages are made with respect and regard at their base, with love to follow. Consider your own match with Lord Crump, and how satisfactorily it is proceeding. If only Lady Enid had put aside her girlish infatuations, as you have done, and persevered with Sheffield! I'm certain that she would have been far happier with a duke than with a parson. Who knows what poor Sheffield will do now?"

Diana didn't answer. Poor Sheffield wasn't poor, and never would be. But she was the one who'd forgotten Mama's cautious wisdom, forgotten her well-reasoned match with Lord Crump, forgotten everything except the empty promise of love that Sheffield had offered her, glittering there like fool's gold.

"I expect he'll find another lady soon enough," Charlotte said, swaying to calm Georgie, who'd grown restless in her arms. "Sheffield does need a wife, and he is a duke, and wealthy, besides."

"That's not what Brecon believes," Mama said. "Brecon fears that this turn of events will quite wound Sheffield, with the most dire of consequences."

"When did you converse with Brecon?" Charlotte asked with surprise, finally passing Georgie to a waiting nursemaid. "I thought you'd gone to Mrs. Cartwright's."

Mama brushed her hand before her face, shooing away an insect, or perhaps Charlotte's question, too.

"I was with Mrs. Cartwright, yes," she said. "But when I was finished there and had heard the news, I happened upon Brecon in the street. He is certain that Sheffield will now abandon us all completely and return to France. He may have gone already, to avoid the talk."

"Who can fault poor Sheffield for that?" Charlotte

said, raising her voice over the baby's howls. "Think of what the men must be saying in the clubs! He has had such a dreadful reputation for tempting ladies to be faithless, and now to have the tables turned upon him!"

Mama waited as the nursery maid calmed Georgie. "What Brecon fears most, of course, is that now Sheffield will marry some French lady instead. Preserve us, a *French* lady!"

Diana gulped and stared down at the grass so no one would notice the truth that must surely show in her eyes.

"Oh, dear," Charlotte said, listening to the servant who had come to whisper a discreet message. "Diana, Lord Crump is here to see you."

"Now?" Diana looked up swiftly. "Here?"

"You can't have him shown here," Mama protested. "He is a bachelor gentleman, and he won't be at ease with the children about."

Charlotte nodded to the servant to fetch the marquis. "He's a bachelor, soon to be a groom. The sooner he learns how to adapt to children, the better it will be for his own."

"But it is the middle of the day, when he is always occupied with his business affairs," Diana said, bewildered, her emotions so confused she could not begin to sort them. "How can he be here now?"

"Because clearly he could not bear to keep away from you, dear," Mama said, smiling fondly. "Now come, gather yourself. Where are your shoes and stockings?"

Diana scrambled to her feet, brushing bits of grass and soil from her skirts. What had been perfectly appropriate for playing with Jamie was not at all right to receive the fastidious Lord Crump. Her clothes were worn, grass-stained, and rumpled, and she looked more like the village goose keeper than a future marchioness.

"My shoes are upstairs," she said with dismay. "I must go have Sarah dress me properly so—"

"There's no time," Charlotte said serenely, as always the very picture of a duchess, even here in the garden. "Here's Lord Crump now."

Here he was indeed, stalking along the garden path behind a footman. Dressed in his customary black mourning and white wig, he did not look so much like an ardent suitor as a determined one. Without so much as a hint of a smile, he first greeted Charlotte, then Mama, before finally coming to Diana.

She sank into as graceful a curtsey as could be managed in bare feet, remaining down until he gave her leave to rise with his usual gesture, an almost impatiently brisk flip of his fingers. The first time he'd done it, Diana had been wounded, wondering why he didn't take her hand to raise her, as more gallant gentlemen would. Now she merely accepted it as only another of Lord Crump's little quirks. At least this one would end when they were wed and therefore of equal rank, and she need no longer curtsey to him.

"Lady Diana, good day," he said, a genteel greeting undermined by his perplexed expression as he stared at her rumpled clothes. "Forgive me for having called at such an inopportune hour. I appear to have disturbed you."

"I was playing with Lord Fitzcharles, Lord Pennington, and Lady Amelia, my lord," Diana said quickly. "The children."

"Ah," he said. "The children."

As if cued by a prompter, the baby loosed a rising wail of unhappiness. Showing empathy for their brother's misery, the twins likewise began to cry, sobbing and blubbering and burying their faces in their nursery maid's skirts. It was a familiar enough racket to everyone in the garden save Lord Crump, whose pale face so filled with horrified repulsion that Diana almost expected him to begin crying, too.

At once Charlotte motioned to the nursery maids to remove the children, giving last little pats and kisses to console them as they were carried past her. Their wails continued long after they had left the garden, echoing distantly from within the house.

"Pray forgive my little ones, Lord Crump," Charlotte said, her smile full of apology. "It is the way of all children, I fear. When weariness seizes them, they must cry, and there is no help for it but to put them to bed."

Mama smiled, too, bending a fraction to one side as two footmen set the tea table before her.

"I know children's voices must seem a savage din now, Lord Crump," Lady Hervey said. "But once you are a father yourself and the children are yours, you will come to believe the sound the sweetest under heaven. Would you care for tea, Lord Crump?"

"Thank you, no, Lady Hervey," he said, finally taking the nearest chair as Diana, too, sat in a chair instead of the grass. He drew his handkerchief from his pocket and tipped his hat back long enough to blot his forehead around the edge of his wig. "I have come not for refreshment, but with purpose and resolve."

He cleared his throat with a ragged rumble, apparently to vocalize that purpose and resolve. "I have this morning learned that I must leave London within the week, and will be away for some months' time. His Majesty has honored me with a special commission to observe and report on the collieries of the Manchester coalfields, and how these mines may be best developed and encouraged for increased usefulness to the country."

Diana nodded encouragingly and tried not to think of how this sounded like the dullest, least interesting topic imaginable. He had not a smidgeon of Sheffield's wit or charm. But Lord Clump was here with her, and not on his way to France; she must remember that.

"What a handsome honor to receive from His Majesty," Mama said, smiling warmly as she poured tea for herself and her daughters. "To be sure, we will miss you whilst you are away, but we must begin wedding plans in earnest so that when you return we—"

"Forgive me, Lady Hervey," he said, interrupting with rare urgency. "But that is exactly why I have come this day. My duty will take me far from London and among strangers, and a wife would prove useful to me. In short, Lady Hervey, I wish to marry Lady Diana as soon as can be decently arranged, so that she might accompany me as my wife."

Diana gasped softly, pressing her hands to her mouth with shock. He wished to wed her at once, within days. He would never know she was ruined, and if in a few weeks' time she found herself with child, she would never know for certain if it was Sheffield's or her husband's. It was not exactly an honorable solution, but it was a kind of salvation, offered by the unlovely hand of Lord Crump.

"You wish to marry my daughter before you leave, Lord Crump?" Mama set the teapot back down on the table with a thump. "Forgive me, Lord Crump, but that is quite, quite impossible! At least three weeks are required for the banns to be read—"

"Not with a special license," Lord Crump said. "I have already taken the liberty of procuring one."

"But we had agreed upon the autumn," Mama insisted, "or perhaps at Christmastide, when you would be done with your mourning!"

"I cannot believe that you would ask such a thing of my sister, Lord Crump," exclaimed Charlotte indignantly. "To make the Manchester coal mines her wedding trip! To expect her to begin her wedded life in some mean lodgings, without a proper household or staff to call her own!"

But Lord Crump ignored them and instead turned toward Diana. He was no more handsome than when they had first met, no more agreeable, no more charming. He wished to marry her now only because she would be "useful." There was nothing of the gallant about him. He'd yet to press those thin, pale lips against hers in a kiss, and she could not begin to imagine him making love to her the way that Sheffield had.

But Sheffield had coaxed and warmed her heart with meaningless promises of love, and then had vanished. With Lord Crump, her heart would be cold and achingly empty, but it would be unbroken. Truly, it was no choice at all.

"I will do it," she said softly, so softly that she feared at first no one would hear her. "I am honored, Lord Crump, by your—your eagerness, and I will wed you as soon as you wish."

CHAPTER
14

Sheffield stood waiting beside the fireplace in Lady Hervey's green room, running his fingers restlessly along the carved marble mantel. On the nearest chair were the flowers he'd brought for Diana, an exuberant bouquet of early roses tied up with silk ribbons, and in his waistcoat, over his heart, was his mother's ring in readiness.

He was determined to do this properly. He had waited one day after Lady Enid had broken their empty engagement, and then another day after that, to make sure that Lord Lattimore failed to find his wayward daughter, and to let the gossip die down a bit. He would first ask Lady Hervey for her daughter's hand, and then, once she agreed (as of course she must; he was confident that a duke always trumped a mere marquis, especially such a sorry specimen as Lord Crump), he'd ask to see Diana. He would propose exactly as he should, pleading his case on his knees the way that poets recommended, and then he'd put his mother's ring on her finger himself.

He would demand a swift wedding, too. Not only did he wish to begin the adventure that would be his life with Diana immediately, but he was also conscious of the possibility of a child. He did not want his child—*their* child—to be branded a bastard and Diana called much worse, and only marriage could prevent it. A hasty wedding would once again make him a seven days' wonder, another golden gift to the London gossips, but he did not care. *He* would have Diana, and nothing else mattered beyond that.

Again he glanced at his watch, shot his cuffs, and smoothed his sleeves. Damnation, what was keeping Lady Hervey? He sighed and swept his gaze around the room. The wallpaper here was dreadful, huge yellow and white tulips fit for nightmares. He hoped Diana didn't share Charlotte's taste and expect to festoon the walls of Sheffield House with monstrous blooms like these. He'd have to speak up if she did. True, wallpapers and such were the ladies' purview, but he knew what was agreeable and what wasn't, and he'd be damned if he let—

A small porcelain shepherd crashed from a high shelf to the floor, the head flying off and skittering under one of the chairs. Startled, Sheffield looked up to the shelf for the reason for the shepherd's sudden, fatal dive. The reason was obvious: a small patchwork mongrel of a cat was sitting there, her tail neatly curled around her paws as she surveyed him.

He smiled up at the little cat, not only because he had a tenderness for all beasts but because this cat must be Diana's pet, beloved Fig. What other excuse could she have to be here, given that cats were not ordinarily given free rein of ducal houses?

"Hey, Fig, hey," he said softly, standing beneath the shelf. The cat blinked and stretched, striving to be nonchalant even as she watched him intently. He held up his hand, which she delicately sniffed. He took that as a welcoming sign, and carefully scooped her into his arms. At once she nestled against his chest, rubbing her head against the buttons on his coat. Clearly he'd won the favor of Diana's cat; now to be equally fortunate with her as well.

He was rubbing his fingers lightly between the cat's ears, a place that, in his experience, all felines enjoyed, when the door behind him swung open.

"Fig, blast you, where *are* you?" Diana said, scowling fiercely until she saw Sheffield. Then she froze, her fingers tight on the door latch and her blue eyes wide with surprise.

"Good day," he said softly, the same voice he'd used to coax the little cat. Only two days had passed since he'd last seen her, yet it felt like an eternity. It almost hurt to look at her now, he'd missed her that much, and yet nothing could make him look away. She wore a plain gown, some pale pink filminess that gave her an ethereal air, or would have if it hadn't clung so splendidly to her breasts and waist. "You're beautiful, Diana."

"Don't," she said sharply, the spell broken. "Don't even begin, Sheffield."

"There's nothing to begin," he said, wishing she'd smile, "considering how nothing ended, not between us."

"Nothing ever began *to* end," she said, her cheeks flushed. "I told you I did not wish to see you again, Sheffield, and I meant it. Now if you please, give me Fig, and leave. Fig, here. Here."

She crouched down and patted her skirt, making a small clicking noise with her tongue to summon the cat. But though Fig twisted her head to look at her, she remained snug against Sheffield's chest.

"You see how it is," Sheffield said, ruffling the cat's fur. "She wishes me to stay, though she wouldn't mind coming to live with me at Sheffield House, either. I believe you'd enjoy it, too."

"Sheffield, please go," she said, an unexpected desperation creeping into her voice. "Please! If you stay, you'll ruin everything."

"I don't wish to ruin anything, Diana." Sensing the

difficulty of making a proper proposal with a cat in his arms, he bent long enough to set Fig on the floor. "I love you, and I want to make things right between us."

Diana clapped her hands over her ears. "No, Sheffield, I will not listen. I will not hear you, not a word."

"Very well, then," he said, reaching into his coat. She was scarcely making this easy for him; in fact, she rather looked as if she might cry, which wasn't encouraging at all. Still, he'd wager the ring would get her attention, and make her realize he was serious in his intentions. "If you will not listen, perhaps this shall prove that I—"

"Sheffield, my dear." The door behind him opened, and Lady Hervey sailed toward him, her arms outstretched to offer a motherly embrace and her face full of sympathy. "Oh, I am so very sorry to hear of your misfortune! I cannot fathom how Lady Enid could behave so abominably as this toward you."

She hugged him and kissed his cheek. Over her shoulder, Sheffield saw that while Diana had removed her hands from her ears, her expression remained less than friendly.

He smiled and winked.

She flushed a deeper pink, but turned away. That blush gave him at least a hint of encouragement. But really, why didn't she smile? Would it tax her so much to show that she was glad to see him?

Unaware, Lady Hervey stepped back, searching his face.

"You are not too desperate, Sheffield, are you?" she asked, clearly concerned. "Brecon is quite worried for you, you know. I know the talk has been merciless, but you must put it behind you and move forward."

"Thank you, Lady Hervey." He sighed manfully. "Your words are a rare comfort to me."

"I am glad of it," she said, giving his chest a fond pat. She really was quite pretty for an older lady in her thirties, with the same blue eyes and golden hair that Diana had inherited, and Sheffield could understand why Brecon seemed to spend so much time in her company.

"There's bound to be another lady in your life," she continued, "one who shall love you as you deserve."

"I can only pray there is," he said. "A lady of beauty, passion, wit, and virtue."

He glanced briefly at Diana, hoping she'd heard that much, but she was pointedly looking in the other direction, as if he hadn't spoken at all.

"Passion *and* virtue?" Lady Hervey repeated, her brows raised with skepticism. "Perhaps you should look more for the virtue than the passion, Sheffield. Passion is not to be trusted, and it inspires unconscionable behavior. Passion is what has led Lady Enid into the arms of that dreadful parson."

At their feet, Fig had discovered the porcelain shepherd's decapitated head, and now batted it halfheartedly toward Lady Hervey. She frowned and picked it up.

"Oh, Diana, see what Fig has done now." The head's painted face stared up glumly from her open palm. "I've told you not to let her come into this room. I hope this wasn't some priceless treasure from March's family."

"You know how Fig is, Mama," Diana said, scooping up the cat with one hand. "She goes where she pleases. Here's the body. I'm sure it could be mended, even though it is surpassing ugly."

Standing before him beautifully dressed in pink, with the scrawny cat in one hand and the headless shepherd in the other, she somehow seemed to perfectly demonstrate why she was his ideal duchess. No wonder he loved her. There would never be a better time to ask for her hand, and once again he began to reach for the box with the ring.

"I'm glad you are here this morning, Sheffield," Lady

Hervey said, taking the shepherd's body from Diana. "You've spared me having to write and invite you to a small family gathering tomorrow night. You must come, you know. We'll even have Brecon's three boys with us. It will all be quite hasty and informal, but we'll celebrate nonetheless."

"He doesn't know yet, Mama," Diana said quickly, clutching Fig tight to her chest. "You must tell him."

Lady Hervey sighed. "Oh, my, I suppose he doesn't," she said. "Dear Sheffield! I hope this won't pain you too dreadfully, considering how you've just lost your own bride."

"I will survive, Lady Hervey," he said gallantly. There was no question that he would, considering he'd have a new bride and one he loved, too, and at last he turned to face Diana. "In fact, if you will permit me, I wish to—"

"I'm marrying Lord Crump on Thursday," Diana said swiftly. "That is what we are celebrating. My wedding."

Sheffield frowned, not believing. "Crump? You're marrying Crump on Thursday? Why?"

She raised her chin, all defiance that he refused to believe.

"Because his lordship wishes it," she said. "Because *I* wish it, and—and it is right, in every way."

The plush box with the ring suddenly felt as ridiculous and without meaning as a chunk of coal, and self-consciously he withdrew his hand.

Lady Hervey nodded in agreement. "At the request of His Majesty, Lord Crump must journey to Manchester almost immediately, and remain there for several months. He decided he could not bear to be without Diana for so long a time, and thus the sudden wedding."

"Manchester," Sheffield said, saying the only thing that came to mind that was fit to say to ladies. "No man who loved his wife would take her to Manchester on their wedding trip."

Lady Hervey laughed. "I will agree that it would not be my first choice, either," she admitted. "But Lord Crump's desire to have Diana by his side can hardly be faulted, nor his eagerness to wed so that she might accompany him. It's all very romantic, isn't it?"

Somehow Sheffield forced himself to nod. It would be romantic if it were true, and if it were any gentleman other than bloodless Crump, and most of all if Diana's eyes weren't brimming with unhappiness and her arms clasped so desperately tight around poor Fig.

She did not love Crump. He would wager his life upon it. But why was she so determined to cast her own life away by marrying Crump?

Lady Hervey was smiling, albeit a bittersweet smile, as she tried to fit the broken head back on the shepherd's body as if it were a puzzle.

"I hope you will join us tomorrow evening, Sheffield," she said. "It may well be the last time we shall all be together as a family for some time to come. Brecon's two older boys are to sail soon to join Lizzie and Hawke in Naples. The youngest will return to school. Diana and Lord Crump will be leaving for the North as soon as they're wed. And then you, too, shall be departing for Paris—"

"For Paris?" he repeated, mystified. "I've no plans to return there at present. Whatever gave you that notion?"

"Not whatever, but whom," Lady Hervey said with hesitation. "Brecon was quite certain that you would return to the French court, and I'd no reason to doubt him."

"This time my infallible cousin is wrong," he said. "I've no plans to return there at present. In time, perhaps, since I've many acquaintances there, but for now I intend to remain in London."

Why the devil would Brecon tell Lady Hervey a tale like that? Of course Brecon had come to offer his solace as soon as he'd heard of Lady Enid's elopement, and though they'd talked long and drunk brandy together in commiseration, there hadn't been any mention by either of them of Paris.

"You are remaining here in London?" Diana asked. "What Brecon said was false?"

"As false as can be," he said, watching her closely. She wasn't blushing now, not at all, and her cheeks were so pale he feared she might faint.

"Then you will be joining us tomorrow," Lady Hervey said. "How fortunate! Perhaps I might also coax you to remain with us now and take tea? We are expecting Lord Crump at any moment. We could make a small party at my tea table."

"Forgive me, Lady Hervey, but I've another appointment that must claim me," he lied. If Diana had accepted his proposal, he'd intended to spend the day here with her. Now that he hadn't even been permitted to ask—and, worse, that he'd be expected to sit to one side while she entertained Crump—he couldn't leave quickly enough. He bid farewell to Lady Hervey first, and then turned to Diana.

"Good day to you, Diana," he said, taking her hand lightly, as any gentleman might. "I wish you joy of your marriage, and every pleasure and happiness with a man you love, and who loves you in return."

He didn't kiss her fingers, but merely the air over them, in a way that not even her mother could misinterpret. But when he looked up at Diana over her hand, he wanted her to know exactly what those words meant to him, and that when he spoke of the man who loved her, it wasn't Crump.

And she knew. He saw it in her eyes, in her mouth, in the very set of her shoulders. She loved him, not Crump. He'd no doubt of it now. Yet still she seemed resigned, even determined, to marry the wrong man, and make the greatest mistake of both their lives.

"Thank you, Sheffield," she murmured. "For—for everything."

Then she pulled back her hand and pointedly turned away.

"Until tomorrow, then, Sheffield," Lady Hervey said, gently patting his arm. "Good day to you, and pray be easy. Put Lady Enid from your thoughts and heart, and look firmly to the future. I'm sure before long you will indeed find the right lady to wed."

He smiled with genuine sadness and bowed, and as his carriage drew away from the house, he hoped Diana was watching behind one of those windows. The bitter truth was that, despite all his clever scheming, he truly had been jilted—just not by the lady everyone thought. And unless he could think of a way to persuade her otherwise within the next two days, he would lose her forever.

"Did Sheffield leave these?" Mama said, picking up the bouquet of roses from the chair. "Strange that he didn't present them. Such lovely roses, too."

"He must have been distracted by Fig, and forgot," Diana said, trying to sound as unconcerned as Mama did herself. Of course she knew that he'd brought the flowers to her, and equally, of course, that she'd made it impossible for him to give them to her. And yet as she gazed at them now, the beautiful roses tied with silk ribbons, she felt only little bursts of wild, inappropriate joy.

Not once had Lord Crump brought her flowers, and the only time she'd hinted that she might like them, he'd sternly dismissed them as a vanity and a waste of money. Yet March still gave flowers to Charlotte, and the obvious pleasure he took in the giving and she in the receiving seemed hardly a vanity to Diana. She still remembered the roses March had sent to her sister before they were married, his first gift: white roses carefully presented in a glass globe, brought all the way from his garden in the country. As young as Diana had been, she'd thought those roses were the most romantic gesture she'd ever seen.

And now Sheffield had brought roses to her.

"I'm sure he meant them for you, Mama," she said, though she yearned to take them and bury her face in their heady fragrance. "He asked for you when he came, didn't he?"

Mama smiled at the flowers, lightly touching the velvety blossoms.

"I would have thanked him earlier if I'd seen them," she said. "It's very kind of him to remember me, especially when he's obviously so distraught himself. Poor Sheffield! Yet how like him, too, to wish to please me with such a pretty token. He truly does possess the heart of a gallant, exactly as Brecon says."

"Is that such a dreadful thing?" Diana asked, still looking longingly at the flowers. "March is gallant to Charlotte, and you don't see anything wrong with that."

"Charlotte is March's wife and duchess, and he honors her by his attentions," Mama said. "But Sheffield puts his gallantry to the sole purpose of seduction and conquest. There's a world of difference between the two. I'd have thought you would have realized that, having spent so much time in Lord Crump's excellent company."

Diana didn't answer, because what she'd realized in Lord Crump's company was that he didn't possess a single breath of gallantry in his entire being. Sheffield had put more care and thoughtfulness into his pretend wooing of Lady Enid than Lord Crump ever had with her. She thought of the amethyst betrothal ring with the antique design that had been perfect for Lady Enid's learned tastes, and then of how Lord Crump had announced that he did not believe in betrothal rings any more than he did in nosegays. To be sure, Diana could hardly quarrel with his reasoning—that the wedding ring he'd give her as part of their marriage ceremony should be paramount, its significance undiminished by a gaudier betrothal ring that was intended more to impress others than to reflect the holy sacrament of marriage.

And yet, and yet . . .

"Have you ever wondered whom Father would have chosen as my husband had he lived?" she asked, gently stroking Fig's head as the cat slept in her arms. "He chose March for Charlotte, and Hawke for Lizzie. It's not so hard to imagine him having chosen the third cousin for me."

"Sheffield?" Mama asked with surprise. "I suppose it is possible. Your father took great pride in aligning the family with dukes. But I could scarce imagine a more wretched match for you! Sheffield is so eager to please, so passionate and with such charm, that it surely would have been disastrous."

"But why?" Diana asked, more plaintively than she should have. "What disaster could come from marrying such an agreeable gentleman?"

Mama sighed, smoothing the rose leaves that had become twisted by the ribbons.

"You force me to be blunt, Diana," she said. "I do not believe Sheffield will be faithful to any wife, whoever he may wed. Gentlemen like him are too fond of variety to be satisfied with one woman alone. Many titled ladies can find it in themselves to ignore their husbands' mistresses and infidelities for the sake of their families, but you—you are too passionate yourself to do that. Oh, yes, it would have been a disaster of the first order, and

I cannot tell you how happy I am that you will marry a steady, devoted gentleman such as Lord Crump."

Diana turned away, unable to bear hearing more. She could see Sheffield's carriage still in the drive, slowly drawing away from the house and from her. She imagined herself running out the door and down the steps, chasing after the carriage with her skirts flying about her legs. Sheffield would hear, and lean from the window to order the driver to stop, and then open the door to gather her up in his arms, and take her . . .

Take her where? Even in fantasy, she could put no happy ending to that tale. Mama was right, as she always was. There could be no lasting contentment with Sheffield. Lord Crump might not bring her flowers, but he had honorably offered to marry her. Sheffield had not. All he'd offered was love.

Love, glorious, intangible love. And where was the future in that?

"Good day, Your Grace," said Brecon's butler, Houseman, as he held the door open for Sheffield.

"Where is my cousin, Houseman?" Sheffield asked, already glancing up the stairs. "I know he's here. He's always at home at this hour."

"I shall tell him you are here, sir," Houseman said, closing the door. "If you would care to wait in the library—"

"Thank you, Houseman," Sheffield said, "but I'll spare you the trouble and tell him myself."

He deftly sidestepped the butler and headed toward the staircase. Brecon was a complete creature of habit, and having completed his letters for the day, he would now be in his bedchamber, dressing and preparing to ride in Hyde Park. This morning would be a bit different, however, for this morning Brecon was going to have to answer a few questions about Lady Diana and

Lady Hervey and why the devil Brecon had told them he was leaving London for Paris.

"Please, sir," Houseman implored, following him. "His Grace does not wish—"

"Do not worry yourself, Houseman," Sheffield said, already bounding up the stairs. "He won't object to seeing me. I know the way to his rooms."

He did, too. Up the stairs, to the passage on the left, to the arch opposite the marble head of Hadrian on a pedestal, and there was the door to Brecon's bedchamber. Not waiting on ceremony—or for a footman to do it for him—he opened the door himself.

Brecon was uncharacteristically late in his schedule this morning, still sitting at the small desk before the window in a red silk wrapping gown and without his wig. He was finishing his coffee and writing a lengthy letter to a lady, doubtless the same lady whose own letter sat open before him, complete with an embroidered silk garter tucked inside. Behind him, his manservant was laying out his riding clothes on the bed.

"Good day, Brecon," Sheffield said, making a curt, perfunctory bow. "I wish to speak to you directly, sir."

Deliberately Brecon finished the sentence he'd been writing before he looked up to Sheffield. He didn't seem surprised to find Sheffield in his bedchamber, but then, Brecon never showed any emotion as vulgarly uncontrolled as surprise.

"Good day to you as well, Sheffield," he said, putting aside his pen and sanding the page. "I'd rather expected you might wish some uncritical company this morning. Would you care to ride through the park with me?"

"I'd rather speak now," Sheffield said. "In privacy, if you please."

"Very well." Brecon pushed his chair back from the desk, waving away both his manservant and Houseman, who was lurking in the hall with two additional footmen. When the door clicked shut, he looked at Sheffield and smiled. "I'm assuming this has to do with Lady Enid. I applaud your discretion in regard to the lady, especially in the circumstances. Would you sit?"

Sheffield shook his head, too restless to sit. "Not Lady Enid, no."

"No?" Brecon settled back, his elbows resting on the arms of his chair. "That surprises me. Another lady, then?"

But Sheffield was in no humor for Brecon's genteel, circuitous conversation, and it infuriated him all the more to see Brecon writing what must surely be a billet-doux to some willing lady or another, while the woman Sheffield loved was slipping away.

"Why in blazes did you tell Lady Diana and her mother that I was leaving for France?" he demanded bluntly. "What was your purpose in a lie like that?"

"It wasn't a lie, Sheffield," Brecon said mildly. "Given the humiliation you had suffered, I believed you were in fact returning to Paris. Apparently I am mistaken."

"It was a mistake the ladies believed," Sheffield said, fuming and pacing back and forth before his cousin, "and a mistake that has caused me great mischief by painting me as careless and inconsiderate."

Brecon raised his brows. "I cannot fathom why. The lady abandoned you, not the other way around. You could hardly be faulted for wishing to leave the sight of such unhappiness."

"Damnation, it's not about Lady Enid," Sheffield said, realizing too late that, in his anger, he was betraying himself. "It's Lady Diana whom I wish to know the truth."

"The truth, the truth," Brecon repeated, and at last he smiled. "I am thankful that we have finally reached that particular article. Have you not a care for Lady Enid and her parson? Are you so wrapped in your own affairs that you don't wish to know if they have arrived safely in Calais?"

Abruptly Sheffield stopped his pacing. "How do you know where they are?"

"Oh, I know a great many things, cousin," he said, idly taking the embroidered ribbon garter from the desk and drawing it through his fingers. There were creases from a knot at either end, showing that the garter had recently graced the phantom lady's leg, making Sheffield uncomfortably imagine Brecon untying it himself. "A great many things indeed. Considering how briefly you have been here in London, you've been remarkably busy."

Sheffield sighed impatiently. Standing here before Brecon, he'd the distinct feeling that he was fifteen again and had been sent down from school, which was also probably what Brecon wished. That was enough to make him sit at last, dropping heavily into the chair beside Brecon's desk.

"Do you know the answer yourself?" he asked. "Are Lady Enid and Pullings safely in Calais?"

"They are," Brecon said. "Though I believe they are now properly styled Dr. and Lady Enid Pullings. Poor Lord Lattimore! Last I heard, he was still wandering about Yorkshire, convinced his daughter was to be found there. I will credit you for your plotting. It was most excellently, if wrongly, done."

"Thank you," Sheffield said warily. "How the devil did you learn of it?"

"Oh, easily enough," Brecon said, weaving the ribbon between his fingers. "Always remember that a gentleman who must buy loyalty has few secrets."

"Not Marlowe—"

"No, not Marlowe," Brecon said easily. "That man's a prize, as silent as a tomb. But others are not so reticent. I have heard not only of your part in arranging

Lady Enid's elopement but also of the very private entertainment you held on a recent afternoon at Sheffield House. Doubtless all you and Lady Diana did alone together was take tea and discuss the weather. No wonder you wish her to hear only the best of you."

"Then you know," Sheffield said, his earlier anger giving way to a rush of relief. He hadn't enjoyed keeping something as momentous as loving Diana from Brecon, and now he leaned forward in his chair, eager to share.

"She is all I wish in a woman, Brecon," he said fervently, "and all I could want in a wife and duchess. I love her more than any other woman, and I'll marry her if she'll have me, and—"

"No," said Brecon. "No."

He'd never seen Brecon's face so stern, nor set so determinedly against him, not in all their times together. It stunned Sheffield, and it wounded him, too.

"Why the devil not, Brecon?" Sheffield demanded. "I love her, and I'd swear by all that's holy that she loves me. She's meant to be my other half, the way the poets say. She's of a suitable rank, and her family's so ancient that not even His Majesty could complain. She's—"

"She's married to another gentleman," Brecon said, his voice hard, "or will be in two days' time. She's not free, Sheffield, and I won't have you ruining their lives and our entire family's peace simply because you imagine yourself in love with the girl."

"But I *am* in love with her," Sheffield protested in disbelief. "I love her a hundred times more than Crump ever could. A thousand times more!"

Brecon shook his head. "In many ways, Sheffield, Crump is a better man than you, and I've no doubt he'll make the lady a far better and more respectable husband than you ever could. I warned you away from her the first night you returned from Paris. Yet you ignored me, and you see the sorrow your petty intrigue has caused."

Abruptly Sheffield rose and turned away, unable to face Brecon any longer. Brecon, who had been like a brother, even a father, to him through much of his life. Brecon, who had always done whatever was necessary to guarantee his happiness, was now denying him the one thing Sheffield most wanted, and needed, too.

He wanted the love of Diana Wylder.

"I am serious about this, Sheffield," Brecon said, continuing as if Sheffield faced him still. "You know as well as I do that His Majesty wished you to marry Lady Enid, and his disappointment was keen when the lady ran off. If he were ever to learn your part in her elopement, and how blithely you contrived to avoid obeying his will, I can promise you his displeasure would make your life here in London very difficult indeed."

"You would do that to me, Brecon?" he asked without turning, bitterness welling up inside him. "You would tell His Majesty?"

"I would not," Brecon said firmly. "No matter what you now believe of me, I would never do that to you. But if you continue to leap from one scandal to another— and disturbing Lady Diana's wedding to Lord Crump for the sake of a fancied passion would definitely constitute a scandal—in direct contradiction to His Majesty's plan for a more respectable court, then I am sure that there will be others willing to tell him a great many things about your behavior. Some may even be true."

The last thing he wished to hear now was Brecon's wry wit. "I do not appreciate your jests, Brecon."

"I do not intend them to be jests," Brecon said. He sighed, and his voice softened a fraction. "Perhaps it is for the best that you return to the Continent for a while. Stay there, amuse yourself, until you have recovered yourself and forgotten Lady Diana. I know that Celia—"

"Celia? Who is Celia?"

"That is, Lady Hervey," Brecon said quickly. "I know she has invited you to dine at Marchbourne House tomorrow night, and to attend the wedding the following day. She is a warm and generous lady, without a notion of your unfortunate attachment to her daughter. If she did, I am certain she would agree with me that it would be better for us all that you stay away. Do you truly want to risk ruining the girl's name?"

As far as Sheffield was concerned, he'd already done far more than that with Diana, which was part of the reason he could not let her marry Crump. Yet he couldn't explain that, not even to Brecon; what had happened on the settee in the Sultana Room was between Diana and him, and no one else.

Lightly he touched his mother's ring, still tucked inside his waistcoat. Brecon could argue the rest of the day as far as he was concerned, but it would not change his mind. Until Diana told him she did not love him, the ring—and his heart—belonged to her.

"Give me your word that you won't behave like a fool," Brecon urged. "Your word as a gentleman, Sheffield."

Slowly the younger man turned back to face Brecon and bowed. "You have my word," he said. "I'll not be a fool."

No, he wouldn't be a fool where Diana was concerned. But he would behave like a man in love, and no man, not even Brecon, could stop him.

CHAPTER

15

Diana stood before the long looking glass in Charlotte's dressing room, letting the lady's maid put the final critical tweaks and touches to her hair, which was styled in a way that Charlotte had declared too fashionably complex for Diana's own maid. Charlotte, and Mama, too, had decreed this night was Diana's to shine, even if the company would only be members of their own ever-growing family.

Diana's gown was a rich silk *robe à la française*, with deep flounced cuffs on the sleeves and the pleated back drifting gracefully from her shoulders. The crisp silk brocade was silvery blue, shot through with metallic threads that glinted in the candlelight, but what Diana liked best about the brocade was its *chinoiserie* pattern of little pagodas and foreign ladies. With such an elegant gown, Mama had even permitted Diana to have her hair dressed high and powdered, with Charlotte's maid now tucking tiny paste brilliants, winking like stars, into the elaborate pale curls.

"That's fine, very fine," Charlotte said, walking slowly around Diana to study her hair. "What jewels are you wearing?"

"You know I don't have any jewels, Charlotte, at least

not that you'd consider," Diana said. "I thought I'd wear my coral beads, with the small pearls for my ears."

"Oh, that's not nearly sufficient for this gown," Charlotte said. "I must give you some things of mine for the evening."

Charlotte unlocked the door in the tall chest that held her jewels. She herself was dressed opulently, a dramatic red and gold brocade gown that showed her famous pearl and diamond necklace and earrings to best advantage. Her pearls *were* famous, too, the kind of jewels that made other ladies stare at balls, having been long ago given to the first Duchess of Marchbourne by her royal lover. Diana was certain there wouldn't be anything like them (or anything as disreputable) in Lord Crump's family.

"Spitalfields silk of that quality deserves diamonds," Charlotte said, returning with a flat blue box. "I believe this will suit you much more admirably."

She fastened a necklace of diamonds set into curling silver loops around Diana's neck—modest stones by Charlotte's standards, but vastly more valuable than any Diana had ever worn. She touched them lightly with her fingers, accustoming herself to the chilly weight of the necklace settling against her skin.

"There," Charlotte said with satisfaction, her reflection smiling with satisfaction beside Diana's in the looking glass. "Now you look like a proper marchioness."

Diana gazed at her image. She did look like a marchioness now, pale and elegant and impeccably dressed, and so composed that she almost didn't recognize herself.

No, there wasn't an *almost* about it. She didn't know herself, not like this. Tomorrow night at this hour she would be married, and the Marchioness of Crump. She would be alone in a coach with her new husband, being carried far away from London and everyone in her life that she held dear.

"Oh, Charlotte," she whispered, still staring at this unknown version of herself. "I'm to marry Lord Crump tomorrow, yet I do not even know his Christian name."

"Poor lamb," Charlotte said, slipping her arms around Diana's shoulders, though taking care not to crush the silk brocade of her gown. "Every noble bride is anxious the day before she weds."

"But what shall I call him?" Diana begged, her voice rising with uneasiness. "How shall I address him?"

Charlotte sighed. "He hasn't told you his name? He hasn't given you leave to use it?"

Diana shook her head, her eyes filling with tears she knew she could not shed.

"Then you must call him 'my lord' until he says otherwise," Charlotte said gently. "I have heard of peeresses who have always employed their husband's titles, even in times of, ah, intimacy, and still have been the most loving and contented of couples."

Yet still Diana shook her head, closing her eyes against her reflection and the reality of the marriage she did not want.

"I do not love him, Charlotte," she said, her words tumbling over one another in desperate haste. "I thought by now I would, or at least feel a fondness, a regard, but though I have tried my best to discover an affection, I feel nothing toward him, Charlotte, *nothing*, and now— now I must be his wife."

She pressed her hand over her mouth to keep from sobbing. It wasn't Lord Crump who made her weep, but Sheffield. If only she had never met him, if she'd never known his laughter, his teasing, his kindness, his passion, then she'd never have realized what love could be.

"Please, Diana, please," Charlotte said, resting her cheek against Diana's temple. "You cannot cry, dear, not now."

"I cannot help it, Charlotte," she said, her voice breaking. "I can't."

"But you must, Diana, you must and you will," Charlotte said, holding her close. "I can hear the carriages in the drive already. You can't show yourself like some pitiful scullery maid, with a red nose and swollen eyes. You're almost a marchioness, a peeress, and you must act like one. You must be beautiful and serene when you walk down the stairs, and no matter what sorrow or unhappiness you feel within, you must never let it show."

If Charlotte only knew how she felt within, or if she could only tell her! Diana held her sister tightly, painfully aware of how much she would miss her after tomorrow.

Because even now, Charlotte was right. She wasn't some hapless girl, but a noble-born woman who'd already made certain choices in her life that couldn't be unmade. She had been a lover, and tomorrow she would become a wife; for all she knew, she might already be a mother as well. Love without marriage, and marriage without love. That was her fate, and all the tears in the sea would not change it.

With a shuddering sigh she raised her head from Charlotte's shoulder, and with another she opened her eyes. She took a handkerchief from the dressing table and carefully blotted the corners of her eyes. She turned toward her reflection in the glass one last time and smiled. A tremulous smile, but a smile nonetheless.

Charlotte smiled, too, and slipped her hand into Diana's to lead her, the way they'd always done as girls.

"Though he doesn't realize it just yet, Diana, Lord Crump is the most fortunate man in all London," she said. "Now come, we've kept the gentlemen waiting long enough."

* * *

Sheffield arrived at Marchbourne House exactly thirty-five minutes later than Lady Hervey had requested. He hadn't anything against Lady Hervey per se, but he didn't like arriving at entertainments along with everyone else, herded from front hall to cloakroom to drawing room like overdressed cattle. Instead he preferred to saunter into a room after the others had assembled and begun to drink, which made for a much better entrance, even for a duke.

Tonight, too, he'd decided to make that entrance even more memorable by bringing Fantôme with him. Lady Hervey had stressed that the gathering would be for the family alone, and at present Fantôme was the sum of his immediate family. Besides, for what he'd planned this night, having Fantôme along could only bring him extra luck.

But as late as Sheffield was when he was shown into the room, to his dismay the ladies—most especially Diana—had yet to present themselves. The room was as thoroughly male as any club, even to March presiding before the fireplace. On his left side stood Brecon, and on his right was Crump, with Brecon's three sons slumped together on a bench, generally ignoring their elders. At least Fantôme felt perfectly at his ease, trotting on ahead of Sheffield with his tail wagging and his tongue lolling in a wide, sloppy grin.

"Good heavens, Sheffield," March said. "You've brought that beast of yours."

"I have," Sheffield said. "Fantôme always enjoys company, you know."

March sighed, patiently submitting to Fantôme's snuffling of his shoes and legs. "He'd better behave himself, or else Charlotte will have him sent down belowstairs with our dogs for the night."

"He'll behave," Sheffield said with more confidence

than he should. "Charlotte is very fond of Fantôme, and so are your children."

"I've heard all about what happened last time he visited," Brecon said, not smiling. "Pray keep him from leaping into the pond again, Sheffield. I can promise you that ladies dressed for evening will not find his antics nearly as amusing."

Sheffield leaned down long enough to pat the dog on the back of his neck. "The pond will hold no allure for him at this hour, Brecon," he said. "He's a staunch believer in morning bathing, with not a drop of water after noon."

He smiled, but none of the other men did. He could understand why Brecon wasn't happy with him, making it clear he'd wished Sheffield had taken his advice and stayed away. He supposed March was simply being his ordinarily slightly stuffy self, and of course he never expected Crump to smile at anything.

"Have you any dogs, Crump?" he asked, idly imagining what Crump would do if he'd known Sheffield meant to steal away his bride.

"No, Your Grace, I do not possess dogs," he said, and that was that. His thin-lipped expression did not change, nor did he so much as blink. How the devil could anyone expect Diana to marry a man as dull and humorless as this?

Even March glanced toward the door with obvious desperation. "I wonder what is keeping the ladies so long."

Brecon, too, looked longingly toward the door. "You know how ladies are," he said. "Every curl and ruffle must be perfect before they can show themselves."

"I should rather not be kept from the table," Crump said. He drew his watch from his pocket, frowning down at the face. "It is neither healthy nor agreeable to the constitution to dine so late in the evening."

Fortunately Fantôme had wandered toward the three young men on the bench, giving Sheffield an excuse to follow. He'd always liked Brecon's sons, partly because they were closer to his age than his older cousins. They'd grown significantly since he'd seen them last, no longer the boys he'd remembered, but young gentlemen in their own right. Lord Hargreaves, or Harry, was the oldest, and Brecon's heir, with Lord Geoffrey close on his heels, both tall and dark-haired and much like their father. Lord Rivers, the youngest, was still at school, and even now had his nose in a book, striving to distance himself from his older brothers.

Which, perhaps, was not such a bad idea. It was clear that Harry and Geoff, newly returned from their tour of the Continent, had acquired a foreign taste for gaudy waistcoats and exaggerated collars, along with a studied swagger that could only have been acquired from pursuing French and Italian ladies of dubious morality. Sheffield recognized the signs at once, and it made him feel nostalgic, and a little old, too.

Most noteworthy, however, were the spectacles that both Harry and Geoff were affecting, square silver frames with dark green lenses that must have made seeing much of anything difficult in the candlelit room. Sheffield could tell by the way they peered over the tops of the foolish glasses, like old scholars instead of young lords, as they dutifully rose to bow at his approach.

"What new fashion is this?" he asked. "Will we all be wearing colored spectacles to balls next season?"

"Father won't," Geoff said with cheerful relish. "He loathes them. He says they make us look like blind beggars."

"All the gentlemen of fashion wear them in Venice," Harry said, more world-weary. "They are excellent protection against the glare from the canals."

"I wager they're also excellent protection against the

morning glare stumbling half-drunk from a brothel, too," Sheffield observed. "Mornings can be like that."

Harry and Geoff laughed, but Rivers only groaned dramatically.

"I wish I had spectacles to protect me against *you*," he said to his brothers, putting aside his book to pet Fantôme. "You two look like a right pair of asses, and you bray like asses, too."

But no one was listening to him, because the ladies had just entered the room.

"Damn," said Harry with hushed reverence. "Isn't Cousin Diana splendid!"

Sheffield could only agree. Diana *was* splendid, so splendid that it made his heart squeeze tight in his chest. He'd never seen her look like this, with her hair powdered and diamonds around her throat and her expression so serene and noble that she was more like a goddess than a mere mortal woman, drifting into the room on a cloud of rustling silvery silk.

A serene goddess, that is, until she glanced his way and spotted him, over the shoulder of her elderly Aunt Sophronia. Her eyes brightened and her cheeks flushed and her lips parted with surprise and eagerness. It was only a second that he'd held her gaze, only a second that she'd dropped her carefully composed mask before she quickly looked away, but it had been enough to tell him what he needed most to know.

When he asked her to marry him, she'd say yes.

He fought the urge to throw himself at her feet and ask her now, before everyone. That, of course, would not succeed. He might be desperate, but he wasn't a fool. If he did that, he'd be locked away in the scullery with the rest of the ill-behaved dogs, and they wouldn't release him until it was too late and she was married to Crump.

No, he'd have to bide his time and let the whole wretched evening progress until the right moment. He'd have only one chance, and like every good thief, he'd have to make it count. Until then, he'd have to keep politely distant, even disinterested, so that no one would suspect him.

One chance, one chance . . .

But was there anything more difficult than watching Diana with Crump as she curtseyed gracefully before him, displaying that dizzying expanse of creamy white breast as she did?

Yet Crump's face remained as impassive as ever. He didn't so much as offer Diana his hand to lift her up, merely flicking his fingers instead to signify she might rise. She did, and while the others smiled their approval, she leaned close to Crump, her hand on his black sleeve, and brushed her lips against his pockmarked cheek with the shyest of kisses. As pretty a gesture as this was by a bride to her groom, for Sheffield it was pure torment, and he couldn't help imagining her kissing him instead, the feather-light touch of her fingers on his arm, the softness of her lips against his cheek, the heady scent of her perfume as she leaned close.

No man outside of his grave could withstand such attention without reacting, and Crump didn't, either.

He sneezed.

He sneezed, and sneezed again, waving his hand to make Diana step back. He sneezed so loudly he seemed to explode with the force of it, groping blindly for his handkerchief. At last he covered most of his face with a small cloud of white linen, wheezing and gasping as his eyes turned red and bulged from his head.

"What is wrong, Crump?" asked March with concern. "What can we do to ease you?"

Crump shook his head and sneezed again, his wig slipping askew from the violence of it. At Brecon's beckoning, a footman hurried forward with an armchair, and Crump sank into it.

"I'll send for a physician, Lord Crump," Charlotte said, her worried voice rising over his sneezing.

He shook his head, wheezing. "Not—not necessary," he gasped. "Will—will pass."

March rested his hand on his shoulder. "No need to be courageous about this, Crump," he said. "A good physician can—"

"I—I beg you not," Crump implored. "It—it is passing already."

Indeed, as he sat in the chair, he did seem to be improving, his sneezes subsiding, while everyone watched and waited around him.

"Cats," he finally managed to say. "Forgive me, Your Grace, but is there a cat somewhere in this house?"

"I have a cat," Diana said, stepping forward. "Her name is Fig, and she is my dearest pet."

He held up his hand to keep her at a distance. "I cannot tolerate cats," he said. "They are the devil's own creatures, and as poison to me. Your cat must be sent away at once."

"No!" exclaimed Diana. "I love Fig! She is coming with me tomorrow. I already have her basket prepared for traveling."

"If you bring that cat, Lady Diana, I shall myself wring its neck and fling its body from the carriage," Crump declared, his red-rimmed eyes so determined that there was no doubt he'd do exactly as he said. "Unless you wish to become a widow as soon as you are a wife, you will never bring a cat near me, nor suffer one to soil your person with its vile scent."

"How dare you even speak such cruelty!" cried Diana furiously. "Fig is like a child to me, my lord, and impossibly dear, and for you to say you would willfully harm her—"

"Hush, Diana, hush," Lady Hervey said, stepping between Diana and Lord Crump. "You can't expect his lordship to risk his own health for the sake of your pet. After you are wed, Fig can continue to live here at Marchbourne House, and you may visit her whenever you are in town."

"She may do no such thing, Lady Hervey," Crump said, displaying more emotion than he ever had before. "I will not permit my wife to have any contact with cats, or let herself be tainted by them."

"You cannot keep me from Fig," Diana declared, anger ringing in her voice, "and if you try, then I—"

"You will come with me, if you please, Diana," Charlotte said, grabbing her by the arm to pull her back. "Mama, may I ask you to lead everyone to the table? Diana and I shall join you shortly."

Unceremoniously Charlotte hauled Diana from the room, while Lady Hervey assumed the role of hostess and saw that March took Aunt Sophronia in to dinner with the rest following. It was rare to have more gentlemen than ladies, gentlemen usually being at a premium at London's dining tables, but because both Charlotte and Diana were absent, Sheffield found himself not only left to walk with Brecon's sons but seated with them, too. He suspected Charlotte had not entirely followed protocol with her chairs—he was, after all, a duke, and entitled to sit as close to the head of the table as possible—and had instead placed Diana and Crump side by side, as the guests of honor, and banished Sheffield to the distant end with the young gentlemen. It rather reminded him—and not in an agreeable way, either—of being twelve and at the children's dining table again. At least he could feel Fantôme beneath the table, settling familiarly at his feet to offer canine solace; not exactly what he wished, but better than nothing.

Matters failed to improve as Aunt Sophronia launched into an unstoppable discourse on the superiority of her dogs over both her late husbands. It lasted through the first remove, giving Sheffield plenty of time to worry that Diana would not return. How would he be able to persuade her to marry him if he didn't see her again?

But as the fish was being brought, she and Charlotte at last reappeared. Charlotte was overly cheerful, while Diana was glowering and clearly still murderous. Sheffield was delighted. When Diana was in a temper and spitting sparks, he found her to be wildly attractive—he'd only to remember her in the pond—and having her still unhappy with Crump would help his own cause.

And unhappy with Crump she was. She took her chair beside her intended without once meeting his eye, nor did she do more than answer his questions with a single curt word.

Sheffield drank his wine, and watched, and waited. Who would have guessed that homely small cat could be of such assistance to him?

"You reek of laundering soap, Diana," Aunt Sophronia announced to the rest of the table. "Is that what Charlotte had to use to make you agreeable to his lordship? Scrubbed you down with lye, did she?"

"Aunt Sophronia, please," murmured Charlotte. "The matter has been addressed and resolved, and need not be discussed further."

"What hasn't been resolved is Diana's poor little pet," Aunt Sophronia said, holding her wineglass up to the nearest footman to refill. "What manner of gentleman is so overnice and dainty that he can't bear his wife keeping a pet or two?"

"Aunt Sophronia, no more," Lady Hervey said, more sternly than Charlotte. "We're here to celebrate the wedding of Diana to Lord Crump, and to welcome him into our family."

Aunt Sophronia grumbled to herself, and whatever she said further did not reach Sheffield's ears. But it was soon clear that what she'd said had left its mark. The conversation for the rest of the meal was dull and forced, with difficult silences that seemed to stretch to an eternity that not even the ever-witty Brecon could fill.

By the time Charlotte rose to signal the end of the meal, the relief was palpable. In honor of the evening, a small group of musicians and singers had been hired to perform love songs in Italian. It was a charming entertainment before a wedding, but especially welcome this night because the music would fill the long, difficult silences, making conversation unnecessary.

Now Sheffield was perfectly content to be among the young gentlemen straggling on their way from the dining table to the music room. It was easy enough to stop one of the footmen in the hall before he joined the others, and easy, too, to take a seat at the back of the drawing room, near the second door. Fantôme squeezed beneath his chair, curling inside the imagined security of the four legs, and promptly fell into a wheezing sleep. Finally everyone else was settled, too, and as attentive as they'd ever be, and the musicians began.

Over and over Sheffield glanced at his watch, praying that the servant wouldn't forget his little errand. The task would be minor enough to the footman (especially considering the half crown that Sheffield had given him), but it would mean everything to Sheffield.

He checked his watch again, sighed, and shifted restlessly in his chair. Beside him, Harry had fallen asleep behind his tinted spectacles and was snoring gently. Sheffield couldn't blame him. Any other night, and the warbling singer would have reduced him to somnolent bliss, too.

Finally the door to the front of the room eased open, and the footman he'd bribed slipped through it, a salver in his hand and the note that Sheffield had given him on it. With the practiced discretion of a ducal household, he

made his way to Diana, and held the salver and the note
to her.

From where Sheffield sat, he could not see Diana's
face, or even if she'd opened the note. His heart racing,
he willed her to follow the instructions he'd written:

My own Sultana,
I beg you come speak with me now in the garden
near the pond. Your happiness & mine depend upon
it. Tell any who may ask that you've been summoned
by your maidservant, & pray do not fail me, else you
will wound my heart to the quick.
  When I see you leave, I shall follow, and join you.
        —The one who loves you above all others

He saw her bow her head, turning slightly away from
Crump. She was reading his note; she was keeping its
contents secret. Sheffield held his breath, daring to hope.

She leaned toward Crump, whispering something,
then rose and left the room. No one turned to watch or
tried to stop her. Instead everyone kept their well-bred
attention on the singer.

Somehow Sheffield kept from shouting with joy, from
leaping about like a madman. Somehow he kept his seat
as he silently counted the sixty seconds that make up a
minute, then rose and walked slowly toward the second
door. To his dismay, Geoff looked up as he passed, and
caught his sleeve to stop him.

"Where are you going?" he whispered, more mouth-
ing the words than speaking them.

"To piss," Sheffield whispered back, the all-purpose
excuse of every man.

Geoff nodded sagely, then closed his eyes and tipped
his head to one side over his folded hands to mimic
sleeping, his critique of the singer. Sheffield hurried away

before Geoff could think of any other great cleverness to pass the time, or, worse, decided to join him.

By the time he'd reached the garden door, his thoughts were racing through every dismal possibility, trying to guard himself against disappointment.

She would not be there.

She would not listen.

She would send him away.

She would refuse outright.

She would declare her love for Crump and her dislike for him.

She would—

But then she *was* there, standing in the opening beneath the trees like a spun-silver fairy in the moonlight, reflected in the pond's inky surface.

She waited for him to join her, her hands clasped tightly at her waist.

"Diana," he said. "You came."

"Only because you called me Sultana." She tossed her head to one side, flipping the single long lovelock back over her shoulder. "I can't stay long."

"No," he said, wondering what had become of the elegant speech he'd been practicing all day long. "No."

"Speak, Sheffield," she said impatiently, "else I'll toss you into the pond for your impertinence."

"I'm not impertinent," he said. "Not about this, anyway."

He dropped to his knees before her, remembering at least that much of his rehearsal. The dew had already fallen and the grass was wet, instantly soaking through the knees of his breeches, but it would all be worth it if only she'd say yes.

But he'd have to ask first, and he could think of not a single thing to say. Every last word and syllable had vanished, leaving him to stare up at her with a head as empty and bereft of intelligence as a summer melon.

"Sheffield," she asked finally, "are you drunk?"

He fumbled in his waistcoat for his mother's ring. Damnation, his fingers were shaking, even as he held the ring up to her. The emerald seemed to glow in his hand, magical in the moonlight, and he remembered his father and mother and how happy and in love they'd been.

And at last the words came, or at least all the words that mattered.

"I love you, Diana," he said, "and I'll never love any other woman as much as I love you. Marry me, and be my love, my wife, my duchess."

She stared at him, her hands still clasped, but her eyes were enormous. "You are serious?"

He nodded. "And my sultana. I forgot that before. Marry me, Diana, and be my sultana."

CHAPTER

16

In an evening marked by grim reality, Diana did not trust any of this to be real. How could it be?

To have the ever-witty and charming Duke of Sheffield, surely the most resolute bachelor she'd ever known and the one (the only one, fortunately) who'd impulsively, wondrously ruined her, kneeling on the grass before her and fumbling and mumbling through a proposal of marriage: could there be anything more unreal than that?

"Are you sure you are not drunk, Sheffield?" she asked. "Even a little?"

"Not at all," he said, almost sheepish. "This would, be vastly easier if I were."

It wasn't easy for her, either. Not the loving part, for that had been easy from the first. She knew she loved him, loved him with every scrap of her being. She always would love him, too, no matter how she tried to love anyone else. But did he truly love her in return, enough to be her only love, her husband, her duke, the father of her children? Perhaps even her sultan? It was an enormous obligation to expect of any man, and Sheffield was hardly any ordinary man.

"You are not marrying me because of—of what we did?" she asked carefully, needing to be certain. "I would never want you to wed me because you felt you must."

"Do you mean if there should be a child?" he asked. "No. And if I marry you now, before you know, then there must never be any doubt in your heart—though it would kill me to see a child of ours raised by Crump. I wish to marry you because I love you, and for no other reason than that."

Then the clouds slid free of the moon and moonlight spilled onto the ring in his fingers, the emerald glittering with a brilliant, otherworldly green. She'd seen this ring before, and with a shock she remembered where: the portrait of his mother, the one that hung in the Sultana Room. This had been her betrothal ring, the one that his father had vowed was pirate's plunder for the prettiest duchess in the world.

Sheffield would not jest about his mother's ring. If he intended to seal his love for her with this ring, then he meant every word of love he'd said, even the part about being his sultana. She could trust him. She *did* trust him.

What else could she do but accept?

"Yes, Sheffield, I will," she said, sinking down to her knees beside him. If he'd humble himself in the grass before, then it seemed only fair that she do it, too. "I will marry you."

She watched as he pushed the ring onto her finger, and then he kissed her. It wasn't like any other kiss he'd given her. It was almost *reverential*, which by her thinking would not do.

"If I am to put aside all other men for you, Sheffield," she said, looping her arms around his shoulders, "then you must kiss me better than that. Kiss me not as a wife but as a sultana."

He grinned and did exactly that, kissing her with such passion and ardor that if she hadn't been holding so tightly to him, she might have toppled over completely. Even when he finally paused, the urge to topple remained strong, and she realized if she didn't stand up now, she'd soon be in exactly the same posture as she'd been in on that settee.

Instead she wisely clambered back to her feet and kissed him that way before finally she pulled away.

"We must go back," she said, breathless with happiness and kissing. "We must tell everyone that you've asked me to marry you and that I've said yes, and I must tell Lord Crump that he's free, and—"

"No," he interrupted. "We won't do any of that. No one wants us to marry, and I've no desire to listen to them offer a thousand sensible reasons why we shouldn't. I've no patience for that, Diana."

"But what else can we do?" she asked. He was right about how unhappy her family would be. Her mother and aunt and sisters would offer endless horrifying reasons for why she'd be happier with Lord Crump than Sheffield any day, reasons she didn't believe but didn't wish to hear, either. Why should she, when she'd heard most of them already? "We have no choice but to tell them."

"Not tonight," he said. "I'll come back for you later, after everyone's asleep, and we'll elope. No one can argue with us if we return as man and wife."

"Elope?" she said, unable to contain her excitement. Eloping was the most romantic thing she could possibly imagine, and if there were any way to improve upon marrying Sheffield, then running away to marry him would be it. "Like Lady Enid and Dr. Pullings?"

"Like my parents," he said, and kissed her again. "Bring only what you must, and only what you can carry. I shall meet you by the servants' stair two hours past midnight, and—"

"Oh, no, not by the stairs," she said. "Someone's bound to see me there. I'll climb from my window and meet you in the garden below."

"Climb from your window?" he asked, mystified. "Diana, I cannot see how—"

"It's no trouble at all," she assured him, pointing up to her bedchamber. "That window, there, second from the end. That's my room. I've done it before. There's a line of bricks that sticks out from the wall beneath my window, and then there's a little porch roof, and *then* I can slide right down, where you'll be waiting. In the country I climbed trees all the time, and the wall is much easier than that."

He frowned. "I would never forgive myself if you fell."

"I won't, I promise." She looked down at the ring on her finger, then reluctantly slipped it off and returned it to him. "You'll have to give this to me again, later. It can be my wedding ring instead if you'd like."

"What I'd like is to have you safely as my wife," he said gruffly, using her return of the ring as an excuse to kiss her fingertips, one by one. "Very well, then. I see now that life with you shall never lack for adventure."

She grinned happily. "Never. It's one of my qualities. You shall never be bored in my company."

"I shall hold you to that, sweet," he said, and winked, the kind of sly wink that could make her do anything, or could if only he realized its power. "At two hours past midnight, I shall be standing beneath that window, waiting for you."

She took a deep breath. "I should warn you that I'm bringing Fig," she said, unable to forget Lord Crump's terrible threat against the little cat. "I cannot leave her behind."

"I never expected you to abandon Fig," he said easily. "I'll be bringing Fantôme as well."

She shook her head, still anxious for Fig's safety. "I shall have her in a basket, but you must be sure she is safe from Fantôme."

"You have my word," he said. "Though I fear far more for Fantôme's sake than hers. For all her size, Fig is very brave and bold, and poor Fantôme is not at all."

"Oh, Sheffield, you are *perfect*." She quickly kissed him again, then hurried back toward the house. She wasn't sure how long she'd been away, yet nothing had changed in the music room. The same pop-eyed woman was singing what sounded like the same mournful song, her sister and her mother and her aunt, Lord Crump and March and Brecon and his sons, were all sitting in the same chairs, dutifully listening as if they cared for the same mournful song—except for the young lords, all three of whom seemed now to be asleep.

She slipped into her chair beside Lord Crump, ready to offer some nonsensical excuse. He glanced at her, noted that she'd returned, and looked back to the singer. He didn't smile, ask where she'd been, or even inquire why she'd damp spots on the front of her skirts. It was the same response she always earned from him, a benign lack of attention that was just shy of ignoring her. Except that this time it didn't fill her with despair or unhappiness. Now she felt nothing but joy, for soon, very soon, she'd be forever free of Lord Crump and married to Sheffield.

But though Lord Crump did not ask where she'd been, her absence hadn't gone entirely unnoticed. Much later, when all the guests had left and Diana was undressed and in bed trying to write the note she'd leave behind, Charlotte came to her bedchamber, a single candlestick in her hand. She wore a flowered silk dressing gown over her nightshift, her long dark hair braided in two thick plaits over her shoulders and her blue eyes filled with concern.

"You are still awake, Di?" she asked, then chuckled ruefully. "Of course you are. You wouldn't be sitting here with the candles lit if you weren't. But what bride sleeps the night before her wedding?"

"Then I am no different." Diana smiled, wishing again that she could confide in Charlotte, and that she hadn't had to shove her unfinished note beneath the covers. "I thought you'd be Mama."

Charlotte climbed on Diana's bed, tucking her feet beneath her dressing gown. "Mama went to bed hours ago. She so feared she'd not sleep that she took a draft, and asked not to be disturbed until morning. The very roof could fall in, and she'd not wake now."

"She might as well sleep," Diana said, wishing she'd been able to say farewell to Mama, too, the way it now seemed she was to Charlotte. She wouldn't be gone long with Sheffield, only the time it took for them to wed, but when she returned everything would be as different as if she'd been gone a year. She glanced around the room at the trunks that were packed for her journey with Lord Crump—the trip that now she would not take. "There's nothing left for me to do, you see. Everything is in readiness."

"I am glad," Charlotte said, also looking about at the trunks and chests. "I won't keep you, then. But I did have one question from this evening."

Diana's smile faded to wariness. If anyone would suspect her plan to elope with Sheffield, it would be Charlotte.

"When you were in my chamber before everyone arrived," she began, "I could see how unhappy you were, and how much you dreaded this marriage. When Lord Crump had his fit, blaming it upon poor Fig, I thought you might break off with him then and there. I haven't seen you so angry for years, Diana."

Hearing her name, Fig appeared, climbing into Diana's lap. "How could I not be angry, Charlotte? You heard him. It was the cruelest thing I've ever heard a gentleman say."

"It was indeed," Charlotte said, nodding. "It did not favor Lord Crump at all. I can only hope that he was shamed and unwell after his fit, and that is why he lashed out at Fig. I do expect him to apologize once he has had time to reflect on his words."

Diana didn't answer, not nearly as confident of that apology. She knew she'd slender experience in the world's ways, but she had observed that men who threatened and beat their horses or dogs were generally the same ones who mistreated their wives and children. Despite Lord Crump's reputation for Christian generosity, she'd been so shocked by his threats against her cat that she had already half resolved to refuse him even before Sheffield had proposed. She wasn't exactly sure how she would have accomplished that, but to save both Fig and herself, she would have found a way, even if it had meant refusing him in the middle of the ceremony itself.

"But what puzzles me is this, Di," Charlotte continued. "You were miserably unhappy. Then during the entertainment, you left for perhaps a quarter of an hour, and when you returned, you were another person entirely. You couldn't stop smiling, and you'd become so joyful that even Aunt Sophronia took note. What caused so sudden a change in you, Diana? What happened to bring about that joy?"

Diana looked down at Fig, tracing the patterns in her fur to avoid meeting Charlotte's gaze.

"I went to the garden to—to order my thoughts," she said, picturing Sheffield, not Lord Crump, and striving to keep her words to be as true as possible. "Marriage is so important to a woman that I wished to be sure. When I asked myself if I respected and loved and trusted the man I was to marry, I realized that I did, and my entire spirit grew light and full of joy. That must have been what you saw."

"Dear Diana, I am so happy for you!" Charlotte exclaimed with relief and joy of her own. "That is all I ever wished for you, to find the same happiness, trust, and love that I have with March."

She leaned forward and kissed Diana tenderly on the forehead. "Good night now, lamb. Try to sleep if you can, for tomorrow will be full of excitement."

Diana hugged Charlotte close, already missing her. Tomorrow would indeed be full of excitement, far more than Charlotte could guess, and when it was done, none of their lives would ever be the same.

Three hours later, that excitement began.

At this time in the night, the great house was still, with highborn and low all asleep in their beds. That alone was exciting for Diana, to be wide awake while the rest of the household was not. She was dressed simply in a plain linen bodice and petticoat, clothes left from the old days at Ransom that were more suited for a London servant than a soon-to-be duchess, but it was more important that she be able to dress herself without a maid than that she impress with her grandeur. Besides, the ordinary clothes would be a kind of disguise, making their adventure even more exciting.

For the last time, she read the letter she was leaving behind for her sister and mother. The letter had been much more difficult to write than she'd thought, and wasn't nearly as noble as she'd wanted to make it. It wasn't even as neat as it should have been, with several blots and crossed-out words.

Dearest, dearest Mama & Charlotte,
When you read this I shall be far away, having
followed my heart & married Sheffield. I know
this will be a terrible shock to you, but I love him
beyond measure & he loves me the same & we
will be most rapturously happy together, which
I would not ever be with Lord Crump. I pray the
scandal will not be too great & that you & everyone

*else will find it possible to Forgive me & offer your
blessings upon us.*

> *Your most affectionate daughter & sister,*
> *D.*

She sighed, wishing she could have explained her decision more clearly. She didn't doubt she was doing the right thing by marrying Sheffield, but she also realized the enormousness of it, and how it would be perceived. She was jilting Lord Crump. There was no nicer way to say it. She was disobeying her family, turning her back on her duty to them, and by her actions, she was causing them considerable unhappiness and trouble. She would become the centerpiece of gossip and scandal, not just among their circle but in the papers as well. While eloping with a duke instead of marrying a marquis would be considered advantageous by some, there would be many others who would see only the shocking circumstances, and even as a duchess, she would not be welcomed in every house, at least not in the beginning.

Most of all, by eloping she would be behaving in exactly the impulsive manner for which she had been faulted and scolded for all her life. Yet now, because she loved Sheffield, it seemed to her that impulsiveness was the virtue and obedience would have been the sin, and she could only pray her family could understand.

The second note, for Lord Crump, was much shorter, and had been much easier to write, too.

To His Lordship the Earl of Crump:
*My Lord, I free you of your obligation to wed me,
for I cannot find sufficient love in my heart to be
the wife you deserve. I thank you for the regard
you have shown me & beg your forgiveness,*

> *Yr. serv't,*
> *Lady Diana Wylder*

She set the two letters side by side on her pillow, where they wouldn't be missed. With a final sigh, she turned away and went to open her window.

The same quarter moon she'd seen earlier still shone in the London night, full of promise and silvery light as it ducked in and out of gathering clouds. A lovely, beauteous moon, she decided, and exactly the ideal moon for eloping. How could anything done beneath such a moon be wrong? With a chirp, Fig jumped on the sill beside her, rubbing her head against Diana's shoulder.

"Here you are, Miss Fig," she said, gathering the cat securely into her arms. "The last thing I wish is to have to chase you about the garden tonight. Come, into your basket now."

She pulled Fig's wicker traveling basket from beneath the bed and tried to lower the cat inside.

"Blast you, stop fighting," she muttered as she struggled to maneuver the cat, suddenly all hissing and rigid paws and claws, into the basket. "Stop this, or I'll leave you behind, and then you'll be sorry."

At last she pressed the lid down and buckled the straps to keep it closed while Fig mewed piteously. Diana flung her cloak over her shoulders and hurried back to the window. She opened the sash wider, wincing a bit at the unavoidable squeak, and leaned forward.

There was Sheffield, standing beneath her. He wore a long, dark cloak and a sword, and had a black cocked hat pulled low over his brow, all wonderfully mysterious.

"Sheffield!" she called softly. "Sheffield, here!"

At once he looked up, his handsome face turned toward her. He smiled warmly, which was very fine, and then pointed to the watch in his hand, which was not quite so fine. Time might be of the essences, but it wasn't particularly romantic to be reminded of the hour like this. She blew him a kiss from her fingertips anyway, and hurried back to gather the valise with her few well-chosen belongings and Fig's basket.

"Gardy-loo!" she called softly, and dropped the valise from the window. Sheffield caught it with a grunt, clearly surprised by how heavy it was, and set it on the ground beside him. He held his hands up, beckoning.

She grinned and set the basket with Fig on the sill. She checked the rope she'd threaded through the basket one more time, and slowly began to lower it from the sill. The frightened cat made the basket swing and jerk, but finally it came within Sheffield's reach. He caught it by the handle, and as he began to coil the rope on top, Fig growled from within.

"What in blazes is in there?" he said, staring warily into the basket. At once Fantôme appeared like a portly ghost in the moonlight, trotting over to sniff at the growling basket. "Is that Fig?"

"It is," Diana said. She sat on the edge of the window-sill and swung her legs over the edge. "You keep Fantôme away from her. She's frightened enough as it is."

"She's making a precious great amount of noise for being frightened," Sheffield said, skeptically peering into the basket along with Fantôme.

Diana recognized the potential for disaster. "Please mind Fantôme, Sheffield."

But her warning came too late. Swiftly Fig's paw swiped through the wicker to catch the bulldog's nose, making him howl with pain and tumble backward.

"That's your fault, Sheffield," Diana called. "Poor Fantôme! Hush him now, if you can, else he'll raise the watch and the kitchen staff, too."

"Your cat's a vicious wild beast," Sheffield said, doing his best to calm the dog, who was slinking far from the basket with his tail between his legs. "I told you my mild-mannered Fantôme would bear the worst of the bargain."

"I did warn you," she said, tossing her shoes and rolled-up stockings to the grass beside him, for it was much easier to climb down in bare feet than in slippery leather soles. She turned and began to slide from the sill, holding on while her toes felt for the brick stringcourse. The architect who had designed Marchbourne House had doubtless intended the neat rows of protruding bricks and pilasters only for their appearance, but Diana had always found them as good as a ladder built into the house's wall, and she moved quickly, with nimble confidence.

"Let me help you, sweet," Sheffield called gallantly. "Jump, and I'll catch you."

"You needn't," Diana said. "I'm almost down."

She edged her way to the roof of the porch, turned on the slates, and then began to lower herself over the edge. She was perfectly capable of making the small drop into the flower bed, but Sheffield charged forward, trampling through the spring pinks and foxgloves to seize her boldly around the waist.

"Oh, my goodness!" she exclaimed breathlessly. Her skirts had flown up when she'd fallen, forcing him to hold her around her bare legs, and as she struggled to pull her skirts down, he did nothing to help her but laugh. In all the times she'd climbed from windows, she had never once been caught like this, as if she were fragile and helpless. It was pleasant enough to feel his arms around her, but it was also a bit disconcerting, too, until he kissed her. That she'd expected, and she twined her arms around his neck to kiss him back, by way of showing she didn't really mind him trying to catch her. He really was excellent at kissing (much better than at catching her), and before long she'd completely forgotten all about how he'd fussed about Fig and trampled Charlotte's flowers, and everything else besides.

Fortunately, his memory was better.

"Enough, Diana, as much as I am loath to say so," he said, disentangling her arms from around his neck and gently setting her down. "I wish to be far away before you're missed."

She hurried to retrieve her shoes and Fig's basket, while he brought her valise and Fantôme. They slipped through the garden gate and back toward one of the streets bordering the park, where a nondescript hackney coach was waiting.

"This is a masquerade, isn't it?" she whispered as he helped her climb inside. The hackney itself was an adventure, for ladies like her never rode in common hired carriages with murky recesses and unspecified pasts. To be in one with a man like Sheffield was almost too exciting to express. "No one will ever guess we're inside."

"That's rather the point, isn't it?" Sheffield said as he hoisted Fantôme on the opposite seat. "Subterfuge and disguise, dissembling and masquerade. All part of a good elopement."

"You say that as if you've eloped before," she said. "You haven't, have you?"

"Why would you even ask such a question?" he said indignantly, settling beside her. "I can absolutely tell you, with no subterfuge or dissembling, that you are the only woman I've ever eloped with, or wished to."

"Ever?" she asked, turning her face up toward his.

"Ever, ever," he said, curling his arm around her shoulders to draw her closer. "The only one. It's a fine thing that I love you as much as I do."

She smiled, and kissed him in such a delicious and leisurely fashion that it was almost as if they were already wed.

"Where are we to be married?" she asked, feeling foolish for not knowing something so important. There hadn't been time to ask for such details earlier in the evening. He had asked her to marry him, she had accepted, they'd agreed to elope, and that had been all. "How long before we arrive there?"

He sighed. As they rumbled along through the London streets, the lights from passing lanterns fell across his face in ever-changing patterns. "It's not so easy as that, sweet."

"I know it's not," she said, twisting about to face him. "The laws are against clandestine marriages, and require couples to have their banns read for three weeks before a marriage can take place. Unless, that is, the couple procures a special license."

He stared down at her. "How the devil do you come to such knowledge?"

"Because Lord Crump had to acquire such a license to wed me," she said. "A perfectly good license that I suppose shall now go to waste."

"A good thing that ours shall not," he said, patting the front of his coat, where she presumed he kept the all-important document. "But I wish there to be no doubt of our marriage, and not the faintest grounds for anyone to challenge it. Therefore we are heading for Oakworth, my house in Hampshire. We'll be wed on my land, in what amounts to my county, and by a nearby bishop who owes me an honorable favor, all making for as ironclad a marriage as can be arranged in a day."

"Goodness," she said, impressed by his diligence. "It sounds wonderfully ironclad to me."

She was thankful for that, too. Although her marriage to Lord Crump was likewise to have been a hastily arranged ceremony, she'd never doubted that it would be legal and binding, not with so many solicitors involved in the settlements and dukes as witnesses.

But an elopement was by its very nature constructed on a less steady foundation. She and Sheffield weren't an ordinary couple, racing off to be wed by the blacksmith of Gretna Green for the sake of love alone. There were nearly royal titles and vast fortunes involved, not just for them but for their children as well. She thought shyly of the child she might even now be carrying within her, who, if a son, could one day become the next Duke of Sheffield. For his sake, there must be nothing to challenge his legitimacy or other entitlement to the dukedom. It would have been far easier if they'd wed in the abbey, the way Charlotte and March had, where there could never be any doubts, but the displeasure of their families had made that impossible.

Still, she liked the thoroughly respectable sound of the word *ironclad*. For an elopement, ironclad was likely the best that could be expected.

"We must change hackneys twice before we reach Oakworth," he was saying. "While we can pause briefly for refreshment, I'd prefer to continue onward rather than stopping at an inn, not until we are wed. Just because I've dishonored you once doesn't mean I intend to do it again."

Her smile turned lopsided with emotion. "Truly? You will wait until we are wed?"

"I will," he said. "Which means you must, too."

She was proud that he would wish to be so honorable and noble in this regard. To her, having been already ruined by him, it did not seem to matter quite so much if she was ruined another time or two before they were married, so long as they finally were. Still, it was admirable that he wished to wait, even if she wasn't entirely certain that either of them would show such resolve.

"However, since we will stop twice to change horses," he said, "it's best we use a false name to cover our tracks. I'll leave it to you to choose one you like."

That was another sobering thought. It had been a fine adventure to climb from the window and run away with him as she had. But in the morning, when Sarah came to wake her and would discover her note, the uproar in the house would be considerable. She didn't doubt that March and likely Brecon, too, would come roaring furiously after them, and it would be better—*much* better— if she and Sheffield were wed before they were found.

"Mr. and Mrs. Hart," she said finally. "Because that is what I have given you."

He chuckled. "Very well then, Mrs. Hart, if that is what you wish to be. But only until I can announce you to the world as my duchess."

"I'll like that, too." She heard a ragged pattering on the roof of the hackney, and she glanced at the first drops as they struck the windows. "Look, Sheffield, I think it's raining."

"Blast, it is," he said, leaning forward. "Pray that it's only a shower, so the roads don't become muck and slow our progress. I want this journey to be a question of hours, not days."

She sighed and pillowed her head against his shoulder. She thought again of Charlotte's wish for her, that she find the same love, trust, and happiness with the man she wed as Charlotte had found with March. She'd no doubt that she loved Sheffield, and already he'd made her happier than anyone else in the world. Now she trusted him, too, not only with her heart but with her future and honor as well. She had to; it was too late to turn back now, even if she'd wished to.

"I do not care how long it rains, Sheffield," she said softly, "so long as I'm with you."

"And I with you, my love," he repeated, pulling her close to kiss. "So long as I'm with you."

CHAPTER

🌺 *17* 🌺

Sheffield was sure he'd thought of everything.

Remembering how easily Brecon had discovered the details of Lady Enid's elopement, he'd planned this one entirely himself, not trusting even Marlowe with the details. He'd only the day to make his arrangements, but still he believed he'd thought of everything, from not hiring the hackney in advance, but simply on the street, to having Bishop Pence waiting at Oakworth to marry them the moment they arrived. The special license had been the most difficult, but he'd managed that, too, though it had cost him a sizable amount. He'd even sent word to have the duchess's bedchamber at Oakworth readied for her arrival, and filled with roses from the gardens. He wished he could have offered her the grand ducal wedding that she deserved with all her family around her, but under the circumstances, he thought, he'd done admirably well.

Earlier this night, Diana had told him he was perfect. He wasn't, not at all, but for her he'd done his best.

If only it hadn't rained.

They'd not even been a mile from Marchbourne House when it had begun, a light spring shower that he prayed would pass. But before long the shower had swelled to a driving torrent that lashed so hard against them that it felt as if entire bucketfuls of water were being heaved against the coach. The weary old hackney was far from a seaworthy vessel, and sprang leaks not only at the windows but through the roof.

At first it all had made Diana laugh, merrily shifting seats to dodge one leak, and then another. But as the storm had continued, there soon were no dry places left, and though he wrapped her in his cloak, he still could feel her shivering against him from the damp. Adding to general gloom was Fantôme, who hated being wet and moaned and groaned like a rheumy old man on the seat across from them; Fig answered with her own yowls of feline misery.

But the worst was happening on the road itself. The hackney's horses were laboring hard against the wind and rain, and Sheffield could feel how the wheels slipped and pulled in the near-flooded roads. Their progress became so slow that it felt as if they were moving only from side to side and not forward at all.

"Where are we, Sheffield?" Diana asked at last. "Can you tell?"

"Not far enough, sweet, I can tell you that." He peered through the rain and darkness, striving to make out any landmarks. "Nearly two hours, and I doubt we're much beyond the city walls."

"Truly?" she asked, the wistfulness in the single word enough to break his heart. She knew as well as he did that speed and distance were imperative, and the last thing either of them wished was to be overtaken before they were legally and finally wed. It wasn't just the humiliation of having to face Brecon and March, either. Sheffield was certain the righteous pair of them would contrive a way to steal Diana from him and perhaps even return her to Crump.

And there wouldn't be one blasted perfect thing about that.

"Perhaps we should step down and walk," she said, only half in jest. "Likely we'd go faster if we did."

"Or swim," he said. "Diana, I'm sorry that—"

"Hush, hush," she said, placing her fingers across his lips to silence him. "Why should you apologize for rain that's not your fault? Do you think Noah apologized to Mrs. Noah for the rain then?"

"Noah had nothing to apologize for, having a better ark than this wretched old vessel," he said, his mood darkening by the minute. "Besides, Mrs. Noah was already Mrs. Noah, which you are not."

"Duchess of Noah," she mused. "You must agree it has a pretty sound to it."

"Not so pretty if we float clear away to Galilee," he said. "We've stopped completely now. What the devil is that rascal of a driver about now?"

"I hope he hasn't drowned," Diana said, then gasped as the man's face appeared at the window. He did in fact look perilously close to drowned, his sodden coat plastered to his body and water streaming from his hat down his face.

"F'give me, sir," he shouted, "but th' horses can go no further, not wit'out droppin' where they stand."

"Damnation, man," Sheffield said crossly. "You can't mean to leave us stranded here. My wife's exhausted, and nearly as wet as your infernal horses."

"Hush now, Mr. Hart, I'm well enough," she said beside him, assuming her new role with remarkable ease. "Is there an inn nearby, sir? A modest place where we could wait out the storm?"

"There is indeed, mistress," the driver shouted, pointing off into the rain. "Not a hundred yards hence. I meant t' suggest it myself."

"That would be most kind of you," Diana said, smiling so warmly that the man tugged the brim of his hat to her before he climbed back up on the box.

"You didn't have to beguile the rascal," Sheffield grumbled. "*Mrs.* Hart."

"Mrs. Hart is not nearly so stuffy as the Duchess of Sheffield must be," she said, drawing closer to him inside his cloak. "Besides, no matter the rank, a smile generally accomplishes more with a man than cursing and name-calling."

She smiled up at him, determined to prove her point. He kissed her, as far as he would go toward admitting she was right, and then turned to peer through the rain at the inn.

"I can only guess what manner of infernal den he's taking us to," he said. "We'll be fortunate not to be robbed and murdered in our bed."

She leaned close to the glass beside him. "Why, it looks quite agreeable," she said. "Not an infernal den at all. Quite welcoming, actually."

But as they lumbered into the inn's yard, Sheffield swore. He couldn't help it. He'd good reason, too. He recognized the inn at once, and while it might not appear an infernal den to Diana's innocent eyes, it was damnably close. The Green Turtle was an inn pleasingly situated on the river, not far from Bagnigge Wells and barely outside the city. The house kept an excellent cellar and better cook, and was famous for the sherry-laced turtle soup that provided its name.

But the Green Turtle was far more famous for ill-fame than soup, and widely known for discretion and for assignations. It was the place where philandering gentlemen brought nubile actresses, and wayward noble wives could meet their latest cicisbeo for an afternoon's dalliance. Everyone in London knew of the Green Turtle, though no one ever admitted to having been there. Sheffield had been there himself, once or twice when he'd been much younger and lured by the infamy of the place—not that he would admit it now.

But to be cast on this particular doorstep with Diana seemed the cruelest of ironies, and the most unseemly. He had wanted to behave as honorably to her as he could, not spend their first night together—or what was left of it—in an expensive bawdy house.

"I cannot wait for a pot of hot tea, all to myself," she said as the hackney finally ground to a halt. "Though I might be persuaded to share it with you, Mr. Hart."

"We can't stay here, Diana," he said. "It's not proper."

She peered out the window as the stable boy came hurrying through the rain to open the door.

"It looks perfectly proper to me," she said. "Beggars can't be choosers, Sheffield, especially wet beggars."

Before he could explain further, the door had opened and she'd hopped out with Fig's basket in her hand. His last glimpse was of her racing toward the inn's door with Fantôme trotting at her side, leaving him to settle with the hackney's driver.

By the time he entered the inn himself, Diana was already addressing the keeper with the horrifying self-assurance of a frequent visitor.

"They've only one room left, Mr. Hart," she said, greeting him. "I took it."

"We're filled up with weary travelers this night, sir," the man said, his face impassive, or merely just wishing he were back in his own bed. "The one room's all we have left, but a fine room it is, sir, with a fine bed and a fine view of the water. The river, I mean, sir, not the rain. We've all had enough of that this night, haven't we?"

"One, ah, bed?" Sheffield asked. "Only one?"

"Aye, sir," the keeper said, patting the front of his green apron. "A fine bed it is, too. There's a looking glass in that room, too, I believe."

"A looking glass?" repeated Diana curiously. "I should expect there would be one."

"Aye, ma'am," the keeper said blandly. "A large one,

secured on a stand so as to be adjusted however one pleases."

"It's for looking, Mrs. Hart," Sheffield said hurriedly, even as his own wicked thoughts raced off to imagine all the things to be seen in that large looking glass. Damnation, why was it being so blasted difficult to behave honorably toward her? "That's, ah, what large looking glasses are for."

"Oh, aye," the keeper said. "You and Mrs. Hart won't complain, I am certain of it."

Yet still Sheffield hesitated, imagining Brecon and March discovering him and Diana in a fine bed at the Green Turtle.

"Is there, ah, no room set aside for ladies' lodgings?" he asked. "My, ah, wife prefers to sleep among others of her sex while we travel."

"I do not, Mr. Hart," Diana said, regarding him suspiciously. "I'm not so odd a duck as that."

"That's well, Mrs. Hart," said the keeper, "since we keep no separate lodgings for ladies alone. We find our guests are all wedded folk like yourselves, and wish to keep to their beds together. This way, Mrs. Hart, Mr. Hart."

Sheffield was sure the man was smirking over those names. Why hadn't Diana called them Mr. and Mrs. Sweetheart and been done with it?

She was already following the man up the stairs when Sheffield called them back. "Stop, keep, if you please. I've, ah, another request."

Slowly the man returned, while Diana waited on the bottom step. "What is it, Mr. Hart? We try to oblige our guests as best we can. Is it a special dish you wish prepared, or a favorite spirit you'd like brought up?"

In silent manful misery, Sheffield shook his head. He thought of the special license in his pocket and the emerald ring beside it, of the waiting bishop and the duchess's bedchamber filled with roses at Oakworth, and he weighed all those good and noble symbols of respectable matrimony against a room with a fine bed and large looking glass at the Green Turtle.

"Honestly, Mr. Hart," Diana said, coming to tuck her hand into his arm. Her clothes were just wet enough that they clung to her body, outlining the curves of her breasts and waist and bottom in a way that was making being honorable almost impossible. "You are being dreadfully skittish this night."

"A reverend minister," he blurted out abruptly. "A gentleman of the cloth. Any fellow from a nearby church will do. That is what I require, at once."

"A minister, sir?" The keeper looked at him dolefully. "Forgive me, Mr. Hart, but while we seek to oblige our guests, there are limits to—"

"You wish to marry me here?" Diana asked, her smile wobbling with emotion. "Now?"

"You wish to marry, ah, Mrs. Hart all over again?" the keeper asked. "Our guests don't usually do that, either, sir, but if—"

"Here." Sheffield pressed three guineas into the keeper's hand. "Find the man as soon as possible. I do not wish to wait a minute longer than necessary, and neither does Mrs. Hart."

Less than a half hour later, an elderly minister was miraculously produced, his eyes bleary from sleep and his jaw unshaven. In that time, too, the word had spread as to the noble names on the special license, and by the time the minister arrived, the Green Turtle's front room was crowded with people from the inn and the nearby village, as well as drovers and farmers on their way to the London markets. All were eager to be witnesses to the wedding, especially after Sheffield announced he'd reward every witness with a dram to drink to his bride's health.

A quarter hour after that, as the first light of day filtered through the front windows, Sheffield had put the ring once again on Diana's finger, and soundly kissed her as his new wife. A cheer of goodwill rose around them and she laughed, all the incentive he needed to sweep her from her feet and into his arms.

She shrieked with surprise and more laughter, too, her legs dangling shamelessly from her skirts as she clung to his shoulders. "Whatever are you doing, Sheffield?"

"I'm going to make you forget that skittish Mr. Hart forever," he declared. "Skittish, my foot."

He carried her up the stairs amidst the general roar of good wishes for their future and predictions for the number of their children. At the top of the stairs, she wriggled free, racing ahead down the passage as he chased after her. He caught her at the door, exactly as he suspected she'd planned, and as he kissed her, they heard the obvious sounds of another couple making noisy love in the next room.

Diana's eyes widened and she giggled. "Very inspiring."

"For us," he asked, leering as he unlatched the door, "or for them?"

He caught her up and carried her through the door, kicking it shut after them. He tossed her on the bed and she laughed again, not caring that she lay sprawled with her skirts already in inviting disarray. Lying on her back, she began to unfasten the front of her bodice, her gaze never leaving his as he tore off his coat and waistcoat.

"I know you'd planned it otherwise," she said, breathless, shrugging free of her bodice. "I know you'd wanted us to wed at Oakworth with a bishop and all, but I wouldn't wish it any other way than this, Sheffield. This is *perfect*."

"I can make it much more perfect than that, sweet," he said, tearing at the buttons on his breeches. He was already hard just from looking at her, aching and ready to make her his wife in the only way that really mattered. "And I'll make you forget that sorry bastard Mr. Hart ever—"

"Listen, Sheffield, listen." She sat up, then rolled from the bed and ran to the window that overlooked the inn's yard. "Oh, by all that's holy, Sheffield, look! It's March!"

"Damnation, no," Sheffield muttered, joining her at the window. There was no mistaking the carriage with the Marchbourne crest on the door, or the half-dozen mounted footmen in livery that rode in accompaniment. Another footman jumped down from the carriage to open the chaise's door, and March himself stepped out, which Sheffield had expected, but then Charlotte appeared as well, which he had not, both of them striding purposefully toward the inn's door.

"Quickly, we must dress again," Diana said, now dressing with the same frantic haste that she'd been undressing only a few moments before. "I don't want them to find us like this."

"Like what? Like man and wife?" Sheffield said, though he, too, was pulling his clothes back on. "They could find us naked and it wouldn't matter now."

"Yes, yes, but they don't know that yet," she said, slipping her feet into her shoes. "How do I look?"

To him she looked like a woman who'd just been caught with her lover, her clothes on but so askew that she might as well have left them off.

"You look fine," he said. "We're only going downstairs long enough to send them away, you know. March and Charlotte are excellent company, but I would rather have you alone."

"And I you, March." She reached up and kissed him, running her hand lightly down his chest to the top of his breeches in a way that made him very nearly toss her back on the bed, March and Charlotte or not. But instead she broke away and briskly threw open the door.

Then stopped and gasped, her hand flying up to her mouth. He followed, curious to see what had so stopped her.

The door to the neighboring room with the noisily amorous couple had just opened, too, and the noisily amorous couple were hurrying from it, in much the same disheveled state of dress.

"Mama?" Diana gasped, staring at her mother. "*Mama?* Here?"

But Sheffield was looking past Lady Hervey to where Brecon stood, fastening the buckle on his neckcloth.

"My God," Sheffield said. "Brecon. I never thought—"

"Diana!" exclaimed Lady Hervey. "Oh, my own daughter, what are you doing here? Where's Lord Crump? Why are you here with—"

"Sheffield," Brecon said. "What in blazes are you doing with Lady Diana?"

"*We* are married," Diana said, thrusting out her hand with the ring. "This morning, with a special license. But you, Mama, you—"

Brecon put his hands on Lady Hervey's shoulders. "Your mother has just agreed to marry me," he said. "We are to be wed early next month. We would have announced it today, at your wedding. At your, ah, other wedding."

"You are married to Sheffield," Lady Hervey said, bewildered, as she looked at the emerald ring. "Diana, Diana, of all I thought for you, I never guessed this."

Slowly she began to curtsey, bowing her head. "I congratulate you on your marriage, Your Grace."

"Oh, Mama, please don't," Diana said, pulling her mother up to embrace her. "If you marry Brecon, then you'll be a duchess, too. We'll all be equal, and then—"

"Sheffield!" thundered March as he came up the stairs

with Charlotte hurrying after him. "How dare you dishonor Lady Diana, you wretched—"

"He hasn't dishonored her, March," Brecon said. "He's married her instead."

March and Charlotte stopped at the top of the stairs, staring at them all.

"I told them you were married, Your Grace," said the keeper, standing behind March. "But they'd have none of it, and wouldn't believe me."

"There is, it seems, a great deal to believe, as well as to explain," Brecon said. "Let us all go below and sort this out properly over brandy."

Over brandy and breakfast, they did indeed sort things out, to the satisfaction of everyone. The gentlemen shook hands, and more brandy was drunk by way of toasts, to the considerable improvement of the general mood.

Yet still Diana found time to pull her mother aside in the hall, dodging the servants carrying dishes from the inn's busy kitchen. "Faith, I still can scarce believe it, Mama," she said. "You and Brecon!"

Mama laughed ruefully. "Meaning that you cannot believe a lady as aged as your mother would fall in love again?"

"No, no, not that at all," Diana said, and in truth Mama's cheeks were so pink and her face so filled with happiness that she did indeed look young enough to be another sister. "But however did you contrive such an—an—*intrigue* without us guessing?"

"Apparently in much the same fashion that you did with Sheffield," Mama said with a tinge of regret. "I suppose we all saw what we expected, and no more beyond. If I'd only paid more heed to you and less to my own affairs—"

"No, Mama," Diana said firmly, linking her fingers into her mother's. "You gave up everything when Father died to look after us. If you have found love again now, it is only what you deserve. And Brecon is such a charming gentleman, how could you not?"

"Thank you," Mama said, her eyes bright with tears. "I didn't intend to fall in love with Brecon. I've known him for years and years, while your father and Brecon's wife still lived, though it wasn't until this spring that we began to see one another in a different light."

"Oh, Mama, don't cry," Diana said, even as her own eyes filled with tears, too. "I want you to be happy with Brecon."

"And you, lamb." Mama blotted her eyes with her handkerchief. "I'll tell you the same that I've already told Sheffield: that if he doesn't keep to his vows and make you every bit as happy as you deserve, then he'll find he must answer to me directly."

That made Diana smile, for Mama was surely the least menacing lady in all London. But the love behind such a rash declaration was real enough, and with a fresh rush of emotion, all Diana could do was hug her mother and hold her tight.

"What has happened?" Sheffield asked with concern as he squeezed into the busy hall beside them. "What is wrong?"

"Not a thing." Wiping her eyes with her fingers, Diana disentangled herself from her mother. "Mama was just wishing us to be happy together."

Sheffield was not entirely convinced. "You don't look happy," he said. "You're both crying."

Diana smiled at his wariness, though his worried frown was nearly enough to set her to weeping again from sheer joy. "I am happy, Sheffield," she said, slipping her arm around his waist. "Perfectly, perfectly happy."

"You have much to learn about wives, Sheffield," March said philosophically as he joined them, with

Charlotte and Brecon close behind. "They only cry like this when they *are* happy. Do you and Diana wish a place in our carriage back to town?"

"There's room enough," Charlotte said, "even with Mama and Brecon, too. We'll be quite a party."

But Sheffield shook his head, tightening his arm around Diana. "I think not. I believe I'd much rather stay here with my wife."

"Oh, the scandal," Brecon said drily. "You do realize that you shall likely be the first true husband and wife in the Green Turtle's history to do so?"

Diana glanced up at her new (and true) husband. "I am the Duchess of Sheffield," she said, grinning even as she strived to look both serene and aloof. "I am above idle tattle and scandal."

"Then come upstairs with me, duchess," Sheffield said, kissing her upturned face, "and prove it."

She did: and together they swiftly returned upstairs to the fine room with the fine bed and the looking glass, too. There they made long, luxurious love to each other, sleeping only to waken and make love again, exactly as newlyweds should.

"My own Diana," Sheffield said softly as she lay across his chest. "My own duchess, my own wife. What would I have done if I hadn't found you?"

"But you did, love," she said, kissing him again. "You did, and it is . . . *perfect*."